What The Crit

Kissed By The Devil
By: Dashawn Taylor

"I loved it...! This was definitely my type of book. Just from the cover...I wanted to read this story. Dashawn did not disappoint with his debut novel!"
- Wendy Williams (Fox Network / BET / UPN) ✶ ✶ ✶ ✶ ✶

"Breathtaking and Shocking! Kissed by the Devil will catch the reader off guard from the beginning. Packed with amazing twists and turns...Dashawn brings his A-Game with his first fiction piece. Kissed By The Devil was a great read."
- Vibe Magazine ✶ ✶ ✶ ✶ ✶

"Kisse... by ... exciting debut novel by Dashawn Taylor. Taylor pulls no punches ... starts with the heart-stopping drama right away ... and the ... epilogue. This pulls the reader in head first into the ... world of Heidi and will have you eagerly flipping the pages.
- Urban Reviews.com ✶ ✶ ✶ ✶ ✶

"An excellent story by newcomer Dashawn Taylor, who seems to have a flair for dramatic twists and turns. Oh yes there is one common denominator that link the characters but when you think you've figured it out Dashawn flips the script on ya! An eye catching cover with a story that will make you determined to uncover the answers to this gripping drama!"
- ARC Book Club Inc ✶ ✶ ✶ ✶ ✶

KN

Kissed by the Devil II

DASHAWN TAYLOR

ISBN-10:   0980015421
ISBN-13:   978-0980015423

Cover Design: UltimateMedia.tv
Publishing Consultation: Nakea S. Murray (The Literary Consultant
Group)
Marketing Consultation: Jahari Vision
Photographer: Maya Guez
Cover Model: Tatiana Harvey
Editor: NewRenaissanceConsulting.com
Typesetting: Shawna A. Grundy
For more info log onto (WWW.KISSEDBYTHEDEVIL.COM) or email
(Publishing_NextLevel@Yahoo.com)

I would like to dedicate this novel
to my ever expanding circle of
Family, Friends and Fans!
Thanks for the continued support.
And as always...
without *YOU*...there is no *ME*!

- Thank You -

Chapter 1

Pearl Kachina Residence
East Orange, New Jersey

Sunday November 4, 2007
1:49 a.m.

"*Now don't be stupid, Heidi. Drop the gun and hand me the money, and we can all go our separate ways. Don't try to be a hero. I will make a mess outta you in this kitchen, Heidi. Trust Me!*"

Heidi's heart buckled as she stood in the middle of her mother's kitchen, processing the violent threat. Vincent "Vegas" Galloway, clearly the most dangerous man that she had ever known, was now pointing his pistol directly at her with sadistic intentions. The cold stare of his grayish eyes momentarily froze her. Every second seemed like an hour as Heidi stiffened with fear. The scene before her was unbelievable. Just a few moments earlier, Vegas had shot and killed Rafeek, one of his partners, right in front of her. She gripped her gun tighter. The terrifying sight of Rafeek's dead body served as a stark reminder of just how dangerous Vegas and his cousin, Shaheed were.

Heidi's mouth opened as she quickly turned and noticed her best friend, Faith was lying unconscious on the kitchen floor. During all the commotion, she'd never noticed that Shaheed had hit Faith over the head with his gun, knocking her out cold. Now Heidi was all alone. Her heart began to race out of control as she started backing away from both men.

"I can't give you this money," she whispered as she gripped the leather briefcase she held with the other hand. Both her hands were shaking, but she continued to point her gun directly at Vegas.

Vegas' face tightened in anger as he looked at his cousin, Shaheed standing on the opposite side of the kitchen. He also had a gun pointed at Heidi. There was a chilling moment of silence as Vegas turned his attention back to Heidi, sizing her up. "What did you just say?" he stuttered.

"If I give up this briefcase, you gonna kill us right here," she continued. "I can't give you this money."

"I'm not gonna hurt you, Heidi," he barked. His deep voice vibrated throughout the room. "Just put down the briefcase. Don't do nothin' stupid."

"No," Heidi hissed as she shook her head. Tears began to flow down her face. She was scared. "I can't die like this," she continued in a whisper. "Not like this."

Vegas choked the gun with his grip as he stared at Heidi. The look in her eyes sent a chill through his body. For the first time tonight, Vegas' heart began to race with anticipation. He didn't know what to expect from her, but he knew she was serious. "Put the goddamn gun down, Heidi," he shouted. "I'm not gonna tell you again."

"No!" Heidi's voice echoed off the walls.

Vegas scoffed at her willingness to defy him. He watched her closely as she wrapped her fingers tighter on her weapon. She took a deep breath, then slowly exhaled, and cut a glare over to Shaheed. She was sizing him up. The deadliness behind her stare pierced Shaheed's strength, making him turn away from her.

As if possessed by a higher power, Heidi's body miraculously stopped shaking. She moved her eyes back to Vegas. Her expression continued to cause him unease.

Heidi recalled a prayer her mother had taught her to chase away bad dreams. In the middle of the kitchen's thick silence, she mentally recited the prayer. *Ye, though I walk through the valley of the shadow* of death, I will fear no evil. For You are with me; Your rod and Your staff, they comfort me... She silently finished but, unfortunately, the nightmare didn't go away. But she was determined. She wouldn't run—she'd confront it. And giving up the briefcase or her gun was not an option. She would have to find a way to pull off the impossible.

"Heidi," Shaheed whispered. His voice trembled slightly with fear. "Just give us the money and we—"

Before he could finish his statement, Heidi made an unexpected decision. A loud gunshot rang out from her pistol. Vegas and Shaheed were both caught off guard by the firing. Shaheed froze. Vegas tried to duck out of harm's way, but the bullet pierced his shoulder, knocking him onto the kitchen floor. He screamed out in pain. Heidi continued blindly shooting at him as he quickly turned onto his stomach and crawled out of the kitchen. Focused on Vegas, Heidi walked backward, trying to make it to the back door. She didn't see Shaheed recklessly pointing his gun at her until he pulled the trigger. She flinched in terror and closed her eyes. Her heart stopped as she tried to brace herself for the bullet.

Click.

There was no shot. Heidi opened her eyes and looked at Shaheed. He was awkwardly glancing at his pistol. The gun's safety must've jammed when he'd hit Faith over the head with it. Heidi took advantage of the mishap and fired a shot at Shaheed. The bullet caught him square in the stomach and forced him to the kitchen floor.

"Oh my God!" he yelled as the hot bullet entered his midsection.

Heidi let off two more shots toward Shaheed, then darted out the back door. A rush of adrenaline went through her body as she stumbled down the stairs, managing to brace herself and regain her balance. She knew she needed to make it to the car and safety in order to save her best friend and family.

Back in the house, Shaheed was still yelling in pain as the hot bullet burned hotter inside his stomach. He squirmed on the kitchen floor, hallucinating from the pain. He began ducking for cover, thinking Heidi was still shooting at him. A loud crash from the living room brought him back to reality. He looked up and noticed Vegas was making the noise. His cousin was stumbling to regain his balance against the doorframe that connected the kitchen and living room.

Vegas grunted in pain as his shoulder burned from the bullet wound. "Fuckin' bitch shot me!" he yelled, nursing his left shoulder. "You good, Shah?"

"I don't think so, man," Shaheed answered, looking down at his midsection. The blood leaking from his wound caused his legs to tremble. "Goddamn, this shit hurts so bad!" he yelled. "She got me right in my stomach."

"Damn nigga, you coulda killed that bitch right there," Vegas barked. "What happened?"

Shaheed ignored Vegas as he continued to press on his stomach.

Vegas stumbled over to his cousin and knelt down next to him. Shaheed's wound was severe. Vegas looked around the kitchen, summoned as much strength as he could, then sprung into action. He made it upstairs, grabbing a few towels from the bathroom. He tried his best to ignore his own injury, but the excruciating pain wouldn't let him. Vegas made it back to his cousin within a few moments, and placed one of the towels over Shaheed's stomach. He took the other towels and wrapped them boxing glove-style around Shaheed's hand, and then placed it on his wound. "Shah, keep these towels over the hole…but don't press too hard. Just try to slow down the bleedin'," he instructed. "I'll be right back."

"What…wait!" Shaheed panicked. "Where you goin'?"

"Gotta get that money from Heidi," Vegas said. He was angry. "I can't let her get away with that briefcase!"

Vegas stood up, then staggered toward the living room. He looked around frantically for his gun. After a few seconds, he saw the weapon tucked in a corner near the staircase. He grunted again as he reached down to pick it up. With pistol in hand, he now turned his attention back to Heidi and headed to the back. As he moved through the kitchen, he looked down at his cousin, Shaheed.

"Don't worry, Shah," Vegas said. "I'm comin' right back."

He reached for the doorknob, and five gunshots exploded from the other side of the door. The gunshots startled him, and he quickly ducked.

"What the hell was that?" Shaheed whispered from across the kitchen. "Was that gunshots?"

Vegas' eyes were wide as he moved from the door to the window, and peered through curtains to investigate the noise. "Nothing just sounds like a gunshot," Vegas mumbled. "Especially that many."

"Is she still firin' at the house?"

"I don't know," Vegas said. "That shit sounded like it came from somewhere on the side of the house. Not the backyard."

Both men remained quiet. Vegas quietly moved to another window to get a better look. It was too dark outside for him to see anything. From his vantage point, the back of the house looked completely empty. He took a deep breath and decided to go outside to find Heidi. His lust for the money overpowered his fear of getting shot. He ignored the possible deadly consequences, and slowly exited with his gun raised.

Vegas looked around the backyard for signs of Heidi. Two more gunshots exploded from the side of the house. Jumping back, he ducked down near the back porch. Cautiously, he waited for another shot to ring, but there was complete silence. He stayed low to the ground, and slowly peeked around the edge of the house to get a better look.

A bizarre feeling came over him as he focused on a strange scene. Heidi was lying motionless on the ground, near the front of the house. A tall man, wearing all black, stood over her, holding the briefcase. Vegas couldn't make out his face. The man looked around momentarily as if he'd sensed Vegas, and then darted off down the street.

"What the hell?" Vegas whispered.

A rush of adrenaline moved Vegas as he stood up and pursued the man. He tried to run as fast as he could, but the pain from his shoulder slowed him. His jaws clinched tight as he passed Heidi's bloody body, headed to the front of the house. It was dark on the street, but Vegas could see the mystery man jogging swiftly down the block about two hundred yards ahead of him. He was still carrying the black briefcase. Vegas noticed the money and gave chase.

The mystery man never saw Vegas running after him as he continued to jog toward the end of the street. Vegas picked up the pace, and as he gained on him, the man ran around the corner and out of sight.

"Shit!" Vegas grunted as he pushed himself to catch up. He could sense the opportunity slipping away to get back the briefcase. Finally, he reached the corner. An unexpected sight surprised him, stopping him in his tracks.

The man was only a few hundred feet away, standing next to a dark-blue Chevy Yukon. He was facing the drivers' side door. Vegas tried to get a look at the man's face, but couldn't make him out. The man's name was Aaron Smith.

Aaron opened the door and tossed the black briefcase inside. Seconds later, he calmly pulled out a cell phone and began dialing a few numbers.

Vegas immediately went into attack mode. He raised his pistol and fired three shots. A loud crash came from the SUV's rear window as bullets shattered the glass. Aaron dropped the phone to the ground and ducked behind the truck. A few gunshots rang out from Aaron's hiding place, causing Vegas to duck for cover. He finally got low and ducked down between two parked cars, continuing to fire shots at Aaron. The loud exchange of fire echoed throughout the quiet streets.

Vegas took a deep breath and braced himself to stand up. He raised his gun in the direction of the vehicle and let off two more shots. Crunching metal could be heard as the bullets entered the truck. Vegas bravely stood, then ran in the direction of the Yukon. As he got closer, he saw Aaron frantically diving into the truck's front seat. Vegas had to act fast. He let off two more rounds as the roar of the ignition fired up. Aaron slammed the truck into gear, and the tires violently spun into motion. Vegas only had one more chance.

The back window of the truck was completely shot out, and he had a clear view of the inside.

Vegas quickly ran into the middle of the street. He raised his gun and took aim at the back of Aaron's head. Vegas was an excellent shot, and he knew he could nail his target. He sadistically smirked, knowing his opponent's life was about to end. The truck got a few yards away from him when Vegas calmly pulled the trigger.

Click.

"Motherfucker!" Vegas screamed. His gun was empty. In frustration, he slammed the pistol to the ground and stared at the Yukon as it sped down the dark street. A cold chill rushed through him. He'd lost the briefcase.

Cautiously, he looked around to see if anyone had witnessed what had transpired. The surrounding houses were dark and the street was completely empty. He searched for his gun, deciding to head back to the house for his cousin. As he went to pick up his piece, he noticed a cell phone a few feet away. A flashback entered his mind. He realized that the man he'd just faced-off with must've dropped the phone during the exchange of shots. Vegas quickly grabbed his gun and the phone, and nodded at the small victory, knowing it would be key in getting back the briefcase.

Chapter 2

Bloomfield, New Jersey

Sunday November 4, 2007
2:01 a.m.

"*K*iss me, Judith. And please don't stop until you make me rise again."

When Judith heard the boyish request come from the mouth of one of the most powerful men in New Jersey, she giggled. For the past seven minutes, she'd been staring out the window of her boss' stretch limousine as it cruised through the empty downtown area of Bloomfield. She was lost in her thoughts as she sat quietly on the leather seat of the SL600 Stretch Edition. Her boss' deep and sexy voice had awakened her from the daydream. Not wanting to send him the wrong message, she instinctively painted a sensual smile on her face, and then turned around to face him. Staring back into her eyes, wearing nothing but a smirk and a pair of silk boxers, sat Max Gordon, the charismatic and always controversial Vice-President of Datakorp.Com.

"Now, baby, you know I can't do that," she whispered in her signature low tone. "Kissing is a no-no, sugar. That's against the rules."

"Not my rules!" Max responded, raising his left eyebrow. Judith smiled at his demanding gesture. "And don't do this to me tonight, cupcakes," he continued. "I want what I want and how many times

I want it. Especially after the last few crazy months that I've been having. This is very therapeutic for me."

Judith suggestively glared at Max without saying a word. She focused on his deep brown eyes that beautifully complimented his bronze skin. From her first encounter with him almost five years ago, she had been highly attracted to his mature and sophisticated features. From the way he dressed to the words he used, Max was clearly cut from a better cloth than many other men. Every time she saw his clean-shaven head and jet-black goatee, Judith was reminded of an oil painting she'd once saw of an Egyptian god. Max was definitely her type of man, and getting paid to have sex with him was a sweet bonus for her.

Judith and Max had a peculiar relationship. They had been working Datakorp together for almost three years before Max had approached her with a proposition. He was a sex-fanatic who could never get enough from his wife. After flirting for almost a year, the two had finally hooked up, and a sexual escapade began. Because Max had a fetish for paying for sex, he'd insisted on shelling out money to her to sleep with him. According to him, being powerful and paying for the goods only added to the excitement. After a few sessions, Judith had agreed to take the payment. Just the thought of getting the extra cash intensified their trysts.

Max looked over to her and gave her small grin. He could see the mood shifting in her eyes. A few goose pimples emerged on his arms as he began to imagine what she had in store for him. He closely watched her gaze as it wandered down his chest to his lower region. She focused on his royal-blue underwear, then nibbled on her bottom lip, teasing him. She smiled, knowing her tease had always driven him crazy. Tonight was no different. As her seductive smile grew larger, so did the bulge in his boxers.

Judith knew every little detail and gesture Max enjoyed. From the right thong to wear, to the toys to use, to the sounds to make, she knew Max much better than his wife. Judith treated Max like royalty. After all, he was a very generous man, and when it came to him, she decided to break all types of rules—but not before first breaking his pockets.

"Maxie, baby…why aren't you dressed yet?" she whispered as the sound of the speeding limousine made her glance out of the window again. "I thought you only needed me once tonight. You're going to be late for your flight, aren't you?"

"Maybe. I'll just catch the next flight," he said as he stared at her sexy body. "I can have the driver cruise around for another hour, then we can go for round two."

"Look at you," Judith playfully mocked. "Round two?"

"Round two!" he responded sternly.

She didn't say another word. His last statement sent a sexual command to her, and Judith found herself calmly lowering her strapless corset, exposing her caramel breasts to him. She slowly leaned back and began to touch herself. Max smiled. Watching Judith caress herself was one of his secret pleasures. He tried his best not to take his eyes off her as he fumbled around to find the car phone. Judith giggled again and shook her head. She watched him finally reach the receiver, then put it to his ear.

"Ross, can you hear me up there?" Max asked as he waited for his limo driver to answer.

"Sure can, Mr. Gordon. How can I help you?" Ross's voice came through the other end of the line.

"Good. Listen. I need you to buy me some time."

"Not a problem," Ross replied, more than happy to grant Max's request. "How long do you need, Sir?"

"About forty-five minutes," Max said as he watched Judith continue to caress herself. He confidently licked his bottom lip, showing her that he approved of her strip tease.

"Okay, Sir," Ross continued. "I will ride through Branch Brook Park and find a private area to rest."

"No Ross!" Max barked. "Absolutely no stopping! Keep the car moving."

Ross was stunned by Max's tone. There was a brief silence on the phone.

"You hear me up there, Ross?"

"Yes, Sir. I understand," Ross uttered. "I'll keep the car moving."

Not wanting to ruin the mood in the back, Max abruptly hung up the phone and focused his attention on Judith. He playfully blew her a kiss and winked his eye. "Round two?" Max whispered.

"In a second," she answered. "I want to show you something." She moved away from Max and stretched out on the butter-soft leather. She made sure she was just far enough away to give him a full view of her sexy body. At five-foot four, Judith was about as tall as the average woman, but she had extremely long legs for her height. And she used every inch of them to her advantage.

Max's eyes grew more intense as he watched her wiggle out of her underclothes. First went the lacey corset, past her hips and down her long legs. Next, it was time to slide off her panties.

Judith knew his building anticipation was driving Max crazy, so she made sure to strip slow, forcing him to savor the moment. "Ooooh," she moaned, catching him off guard. She smiled when his face lit. He was getting there. Slowly, she raised her knees to her chest and slid off her panties. She made sure she took her time and removed them very smoothly, never breaking her rhythm or seeming awkward. That was important when seducing Max. In fact, she believed, that was important when alluring any man.

Before their arrangement had become official, Judith made Max agree to three rules. One: She would never get naked before being paid. Two: They'd never visit each others homes. And Three: no kissing. Judith smiled, thinking of how she was about to break the third rule—for good reason. Financially, Max would make it all worth it. Whatever he asked, Max got—no matter the request. Being the Vice-President of a multi-million dollar company gave him obvious advantage. Not to mention, he was the sexiest man that she'd ever known over forty-five.

"You need some help with those?" Max joked as he watched her silk drop panties to the carpet.

"No, I don't," she responded with a playful attitude. "And why are you all the way over there, baby? I thought you wanted a kiss."

Max froze, stunned that she'd acquiesced, then smiled at the

11

sensual cat-and-mouse game. He watched as she teased her soft skin with the tips of her fingers, then invited him to join her.

"Don't you move," he whispered as he crawled on top of her, his strong body covering hers like a warm blanket.

Her heart started to race uncontrollably. She felt Max's hand run up the side of her body, and moaned from the chilling sensation. She wrapped her arms around his broad shoulders and pulled him closer.

"You are so beautiful, Judith," he whispered.

She gave Max a peculiar look. Something in his tone sent trembles through her, and before she could respond to his compliment, his lips were softly locking with hers. Judith moaned in pleasure, and her body jerked from the impact of his kiss. Max became more aggressive as he placed his hands around her lower back and yanked her closer. Her heart skipped another beat. Max pushed his hips closer to hers, and she could feel him growing as he got more excited.

Judith knew that Max could be an aggressive lover, and she'd liked it. But tonight she enjoyed his forcefulness even more. His lips were so electrifying and sensual; she grew hotter by the second. She couldn't help but smile as she realized that breaking the kissing rule suddenly became a silly superstition.

"Damn Maxie, where did that come from?" she whispered as she slowly pulled her lips away from his. She leisurely ran her index finger across her bottom lip and smiled at him. "You know that's gonna cost you extra."

"It was worth it," Max responded.

She felt him poking her from below and realized he was ready for more of her. "So you got a half-hour?" she asked quietly as she looked around the backseat of the limo.

"Yes," Max answered, nodding his head.

"Okay. Sit over on the other seat for a second," Judith said, pointing to the other side of the limo. "I want to try something with you."

A devilish smile grew on Max's face. He calmly lifted his body from hers and obeyed the order. Judith sat up on the sofa and reached for her Chloe Cyndi Tote bag.

Max's entire mood changed when he noticed her pulling out a pocket knife. "And what is that for?"

"Relax, sweetie," she said. "A girl can never have too much protection."

"Excuse me?" Max grunted nervously.

"I'm joking, baby," Judith reassured, giggling. "I think you're going to like this."

An uneven smirk emerged on Max's face. Judith could tell he was taken aback by the site of her stark naked, wielding a knife. She slowly reached down and picked up her silk panties. She playfully dangled them in front of her own face, then winked. He smiled at her. He was still watching her closely as she used the knife to slice one side of the underwear. She tossed the knife to the side and slowly approached Max, giving him another sensual kiss on the lips.

"I want to tie you up, baby," Judith whispered.

"You want to tie me up?"

"Is there an echo in here?" she joked. "I want to tie you up."

"With what?" Max responded.

"With these," she said, showing him the panties.

Another wide smile emerged on his face. She noticed some movement in his boxers again, which told her Max was exited about her idea.

"Sit back, baby. Imma get on top of you," she whispered.

Max backed away and obeyed her once again. Judith climbed on top of the seat and straddled him. She started grinding on his lap, making him more excited by the second. If it wasn't for his boxers, Max would've slipped inside of her without so much as an apology. She gave him another kiss as she grabbed both of his hands and raised them above his head.

"Hold on to the grab-bars, Maxie," she whispered.

Again, he obeyed her.

Judith gave him a quick kiss on his lips and proceeded to tie his hands around the grab-bars. "Is that too tight, sweetie?" she asked playfully.

"No baby, it's just right," Max said. The feeling of being sexually restricted was a brand-new experience for him. Judith gave him a reassuring smile to help put him at ease.

Max helplessly watched her as she slid down his body. She moaned as her nipples grazed over his bare chest. She continued to move down until her knees touched the floor.

"I have been dying to do this all night," she whispered, keeping her soft brown eyes fixed on his. The intensity and fervor in her look made him even more excited. He continued to watch Judith as she reached for his boxers, and then pulled them down his legs. "Whoa," she mumbled.

Max was rock solid, and she couldn't help but react to the sight. She'd seen his dick over a hundred times, but always marveled at how strong it appeared. She gently took her hands and wrapped her palms around it. He reacted to the sensation.

"Yeah Maxie, you like that?" Judith asked rhetorically. Her eyes shifted to his throbbing shaft. She continued to stroke him, causing him to moan her name. Another seductive grin came over her face when he began melting into the feeling. She stroked him harder.

"Damn," Max whispered. He moaned her name again and started moving his hips in rhythm with her stroke. She sensually nodded her head at the intense look on his face.

"You want me to suck it, baby?" Judith asked.

Before Max could open his mouth to speak, she'd opened hers and covered the head of his dick with her lips. Max's body trembled from the sensation.

"Oh my God, girl," Max whispered. He looked down in ecstasy, watching as Judith orally pleased him. The sight of her beautiful lips moving back and forth turned him on tremendously. He was getting into it. He closed his eyes and took a deep breath when her soft tongue began to hit his spots. "Okay, baby. Goddamn!" he moaned as a sexy grin surfaced. "You know I like that. Don't stop, baby." He took another deep breath and looked at Judith. He instinctively tried to reach down and grab her hair, but forgot he was tied up.

"Mmm…hmm," Judith mumbled. She noticed he was trying

to move his hands and smiled. The idea of a helpless Max made her excitement grow. She became more aggressive as she felt him becoming harder. Up and down, her face went. Faster and faster. She was taking all of Max in her mouth now. He tasted so good. Judith felt a tingle between her thighs and let out a loud moan. "Damn, daddy," she whispered as Max grew. It felt like he was literally getting larger in her mouth. Judith squeezed his thighs and began sucking and stroking him harder. Another tingling sensation shot from between her legs and straight up her spine. She let out another loud moan. "Oh shit, Max…I…mmm…" Judith tried to speak, but couldn't finish her statement. She didn't want to break her rhythm so she quickly put him back in her mouth and kept going. Another tingle made her moan again. She began to feel slightly guilty as she realized she was enjoying the oral sex just as much as he. Her nipples were getting harder and her pussy became wetter.

"Yes…Judith…please keep doing that," Max moaned. "I'm close."

Judith responded to Max's statement by grabbing his dick with both hands. She moaned louder as Max began thrusting himself deeper into her mouth. "Damn Max, I can't take it anymore," she uttered as her body began to shake. She grabbed Max tighter and stroked him faster.

Max tried to stop himself from yelling as he started climaxing. "Oh my God…Judith…hell yes!" Max uttered.

Judith trembled, climaxing with him. "Holy shit, Max. I can't believe this!" she sang. "I'm cumin', baby."

"Me too!" Max mumbled as he gritted his teeth.

She never heard Max's words because her own orgasm had caught her off guard. Her body quivered uncontrollably. A burst of pleasure made her scream with passion. She was almost whimpering as the multiple orgasms shook her body like an earthquake.

"Oh…my…God…Max," Judith moaned as she shivered again. With every eruption, her body clinched with satisfaction. She felt Max's body trembling and opened her eyes. In the heat of the moment, she hadn't realized that Max had had an explosive

15

orgasm of his own. She slowly wiped her face and looked down at her cream-covered breasts. He'd made a mess of her, but she loved every bit of it. She nibbled on her bottom lip again and smiled at Max. He seemed to be out of it. "Damn, daddy! That was a lot," Judith whispered, then gently kissed his stomach and rubbed his thighs.

"I know, baby," Max mumbled. "I was saving all that for you." He chuckled for a second and took a deep breath. "Whoa…that was good."

Judith could feel his entire body shift as he relaxed. She smiled at him again and playfully smacked him on the leg. "Be right back, sweetie." She crawled over to her bag and grabbed a small towel. Max watched her as she cleaned off herself. He marveled at how beautiful and sexy she was. Judith noticed he was looking at her and gave him a sexy glance. "You okay, baby?" she asked.

"Yes…I'm perfect. That was wonderful. I'm just sitting here trying to figure out why you put up with me?"

Judith laughed at the question and crawled back over to him. She rubbed the towel over his stomach and started cleaning him. Before she finished, she looked at him. "Because you pay me, baby," she said, and they both started to laugh.

Max shook his head. "I guess I walked right into that one," he joked. He continued to watch Judith as she grabbed the knife from the floor, and then cut him free from the pair of panties.

"That was fun, right?" she said in a playful voice.

"Oh yea…I love when you get creative," he answered as he reached for his clothes. They both started to dress.

"I have a confession to make."

"Is that right?" he asked as he slipped back into his pants. "A confession?"

"I sure do. You know that this is the first time that's ever happened to me?"

"What's that?"

"I came so hard just now. I mean… that was a serious climax, and you never even touched me," she said, astounded. "That was amazing. I guess I was really horny tonight."

"Well damn...that *is* something. I guess you should be paying me now," Max joked.

Judith smiled, and turned away from Max, who was still laughing at the joke. He was putting on his shirt when a loud ringing blared from the rear of the limo. The sound startled Judith. It was his cell phone.

Quickly, he looked at his watch. "Give me one second, honey," he said. "Let me answer that."

Max moved to the rear of the limo and fumbled with his things until he found his cell in his coat pocket. Judith watched him and noticed his body stiffen when he looked phone.

He flipped it opened and answered the call. "This is Max Gordon."

A frantic voice began screaming from the other end of the line. "Where you at, motherfucker?"

Max quickly pulled the phone away from his ear and looked at the display again. The call was coming from an unidentified number. Max put the phone back to his ear. "Who is this?" he shouted.

"This is Aaron!" the voice yelled from the other line.

"Aaron?" Max responded. "Where are you? Where are you calling me from?"

Judith heard Max's conversation and turned to him. She became nervous as she noticed his mood continued shifting.

"Somebody just tried to blow my head off, nigga!" Aaron yelled. His voice cut through the receiver. "Did you try to set me up?" Max's heart started to race. "Hello?" Aaron barked from the opposite end of the call. "Max, we need to talk. Right now. You fuckin' asshole! I don't care where you at. If you want to see this money, you got exactly twenty minutes to come see me or I'm gone like the wind. You hear me?"

Max froze with momentary shock as he tried to figure out what went wrong. He took a deep breath and put his mouth to the phone. "Okay, man, listen...don't panic," he said, his voice trembling. "I don't know what went wrong, but I didn't set you up. Where are you? Where are you calling me from?"

"I'm at a pay phone now," Aaron answered. "But meet me on Frelinghuysen in Newark, behind the DMV. Remember, you got twenty minutes."

The call disconnected.

Max's heart dropped to the floor as he looked out the window. He picked up the car phone and dialed the driver.

"Hey, Boss. All set to head home?" Ross asked from the other end of the phone.

"No Ross," Max stuttered. "How far are we from Newark?"

"About thirty-five minutes away, Sir," Ross answered.

"Okay, you got fifteen minutes to get us there," Max sternly ordered. "I need to make it to the DMV on Frelinghuysen in fifteen minutes."

Ross chuckled from the other line. "At this time of night, Boss? I think the DMV is closed, Sir."

"Just do it," Max barked. He was not amused. "This is not a game, Ross. Fifteen minutes, okay?"

"Yes Sir," Ross responded.

Max hung up the phone and looked over to Judith. She looked very worried. She could tell that something was weighing heavy on Max's mind, but decided to stay silent.

"I need to drop you off, Judith. I'm sorry," Max whispered as he slowly turned to look out the window. "Looks like I need to rush and see what happened."

"Is everything alright, Max?" Judith asked. "Is there anything I can do?"

"I don't think so. But I need to get you somewhere safe," Max whispered. "Get dressed, honey. This could certainly get ugly."

Chapter 3

East Orange, New Jersey

**Sunday November 4, 2007
2:28 a.m.**

*F*orty-eight year-old Rick Miller slowly pulled into the dark driveway of his girlfriend's house, and shut off his engine. He'd been in front of the house only seconds when he realized something was terribly wrong. In the six years since he had been dating Pearl, he'd never known her to turn off the porch light before he got home. He ducked his head under the rearview mirror to get a better look at the house. Most of the second story lights were on, indicating something was obviously different tonight.

Warily, he got out of the car. The fall wind blew more than just cold air his way; a strange feeling overcame him as he cautiously looked around the quiet exterior of the house. Following his better judgment, he decided to use the back door instead of the front. As he walked around the car, Rick made a gruesome discovery. A woman was lying motionless near the side of the house. He quickly ran over to the body.

"Jesus Christ!" he mumbled. He stood over her body in shock, becoming more nervous as he recognized the woman's face. It was his girlfriend's daughter, Heidi Kachina. She was bleeding from a number of gunshot wounds to her chest.

He was tempted to kneel down next to Heidi, but decided against it. He frantically looked around the quiet backyard. A loud bang came from inside the house, causing Rick to turn around in a panic. He rushed back to his car and popped the trunk. Something was going on inside the house, and Rick wanted to be prepared for anything. He reached for a black toolbox and removed a small handgun from it. He closed the trunk of the car and jogged around to the rear of the house. With gun in hand, Rick quickly approached the backyard. He noticed the door was slightly ajar. A nervous chill ran through him. He slowly opened the door, and walked into the rear of the kitchen.

"What the fuck?" Rick stuttered. He stood in awe at the sight of the carnage in Pearl's kitchen. Blood was everywhere. His heart dropped to his stomach as he found himself staring at three bodies laying in succession on the kitchen floor. "What the fuck?" Rick unconsciously repeated. His mind raced as he tried to put a story to the madness. A young woman lay dead near his feet and a young man's lifeless body was on the other side of the kitchen floor. Both were shot in the head. Another man lay in the corner of the kitchen with his hands on his stomach, and Rick couldn't tell if he were dead or not. Slowly, Rick walked over to the man and noticed that his face was familiar. Before he could kneel down next to the young man, Rich heard a noise come from the living room. Rick turned around just in time to see a huge man with grey eyes pointing a gun directly at him.

Vegas.

Rick raised his gun, staring at him. There was a silence between them. A few moments passed and Vegas said nothing. His shoulder was bleeding badly, but he seemed unfazed by the injury. He continued to stare at Rick intensely, his gun still pointed. Rick didn't know what to expect. He decided to break the silence.

"What the hell is goin' on in here?" Rick nervously mumbled.

"You tell me, Rick!" Vegas countered. His voice was angry.

"I said *no bodies*, Vegas," Rick said as he looked around the kitchen.

"And I said *no* surprises," Vegas reminded.

Rick's left brow lowered at the statement. He was confused. "What are you talkin' 'bout, young blood? Everything shoulda went smooth."

"Well, it didn't! Now my cousin, Shaheed is shot over there and we don't got the money. So whatever game you playin' is gonna stop now."

"Wait a second. What?" Rick stuttered. He became increasingly worried after hearing the news. "You don't got the money? Where is it? Is that why you shot Heidi?"

"I didn't touch her!" Vegas barked. "Somebody robbed and shot her. I thought it was somebody you sent over here."

"Vegas, wait! You not makin' no sense," Rick said. "Put the gun down, man, and let's talk."

Vegas shook his head. "Nah, nigga. You put ya shit away, and then we can talk."

Both men fell silent. Rick gritted his teeth and stared at Vegas, contemplating his offer.

"Okay, young blood. Don't shoot me now. Imma put my gun away. Just relax, okay?"

Vegas didn't budge as he watched Rick lower his weapon, and then tuck it away in the small of his back.

"Okay?" Rick whispered, showing Vegas his empty hands. "Now what happened in here, man? This is a fuckin' mess."

Vegas frowned his face and lowered his gun. He slowly walked all the way into the kitchen and sat down. He was badly hurting, but he tried not to show any weakness in front of Rick. "You know some nigga with a blue Yukon?" he asked as he looked over to a visibly stunned Rick.

"Nah," Rick whispered as he backed away from Vegas and leaned against the kitchen counter.

"Well, we gotta find this nigga. He got the money," Vegas said, looking down at Shaheed, who still lay unconscious. "He shot Heidi and took the briefcase from her. I tried to chase him, but the snake got away."

Rick let out a loud gasp. He was frustrated.

"But it's cool because he dropped his cell," Vegas mumbled as he pulled out a phone from his pocket. "He dropped this out there, so I will definitely find his ass." He set down the phone on the kitchen table.

Rick looked at it and immediately turned his focus to a smaller red one that was inches from the first. "Wait…whose phone is this?" he asked, picking up the red one.

"I took that one off of Heidi's friend," Vegas said, nodding his head toward the dead woman on the floor.

Rick didn't say a word as he put Faith's phone back on the table.

Vegas turned and stared at his cousin. He became angry. "And my bitch-ass cousin could'a shot that fuckin' girl while she was in here," he snapped as he turned to Rick. "Man, this nigga had a clean shot at Heidi and fuckin' bitched up. I don't know what the fuck is wrong with this dude."

"Vegas, where's Pearl?" Rick nervously asked.

"Who?"

"Pearl," Rick repeated. "Heidi's mom. Where is she? You didn't hurt her did you?"

"No, she got away," Vegas barked, cutting his eyes at Rick. "Why you ask me that?"

A feeling of relief came over Rick as he learned of his girlfriend escaping. He cautiously looked at Vegas, then began to speak again. "Because all of this shit wasn't part of the plan," he said, looking around the kitchen. "You was suppose to tie everybody up, wait until Heidi came back with the money, and that's it. It was a simple plan."

"Yea?" Vegas said, cutting off Rick. "Well, shit got really fuckin' complicated, didn't it? But like I said, Heidi was here and she had the money," Vegas continued. "But my cousin fucked this up. She started bustin', and he didn't shoot back. She fuckin' got away with the money after that."

"So, what now?" Rick asked.

"Shit. You know what's next. I'm not waitin' around here for the cops to come. So help me get his bitch-ass up, then we out of here. Everything is done here. I just took care of her brother, so we done."

"Lamar?" Rick nervously asked. "What do you mean *took care* of him?"

"Stop being a bitch, Rick," Vegas snapped. "You know what I mean. He's game-over."

Vegas' cold tone shook Rick. He put his hand on his head as he thought about the rising body count in the house. "Jesus Christ, young blood," Rick whispered. "You out of control."

Vegas shook his head and waved his hand at Rick. "Whatever, man. Let's go."

Vegas grunted as he forced himself to his feet. The loss of blood was causing him to become weaker by the minute. He grabbed one of the towels from next to his cousin, and then wrapped it around his shoulder. "Help me pick him up and take him to the car." He pointed to his cousin. Rick stood up as Vegas grabbed Shaheed by the legs. "Wait a minute, Rick. Grab that phone for me before you pick him up. I need to find this dude."

Rick turned around and looked at the kitchen table. He mistakenly grabbed the red phone instead of the phone of the man who'd taken the money. He put phone in his pocket, then grabbed Shaheed by the shoulders.

"So where you gonna take him?"

Vegas took a deep breath as he finally got a good grip on Shaheed's legs. He looked at Rick. "Just help me get him to the car. I'll let you know where we goin' on the way."

Chapter 4

2:48 a.m.

*T*he loud clanging of a falling trashcan echoed off a quiet alley just off Central Avenue. The tit-tat-tit-tit-tat sound of the clanging metal caused a couple of late night streetwalkers to investigate the annoying noise. A ragged old man, posted on a park bench across the street, tried to focus his drunken eyes on a silhouette emerging from the dark alley. Another loud crash blared as a second garbage bin toppled over. The old man continued watching as someone tried to unsuccessfully regain their balance against the falling trashcan. The person stumbled from the dark alley. The old man tittered at the sight and rolled his eyes. He was surprised to see a woman coming from the darkness. She was visibly injured as she made her way to the street. The woman was in her mid-fifties, but moving very gingerly. Her black trousers and rococo-red sweater were too thin for the fall weather. The woman's aging, yet attractive face shivered in the cold as she suspiciously looked around. Her name was Pearl Kachina.

Pearl carefully stumbled to a nearby car that was parked near the edge of the alley. She rested against it and took a deep breath. The fractured bone in her right leg caused her to grimace in pain. She was near tears as she reached down and lifted her pants leg to get a better look at her injury. She frowned. The dark burgundy and blue marks around her ankle were a stark reminder of what had transpired at her house not long ago.

Pearl was just an hour removed from a home invasion that had shaken her world. The lives of her son, Lamar and her only daughter, Heidi were in danger. The images of three men holding her family hostage in her home flashed into her mind. In order to get away from the mayhem, Pearl had made a bold escape. She'd jumped from her second-story bedroom window, breaking her leg in the fall. Despite the pain, she'd driven herself to the East Orange General Hospital where she was now desperately making her way to the entrance. She stopped, taking once last look into the alley. She had to be sure no one could see the car she'd arrived in. She'd hid it in the alley for fear of the kidnappers finding her.

Seeing no one, Pearl gathered herself, then limped toward the emergency room. She could feel her injured leg buckling from the pressure, and began to move with more urgency. The area just outside the entrance was very quiet for a weekend night in East Orange. She felt relieved. Usually the ER would be clustered with shooting, drug overdose, and car accident victims. But tonight the area was eerily silent. Pearl walked through the automatic doors and stepped into the waiting area. A female receptionist sat on the far side of the room chatting on a cell phone. Pearl limped over to the registration cubicle and tried to speak to her.

"Excuse me, Ma'am. Do you have a policeman on duty tonight?" Pearl whispered to the receptionist.

The receptionist took one look at Pearl and rolled her eyes.

Pearl was immediately taken aback by the clerk's attitude. "Did you hear what I just asked you?" Pearl patience was quickly wearing thin.

The woman put her hand over the mouthpiece of the cell phone and looked around the waiting area. "There's a few cops on duty," she said. "But all of 'em are busy." The clerk turned away from Pearl and continued her conversation.

Pearl became annoyed. The rude behavior of the young lady was making her uneasy. She quickly calmed herself and spoke again. "I really need your help," Pearl whispered as she decided to take the high road.

"Okay, Ma'am," the lady responded as she turned around. She nodded her head and handed Pearl a clipboard with a few papers attached to it. "I'm gonna need you to take this and have a seat," the employee snapped, pointing to the waiting room. "Fill this out completely, then come back once you're done."

Pearl tossed the clipboard to the side. "Young lady, you don't understand. I need you to—"

"Wait a second," the receptionist said, cutting off Pearl. She slammed her cell phone on the desk and looked at Pearl with an attitude. "Lady, it's been a long night. Now all you have to do is take these forms, fill them out, and someone will help you in a minute, okay?"

"It's not okay!" Pearl snapped. She immediately turned her attention to the desk and looked at the cell phone. Pearl grabbed it and put it to her ear. "Hello? Yes...she's gonna call you back!" Pearl yelled. She disconnected the call and threw the mobile phone against the wall. It seemed to shatter into a thousand pieces. The loud noise startled everyone in the waiting room. Pearl turned back to the receptionist with fire in her eyes. Her expression caused the lady to become visibly nervous. "Now listen to me, you rude bitch!" Pearl growled. "You lucky this ain't ten years ago. I would'a smashed that goddamn phone against the side of your ridiculous weave. Now get on that phone and call the police down here. Tell them I got people in my house and they are holdin' my family hostage."

The receptionist gave Pearl a blank stare. She was frozen by the news.

"Do it!" Pearl yelled, startling the receptionist again.

Everyone in the waiting area watched the commotion at the cubicle. The receptionist quickly grabbed the desk phone. Her entire mood changed within seconds. She dialed the security office and humbly looked at Pearl.

"I'm sorry, Ma'am," she whispered. "What's your address?"

* * *

Newark, New Jersey

Sunday November 4, 2007
2: 56 a.m.

About fifteen miles away, back in Newark, a million thoughts were running through the mind of Max Gordon as he sat in the back seat of his limousine. He was amazed that his driver was able to drop off Judith at the train station and make it down to the old DMV in less than twenty minutes. As he looked down the dark street, Max didn't know what to expect. He slowly got out of the limo and headed up the street. He was nervous. This particular section of Frelinghuysen Avenue was very dark and desolate. Abandoned warehouses lined the broken sidewalks and a trail of garbage was sprinkled throughout this deprived stretch of road. Max slowly walked up the street. He balled up his lip and suspiciously looked at every car that passed. A feeling of regret came over him as he approached a side street.

"I know this is not a good idea," Max whispered to himself.

He was now making his way to the rear of the building. The side street was unpaved and it appeared as if it hadn't been used in years. Broken glass, bricks and trash were everywhere. Max even found himself holding his nose as he stumbled closer to the back. A strange noise made him stop dead in his tracks.

"Hello?" he whispered, hoping he wouldn't get a response. After a brief moment, he heard nothing. He slowed his pace, but continued on to the rear of the building. The strange noise sounded again. This time Max heard which direction it was coming from. Turning his attention, he focused his eyes on a young man walking toward the back of a SUV, holding a large container. The man, dressed in black, moved with a purpose. Upon closer inspection, Max saw the guy sloshing gasoline inside and outside of the truck. Visibly upset, he was talking to himself. As the young man walked around the other side of the truck, Max got a clearer look at his face. He recognized him. Aaron Smith.

27

"Aye!" Max yelled, trying to get Aaron's attention. To Max's surprise, Aaron turned and pointed a gun at him. Max immediately put up his hands. "Whoa gangster…it's just me!" Max yelled.

Aaron peered though the darkness and noticed Max. He shook his head and put his gun away. "You're late!" he barked.

"And you're trippin'!" Max countered. "What the hell are you doing talking to yourself? Don't tell me you getting mental on me."

Aaron didn't respond. He continued to pour the pungent gasoline on the hood of the truck.

Max curiously walked over to the SUV and inspected the damage. As he looked at the bullet-riddled metal, he took a deep breath and slowly let out a lung full of air. "Sheeeese…good thing I took the license plates off this damn thing," he whispered. "So what happened out there? And who the hell was shooting at you?"

"Obviously, somebody didn't do their homework," Aaron barked.

"What?" Max questioned as he covered his nose. The strong smell of gasoline was making him nauseous.

"One girl!" Aaron yelled. "Ain't that what you said? You said it was gonna just be Heidi, right? One girl! That was you…saying that to me, right?"

"Right! One girl," Max confirmed. "All you had to do is take the money from Heidi and disappear. What happened?"

"All this!" Aaron yelled, pointing at the truck. "All this is some cowboy shootin' at me at Heidi's house."

"Whoa…whoa…backup just a second," Max said. His tone grew very cold. "You went to Heidi's *house*?"

"I had to," Aaron exclaimed. "By the time I got downtown she was already leaving the building. So I had to follow her home. And who the hell was that shooting at me. Do you know him?"

Max rubbed his temples and started pacing back and forth. He shook his head uncontrollably as he processed Aaron's words. Without warning, he stopped and turned to Aaron.

"So somebody saw you take the money?"

There was a brief silence in the back of the building. Aaron didn't say a word. He looked away from Max and nodded his head.

"Goddammit Aaron!" Max said. "I'm fucked, man!"

"What are you talking about?"

"You just killed me! I'm fucked for real," Max repeated. He was nervous. He walked over to Aaron. "Do the math, Aaron. Heidi was never supposed to make it back to that house. You understand? She was never supposed to show up *at all*. So if somebody saw you take the money, then they know that somebody else was involved with this shit."

"And what that mean?" Aaron asked aggressively.

"Jesus Christ, Aaron. You got to be the smartest idiot I know," Max said. "Where's the first place they gonna look to get the money back?"

Aaron remained silent.

"Yeah…that's right," Max continued. "Me!"

Both men fell silent as Max's last statement sunk in. Aaron unconsciously began to rub his chin as he looked around the dark lot. Max was frozen. He put his hands on his waist and tried to catch his breath.

Aaron looked at him and realized Max was clearly shaken up. "So who are these guys anyway?"

"Not the kind you want to fuck with," Max responded.

"Or not the kind that wanna fuck with me!" Aaron snapped.

Something in Aaron's tone made Max turn to him. Aaron was clearly getting angry about the news.

"So let me get this straight," Aaron continued. "You sent me over there knowing that I could get my goddamn head blown off?"

"Wait a minute. I didn't send you to Heidi's house," Max nervously said.

"No, but you didn't tell me everything, Max!" Aaron said as he turned away and walked toward the SUV.

"Look…Aaron…here's the deal," Max began laying it out. "Rick asked me could he bring in some guys to help him out. So I let him do his thing. He told me that they were dangerous, but they would make sure Heidi did what the hell she was supposed to do,"

Max began to grow more nervous as he continued to speak. "Now remember…the original deal was supposed to be me, you and Rick. I know you remember this. You was suppose to get close to Heidi to find out the account number. Rick was suppose to take care of her family. That's it!"

Aaron continued to walk toward the SUV. He remained silent as Max continued to talk.

"Aaron…now…I told you to beat Rick to the punch and take the money from Heidi. That way we could split the money two ways and Rick would've never known nothing about it. And that's it. Simple and plain. But you—going to her house—definitely complicated things, Aaron. Come on, man, you gotta know I'm right on this one."

Aaron's mood grew colder, and Max could sense a change in his tone. Max slowly followed him toward the truck, but kept a safe distance. After a brief moment of silence, Max tried to diffuse the misunderstanding. "Actually… you know what?" he said. "Forget about it. It's no big deal."

Aaron remained silent as he opened up the drivers' side door of the truck.

Max continued to try to reason. "Just give me some time, Aaron. I'll handle those guys. That's my problem. Let's just forget about that and split the money now. In fact, why don't you take another ten percent and add it to your share. To be honest, I only need about five hundred to take care of what I got to take care of. We can negotiate the rest."

Aaron was still quiet as he sat down in the front seat. He leaned over and grabbed the black briefcase from the passenger seat. Max became more nervous. He leaned up against the truck and took a deep breath. Aaron grabbed a few more things from the front seat and got out of the SUV. Max's eyes lit up once he saw the briefcase. Aaron stood near the front door of the truck and stared at Max. There was a blank expression on Aaron's face that scared Max.

"So we good?" Max whispered. The fear caused his heart to race.

Aaron's blank expression slowly shifted to disappointment. He looked away from Max momentarily, then turned back to him. "So…as of right now…the only link between me and this money and Datakorp…is you?" he asked in a low tone.

Max raised his eyebrows in shock. He was taken aback by the timing of the question. "What's that suppose to mean?" His voice cracked.

"Just a question, Max," Aaron said. His voice became cold. "Who else knows about me?"

Max was reluctant to answer. Aaron's sharp stare was making him more nervous by the second. After a brief moment, Max opened his mouth to speak. "Nobody else, Aaron," he began. "Just—"

Before Max could finish his statement Aaron quickly pulled out his gun and pointed it at Max.

"Shit!" Max yelled, but it was too late.

A blinding white flash lit up the dark lot as Aaron pulled the trigger. The bullet mercilessly ripped through Max's right cheek, causing him to double over to the ground. He never knew what hit him. He died instantly.

Aaron looked at Max's lifeless face, and then shook his head. "I can't trust you no more." His tone was sadistic. He looked around the dark lot and dropped his gun to the ground. The area fell silent. He walked around Max's body, and twisted his mouth. He could see the thick blood leaking from Max's face. He continued to talk to himself as he put down the briefcase. "I mean…if I'd let you live, then who knows what else could happen," he continued to whisper under his breath. "Right?"

Aaron knelt down near Max's body and turned him around. "You see…I can't take that chance. Who knows if you got another little surprise waiting me somewhere else?" Grabbing Max by the arms, he began to drag him across the dirt toward the drivers' door of the truck. He took one last deep breath before he picked up Max's limp body, then shoved him into the front seat. "So Max, I have to apologize," he said, reaching down and grabbing the gun. He tossed the weapon in the front seat of the truck and slammed shut the door.

He backed away and picked up the black briefcase. He took another look at Max's dead face.

"Okay partner…this is where we part ways. And Max, you are right. A deal is a deal. Here is that five hundred you need." He turned around and pulled out a book of matches. He opened the briefcase and took out five one-hundred-dollar bills, and lit them one by one, then tossed them into the SUV. The gasoline immediately ignited the truck. The fire spread into an intense blaze within seconds. Aaron quickly turned his back on the burning truck and sprinted toward the dark street.

Chapter 5

East Orange General Hospital
East Orange, New Jersey

Sunday, November 4, 2007
5:03 a.m.

*T*here was a loud crash near the front entrance of the break-room at the Forrest E. Brower Emergency Department. Kevin Blackman nearly stumbled to the floor as he rushed past a few employees of the hospital, making it to the time clock. The thirty-two-year-old Medical Technician fumbled with his belongings as he grabbed for his identification card that hung from his neck. He took another frustrated look at the clock and almost yelled out loud as he discovered the time. He frantically grabbed his swipe card and ran it through the slot. A bright green light signaled that he was officially signed in to begin his shift, despite the fact that he was late.

"Shit!" he mumbled, palming his forehead in frustration.

"That's the fourth time this month, Kevin," a female voice echoed from the other side of the break room.

Kevin turned around and followed the voice until his eyes landed on his shift-supervisor, Makia. She was sitting at one of the round tables finishing her lunch and giving him a hard look.

"I know Mak," Kevin said, wearing a defeated expression. He slowly walked over and sat next to her.

"You know if you don't want to do the third shift, you should just request a schedule change," Makia suggested, taking a break from her tuna-on-rye. "Trust me, I will understand."

"Are you going to write me up again?"

"You know I have to, Kevin. It's my job," Makia answered. "You are making a habit of this."

"Mak, come on," Kevin interjected. "I was three minutes late. I can't believe that this is such a big deal."

Makia put her soda down and gave Kevin a disappointed look.

"You know I hate to hear you talk like that, Kevin," Makia said, obviously upset with his attitude. "You're an EMT now. You, of all people in this place, should understand the difference of three minutes, two minutes or even three seconds."

Kevin twisted his face and remained silent. Makia knew he didn't appreciate the lecture, but decided to continue regardless of his expression.

"Let's say that one day it's you out there bleeding and waiting on someone like *you* to come and save the day," Makia continued. "Do you think you will sit there and say that you can spare three more minutes while someone takes their time to get to you? *Hell no*, right?"

Kevin remained silent.

"Exactly," Makia mumbled, using his silence as a green light to continue. "Three minutes is an eternity. It's the difference between life and death, in some cases. And don't you forget that."

After her last words, Kevin felt compelled to turn to her. His facial expression changed, causing Makia to stare back at him.

"You know I know that," he said. "I'm not stressing about the write up."

"I know, Kevin," Makia said, grabbing her sandwich and wrapping it up. "But the time clock is going to show that you were late again. Just be on time and we won't have this problem in the future. I'm sorry." Makia stood up and left Kevin sitting alone at the table.

He looked at his watch again and shook his head. "What if that was *you*...waiting on *you*...and don't you forget it...blah blah blah," he squeaked in a comical voice, mocking Makia , who had already left the room. A few employees started laughing at his antics as Kevin gathered his things and stood up. He totally ignored everyone and exited the break room.

Kevin had been an Intermediate Technician at the East Orange General Hospital for almost a year now. His lust for excitement, along with his quick thinking skills made him a natural at the position. But his lack of focus and tendency to challenge authority made it difficult for him to advance in his department. The strain of his home life and the late hours were slowly eating away at his sanity. But he was no quitter. A few years before, he'd decided to turn his life around and become very successful. His overnight gig at the hospital was just a stepping stone to his ultimate goal. As he entered the locker-room to change into what he often called his monkey-suit, he couldn't help but reflect on the reason why he was there and why it was important for him to stand his ground and keep his head on straight.

Kevin was still changing when he heard a loud banging on the door.

"Damn already," he mumbled under his breath.

"Let's go, Mr. Blackman," Makia yelled from the other side of the door. "You're up!"

Kevin grabbed the rest of his equipment from his locker, then slammed it shut. He didn't even bother to put his padlock on as he rushed out into the hallway. He noticed most of the first responders were already rushing to the exits and he looked over to Makia.

"You see that," she said, pointing to Kevin. "If you would have been ten minutes late, you would have missed that call."

Kevin didn't respond. He simply nodded his head and rushed toward the exit. His expression changed as his adrenaline kicked in. The first distress call of the evening blared through his radio. His blood started to simmer. He followed two fellow EMTs to the first available ambulance and hopped in. As he began to prepare the back of the vehicle, he immediately noticed that another crew was preparing to head out in an ambulance right next to them.

"I didn't get the entire call," Kevin yelled to the driver. "What's going on? And where are we headed?"

"I don't know exactly what it is, but it seems to be pretty big," the driver yelled as he turned on the sirens. "We are the second unit of three."

Kevin closed the rear ambulance doors and prepared for a fast ride. Because he didn't hear the full dispatch, he couldn't help but speculate on what type of call he was going on. Every night was different for the Emergency Response Team. His unit responded to all types of calls. One night, it could be helping out an elderly person with chest pains. The next, it might be trying to revive a child on the highway who'd been involved in a multi-car collision. Something deep within Kevin gave him the feeling that this was not going to be an ordinary call.

Kevin grabbed onto anything he could as the ambulance went flying down the quiet streets of East Orange. The loud screaming from the sirens was a painful reminder that he'd forgotten his ear-plugs back in his locker.

"Maybe I need to be on time," he mumbled. "I'm pretty sure my ears will thank me for being late."

Glancing out of the back of the ambulance, he saw that they were heading deep into a dark neighborhood. The sight instantly told him this was not going to be a highway incident.

"Kevin, I just got word that his is a crime scene," the driver confirmed his thoughts, yelling to the back of the ambulance. "The location is just ahead."

Kevin became more anxious as he heard the news. He grabbed his equipment bag when they slowed to a stop.

"It's a multiple shooting," the driver informed Kevin, and then looked over to another paramedic that was sitting in the passenger side of the ambulance. "We haven't had one of these in the city in a while, so you know what to do."

"Be alert and keep your eyes open!" Kevin and the other two team members recited the command they'd all committed to memory, in unison.

Kevin was the first to exit the ambulance. Police were everywhere. The crime scene seemed to stretch from one end of the block all the way to the three-story house where Kevin found himself trying to make sense of it all. Ducking under the yellow police tape, he made his way to the front entrance of the house. He was quickly greeted by a female police officer.

"I'm Officer Richards," the policewoman said, introducing herself. "I know you guys see a lot of things, but please brace yourself for this. I hope you didn't eat this morning." Officer Richards' words were lifeless as she turned around and led Kevin into the house.

The house was a mess. The furniture was toppled over and most of the pictures and wall fixtures were smashed on the floor. He stepped over mounds of trash as he and the officer made their way through the living room. As they neared the kitchen, Kevin noticed that the trash was just the beginning of the calamity. A bone chilling sensation ran through his body as he came face to face with carnage. Blood was everywhere. Officer Richards looked over to him and gave him a blank stare. He took a deep breath when he saw two bodies lying on the kitchen floor.

"In my six years, I've never seen nothing like this," Officer Richards mumbled as she shook her head. "Senseless murder. People are so wicked in this world."

Kevin gritted his teeth. He couldn't shake the ugly feeling as the faces of the dead already began to haunt his mind. "So both of these individuals are already gone?" he quietly asked.

Officer Richards nodded her head and confirmed his suspicions. "I checked the vitals, but you know we have to do this by the book," she pointed out. "Actually, there is really not a lot for you guys to do here. Just confirm the statuses."

Kevin nodded his head and bent down next to the first dead body. It was a young man who appeared to be in his late twenties to early thirties. Kevin had to numb himself as he noticed an enormous exit wound in the victim's head. He grabbed the victim's right wrist and checked for a pulse. There was none. He looked at his watch and made a note in his pad, then moved on to the body of a young lady. She was clearly older, and looked to be in her late thirties. He felt a strangely disturbing vibe as he knelt down beside her. He took another look at her peaceful face and to hold back his emotions. He grabbed her right wrist and checked for a pulse. She, too, was unresponsive. There was a close range entry wound on the side of her head, indicating that she was also a victim of a gunshot. He couldn't imagine what this woman had done to warrant such a gruesome demise.

Slowly, he stood up and looked over to the officer. "It's confirmed," Kevin said quietly. "These two are definitely dead."

Officer Richards nodded her head. "I have one more downstairs. A male victim."

Kevin was shocked by the news. He wasn't ready to see another body. He gave the officer a peculiar look. She picked up on the vibe and nodded her head.

"I will grab your partners and ask them to confirm for me," she said.

"Thanks," he whispered. He noticed the back door of the house was opened, and decided to grab some air. All of the classes and training he'd taken couldn't prepare him for the experience of death. Victims of violent crimes were always tough for him because of the chaotic nature of the aftermath. Fear, anger, aggression, and rage were some of the emotions felt at crime scenes. And tonight, the mix of emotions was quickly getting to the young paramedic.

Kevin slowly walked down the back porch stairs. After taking a few deep breaths, he headed around to the front of the house to gather himself. He'd only made it a few steps before he made an unexpected discovery. A third body lay motionless a few hundred feet away. "What in the hell?" he mumbled.

Instinctively, he rushed over to the individual lying on the ground. He froze as he stood over the victim. It was another young woman. She had multiple gunshot wounds in her stomach and chest area, and her body pooled in blood. Kevin involuntarily covered his mouth as he looked down at the woman in shock. He couldn't believe the destruction her frail body endured. He didn't know it at the time, but the young woman's name was Heidi Kachina.

Looking around the backyard, he couldn't believe how the police were carelessly treating the secondary crime scene. The nearest officer was nearly one hundred yards away, and it appeared that no real effort was being made to secure the area. Kevin shook his head and knelt down next to Heidi. He gingerly grabbed her hand and noticed that she was still warm. He suddenly felt optimistic. He grabbed her right wrist to check for a pulse. *She's alive!* Her veins gently pulsated against his finger tips. Her response was weak, but Kevin was getting the message. She wasn't dead. Yet.

"Preston, I need you to come out to the side of the house," Kevin yelled into the radio as he called for assistance. "I found a woman out here. She appears to be in her late twenties or early thirties. Multiple gunshot wounds to the chest and abdomen. Victim is unresponsive, but has a pulse. I repeat, victim is unconscious, but showing a pulse. I need a stretcher and preparation for transport immediately!"

"Roger that," a strong voice confirmed from the other end of the radio. "I'm on my way out."

Less than a minute later, two additional paramedics were rushing over to assist Kevin. Kevin prepared Heidi's limp body to be rushed to the hospital. As his partners worked on her, he stood and headed back into the house. He wanted to deliver the news of the surviving victim to the officer in charge of the crime scene. His adrenaline pumped heavy as he approached the rear of the house. He ran up the backstairs and darted inside.

Officer Richards was still in the kitchen, but was now accompanied by a male officer. He was dressed in a sharp black suit, and his grayish beard gave the impression that he was clearly more experienced than Officer Richards. His name was Detective Harold Williams. Before Kevin could get a word out of his mouth, Detective Williams approached the young man and spoke to him in a stark tone.

"What is it?" Detective Williams asked.

"Who's in charge here?" Kevin asked, trying to catch his breath.

"I'm Detective Harold Williams," the detective responded. "I'm in charge for the moment."

"Good to meet you, Detective," Kevin said. "You gotta see this."

Kevin turned and headed back outside.

Detective Williams and Officer Richards followed close behind as he led them to Heidi, who was now being tended to by the other paramedics.

"What's going on here?" Detective Williams frantically asked.

"She's hurt up pretty bad, Detective," Kevin whispered as he knelt down near Heidi. He grabbed her hand. "But miraculously, she is still breathing."

Detective Williams groaned as he looked at Heidi's beautiful face. "Is she going to make it?"

"I believe so," Kevin responded. "She seems to be a strong woman. I believe she's going to make it."

Detective Williams nodded his head. He watched as the paramedics loaded Heidi onto the stretcher and hustled her over to the ambulance.

Detective Williams and Kevin walked over to the ambulance. "What's your name?"

"Kevin, Sir. My name is Kevin."

"Okay, Kevin. Where are you guys going to take her to?"

"East Orange General."

"Okay, I'm coming to," Detective Williams said, inviting himself. I need to know what happened here." Kevin nodded his head as he got into the ambulance. Detective Williams headed to his car and looked at Officer Richards. "You are in charge here until I come back."

"Okay Detective," Officer Richards answered.

Detective Williams drove off ahead of the paramedics while Officer Richards watched the ambulance speed behind the police vehicle en route to the hospital.

❖

Chapter 6

East Orange, New Jersey

3:20 a.m.

"*C'mon Rick, you gotta floor this bitch!*" Vegas yelled. "*He's losing a lot of blood back there. Get us to the hospital man.*"

The tension in Rick's car was mounting as the vehicle sped down Central Avenue. The urgency in Vegas' voice made Rick turn around to the backseat and look at Shaheed. His eyes lit up when he saw the blood leaking heavily from his stomach.

"Goddammit man, this is all fucked up," Rick yelled back, turning back to focus on the road.

"No shit, nigga," Vegas said from the passenger seat. "Just drive."

"What the fuck are you snappin' at me for?" Rick questioned. "I'm not the one who told y'all to start tradin' shots with that bitch."

Vegas shook his head and looked back at his cousin. He turned to Rick and gave him a hard stare. "Let me get that phone I told you to grab back at the house."

"Right now?" Rick responded.

"Yes…right now!" Vegas raised his voice. "I need to find out who this nigga is that took the money!"

Rick dug into his pocket and pulled out the red mobile phone and gave it to Vegas.

"Wait a minute…please tell me you grabbed the other phone too?" Vegas shouted.

"What…you told me to grab the phone from the table," Rick responded with a confused look on his face.

"This is not the dude's phone. This is that other girl's phone. Heidi's friend," Vegas said.

"Damn…I grabbed the wrong one," Rick mumbled.

"No shit!" Vegas snapped. He put the phone in his pocket and turned away from Rick. "Nigga, I knew you was bad luck from the time we hooked up with you," he mumbled. "I don't know why I agreed to do this shit with such a lame ass nigga."

"What?" Rick snapped. "What in the hell does that have to do with anything? How in the hell is that helpin'?"

"Man, just drive," Vegas barked. "Before somebody else get shot tonight."

Before Rick could engage Vegas any further, a frail moan from the back seat startled both men. Vegas turned around and noticed Shaheed was waking up again.

"Don't worry about it, Shah'," Vegas said. "We are almost there, big homie."

"This shit hurts, man," Shaheed moaned as he squirmed around in the backseat. He tried to sit up, but the pain from the gunshot was punishing him.

Vegas didn't say a word. He was clearly becoming more agitated. He turned around and focused his attention back to the road.

Shaheed continued to groan in pain. "I'm serious, Vegas," Shaheed moaned again. "I think I'm dyin'."

"Nigga, don't say that shit!" Vegas yelled. "We almost there! Don't start talking that dyin' shit. Nobody's dyin' tonight! Stop bein' a bitch!"

"Vegas, what the hell is wrong with you, man," Shaheed grunted. "I'm shot. I'm not being a bitch. Shit…this hurts!"

Vegas turned around. "Nigga, I can see that. And you wouldn't be shot if you gave it to that bitch before she hit you."

"What?" Shaheed whispered. He didn't recognize the tone in Vegas' voice.

"Heidi! She got away with the money, man. All you had to do

was pull the trigger, and you didn't, Shah! What the fuck is up with that?"

Shaheed was frozen. He didn't know what to say to his cousin. Vegas' tone was filled with resentment.

The tension in the car was mounting, and Rick tried to deescalate the mood that was building. "Chill, Vegas," Rick whispered from the driver's seat. "We almost at the hospital."

"Nah man, don't tell me to chill," Vegas snapped. "You wasn't in there. Alright? So don't tell me to chill."

Rick didn't say a word.

Vegas turned his attention back to his cousin, Shaheed. "The bottom line, Shah…man, you fucked up." Vegas stared his cousin directly in the eyes. "You had a clear shot at Heidi and you didn't bust on her. Why not?"

"Vegas, go 'head, man," Shaheed snapped. He tried to give off a more aggressive tone, but he was growing weaker and weaker by the minute. "This ain't the time for your crazy shit. I need to get to the hospital."

Vegas gave his cousin another hard stare. He was clearly angry with Shaheed. "Yeah okay, nigga. Just know that you the reason we don't have that money," he said and turned around. "I still think you bitched up in there."

Shaheed decided not to respond. He was growing more concerned for his life as he felt himself growing weaker from the loss of blood.

"Nigga, just get us there," Vegas snapped again at Rick. The entire car fell silent. The only sound that could be heard was the engine roaring as Rick punched the gas to make it to the hospital.

* * *

Langhorne, PA

3: 30 a.m.

About seventy miles away in Langhorne, Pennsylvania, an ugly feeling came over Melissa Davis, causing her to awaken from a dead sleep. She felt her heart racing, and quickly sat up in her bed. It took her a second to catch her breath and to calm her nerves. She looked around her dark bedroom and noticed that she was all alone. Her thoughts quickly shifted to her boyfriend, Lamar, who was the last person on her mind before she'd decided to turn in for the evening. She instinctively became worried. Lamar hadn't returned yet from visiting his mother. She grabbed her cell phone and scrolled through her calls. Strangely enough, she had no missed calls from him. He was usually good at calling her or sending her a text message to let her know he was okay. But tonight, Lamar was missing in action, and the thought made Melissa jump to her feet and turn on her bedroom light. She nervously dialed his cell phone and waited for him to answer. Melissa felt relieved when she heard his voice calmly speaking from the other line. Unfortunately, it was his voicemail.

You just reached Lamar. And unless you been on the Moon for the past 80 years, you know what to do after the tone. Leave it!

Melissa worried more. She decided to leave a message for him.

"Baby, it's me. I'm starting to get worried now," Melissa said. "You haven't called me in almost two days. I'm trying not to be a pain in the ass, but you gotta call me back, baby. I don't know what's going on. When you get this message call me. Please—" she ended, deciding not to say another word. She hung up the cell phone and sat down on her sofa. She looked at her clock and noticed it was almost four in the morning. "Where the hell is he?" Melissa whispered.

She thought back to the last time she'd seen Lamar. She remembered them having a loud argument about his running off to save Heidi, his sister, every time she'd called. Melissa's temper got the best of her that night and, as a result, things skidded down hill. She thought about the look on Lamar's face when she'd stormed out of his apartment. He'd looked disappointed and hurt, but Melissa was determined to be selfish that evening. She'd begged him not to leave, but he'd disobeyed. Now Melissa feared that maybe he was staying away on purpose. Maybe he was finally fed up with all of her demanding ways. Her mind raced with many negative thoughts. She looked at her clock again, then decided to take a chance and call the one person that might know where to find her boyfriend.

Melissa scrolled down the contacts on her cell phone. When she came to Heidi's phone number, she shook her head. "This bitch," Melissa mumbled.

Her relationship with Heidi always seemed to be on the rocks. From the first day she'd met Lamar, she'd always felt like she was competing with Heidi for his attention. And although she was in competition with Lamar's flesh and blood, Melissa felt she'd earned the right to be closer to him. Especially after almost nine years of being his girlfriend. She decided to phone Heidi despite the tension between the two. She thought back to the other day when Lamar had asked her to bury the hatchet with his sister. Maybe now would be a good opportunity to do just that. Not to mention she could finally find her man.

After a few rings, Heidi's phone unrepentantly disconnected. Melissa looked at her phone and tried it again. This time Heidi's phone went directly to voicemail. Melissa instantly became frustrated. *What the hell is going on?* She dialed Heidi's phone one more time and, to her surprise, someone answered the phone, but it wasn't Heidi. A weak voice spoke from the other line. It was Lamar's mother, Pearl Kachina. Melissa was surprised that Pearl answered the phone and instantly changed her tone.

"Hey Ms. Pearl, is that you?" Melissa stuttered.

"Yes, this is me," Pearl softly answered.

"I apologize for calling so late," Melissa said. "I was expecting Heidi to answer."

"It's okay," Pearl said. "I have my daughter's phone."

"Oh okay. I'm so sorry, I didn't know," Melissa apologized. "Did I wake you?"

"No, no…no child. You didn't wake me," Pearl answered. Her tone sounded distant. "You're looking for Lamar?"

"I am," Melissa quickly answered. "And I hate to call over there at this hour. But Lamar hasn't called me in a couple of days now. And the last time I heard from him, he was at your house."

"I know. He's still there," Pearl whispered. Her voice began to crack with emotion.

"Ms. Pearl…are you okay?" she asked. "What's all of that noise in the background?"

"I'm in the ER at East Orange General," Pearl whispered from the other line.

"Oh, my goodness. Are you okay?" Melissa uttered.

"Not really. Something happened at the house," Pearl became emotional as she revealed the news.

Melissa stood up and covered her mouth. She felt her hands beginning to shake. The only thing she could think about was her Lamar getting into trouble again. She was afraid to ask the next question, but the words were falling out of her mouth before she could catch them. "Is Lamar okay?" she quietly asked.

"He's not, Melissa," Pearl mumbled. Her voice was filled with concern. "Something terrible is going on at the house."

Melissa closed her eyes and slowly sat back down on the sofa. She tried her best to fight back her tears, but a few began to trickle from the corners of her eyes. "Tell me, please," Melissa pleaded. "Tell me what's going on? Is my baby okay?"

"Melissa I have to go," Pearl interrupted her. "I gotta talk to the police now."

"The police? What's going on up there? I'm coming up." Melissa frantically made her way back to her bedroom to get dressed.

"Coming up where?" Pearl quickly asked.

"I'm coming up to Jersey. I'll be up there in less than an hour," Melissa snapped. "I'm 'bout to go over to your house to see what's going on."

"No!" Pearl yelled. Her motherly voice made Melissa pause for a second. "Don't go to that house, Melissa. I don't want you to get hurt. Please. I will call you back in a few and let you know everything that's going on. I have to talk to these cops now."

Before Melissa could say another word, Pearl hung up. "Shit!" Melissa yelled, realizing that the call ended. Despite being warned by Pearl, she continued to get dressed. It took her less than five minutes to put on her clothes, grab her bag and bolt out the door. She fired up her engine and made her way to the East Orange General Hospital to see exactly what was going on with her boyfriend, Lamar.

* * *

East Orange General Hospital
East Orange, New Jersey

3: 43 a.m.

Back at the East Orange Emergency Room, Pearl hung up the cell phone in frustration. Melissa was the last person she'd expected to call Heidi's phone. She became even more worried for Heidi as she realized that she hadn't heard from her daughter or Faith since leaving the house. She tried her best not to focus on the worst. She gathered her emotions once again, and tucked the cell away in her pocket. She took a deep breath, then noticed a large policeman approaching her as she sat in the waiting area.

To Pearl's surprise, the officer looked extremely young to be handling a gun and a badge. She immediately assumed he was close to twenty-years old and fresh out the police academy. She could tell that he was a rookie by his nervous demeanor. His tall frame and massive weight were almost a comical opposite of his baby face. Pearl stood up to greet the young policeman.

"Okay Ma'am, you said there's some sort of disturbance at your house?" the young officer blurted.

Pearl was taken aback by his rough tone. She didn't know how to respond to him. "Umm… yes," she answered nervously as she waited for the officer to introduce himself. After a few moments, she was stunned that the officer never made a formal introduction. He began to write something down on his note pad.

Is everybody at this place a rude ass? She stared at the officer's face and instantly became disgusted. The lower half of his face was dotted with razor bumps, Keloids and scars. Pearl found herself uncomfortably staring at what seemed to be his first rookie mistake; shaving with a dirty razor. She shook her head and turned her attention to his notepad. Since the officer never revealed his name, she decided to assume his friends called him Officer Bumpy.

"And you are an East Orange resident, right?" Officer Bumpy sternly asked.

Pearl was tempted to ignore the remedial question, but decided to cooperate with the beginner. "Yes, Officer. I live in East Orange," Pearl responded. "If I'm not mistaken though, I think one of your fellow officers took my information earlier."

"Is that a fact?" Officer Bumpy asked with a shocked expression. His tone made him appear even more inexperienced.

"Yes," Pearl quickly answered before the officer could write another word. "I spoke to an Officer Richards about an hour ago, and she told me your police department was going to dispatch a unit over to my house."

"Okay, that is a possibility," Officer Bumpy conceded. "I just started my shift, and my supervisor instructed me to come speak with you."

"Oh okay," Pearl mumbled.

"Give me one second," he said as he grabbed his radio from his left shoulder. "I will call this in and get a status report."

"Thank you."

The officer abruptly turned around and walked away from Pearl. She watched the rookie return to the security station, and couldn't help but feel apprehensive about his antics. She thought about Heidi again, and grabbed the cell phone from her pocket. There were still no calls from her. Pearl began to get antsy. She waited patiently for a few minutes, then decided to walk over to the security desk where the officer was posted.

"Excuse me," she politely said, trying to get the officer's attention as he sat at the desk. "I was just wondering if you heard anything back from your people?"

The officer looked up to Pearl with a slight attitude. "What?" he grunted, pretending he didn't hear her question.

Pearl felt a sense of déjà vu, realizing this was the second person snapping at her at the hospital. "Did you just say *what* to me?" she questioned fiercely. Her temper flared as she continued to scold the young officer. "That is extremely rude."

"Wait a minute," Officer Bumpy said, rising to his feet. "First of all, I need you to calm down, Ma'am."

"And second of all, Sir!" Pearl snapped, interrupting the officer. "I need you to show me some respect. I'm old enough to be your grandmother, boy. So don't say *what* to me. I asked you a simple question, and I think I deserve a simple answer."

"Ma'am relax," he boldly said. He was clearly becoming more agitated.

"I am relaxed," Pearl yelled. She didn't realize how loud she was. A few people in the waiting area immediately turned their attention to the commotion. "It's like no one wants to do their goddamn job around this place. Now I need to know what's going on at my house, and I need to know now."

"Ma'am, I understand that," Officer Bumpy interjected. "But you won't give me a chance to speak."

Pearl remained silent and stared at the police officer. She coolly folded her arms and waited for him to speak again.

"Are you calm now?" the officer asked.

Pearl nodded her head.

"Okay good." The officer was relieved. "I called to my supervisor and he couldn't give me any additional information from the scene. Now that can mean one of two things. Number one…that could mean that there's nothing going on at the house that would warrant some sort of major report from the premises. Or number two…they are still trying to put things together over there."

"And what the hell does that mean?" she yelled again. Here

voice echoed off the walls of the waiting area like an opera house. "This is bullshit. You are not telling me anything!" she continued her tirade at the officer.

"Goddammit, Ma'am!" he shouted. "You are making a scene. And we really don't have to take it there."

"Take it where?" Pearl fired back. She took extreme offense to his threatening tone. "Take it *where?*"

In the mist of the argument, neither Pearl nor the policeman noticed three men stumbling into the front entrance of the emergency room. Two men were carrying another man, who seemed to be in serious condition from the thick stream of blood flowing into his already soaked t-shirt. The men held him up as they slowly made their way into the waiting area.

"I need some help over here," the larger man yelled. "Nurse? Somebody…hurry up in there…please. I need somebody to help my cousin now!"

The familiar voice yelling from across the room hit Pearl's ears like a sharp bolt of lightning. She momentarily froze where she stood. Her mouth remained opened, but nothing was coming out. Her eyes were as wide as two silver dollars. Officer Bumpy didn't know how to respond as he watched Pearl slowly turn away from him.

"Hey, where's the nurse?" the larger man yelled again. "Will somebody come out here and help us!"

Pearl nearly pissed herself when she saw the man's face. "Oh my lord," she whispered as she stared into the man's grey eyes. All the blood rushed from her head into her stomach. She felt like she was about to faint as she recognized the men. Vegas. Shaheed. And her boyfriend, Rick.

Vegas saw Pearl across the room and stared at her. He stood motionless. Rick picked up on Vegas' vibe and turned her way. He looked at his girlfriend in shock. He didn't know what to say. Pearl was horrified at the sight. Rick watched her as she fearfully backed into the police officer, causing the officer to move away. Rick let go of Shaheed and immediately ran out of the hospital.

"Sir, that's them," Pearl mumbled to the officer. She was beyond terrified. Her voice cracked with each word as her emotions took control of her body. "That's the men who were at my house, Sir. Please…that's them."

It took a brief moment for the young officer to understand what Pearl was saying. She looked over to the rookie, who gave her an unsure gesture.

"That's them!" she screamed at the top of her lungs. She pointed directly at Vegas and Shaheed, who were now in the middle of the waiting area. Pearl was near tears. She yelled at the officer again. "That's the men who were at my house, please...get them. They're right there!"

The officer finally picked up on the message. He quickly drew his service weapon and pointed it at the bleeding men. "Put your hands up!" the young officer yelled at the men. "Do it now!"

Vegas didn't budge as he watched the officer make his way over to him. Shaheed was in too much pain to obey the command. "Officer, my cousin and I were the victims of a robbery," Vegas pleaded as the officer moved closer. "We are just here to get some medical attention."

Pearl watched in fear from the other side of the room as the young officer approached Vegas and his cousin. She couldn't believe how cool Vegas was, even with the policeman pointing his gun at him.

"I'm not going to tell you again. Put your fucking hands up. Both of you!" The officer commanded.

"I'm shot!" Vegas said vehemently. I don't know if you see that but I can't put my hands above my head.

The young officer was now only a few feet from Vegas and Shaheed. He squeezed his gun tighter and pointed it directly at Vegas' face. He gave him an unflinching stare. "Ask me if I give a shit, nigga," the officer whispered. He wanted to show Vegas that he was not intimated by his size. "Now put your fucking hands up!"

Vegas almost lost control. The words from the officer's mouth infuriated him. He kept his cool and looked over to his cousin. He let Shaheed go, and raised his hands. The pain was excruciating, but

Vegas didn't grimace for a second. Shaheed almost fell to the floor as the gunshot wound continued to do major damage to his body. He leaned against a chair in the waiting area and looked over to the cop.

"I can't raise my hands, Officer," Shaheed mumbled. He continued to hold his stomach. "I'm dyin'."

Vegas looked over to Shaheed and gave him a disgusted look. He balled up his lips and turned back to the officer, who was now calling for backup.

"I need officer assistance in area three of the emergency room," the young officer requested from his radio. "I also need a nurse down here too. We have two injured suspects that will need medical assistance before transporting."

The officer waited for confirmation and put away his radio. He turned his focus back to Vegas, who continued to stare at him. Pearl felt relieved that the officer finally had the situation under control. She watched closely as the officer got closer to Vegas.

"Turn around, and put your hands behind your head," he instructed. "I don't care what kind of injury you got. Let's go!"

Vegas took one last look at the rookie's young face, and turned around. He raised his arms higher and placed his palms firmly on the back of his head.

The officer grabbed Vegas and pushed him against the nearest wall, face first. Vegas didn't put up a fight. Everyone in the waiting area was now watching the incident. Vegas listened closely and heard the officer holster his weapon. "This is it," Vegas thought as he heard the sharp clicking noise of the handcuffs behind him.

"Officer, please call the nurse," Shaheed moaned. He stumbled against the chair again. "I'm in so much pain."

The young officer took his attention away from Vegas for a second and turned to Shaheed. Pearl gasped as she watched the officer make a monumental mistake.

"What the hell are you doing?" Pearl whispered. "Just arrest him!"

"Please…Officer, can you call the nurse again?" Shaheed pleaded.

"Shut the fuck up!" the officer yelled.

The momentary lapse in judgment was all Vegas needed. He made a quick decision. Before the officer could turn back to him, Vegas summoned every pound in his enormous frame to his elbow. In one motion, Vegas twisted his body around and broke free from the officer's grip. The rookie was stunned by the move and didn't have time to react. Before he could grab hold of Vegas again, Vegas smashed the young officer flush on the side of his face with a stiff elbow. The rookie was dazed from the wrecking-ball effect of the hit. Vegas quickly turned around and grabbed the officer by the collar. He punched the rookie three times in his face and head. The massive blows knocked the officer unconscious. Vegas tossed the young officer's limp body to the floor. Pearl screamed in horror. Her mouth fell wide opened as she watched the massive policeman crumble to the hospital floor like a house of cards.

"Oh my God…somebody help!" Pearl screamed. She quickly turned around and ran toward the Telemetry Unit of the hospital.

Vegas stepped over the officer's body, rushing over to Shaheed.

"C'mon Cousin…we gotta go!" Vegas ordered as he reached down to grab Shaheed.

Shaheed tried to get up from the chair, but he couldn't move. The continued loss of blood was catching up to him. Vegas reached down again and tried to grab him. His injury was also worsening. It was impossible for Vegas to pick up Shaheed.

"Shah…I need you to help me," Vegas pleaded. "Stand up, man. We gotta get out of here." Vegas got a good grip on Shaheed and tried to pull him. He grunted in pain as he attempted again. "Goddammit, Shaheed!" Vegas yelled. "Get the fuck up, man! We gotta bounce outta here or we goin' to prison, homie!"

Shaheed tried to push up himself. His arms were so weak. The cousins were running out of time. There was a loud commotion from just beyond the emergency area of the hospital. Vegas' eyes lit up when he saw three police officers running down the hall toward the waiting area.

"Fuck!" Vegas grunted. He looked down to Shaheed, who

fluctuated between being in and out of consciousness. He looked up again and saw the officers were closing in fast on them. Vegas had to think quickly. He tried to pick up Shaheed one more time, but his arms buckled. Shaheed fell back into the chair, the impact waking him. Helplessly, he looked at Vegas staring back at him. Vegas could hear the officer's boots as they ran down the hall. He knew they were getting closer.

Shaheed saw something in Vega' eyes that he'd never seen before. *Fear*. Vegas looked at the officers, then turned to his cousin again. Shaheed could sense what was coming next.

"I'm sorry, Cousin," Vegas whispered.

Before Shaheed could open his mouth, Vegas turned around and darted out of the ER and into the street. The officers drew their weapons, and tried to give chase, but Vegas was long gone. Shaheed was stunned. He couldn't believe his cousin left him all alone to face the music. A burly officer, who was trailing behind the pack, approached the waiting room and surveyed the area. He saw the young officer stretched out on the floor near the far wall, and became beet-red. He turned to Shaheed, who continued to bleed on the chair. The burly officer was enraged. Shaheed tried to say something in his defense, but it was too late. The officer cocked his arm back and slapped Shaheed on the side of the head with the butt of his gun. Despite his crushing injuries, the officer shoved Shaheed to the hospital floor, turned him over, and placed handcuffs on him. The last thing Shaheed saw was the butt of the officer's gun, violently banging against his face.

Chapter 7

East Orange General Hospital
East Orange, New Jersey

6:18 a.m.

D etective Williams pulled up to the parking lot located in the rear of the hospital. Unconsciously, he grabbed his stomach as he emerged from the unmarked police cruiser. In all the excitement from the crime scene, he'd never realized his stomach had been empty for most of the morning. He turned his focus from his hunger to the speeding ambulance as it blew by, then parked near the hospital's emergency entrance. The paramedics wasted no time hopping out of the ambulance and rushing Heidi into the hospital. The detective slowly shook his head as he watched the all-too-familiar scene.

He'd spent most of his career chasing violent criminals. During his twelve years as an East Orange policeman, he'd encountered hundreds of burglars, rapists, and even murderers in the Essex County area. Of all the crimes perpetrated by unlawful men in his jurisdiction, his most loathsome crime was violence against women. He despised it. He took it personal when a woman was beat-up, raped, or murdered in his city. The disturbing image of a woman's mutilated body instantly made the detective set his sights on vengeance. And tonight, seeing Heidi's bloody frame clearly made him furious.

He glanced at the blue neon lights of the entrance and took a deep breath. A feeling of anxiety came over him as he hesitated to walk inside the hospital. A number of dark memories came to his mind. He pictured all the faces of the many victims who'd lost their battle to death inside of East Orange General. He shook his head for a moment, then prayed that this latest victim would survive. He was slowly making his way to the entrance when his phone began to buzz on his hip. He stopped in his tracks and answered the call.

"Go!" the detective barked as he answered the phone.

"Detective, this is Officer Richards," A female voice responded.

"What happened?" he mumbled, rushing the officer to the point.

"There was a call that went over the radio about a disturbance at the hospital," Officer Richards informed.

"At East Orange General?"

"Yes Sir," Officer Richards answered. "The victim's mother reported seeing the suspects at the hospital."

"No shit? I'm at the hospital now!" The detective's adrenaline kicked in. "Are they still here?"

"Yes. They have one in custody as we speak," Officer Richards said. "He's receiving medical treatment for an apparent gunshot wound."

Detective Williams abruptly disconnected the call and rushed into the hospital. The news of a viable suspect made his blood boil. He became angrier as he thought about confronting the man. He rushed through the automatic doors, and took a quick survey of the hospital. The lobby was buzzing with police activity. Flashing his identification card to a uniformed officer, he immediately began asking questions.

"What happened here, Officer…" He looked at the officer's name tag. "Officer Green, is it?"

"Yes Sir," Officer Green responded. "It was total chaos in here, Detective. We have a gunshot victim prepping for surgery. His story is that he was the victim of some sort of robbery. But then we have another E.R. patient here who has identified him as a suspect in a home invasion in the city."

Detective Williams looked around the lobby and nodded his head. "Yes. I just came from that home invasion scene," he informed. "It has turned into a murder scene."

The officer's mouth fell open at the news. "One more thing, Sir," Officer Green whispered.

"What's that?"

"They assaulted an officer. They knocked the rookie out cold!"

Detective Williams dropped his brows. He became angrier. "Where is the suspect now?"

"They have him in the trauma unit now," Officer Green responded and pointed down the hallway. "Like I said, they are prepping him for surgery."

"Well…let's go make sure that he's *properly* prepped!" Detective Williams mumbled as he turned around. Officer Green instantly picked up on the detective's sarcastic tone. He followed closely behind the detective as he made his way through the lobby. A few officers joined the pair as the detective moved through the hospital. By the time they reached the suspect's room, the group had grown to over ten policemen.

"What's the suspect's name?" Detective Williams asked as they reached the room.

Another uniformed officer stood near the entrance to the unit and greeted them. "Good morning, Detective," the other officer said. "The suspect's name is Shaheed Porter. There was another suspect with him but he fled on foot. We are still looking for him, Sir. And as for Shaheed, he does have an arrest record…but we could only find a juvenile—"

Thank you," Detective Williams snapped, cutting the officer short. He looked over to Officer Green and motioned for him to follow him inside the trauma unit. A couple of officers continued to follow the detective as he looked for Shaheed's bed. The detective felt relieved when he saw a nurse working on Shaheed. He was still conscious.

"Excuse me, nurse, we need to speak with this gentleman," Detective Williams ordered forcefully.

The RN turned around and looked at the officers. "Excuse me?" "Right now, Ma'am," Officer Green added as he tried to backup the detective's orders.

"He's about to go into surgery," the nurse offered. "I don't think this is possible."

"Just give us two minutes with him," Detective Williams said with an assuring tone.

The nurse hesitated to move. One of the officers behind the pack walked over and grabbed her by the arm, and removed her from the hospital room.

Detective Williams walked over to Shaheed and looked at him. "This is him, right?" he asked, making sure Shaheed was handcuffed to the bed.

"Yes Sir...that's him!" Officer Green responded. He walked over to the other side of the bed.

Shaheed looked up to the detective. The monitor tracking his vital signs started to beep off the charts as his heart rate increased.

"I'm only going to ask you this once," Detective Williams said. "Who did it?"

Shaheed trembled with fear. He tried to yell for the nurse, but Officer Green covered his mouth.

"Don't make me ask you again, you little rat bastard!" Detective Williams said as he got closer to Shaheed's face. "Who killed that girl at the house?"

Officer Green removed his palm from Shaheed's mouth and looked at him. Shaheed was nearly in tears. He looked over to the detective, slowly shaking his head. "It wasn't me...I swear!"

"Give me that stick!" Detective Williams ordered as he pointed to Officer Green's baton. The officer snatched the nightstick off of his utility belt and handed it over. The detective quickly pulled back the sheets, exposing Shaheed's bare feet. Before Shaheed could mumble another word, Detective Williams swung the wood baton from over his right shoulder and smashed the bottoms of Shaheed's feet.

"Owww fuck! Please stop!" Shaheed yelled. Officer Green quickly covered Shaheed's mouth as Detective Williams continued to strike. The pain felt like the impact of a sledge hammer. Tears came to Shaheed's eyes as he became defenseless to the punishment.

"Now I'm going to ask you again…!" Detective Williams shouted as he tried to catch his breath. "Who killed those people back at that house? Was it you?"

A few nurses in the trauma unit heard the commotion in the room and tried to investigate the noise. Two officers near the entrance of Shaheed's room stopped and turned them away.

"I got all night…and judging by this bullet…you don't!" the detective taunted. "Now answer my question…who did it?"

"It wasn't me. I'm tellin' you the truth," Shaheed uttered. He was crying now. The bottoms of his feet felt like he was standing on a bed of nails.

"Wrong answer!" He cocked back the baton and whipped the bottom of Shaheed's feet again. Shaheed yelled to the top of his lungs. A few officers giggled at the sight of him in pain.

"You not tellin' me what I want to hear!" The detective yelled. "Who killed them!"?

Shaheed's mouth was moving, but no words were coming out. He was too weak to speak. The pain from the bullet and the soles of his feet were taking a toll on him.

"Don't die on me yet…you bastard…you hear me?" Detective Williams shouted. "Just tell me who did it!"

"I did," Shaheed whimpered. "I killed them." His voice was barely loud enough for anyone to hear the admission.

Detective Williams looked at the other officers. "I have three uniformed witnesses here that can verify that they heard you confess to these crimes," he said as he stood over Shaheed. The other officers nodded their confirmation in unison.

"I heard it too," Officer Green mumbled. "He definitely con-fessed."

"Just to let you know, Mr. Shaheed, after your surgery you *will* be arrested and charged with murder," the detective pointed out. "And you better pray that this other girl makes it. Or you will be charged with her murder too."

A commotion came from the entrance to Shaheed's room. Two nurses and three doctors rushed into the room.

"What the hell is going on in here?" a doctor with a Middle Eastern accent screamed.

"It's okay, everybody…we're done here." Detective Williams smiled as he tried his best to conceal the baton. "Our suspect just wanted to confess his sins." He gave Shaheed a devious gesture.

The officers began to file out of the room. Shaheed was still moaning in pain as the detective left his bedside and walked over to one of the doctors, pulling him a side.

"Do what you got to do to keep him alive," he said to the doctor. "We need his ass alive so we can charge it with murder…okay?"

The doctor gave him a strange look and nodded his head. "Okay, we'll do our best," the doctor uttered.

Detective Williams calmly gave the doctor a small nod and left the trauma unit.

* * *

Garden State Parkway

6:31 a.m.

About seven miles away, on the Garden State Parkway, Melissa Davis broke every moving violation there was, trying to make it to the East Orange General Hospital. She'd spent the last hour dodging cars and avoiding police detection as she pushed her truck well past the legal speed limit. She'd repeatedly tried to contact Pearl, but was unsuccessful. As she approached her exit, Melissa grabbed her phone from the passenger seat and tried Pearl once again.

"Dammit!" she yelled. The phone went straight to voicemail. She decided to try her boyfriend Lamar's phone again. No luck. It was turned off. *What the hell is going on up here*! A million scenarios raced through her mind as she exited the highway and entered the city limits of East Orange. She continued to speed until she saw the

General Hospital. Melissa approached the parking lot of the hospital and became numb. Her chest pounded with anxiety. She didn't know what to expect as she parked her truck and rushed into the emergency entrance.

The waiting area was crowded. Melissa frantically looked for a familiar face, but there was none. Immediately, she rushed over to the reception desk and motioned for the desk clerk. Before she could ask a question, she heard a familiar voice just over her left shoulder.

"Melissa, what are you doing here?" a woman shouted.

Melissa immediately turned and saw Pearl. She rushed over and hugged her. "I had to come up here …you didn't sound right." Melissa turned back and took in the waiting room. Police officers, nurses, and patients were buzzing about the area. The scene made her very nervous. "So what happened? Are you hurt?"

Pearl slowly nodded her head. She sat down, then pointed to an ankle brace. "They shot my baby," she whispered as she wiped a few tears from her face.

"What?" Melissa stuttered. "What happened?"

"They shot Heidi," Pearl mumbled. "They tried to kill my babies."

"Oh God…no!" Melissa groaned. She was in shock. "What happened up here? Where's Lamar?"

"Melissa. I'm so sorry, sweetie…" Pearl stammered. "Some men broke into my house. They really hurt Lamar bad."

Melissa covered her mouth with both hands. She became numb as Pearl continued.

"I don't know what's going on now. I've been waiting for someone to tell me where he is. The cops are at my house, but nobody will tell me what happened to my son."

"Do you think Lamar is still at the house?" Melissa asked as she tried to fight back her tears.

"Baby, I have asked every policeman here," Pearl continued. "No one is saying a word. They don't know what's going on at the house."

Melissa's heart buckled from the news. She slowly sat down across from Pearl. "I told him," Melissa mumbled as her face turned red with pain. "I told him not to go over to your house. I don't know why I felt like something bad was going to happen to him, but I told him." Pearl looked over to Melissa, who was crying now. "Goddammit!" she shouted as she became frustrated. Before Pearl could console her, a nurse walked into the waiting area and looked at the women.

"I'm sorry to interrupt," the nurse humbly apologized. "Are you Pearl?"

"Yes!" Pearl quickly answered as she stood up.

"They told me to come out here and let you know that your daughter is stabilizing."

"Oh…thank God!" Pearl shouted. "So she's alive?"

"Yes. Your daughter is incredibly strong, Ma'am," she told Pearl with a warm smile. "She lost a lot of blood, and is going to need another operation. The doctors have ordered that she to airlifted to another hospital."

Pearl moved closer to Melissa and grabbed her hand. "Where are they going to take her?" she asked.

"Riverview Hospital in Red Bank," the nurse continued. "It's a great hospital, Ma'am. Trust me, your daughter is going to pull through."

Pearl's eyes erupted into tears of joy. She was elated to hear Heidi was alive. She glanced over to Melissa and smiled.

Melissa continued to struggle with her emotions. She looked over to the nurse. "What about Lamar?"

"I'm sorry?" the nurse stammered.

"Lamar…is he in here, too?" Melissa asked. Her voice shook with emotion.

"I'm sorry. We don't have a patient here by that name—"

"Well…where is he?" Melissa quickly asked, cutting the nurse short.

"I don't know."

"What do you mean *you don't know*?" Melissa snapped. "Where are the police? Do they know?" She became infuriated. She stormed past the nurse and headed toward the exit.

Pearl tried to follow her, but struggled to keep up. "Where are you going?" she yelled to Melissa.

"I need to find Lamar," Melissa answered as more tears came to her. "I'm going to your house!" She rushed out of the emergency room doors and headed to her car. Pearl struggled with her leg, but managed to follow her to the parking lot. The women got into the car. Melissa fired up the engine and sped out of the parking lot. Pearl felt nervous as they headed to her house to find out what happened to her son, Lamar.

* * *

Pearl's House
East Orange, NJ

7:02 a.m.

Officer Richards walked out of Pearl's and noticed the morning sun was slowly creeping through the amber sky. She let out a much needed yawn as she realized she had been working almost twelve hours straight tonight. The officer was clearly ready to end this night as she walked over and spoke to a driver from the Medical Examiner's Office.

"We are good to go, Sir," Officer Richards said. "You can remove the bodies from the house now. Please notate the time."

The driver nodded his head and walked into the house. He was followed by two co-workers as they carried a mortuary-style gurney through the living room. Officer Richards walked off the porch, grabbing her cell phone. She dialed Detective Williams' phone and waited for him to answer.

"We are getting ready to wrap up here," she said when she heard the detective's voice.

"Did you find another gun at that house?" Detective Williams barked.

"We have searched everywhere, Detective. The basement, upstairs, and even in the yard. I'm telling you…" Officer Richards continued to speak. She sounded aggravated. "We didn't find a single weapon here. It's like somebody took all the guns off of the scene already."

"Well, how in the hell can we have three goddamn bodies and no guns?" Detective Williams yelled.

"Why are you yelling at me?" Officer Richards snapped. She moved away from the house and walked toward her police cruiser.

"I'm not yelling. Yet!" Detective Williams shouted. "It *don't* add up! Three bodies, almost ten goddamn bullets, and no guns?"

"That seems to be the case here, Detective," the officer responded. "We haven't found a single gun here."

"Well, before you leave…there better be a gun showing up miraculously somewhere," Detective Williams strongly ordered.

Officer Richards was shaken by his tone. Something in his voice was malicious. "What are you saying?"

"What I am saying is this," the detective continued. "I don't care how it gets there. But a non police-issued weapon better show up in that house and in an evidence bag before you leave."

Officer Richards became nervous. She looked at her cell phone for a moment. "What are you asking me to do?" she whispered. She looked around to make sure no one was listening to her.

"How long you been a cop?"

"Almost four years."

"So…you know the routine. You're a big girl. Use your imagination. When you find that gun…make sure it gets to me first. I will get it to the crime lab myself!"

The officer put her palm on her forehead as she heard Detective Williams disconnect the call. She looked around to the other officers and shook her head. She couldn't believe what the detective was ordering her to do. Officer Richards put her cell phone back in her pocket, then walked over to her police car. She opened the trunk of the cruiser and grabbed another evidence bag. The officer looked around one last time before she pulled the cover off a false bottom in the rear of her trunk. She quickly pulled out a jet black .40 caliber pistol.

Officer Richards hadn't seen what she referred to as her *insurance gun* in over a year. She took a deep breath, and tucked the dummy gun inside of the evidence bag. She tried to ignore the consequences of her actions, but the thought of being fired and brought up on charges could not escape her mind. The officer sealed the evidence bag and slammed the trunk shut.

A loud commotion startled her for a moment. She turned around and saw a car speeding recklessly down the quiet street. The officer rushed to the front of the police cruiser and tossed the evidence bag inside. She turned around just in time to see a female driver pulling over directly in front of the house. Officer Richards approached the car, and two women frantically exited the vehicle. It was Melissa and Pearl. Officer Richards immediately recognized Pearl from the family photos inside the house. She put her hands up, trying to stop the women.

"Wait a minute, ladies…this is still a crime scene," Officer Richards shouted as she moved closer to Pearl.

"This is my house!" Pearl snapped. "Where's my son?"

"Can I get some help over here?" Officer Richards yelled as she looked over to a few cops.

"Where's Lamar?" Melissa shouted. She rushed past Officer Richards and was intercepted by a number of policemen who were determined not to let her enter the house.

"What happened here?" Pearl screamed. She tried to force by. "Please tell me what happened. Is my son okay?"

"Please calm down, Ma'am," Officer Richards said as she struggled with Pearl. "We are still doing an investigation here—"

"Fuck your investigation!" Melissa shouted at the top of her lungs. "Who's in charge here? We are his family…what happened to him?" She continued to battle with the officers.

"Oh my God. Please no!" Pearl yelled. The pain in her voice froze everyone in the front yard, even the officers. Melissa turned to the house and was immediately gripped by emotion. She watched in horror as two men carried a lumpy body bag out of the front door. Her face exploded with tears. Melissa ran toward the house, but her legs buckled, stopping her. She couldn't breathe as the rush of emotions had gotten the best of her. She collapsed in the arms of a male officer and shouted in anguish.

Pearl started to shake like a leaf as she rushed toward the black bag. "No…no…no. No…no!" she screamed as she forced her way by Officer Richards. "Is that him?" Pearl hollered. "Please tell me that's not my son!" She continued to scream as she rushed toward the gurney. A few officers tried to hold her back, but her motherly pain gave her the extra strength she needed to break free from the officers' grip. "Please…Lamar…No…!" Pearl continued to yell as she got closer to the body bag. As the men rolled the gurney through the yard, Pearl jumped in front of them and reached for the black bag. The men froze as Pearl frantically grabbed the zipper and tried to open the bag. Before she could expose the body, Officer Richards dove on Pearl and knocked her to the ground.

"Please Ma'am…you don't want to do that!" Officer Richards yelled. She held Perl down while the men continued to roll the gurney toward the van.

"Please don't tell me that's my son…please," Pearl cried out. Her face was twisted with pain as the tears ran down her face.

"I'm sorry," Officer Richards whispered as she began to feel sorry for Pearl.

"Please tell me that Lamar is not in that bag," Pearl groaned.

"Ma'am…I feel so terrible to be the one that has to tell you this," Officer Richards whispered. "But your son, Lamar…has been… murdered."

The news knocked the wind out of Pearl. Her face froze like a portrait as the loss cut deep into her soul. A collage of images flashed into her mind as she thought about Lamar. Pearl couldn't feel her body. The combination of falling to the ground and receiving the horrific news caused the blood to flush from her head. She was on the verge of fainting. She watched as the men placed her son in the back of the coroner's van. She tried to speak again, say something to her son, but it was too late. Everything went black.

❖

Chapter 8

Edison, New Jersey

Wednesday November 5, 2008
5:54 a.m.

1 Year Later

*T*he bright morning sun calmly crept over Pearl's peaceful face, causing her to open her eyes. She was finally awakened from a long overdue slumber. She took a deep breath and slowly exhaled a lung full of air onto her pillow. Ten hours ago, she thought she was going to be in for another sleepless night. But a change of scenery was just what the doctor ordered after a long and stressful weekend. Rolling over onto her stomach, she escaped the intense sunshine. After a few moments, she realized she was no longer contorted in a hospital chair like she'd periodically been for the past twelve months. With Heidi being in and out of the hospital, it was difficult for Pearl to enjoy a good night's rest. But this morning, Pearl was finally on a comfortable mattress. And although she was not resting in her own bed, the familiar surroundings helped to put her at ease.

There was a gentle knock on the bedroom door. The tapping momentarily jolted Pearl. She thought she was half-sleep and ignored the knocking. After a few seconds, the tapping returned with a bit more force. Pearl was fully awake now. She twisted her neck around and looked at the door. "Come in," she groaned.

The bedroom door slowly opened, and an older woman entered

the room. Despite the early hour, the woman was already dressed. Pearl watched her as she walked to an oak dresser on the opposite side of the bedroom. The woman moved with an assured grace about her. Her well-maintained figure, smooth skin, and perfect posture defied her age. At fifty-one years young, the woman continued to turned heads, even one of her own siblings. The woman's name was Valerie Kachina. She was Pearls younger sister.

"Damn Sis, you sounded like my ex-husband for a minute with that deep ass voice," Valerie teased as she reached for her White Diamonds perfume. "How are you feeling this morning?"

"A lot better than last night," Pearl responded, trying to clear the frog out of her throat. "This bed is so damn comfortable. Thanks for letting me stay here. I was getting so tired of rotating between the hotel and the hospital."

"It's okay, Sis," Valerie said, turning to Pearl, who was still lying on her stomach. "I'm just glad you're feeling better."

"I am," Pearl grunted as she stretched out her aging bones.

"And my niece? How's Heidi doing?" Valerie questioned.

"Well, you know it's an everyday battle for her," Pearl said. She rolled over once again, and then sat up on the bed. "I feel so bad watching her go through all of this nonsense. And now she has the rehabilitation and testing stuff to do. I know she's 'bout drained at this point."

"I know. That poor girl…it's just so sad," Valerie responded. She put the finishing touches on her outfit in preparation for a long work day. "So are you heading back up there later on?"

"Oh yes," Pearl quickly responded. "I'll go back up there after two. I want Heidi to rest up and get some time away from me. I know she's tired of seeing my worried face all damn day."

"Trust me, your daughter appreciates you even more now," Valerie said as she turned to her sister. "I think this will bring you guys closer together."

There was a silence in the room. Pearl thought about Valerie's wishful thinking for a moment. Although her relationship with Heidi seemed to become more strained with each passing year, Pearl found herself hoping that this unfortunate ordeal would put them both on a path to a more healthy relationship. She turned to her sister, who continued to groom herself. "I hope so," she whispered. "I really do hope so."

"You doubt it?" Valerie asked.

"You wouldn't believe how bad we were going at each other before all this shit happened," Pearl quietly confessed. "We had a huge fight. I can't get that argument out of mind."

"You and Heidi?" Valerie was surprised.

"Yup. Scared the hell out of me too," Pearl continued. "Thought she wanted to fight me for real."

"Holy shit," Valerie said. "Not my niece. Are you serious?"

"Yes…your niece!" Pearl responded. "I was ready to smack fire out of your niece's ass."

Valerie chuckled. "I'm sorry I don't mean to laugh. But that is crazy."

"Crazy is not the word," Pearl said, shaking her head. "It's always the girls, right? The boys will grow up and at least respect you. But the girls want to rebel and raise up against you. It's such a shame."

"I know what you mean," Valerie said. She turned back to the dresser and grabbed a few more items. "Speaking of which, I'm taking my granddaughter for a while."

"Awww…Janaya is coming up? How is she doing? Lord, I haven't seen her in a while now."

"Janaya is good. It's the dog 'gon parents who are wacko. I swear my son and his wife are both a hot-ghetto-mess with butter on it."

Pearl smiled at her sister and shook her head. "Damn, Sis. Looks like you will have your hands full for the next couple of months."

"I know. So it's going to be good having you and Heidi around."

Pearl twisted her face as she thought about her sister's last statement.

Valerie kept her focus on the mirror and never noticed the hard stare that Pearl was giving her.

"What are you talking about?" Pearl firmly asked. Her mood

instantly changed.

"This is not up for discussion, Sis," Valerie said, still looking into the mirror.

"I am not staying here," Pearl said. She was growing more upset.

"Pearl, don't be so damn stubborn." Valerie turned to face her sister. "When Heidi gets out of the hospital, where are y'all supposed to stay?"

Pearl didn't answer.

"Heidi lost her apartment, right?" Valerie asked.

Again, Pearl didn't answer.

"And I hope you wasn't going to try to move back into *your* house," Valerie continued. "That would be a nightmare for the both of you."

"I wasn't going to move back into my house," Pearl snapped. "I've been looking for a place for the past few months. I'm getting closer."

"Sis, look around," Valerie said, raising her voice. "There is more than enough room for you and Heidi here. My kids are grown and they are never moving back into this house. So y'all can stay here. I think it will be good for Heidi to be around some more of her family now. Especially while she's recuperating from all of this."

"So are you telling me what's good for my daughter now?" Pearl asked with a bitter attitude. She turned away from her sister.

"Stop it, Pearl. Dammit!" Valerie blurted. "Why are you so damn stubborn? You are just like Dad, I swear. This has nothing to do with whether you can take care of Heidi or not. I'm just saying that you don't have to worry about mortgage or getting around while you're here."

Pearl remained silent. After a few moments, she turned and looked at Valerie.

"And when I said Heidi should be around more of her family, I think the same goes for you too." Pearl closed her mouth. She continued to stare as Valerie looked at her watch. Realizing she was running behind, Valerie quickly began to fill her handbag with a few cosmetics. "I'm just saying," Valerie continued, shrugging her shoulders. "Just think about it. I just thought I would offer."

"I will," Pearl said quietly. She decided not to press forward with the argument.

Valerie zipped up her small bag and took one last look in the mirror. Pearl lay back down on the bed and got more comfortable. Valerie quickly walked to the bedroom door. Before she left out of the room she turned around.

"Hey," Valerie said, trying to get her sister's attention.

Pearl rolled over, facing Valerie.

"You know what Mom told you right before she died that night at Beth Israel?" Valerie quietly asked.

"Yeah," Pearl answered. "She said take care of your sister."

"That's right," Valerie said, nodding her head. "And you know what she said to me?"

Pearl didn't answer the question as she realized what was coming next.

"She told me..." Valerie said.

"The same exact thing," they said at the same time.

"That's right, and don't you forget it," Valerie teased as she playfully pointed her finger at her sister.

Pearl smiled as Valerie returned the gesture. She decided not to say another word. Valerie turned around and left the room. Pearl felt good knowing her sister was there to help. She turned around and closed her eyes. She decided to rest up knowing that she was in for a long road, helping her Heidi make a full recovery.

Chapter 9

Riverview Medical Center
Red Bank, NJ

Wednesday November 5, 2008
6:08 a.m.

Good morning, sweetie. I just wanted to check in on you before I start my long day of therapy in here. I want you to know that I still continue to have these terrible headaches. They will not go away. I don't know what it is about them, but they continue to keep me up at night. I thought about you this morning, and I wanted to say that I'm so sorry I wasn't there at the end. I know I made a bad decision by leaving you in that house all alone, and for that I am truly sorry. You know you will always be in my heart. My road dog...my best friend...and now...my angel. Please don't be mad at me. I will text you later. I miss you...I love you...your road dog...Heidi!

Heidi sat quietly on the edge of her hospital bed for a moment and stared at her cell phone. She re-read the text message a few times before she scrolled down to find the recipient. *Faith Jowler* was the contact name she clicked on. Heidi closed her eyes and sent the text message. After a few moments, she took a deep breath, and then slowly exhaled. Sending her best friend, Faith an apology through her cell phone was becoming an everyday routine. After nearly seven months of intense treatment and rehabilitation, Heidi was slowly recovering from the horrific shooting at her mother's house. Although her body was getting better, emotionally she was far from a full recovery. Despite her family's efforts to get her to believe otherwise, she continued to feel that she was exclusively responsible for Faith being killed. Her heavy guilt bogged her down until she was on the brink of clinical depression. She forced herself to battle back. Sending Faith messages through her cell phone was one of the many coping tools Heidi used to push forward. Somewhere deep inside her, she truly believed Faith was somewhere in Heaven reading the messages.

"Good morninnngggg," a female nurse sang as she walked into Heidi's room.

"Good morning, Nurse Sonya," Heidi responded. She looked up and gave the nurse a half smile.

"And how are we feeling this morning?" Nurse Sonya asked as she made her way over to Heidi.

"Still can't get no sleep," Heidi answered as she put her cell phone away.

"Headaches?" She flipped through a few sheets of paper that were attached to her clipboard.

"Yes," Heidi responded. "These headaches are getting more serious. Do you think it's from all of these procedures I have to do?"

"Oh no, headaches are very common with people who had your similar injuries."

"Okay…but are they suppose to last this long?" Heidi asked. "I have been having them for almost two months straight."

"No…they usually don't last that long. Not continuously," Nurse Sonya said. "On a scale of one through ten, what would you say the pain is?"

"A twelve!" Heidi joked. "But if I had to keep it up to ten, I would say at least a ten."

The nurse nodded her head and started writing notes on the clipboard. "Okie dokie. I will get you some more medicine after you have your breakfast. Before you go home I will make sure the doctor writes a prescription for a strong pain medication for you."

"Wait a minute. Back up," Heidi interjected. "Before I go home?"

"Oh yes, Heidi. You are almost done here," Nurse Sonya said. A smile came to the nurse's face as she continued to read through her files. "You are rehabilitating at an amazing rate. I mean, don't get me wrong, I've seen people go through this process faster. But it's always good to see our patients go through this without any major complications."

"So when can I go home?" Heidi anxiously asked.

"Doctor Patel has you being discharged next week. Friday to be exact, if everything goes as planned."

"Oh my God," Heidi whispered.

"Yes, He is good!" Nurse Sonya responded.

"That is great news." Heidi stood and walked over to her bag, and grabbed her toiletries. "Does my mother know?"

"We called and left her a message this morning," Nurse Sonya continued. "She left last night to get some rest and she told me to tell you that she will be back up here later today."

"Okay thanks. I'm glad she went to go get some rest," Heidi said as she made her way to the bathroom. "I don't know how in the world she slept on those hard chairs out there."

"I know what you mean, but people do it all the time," Nurse Sonya said as Heidi walked by her. "Before you get dressed I also wanted to tell you that you had another visitor last night."

Heidi turned around in shock. "A visitor? Who was it?" she nervously asked.

"I don't know. He didn't leave his name."

"He?" Heidi blurted, almost gagging on her own words.

"Yes, it was a guy," the nurse whispered. She was caught off guard by Heidi's reaction.

"And he didn't leave his name?" Heidi rhetorically asked. "Did he say what he wanted?"

"I'm sorry, Heidi. We didn't give him a chance to say what he wanted or why he was here. We just turned him away."

A dozen faces entered into Heidi's mind as she tried to figure out who could've been visiting her. Especially here. She wasn't even registered under her own name. Pearl had set her up real safe. In addition to the alias, Pearl had made sure no one besides the nurses and the doctors even came close to her daughter. And now on the first night Pearl was away, someone came to visit her. Heidi turned back to the nurse who tried her best to figure out why Heidi was so uptight.

"I'm sorry, Heidi," Nurse Sonya continued. "If I would have known you needed the information, I would have gotten his name at least."

"It's okay," Heidi assured. "I'm just surprised that anyone even knows I'm here."

"Well, that's not the first time he was here."

"What? Are you serious?" Heidi gasped.

"Yes, Heidi. He came up here about a month ago, but your mother turned him away that time." Nurse Sonya said. "But if it's worth anything to you, he looked very harmless and, frankly, he looked genuinely concerned about you."

Heidi slowly shook her head. Her heart started racing as she thought about everything that unfolded in her life over the past few years. Things were very cloudy, and Heidi couldn't imagine who would be coming to see her. She looked at Nurse Sonya. "Sonya... please do me this favor," Heidi asked. "If this guy comes back up here before next Friday, tell him that I want to see him and make him wait in another wing of the hospital. Then call the police and let them take care of it, okay?"

"Yes. I will do that," Nurse Sonya nervously agreed. "You got my word on that."

"Thank you, Sonya." Heidi said. "You're an angel."

Sonya nodded her head and closed up her clipboard. "I'm going to let you get dressed now. You have a long day ahead of you."

"I know," Heidi said, nodding her head.

"Good deal. See you in Room 412 in twenty minutes okay?" Nurse Sonya asked.

"Okay. See you in twenty."

Chapter 10

Newark, NJ

Wednesday November 5, 2008
11:18 a.m.

"*O* samaaaa!" a little boy's voice yelled from a second story window on the corner of Clinton and Osborne Terrace. "Osama, y'all…two lights away, and they comin' down fast!"

The eleven-year-old's warning from above triggered a massive scramble on the ground as drug hustlers and fiends tried their best to disappear out of view of the Newark Police. Three police vehicles and two unmarked cruisers sped through the red lights, tearing down the busy street. Everyone on the block except a young teenaged boy rushed away from the corner. In the midst of all the commotion, he didn't budge. Fifteen year-old Steven "Hammer" Chiles stood his ground as the screaming sirens got louder. Instead of running, Hammer walked to the edge of the street and watched the oncoming police cruisers. He could smell the burning rubber as the speeding vehicles passed by the building. None of the police cars stopped. The entire convoy of cruisers continued past the corner until they disappeared down the block. Hammer calmly put his hands in his pockets, and then turned around. He chuckled when he noticed he was the only person left standing on the street corner.

"Man, fuck them," Hammer said, waiving his hands toward the distant cop cars. They were long gone. "Back to business!" he yelled. "Where the money at?"

Hammer was not the typical Newark drug dealer. He was more of a daredevil than a hustler. He was only a few months away from his sixteenth birthday, but moved like a grown man. Standing at only five-foot two, he was shorter than a lot of his rivals, but his fearless heart made up the difference. He'd received his nickname Hammer for two reasons. Since his diaper-days, people had made fun of his oddly shaped hammerhead. Then he'd entered into his pre-teen years and developed a fetish for guns. Soon after he'd started flaunting his weapons, people eased up on the jokes about him. His short life was already filled with robberies, arrests, and even a number of major assaults. He had absolutely no fear when it came to the streets. But this posed a problem for the other hustlers in his neighborhood who viewed his reckless ways as a magnet for trouble. One hustler in particular, named Ray, had zero tolerance for Hammer and his antics. Ray was only twenty-two years old, but he was already considered a veteran on the street. And although both Hammer and Ray hustled on the same block, a stark tension between the two constantly loomed.

"Hammer, what the fuck is wrong with you?" Ray yelled as he stormed out of the building. His eyes were cold as ice as he walked up on Hammer. "All you got to do is walk away, my nigga. Stop toyin' wit' them cops."

"Man, fuck them," Hammer barked. "They not gonna do shit out here. This is my block!"

"Nigga, this is *our* block," Ray corrected. "And don't you get that shit twisted again. You sharin' this shit with us, and you need to stop playin' with them cops like I said. When they make a move... we make a move! Got it?"

"Ray, look at the block right now...they wasn't comin' for us anyway," Hammer snapped. "Stop bein' so fuckin' paranoid."

"And how you know they wasn't comin' for us?" Ray quickly asked.

"C'mon man...use your brain, nigga," Hammer continued. "If they was comin' for us those goddamn sirens would'na been blazin' like that! You know they creep up on us and hop up outta shit. They never announce they comin'. Damn Ray, I think you slippin'!"

"Nigga, fuck you!" Ray yelled, obviously taking offense to Hammer's last statement. "How 'bout I show you just how much I'm slippin', nigga?"

The heated exchange on the corner quickly attracted a crowd of onlookers. Another hustler quickly ran over to the scene and got between the two men.

"Whatever, Ray," Hammer yelled. "It's whatever! I'm not scared of you!"

"You ain't gotta be scared of me!" Ray continued to yell. "But imma make ya young ass respect me!"

Ray took off his watch and chain, and handed them to another onlooker who'd run over to try to break up the fight. Ray took off his t-shirt and tossed it to the ground. Another onlooker rushed over and got between the two men.

"Chill y'all," somebody said from a few feet away. "Y'all niggas bout to bring more heat over here!"

Hammer backed away from Ray. He quickly took off his shirt, revealing a silver .38 that was tucked snuggly between his belt and his stomach. Everybody except Ray backed away from Hammer. A few fiends turned and ran away from the scene. Things quickly escalated on the corner, but neither man backed down.

"What the fuck you gonna do with that?" Ray said. He tried not to show it, but he was surprised that Hammer was carrying a weapon on him today.

"I told you, nigga!" Hammer said. "I'm not scared of you, so it's whatever."

"So what the fuck, you a killer now?" Ray snapped.

Hammer didn't say a word. His young face was frozen with intensity as he stared back at Ray, who was becoming angrier by the second.

Ray felt all eyes were on him on the street corner. He decided to make a move. He knew his reputation was on the line. "Fuck you, nigga," he snapped. "You just gonna have to shoot me."

"Nah, Ray…chill!" an onlooker shouted.

Everyone watched as Ray rushed toward Hammer, who took a few steps back in shock. He hastily reached for his gun. But before he could get a good grip on the pistol, Ray was up on him. He grabbed Hammer's arms and rammed him into a parked car.

"Fuck!" Hammer yelled as he felt the back of his elbows smash the window of the park car. Ray made the only move he could, head butting Hammer. The move proved to be costly for both men as the pain shot through Ray's entire body. Before the fight could intensify, a white unmarked police car flew around the corner, screeching to a halt in front of the building. The red-flashing lights alerted the street corner, and people began to flee the scene again. A plain-clothes officer jumped out of the vehicle with his service weapon drawn. His older appearance proved deceptive as the officer moved with surprising agility. He ran around the police car to the fighting men. It was Detective Harold Williams from the East Orange police department.

"Police!" Detective Williams yelled. "Break this shit up!"

Hammer grabbed his head and pushed Ray off of him.

Detective Williams ran behind Ray and grabbed him. "What the fuck is going on here?" he yelled. "Break this bullshit up over here!"

"Imma fuck you up, nigga!" Ray yelled as he also grabbed his head. His left eye instantly swelled. Ray's adrenaline made him go after Hammer once again, but Detective Williams put his body between the men.

"Ray!" Detective Williams yelled, grabbing him by the neck with one hand. He pushed Ray a few feet back with one shove, surprising Ray with his strength. "It's over! Now get the hell away from here before I make it a fucked up day for you!"

Ray froze for a moment. He started to calm down as he realized that the detective meant business. Everyone in Essex County knew Detective Williams for being a hardnosed police officer. He had been the type of cop who thrived off bringing pain to criminals in and out of his jurisdiction—especially drug dealers. And now that he was a detective, people knew to stay out of his way or become a victim of his wrath. Ray didn't think twice about leaving. He realized that going head up with the detective was no good for his business. He grabbed his t-shirt from the ground and walked up the block to cool off.

Detective Williams turned his attention back to Hammer, who continued to grimace in pain. The detective looked down near Hammer's waist and saw the gun.

"What the hell is this…just what the world needs right now," Detective Williams said as he grabbed Hammer's pistol and put it in the small of his back, then holstered his own gun. "Another young-ass…dumb-ass cowboy." He turned Hammer around and threw him against the car.

Hammer groaned from the pain. "Owww…man…take it easy."

"Shut your mouth!" Detective Williams snapped. He grabbed his handcuffs and swung Hammer's arms around. Quickly, he cuffed him and shoved his face against the car again. This time Hammer remained silent. Detective Williams searched Hammer's pockets. He found twelve small bags of dope and a few thousand in cash. The detective put the money in his jacket pocket, keeping the drugs in his hand. After he completed the search, Detective Williams grabbed Hammer's left arm and forced him over to the front of the building.

"Sit down!" Detective Williams ordered.

"Huh?"

"Sit the fuck down!" Detective Williams repeated. "Right there on the stoop. Sit down."

Hammer sat down, then looked up to the detective. He watched him closely as Detective Williams searched their surroundings, then summoned a dope fiend, who was watching from across the street.

"Bring your raggedy ass over here," Detective Williams yelled to the scruffy man.

The fiend noticed the detective, and slowly walked over to him. The fiend didn't know what to expect. He was praying he wasn't about to get arrested. When the dope fiend got close enough, Detective Williams gave him the twelve bags of dope that he took from Hammer's pockets.

"What the fuck?" Hammer protested.

"What did I say?" Detective Williams barked. "Shut the hell up!" He turned back to the dope fiend, and nodded his head toward the other end of the street. "Now get the hell away from here. And if I see you again, I will bag and tag your ass!"

The dope fiend said nothing. He ran up the street and never looked back. Hammer was staring at Detective Williams when he turned his attention back to him.

"Do you know who I am?" Detective Williams asked.

"Yes."

"Who am I?" Detective Williams continued to toy with him.

"You set my uncle up!" Hammer snapped. "Ace Chiles…you set him up. You did him dirty."

"Allegedly!" Detective Williams said as a shifty grin came to his face. "Well, I'm glad you know who I am. And now…I know that you will never forget me."

Hammer just stared at him.

Detective Williams looked up the street and saw a few people were beginning to take notice of the scene. "I wanted Ray, but I think you will do a lot better," he continued. "You know a guy name Vincent Galloway? They call him Vegas."

"Man…I ain't no snitch!" Hammer snapped. He looked around to see who was watching him as he talked to the detective.

"Not yet, you not!" the detective responded. "But when I get done with your name, you will be the poster boy for snitches. So imma asked you again. Ever heard the name Vegas around here? Ever met him? Anybody you know do business with him?"

"Man…I ain't never heard that name around here," Hammer snapped. "Never! Don't know him. Never saw him and never heard of him. The only Vegas I know is the state!"

Detective Williams shook his head at the young boy's ignorance. He walked closer to Hammer, then grabbed his arm. "Stand up," he ordered as he pulled Hammer to his feet. "Just to let you know…I found enough shit on you to lose you in the system for while. You know that, right?"

Hammer didn't answer.

"You know who I am, so you know where to find me. You got two weeks to find out something about this Vegas dude. And if you hear of the name or meet him or see him, you better find me."

"What the fuck…so I work for you now?" Hammer asked with authority.

Detective Williams chuckled to himself as he took the handcuffs off of Hammer. He put them away, and turned him around.

"All you niggas work for me," Detective Williams said. "You just don't realize it yet."

Detective Williams turned and headed to his car. Everyone on the corner watched as he got into the unmarked cruiser and sped off. He'd made it halfway down the block, then grabbed his cell phone. He dialed ten digits and waited for someone to pick up on the other line.

Chapter 11

Edison, New Jersey

Wednesday November 5, 2008
2:00 p.m.

Whoo..hoo....I'd rather live in his world, than live without him...in mine.
Go...go..gonna board, for love I got' ta board... gonna board, Gonna board...the midnight train to Georgia...

Pearl stood in front of the bathroom mirror, singing along to the classic melody as if she was the great Gladys Knight herself. *Midnight Train to Georgia* was a song she'd heard over a thousand times since she was a child, but still got goose bumps, reflecting on the deep meaning of the words. *My world...his world...our world... mine and his alone.* Pearl continued to sing as the music faded from the stereo in the bedroom. Emphatically, she shook her head and continued to get dressed in the mirror.

"Damn...sing that shit, Gladys!" Pearl whispered. She always found herself thinking back to her past relationships whenever she heard the song. The common theme of lost love and shattered dreams replayed in her head like a broken record. She thought back to the many men that had come and gone in her life. Some of the men were *friends*, some boyfriends, and two were lucky enough to be fiancés. But never had a man been referred to as *husband*. The dim reality that there was no significant one in her life was a hard fact for her to accept.

Pearl's thoughts immediately switched to Rick. She hadn't seen or spoken to her so-called boyfriend since the night her son, Lamar, died. Rage filled her heart every time she thought about that night at East Orange General, seeing Rick with Shaheed and Vegas. She could only imagine how much Rick had been involved with her son's death. The very thought of him betraying her family made her angry. She wanted answers. And with each passing day, her need for closure grew larger and larger.

After a few moments, Pearl shook the ugly thoughts from her head. She continued to get dressed, preparing herself for another long day at the hospital with Heidi. A loud ringing from her cell phone brought her back to reality. She looked at her watch and rushed to answer the phone. She assumed the hospital was calling her with another update about Heidi, and she did not want to miss the call. As she grabbed her cell phone, her mood immediately changed when she read the caller's name.

"Yes," she answered with a slightly bitter edge.

"Hello Pearl, this is Detective Harold Williams," a strong voice said from the other line.

"I know who this is," Pearl uttered. "And please call me Ms. Kachina."

"Okay, Ms. Kachina. I'm glad I caught you in a good mood today," Detective Williams responded.

"What do you want?" she quickly asked.

"I was just doing my rounds today and found out some more information pertaining to your case," the detective informed. "I would like to meet up with you today to discuss the details."

"Did you find Vegas yet?" Pearl snapped.

"I'm sorry to say that we haven't yet, Pearl—I mean, Ms. Kachina."

"So what is there to discuss? There are only two things that I care about right now. My daughter, Heidi is one of them. And number two is watching them animals pay for what they did to my family."

"I understand that," Detective Williams said. "And believe me, I'm going to do everything in my power to see that those men are

84

brought to justice."

"Don't give me that *Law and Order* shit today," Pearl quickly said, interrupting him. "This is not some damn cop show, and I don't care about that legal talk."

"Ms. Kachina, I understand your frustration. Can we just meet so that we can talk in person about the information I have? I think you will be interested to hear this."

Pearl didn't say a word. She thought about his offer for a moment.

"Are you still there, Ms. Kachina?" Detective Williams asked.

"I'm here, but I won't be for long," Pearl responded. "I'm heading to go see my daughter, if you don't mind. And if you want to meet…it will have to be after I get back."

"You know what, Ms. Kachina…I will make it a lot easier for you. I'll come up to the hospital to speak with you. That way, I won't take up too much of your day."

"Okay," Pearl said. "I guess I will see you later."

"Great."

Pearl hung up the phone without saying goodbye.

Detective Williams was taken aback by her abrupt manner. He tossed his cell phone to the side and turned his attention back to the road. The detective found himself trying to figure out why he and Pearl were off to such a rocky start. She didn't have a lot of respect for the detective, and both parties were fully aware of it. He was baffled by her attitude. Every call and visit seemed to bring about more ill feelings toward him. He decided today was going to be the day he would have a serious talk with her. He knew that they would have to work together to bring justice to the men who killed her son.

* * *

Newark, NJ

2:39 p.m.

Back in Newark, Hammer pushed his legs to the limit as he rode his mountain bike through the busy streets. He was still fuming over his fight with Ray, and had to get away from the street corner. Although the two had minor disagreements and arguments in the past, today was the first time things became physical. Hammer decided to take a break from the block and put an end to his feud with Ray. The beef with his new rival could have escalated into something more if it had not been for Detective Williams' breaking it up.

In Hammer's neighborhood, hustlers died every week over petty issues. And Ray was the type of person that would never forgive Hammer for flaring up against him, especially around so many of his friends. Hammer knew he would have to eliminate Ray in order to protect himself. He refused to be another forgotten soul on the block that died for something small, like an argument. He peddled fiercely, deciding to go see the one person he could trust to handle this problem for him.

Hammer let out a gasp of air as he got off of his bike. He was beyond tired from peddling almost three miles to the North side of Newark. He took a moment to catch his breath, and then walked around to the rear of a dilapidated building. To the naked eye the structure seemed to be abandoned. But Hammer knew he was at the right location. He walked toward the back door and cautiously looked around. After realizing that there wasn't a soul in sight, he banged on the wooden door. Without warning, the back door slightly opened. His heart dropped when he saw a dark hand emerging from the opening, holding a pistol.

"Who?" a roughed voice yelled from behind the door.

"What the fuck, man!" Hammer screamed as he ducked away from the gun. "It's me.....your nephew." He started to breathe easier as he watched the gun disappear behind the door. "C'mon, man… let me in."

The door swung opened and revealed the person behind the gun. The large man gave Hammer a hard stare, then dropped the weapon to his side. It was his uncle, Vegas.

Hammer gave him an uneasy grin. "Don't flip out, Unc'...I know you told me never to come here, but I got a problem."

Vegas eyed his young nephew and shook his head. He looked around, then motioned for Hammer to come inside. He was clearly upset, but he couldn't turn him away.

They weren't related by blood. Hammer's father and Vegas had been partners in the late '90s until his father was killed by a New Jersey State Trooper. Vegas, having vowed that he'd look after Hammer, took him under his wing and treated him like blood. They hadn't seen much of each other since Vegas had been on the run, but Hammer decided to roll the dice and ask his uncle for help.

"What's goin' on, Vegas?" Hammer asked as he walked in.

"Not a thing!" Vegas answered. "Just tryin' to stay away from the spotlight."

"I feel you, Unc'. That's one reason why I needed to slide through here," Hammer continued. "This cop asked about you today. That nigga knew ya government and the whole nine."

"Damn...*word?*" Vegas grunted.

"True," Hammer responded.

"You didn't tell him shit, did you?"

"Come on, Vegas...do I look like a nigga tryin' to win the Snitch of the Year award?"

Vegas laughed at his nephew and sat down. "So them boys are gettin' close, huh?"

"Yeah...but fuck them cops. They still a bunch of dumbasses out there," Hammer joked. "They couldn't find they assholes in a bathroom stall."

Vegas smiled at his nephew, shaking his head at the clever joke. Although they didn't share the same blood, they shared the same disdain for law enforcement.

"So what's your problem?" Vegas sharply asked his nephew.

"What you mean?"

"You said you had a problem when I opened the door," Vegas reminded. "So what happened?"

"Pssssss...oh yea...I had to get away from the block today before I bodied somebody out there."

"What!?" Vegas angrily responded. He hated to hear that his

family had beef. "What happened?"

"Me and this dude Ray got into it again today. It got so crazy that I was about to pull out on him."

"Damn, nephew…like that?"

"Hell yeah," Hammer exclaimed. "Dude tried to rush me, so I was gonna lay him down."

"So y'all just fought?"

"Yea...but then that same cop that was askin' about you...broke up the fight."

"Damn, I see the streets ain't change a bit!"

"Yea…but I can't go back around there no time soon. We gonna get into it again, and who knows what's gonna happen next time."

"So what's the problem?" Vegas asked again. "What do you want me to do?"

"Fam…look, that nigga Ray don't know how to run that spot over there. And all them niggas respect me. So with Ray out the picture, I can take over."

"You want me to kill this dude for you?" Vegas asked with a hardened smirk.

"Hell yea...this dude needs to be put to sleep."

"And what's in it for me?" Vegas asked.

Hammer shook his head at his uncle. "You ain't nevva gonna change, Vegas. I thought about that on the way over here." A sadistic smirk came to Hammer's face as he continued to speak. "Ray keeps a lot of money around. In his pockets...in his crib, and even in his car. "

"So...?" Vegas said as he gave Hammer a shifty look.

"We don't have to split the money...I don't need his money....I just want him gone from Osborne," Hammer coldly said.

Vegas sat back in his chair and thought about Hammer's proposition for a minute. "Where does he live?"

"Nobody knows," Hammer replied. "Dude is real secretive. He keeps shit like that on the low."

"Cool... I will find that out."

"So...you gonna do it?"

"Why not? Fuck it....I need the fuckin' money," Vegas said as he looked around his rundown living space.

"That's what's up. So how you gonna do it?"

"Does it matter?" Vegas snapped as he stared at his nephew. "Just as long as it gets done, right?"

Hammer put up his hands. "You right...imma fall back. Good lookin' on doin' this for me."

"It's cool. So just lay low for a couple of weeks...and let me do what I do. I will find you when it's done."

Hammer nodded his head and gave his uncle a pound. "Okay... I'm goin' to skate. Hit me up if you need anything."

"Actually, leave me some money," Vegas ordered. "Shit is gettin' tight around here. I can't make no fuckin' money with all these cops lookin' for a nigga."

"Cool!" He pulled out his money roll and peeled off five hundred dollars. He shook his uncle's hand and left him with the money.

As his nephew left the house, Vegas recounted the money, thinking about his new job and how badly he needed to make some cash.

Chapter 12

Essex County Correctional Facility
Newark, NJ

Wednesday November 5, 2008
4:18 p.m.

$\mathcal{S}$ haheed Porter calmly sat in the dayroom of the Essex County Correctional Facility. Despite all the noise from the other inmates behind him, he continued to stare at the television screen above his head. His eyes were fixed on the monitor, but his mind was in another world. After almost a year inside the county jail, Shaheed was coming closer to his day in court. He was facing a mountain of serious charges filed against him by the State of New Jersey. With the first day of his trial only a couple of weeks away, he found himself clinging onto a tiny grain of hope that the bleak situation would turnover in his favor. But like many inmates in the county lockup, his odds of a Federal Prison becoming his home was more of a sure bet.

An inmate next to him chuckled at the television, making Shaheed cringe. The boisterous laughter momentarily shook Shaheed, and brought him back to reality. He turned his attention back to the TV show. Ironically, Judge Marilyn Milian of The People's Court was handing down a civil dispute verdict over money. He shook his head as he watched the famous judge make her decision and slam the walnut gavel. *If only my problems could be fixed with a half hour show*. He sat back in the metal chair and continued to daydream. He never noticed a male corrections officer walking up behind him.

"Porter, let's go!" the officer commanded. "You got visitation. Right now!"

Shaheed's expression never changed. He quickly rose to his feet and walked toward the guard. The officer turned around and summoned a few more inmates. He instructed them all to line up single file, next to the dayroom's main exit.

Shaheed was not surprised that he had a visitor today. In fact, he'd known exactly who it was and what time they were coming.

His girlfriend, Rhonda.

For the past eleven months, she'd never missed a Wednesday visit. No matter what was going on in her world, she'd made sure she'd be there to see him. Even when her car broke down and there were no other cars to borrow, she'd proudly boarded the No. 25 bus and made her way to the county jail. After a while, she'd become Shaheed's only visitor. The fifteen minutes he'd shared with Rhonda was his only proof that something beyond the cold walls waited on him.

He took a deep breath as the steal doors opened. The inmates filed out of the dayroom and entered the visiting area. Shaheed took a seat in the corner and waited for Rhonda. After a few minutes, a crowd of mostly women and children entered the visitation room. He scanned the flock, looking for a familiar face. After a few moments, he spotted her. *There she is.* Shaheed smiled and stood up. Rhonda gave him a soft grin from across the room, quickly walking toward him. She greeted him with a tight hug, and then kissed him on the lips. She definitely missed being close to him.

He quickly let go of Rhonda, then sat back down. He didn't want to draw too much attention from the officers who were always looking for an excuse to cut short an inmate's visit.

"So how are you holdin' up, baby?" Rhonda asked as she sat down next to him.

"You know me. I'm a soldier. I'm takin' it one day at a time."

"You look a lot better than you did last week," she complimented. "Are you eatin' the food now?"

Shaheed chuckled as he thought about his reluctance to eat State issued food. "I started eatin' it again. I had no choice. I was gettin' sick in this bitch."

"I just bet you was," she said. "But you know you gotta eat that shit just to keep somethin' in your stomach, baby."

"For sure. But I don't wanna talk about that damn food."

"I know," Rhonda mumbled. "And I know what you are about to ask me."

"Did you speak to him yet?" Shaheed quickly asked.

"Baby, I don't know where Vegas is," Rhonda continued. "This dude totally disappeared off the map. And I asked everybody that knows him."

"*What?*" He was disappointed. "And nobody saw him around the streets? No nothin'?"

"Baby, I have asked everywhere. I went into the barbershop y'all use to go to. Everywhere! I think I checked every little club and bar in Newark asking around for him."

"And nobody saw him?" Shaheed interrupted her.

"Nobody."

"I can't believe this shit."

"Me neither," Rhonda whispered as she grabbed onto Shaheed's hands. "I'm gettin' nervous for you, baby."

"What do you mean?"

"I know you're goin' to court soon, and a lot of people are talkin' on the streets."

"Talkin' about what?"

"They think you should take a plea," Rhonda said.

Shaheed shook his head and looked down. "Nah…we can't talk about this, Rhonda," he whispered.

"I'm just sayin'…think about it." She totally ignored his last statement.

"Rhonda!" Shaheed snapped, raising his voice just enough to let her know that he was getting agitated. "I didn't kill nobody! Period…it wasn't me! And I'm not takin' no goddamn plea so I can rot away in some prison cell. I can't do it."

"I understand, baby," Rhonda conceded. "I'm sorry...I didn't mean to get you upset. But think about it when you can because there's another problem."

Shaheed closed his mouth and looked at Rhonda. As he made eye contact with her he could tell that something heavy was weighing on her mind. He was almost afraid to ask. A knot formed in his stomach. "What happened?" He tried to brace himself for the news.

"We are runnin' out of money, baby." She dropped her head as if she was ashamed to deliver the bad news. "I thought we was goin' to have enough to make it until the trial, but it's runnin' thin now."

"Goddamn." The bad news hit him harder than he'd expected. "How much is left now?"

"We only got three thousand left, but the rent is due in a few days. After that we will be down to about twenty-four hundred," she informed. "But for real...that attorney is killin' us. I don't think we're gonna be able to afford her once the trial starts."

"What?" Shaheed raised his voice again. "I thought she was paid up."

"She was paid up for the first year. But it's goin' into the second year now; it's a whole 'nother ball game. And she is houndin' me for the money too!"

"Fuck!"

"That's why I was thinkin' that maybe a plea would work. The lawyer said you would be lookin' at no more than six years...maybe even five."

"Fuck that!" Shaheed's voice echoed off the walls. "Hell no! I'm not doing no fuckin' six years without puttin' up a fight!"

"Baby, calm down." Rhonda looked around the visitation room.

"I gotta fight this bullshit," he continued. "I'm not doing no goddamn six bullets for this case. You hear me?"

"Baby, I hear you." Rhonda grabbed his hands again to calm him down. "I'm sorry I said anything about the plea."

"I'm not takin' no plea!" Shaheed repeated. "You hear me? No plea. If I have to get another lawyer, then that's what it is. No plea! Damn Rhonda... who side are you on, anyway?"

"Nigga, don't give me that shit!" Rhonda snapped back. "I'm on your side. You know that! Don't even start this shit today. I'm here. And I'm not goin' nowhere! I'm on your side."

Shaheed gave his girlfriend a long stare and nodded his head. "Rhonda, don't fold on me," he lowered his voice as he began to calm down. He squeezed her hand and continued, "Right now is where we need to be strong. I can't take no plea. Not now. If I take a plea, they are goin' to add more time to that behind those damn chambers. They don't give a fuck about me. All they care about is the money. So let's concentrate on that. The money! Okay?"

"Yes, baby, I understand," she assured as she nodded her head. "So what do you want me to do? Just point me in the direction, and I'm goin'. I can try to get a job if you want me to."

"Nah…fuck that. That money is too slow."

"So what do you want me to do?"

"I don't know. Seriously…I don't know," he answered. "But there has to be a way to get some money to this lawyer. I just have to think about it."

"So, in the meantime, what do you want me to do?" Rhonda pressed.

"Look for Vegas. Look under every rock you can for his ass. I gotta find him."

"Okay, baby. I will keep lookin' for him."

"As a matter of fact…" Shaheed whispered as he thought for a second. "Remember where I used to work at in Hillside?"

Rhonda gave Shaheed a confused look. "You never had a job, baby."

Shaheed became frustrated. He looked around at the guards who were keeping a close eye on all the inmates and visitors in the room.

"C'mon, baby…think," Shaheed said. "It was a while ago, but I used to work there with Vegas. Rhonda, you gotta remember that." He gave his girlfriend a guarded look. He didn't want to reveal the exact location of the place just in case there were some unwanted ears listening in on his conversation. He cautiously looked around again. He made a motion with his hand to Rhonda as if he was turning a key in a car ignition. Rhonda looked down at his quick clue and smiled. "You remember now?"

"Oh yes, baby," Rhonda confirmed. "I do remember."

"Cool. Go over there and see if they've seen him. If I know him right, he is trying to stack a lot of money, and that's the best way he knows how."

"Okay...I will do that tomorrow. And I'm goin' to try to put some money together for the next few months for us. Do you need me to leave you some today?"

"Nah...I'm okay for now," Shaheed answered. But he knew that Rhonda was going to drop some money in his commissary anyway. She never left the jail without doing so. "Just make sure you find Vegas. Even if he's dead, I need you to find that nigga."

Rhonda nodded her head. She knew he needed her to deliver, more than ever. She was going to do everything in her power to be there for him.

As the visitation came to an abrupt end, he stood and hugged her. "You still my girl?" he asked as he gave her a smile.

"Through hell and hot water, baby," Rhonda sweetly responded.

"That's what I like to hear." He kissed her on the forehead. "I'll see you next Wednesday, baby."

Chapter 13

Riverview Medical Center
Red Bank, NJ

Wednesday November 5, 2008
5:08 p.m.

"You are doing an excellent job, Heidi. Just give me three more laps like that, and you're done for the day."

Heidi quickly wiped her swimming goggles clean, then gave her physical therapist a confident thumbs-up. She took one last deep breath and submerged herself in the shallow end of the pool. Her aquatic therapy sessions were doing wonders for her recovery. After nearly two months of intense rehabilitation and training, she had finally graduated to swimming underwater laps and holding her breath for an extended length of time. Today, her instructor, Dorothy Smith, was overly impressed with Heidi's focus and determination to get better. Dorothy proudly watched as Heidi moved through the water like a professional. She smiled when Heidi completed the three short laps and got out of the pool.

"Well done," Dorothy said, applauding Heidi. "That was a great session. As far as I'm concerned, I don't think you need anymore lessons from me. You have made me a believer."

Heidi smiled. She walked over to Dorothy as she dried off herself.

"How is your body feeling?"

"It feels a lot looser now," Heidi responded. "I feel great. On that last lap I felt my body cramping up a little bit, but the pain is gone now."

"Well, that's normal," Dorothy assured. "You have been pushing yourself pretty hard these past few weeks."

"I know. I'm so ready to go home."

"Well, don't you worry. As far as I'm concerned, you have exhibited an immense amount of body control and balance. I have to say, in my professional opinion, you have fully rehabbed."

"Are you serious?" Heidi gasped. "Thank you so much, Dorothy. You have been so much help to me."

Dorothy chuckled at Heidi's excitement. "I didn't do it all alone. I had a lot of help from my patient. You did a great job in here. You deserve to go home and rest."

Despite her damp body, Heidi hugged Dorothy, who was surprised by the gesture. Heidi was happy about the news of finally being cleared to go home.

"I will give Dr. Patel my recommendations and, hopefully, he will give you a discharge date."

"Thanks again," Heidi said. "I can't thank you enough."

Dorothy smiled at Heidi and patted her on the back. She grabbed a few things from the pool area and made her way to the exit. "Don't forget to stop and check in on us every once in a while."

Heidi nodded her head toward Dorothy as she left the pool. She felt lucky to have such a caring aquatic therapy instructor. Dorothy's confidence in Heidi had helped her believe in herself when her esteem was deteriorating. With her physical and water therapy complete, it was time for Heidi to move on to the next chapter of her recovery.

She walked into the locker room to shower and change. On a normal day, she would have taken nearly twenty minutes to wash off the chlorine. But today, Heidi had an extra pep in her step. She swiftly showered, returning to her locker in less than ten minutes.

She retrieved her blue sweatpants, then let out a perturbed gasp. As she pulled the polyester fabric up and over her waistline, she couldn't help but think about how much she missed her clothes. All of her always-too-tight-jeans and beautiful dresses were waiting for her back in her storage lot. But there was nothing Heidi missed more than her extravagant shoe collection. She had enough shoes and boots to make Michelle Obama jealous. She nearly cringed at the awful thought of all of her Gucci, Jimmy Choos, Versace and Marc Anthony shoes sitting inside the rented space collecting dust. She couldn't wait for the day to finally feel like a woman again, and step out of the dreadful clothes she'd been forced to wear at the hospital.

Heidi shook her head, and reluctantly grabbed the matching blue sweatshirt from her gym bag. She unfolded the polyester sweater, and walked in front of the mirror to get a better view of her body. She momentarily froze as she looked at herself in amazement. In addition to helping Heidi with her balance and body control, the water therapy had whipped her figure into better shape than she'd ever recalled having. She turned to the side, noticing she had lost most of her stomach fat, shedding what she'd affectionately referred to as *muffin-top*.

"Damn…you a bad bitch!" Heidi whispered as she continued to check out herself in the mirror. She was stunned at how much weight she had lost since the shooting. She tried to imagine just how sweet some brand new clothes would look on her brand new body. However, it didn't take long for her euphoria to be erased.

Her mood darkened when she turned back, facing front in the mirror. Her heart twisted with pain as she looked at her bare chest. Her face stiffened. She found herself coldly staring at the numerous bullet scars scattered across her torso. Her mangled skin was a callous reminder of how she'd landed in the hospital. She tried to shake the memories, but her mind violently tore away from a peaceful state, and hurled back reminders of Vegas, Shaheed and Aaron. She ran her fingers across the scars. The surgeons were successful in sewing her chest back together, but Heidi knew they couldn't heal the wounds that were too deep for stitches or staples. She had spent the last few months of her recovery trying her best to erase the incident from her brain. But every time she looked at the grotesque scars, her thirst for revenge grew even more.

Heidi was unexpectedly brought back to reality by a loud knocking on the door. She quickly put on the polyester sweater, and turned around just in time to see Nurse Sonya walking into the locker room.

"Hey, Heidi. Sorry to barge in on you," Nurse Sonya apologized. "I just wanted to let you know that your mother just got here. She asked me to tell you."

"Oh okay," Heidi stuttered. "I was just finishing up in here. I will be up to my room in a few minutes."

Nurse Sonya picked up on the uncomfortable vibe in the room, but decided not to be a pest. Heidi watched Sonya as she turned around and left her alone again in the locker room. She gathered her things and slowly sat down next to her locker. She needed to take a moment to calm herself before she headed back up to her room.

* * *

5:42 p.m.

Pearl sat patiently in the waiting area of the Inpatient Rehabilitation Unit, reading a magazine. She didn't mind waiting for her daughter today, especially after receiving the good news that Heidi would be discharged soon. The long rehabilitation process was not only doing a number on Heidi, it was working on her nerves as well. Pearl tried her best not to worry about her daughter while she was in the hospital's care. But Pearl refused to be absent while her only daughter was going through the worst time in her life. She decided that she was going to do something nice for her daughter once she'd left the hospital. She'd been itching to let the cat out of the bag on a number of occasions, but held back. After receiving the message that Heidi was near the end of her hospital stay, Pearl had decided today was the day she'd break the news.

The loud beeping of the elevator doors made Pearl look up from her magazine. She smiled when she saw Heidi exiting the elevator, holding a black gym bag. She put the magazine down and walked over to Heidi, who met her halfway.

"Hey Munchy..." Pearl said as she hugged her daughter.

Heidi hugged her mother and smiled at her. She'd only heard Pearl call her Munchy a few times since she was a child. She'd given Heidi the nickname after Heidi had developed an addiction to junk food. Whenever Heidi heard her mother call her by her pet-name, she knew that Pearl was in an extreme motherly mode. Munchy could've only meant one of two things: Pearl had some very good news for Heidi or she had a very big gift in store. Either way, Heidi was anxious to see what her mother was up to.

"Hey Mom," Heidi greeted. "They didn't give you a hard time at the front desk, did they?"

"Absolutely not. I don't even pay attention to those visiting hours. They should know who I am by now."

"I know that's right," Heidi joked. "So did you take care of that phone bill for me?"

"Faith's phone bill?" Pearl rhetorically asked. "Yes, Munchy. I paid it already. I know you would kill me if I didn't pay Faith's bill."

"Nah, Mom...I wouldn't kill you. I just want to make sure nobody takes my baby's phone number. I will pay it after I get out of here. Thanks, Mom." Both women turned around and walked to Heidi's room. "So what exactly are you up to, Mom?"

"What do you mean?" Pearl asked with a precarious smile.

Heidi laughed at her mother's terrible poker face. "Come on Mom...I know you. Munchy? I haven't heard that in almost ten years. I know you're up to something. You just need to let it out. You know you can't keep a secret."

Pearl smiled at her daughter as they entered the room. "Dammit... and I was trying not to give myself away," she said, laughing at herself. She waited for Heidi to put her stuff away, then walked over to her. "Okay, I know this has been a bad year for the both of us, but I received news you'd be leaving soon, so this is what we are going to do. After you get discharged from the hospital, we are going to have a big party at your Aunt Valerie's house."

"Seriously?" She was growing more excited.

"Yes, I'm inviting everybody, sweetie," Pearl continued. "She wants us to stay with her for a few months, so I was thinking we can do the party right around Christmas time. What do you think?"

"Oh my God...I love it. Let's do it," Heidi said. She was smiling from ear to ear.

"I think I'm more excited about the party than you are," Pearl joked. "It's going to be a nice Christmas this year...I know it. This is going to be fun."

"I can't wait," Heidi said. "So tired of being in this hospital."

"I know you are. But this party is just what you need when you get out. Some good food, some good music and, of course, your family is going to be there."

"I know...I can't wait. Thank you, Mom."

"Well, I can't take all the credit. Valerie had a lot to do with that idea."

A gentle knock at the door interrupted the conversation in the room. Heidi spun around and turned her attention to the entrance. "Come in!" Heidi yelled, looking at her watch. "I may have to order my dinner now."

Nurse Sonya nervously poked her head in the room and smiled at Heidi. "Hey ladies, so sorry to interrupt. But you have a visitor, Heidi."

"Right now?" Heidi uttered as she looked at her watch again.

Pearl was the first one out of the hospital room. Heidi followed close behind as Nurse Sonya led the women to the visiting area. She couldn't imagine who would be coming to see her today besides her mother. As they walked into the waiting area, Pearl instantly became irritated.

"Detective Williams!" Pearl announced. "Why am I not surprised?"

"Hello, Ms. Kachina," Detective Williams said as he stood up to greet Pearl and Heidi. "I hope I'm not coming at a bad time."

"Sir...anytime you come around is a bad time," Pearl said with a slick edge.

Heidi quickly elbowed her mother in the side. "Mom...stop it. Detective, I'm sorry for my mother. Not quite sure why you keep rubbing her the wrong way. But don't mind her."

Pearl rolled her eyes at her daughter, and then sat down in the waiting area.

Heidi shook the detective's hand and sat down next to her mother. "How can I help you?" Heidi asked as the detective sat down across from the women.

"First of all, how are you feeling today, Heidi?" he asked.

"I'm doing great. I just finished my pool exercises, as you can tell," Heidi said, referring to her wet hair. "I'm ready to get the hell out of here and back to the real world."

"That should be soon, right?"

"Yes...I should be out of here any day now."

"Why do I get the feeling you already knew that?" Pearl quickly asked as she readjusted herself in her chair.

"Well, I am a detective, Pearl," Detective Williams said.

"Hey!" Pearl snapped, pointing her finger at him.

"I'm sorry," Detective Williams apologized with a playful smile. "Ms. Kachina. I keep forgetting. My apologies."

Heidi waved at her mother. She shook her head and turned her attention back to the Detective. "So how is the case looking? Have you found Vegas yet?"

"Unfortunately, that is why I'm here," Detective Williams continued. "We are working around the clock to find this guy. And in all honesty, he is really off of our radar. His cousin, Shaheed apparently doesn't know where he is at this point."

Heidi shook her head in disappointment. She looked over to her mother, then back to the detective. "So what are we going to do?"

"Well, that's another reason why I wanted to come see you tonight, Heidi," Detective Williams said. "The lead prosecutor on the case is trying to get Shaheed to plead out."

"Plead out?" Heidi asked. She was confused.

"Shaheed is insisting that he was a victim in all of this," Detective Williams continued. "He is maintaining his innocence in the murders of Faith Jowler and your brother, Lamar. And, at this point, all of the evidence is in his favor. We have no murder weapon that links him to the actual shootings and, also, there was no physical evidence on him that would indicate that he was the trigger man."

"So what does that mean?" Pearl snapped. "He was there. I saw him there."

"I know," Detective Williams said. "He was there. There is no doubt about that. So the most we can get him on is an accessory charge."

"But he won't walk from this, right?" Heidi nervously interjected. "He is going to prison for what he's done, right?"

"Heidi…don't worry he's going to jail for a long time, if there is anything I can do about it. But we have to find Vegas. He is the key. If he is as dangerous as you made him out to be, we need to get his ass behind bars soon. If we get him, maybe we can get both of them to tell us more details about that night that would land both of them behind bars forever."

Heidi put her head down. She was becoming scared for her own safety as she thought about the Detective's words.

"There is something else I need to ask you, Heidi," he whispered.

Heidi looked up to the detective and waited for him to continue.

"Is there anything else about your connection to these men that we could use in order to help us out in this investigation? Anything that you haven't told us before?"

Heidi's heart dropped to her stomach. She felt herself growing more nervous as she thought about the first time she'd ever laid eyes on Shaheed. The horrific crash flashed into her mind. She'd never told the police about that night fearing that she, herself, would be facing prosecution for leaving the scene of a fatal accident. Nervously, she rubbed her face and tried to erase the chaotic images from her mind. She looked up to the detective, who was still staring at her. She calmly swallowed an imaginary lump and opened her mouth to speak.

"No Detective," she lied. "I have told you guys everything that I know."

Detective Williams slowly nodded his head and looked at Pearl.

"Ladies, I don't want to keep you." He stood up and extended his hand to Pearl. "Thanks for taking the time to speak with me tonight. I will keep you guys informed on what is going on with the case and, hopefully, the next time I speak with you two, I will have some good news."

Heidi and Pearl stood up.

"I hope so," Pearl said. She reluctantly shook the detective's hand and turned to her daughter, who was still looking uneasy. Heidi shook his hand, then watched the detective as he left the waiting area and headed to the elevator.

"You okay?" Pearl said as she tried to console her daughter. The women walked back to Heidi's room.

"Yea, I'm okay. I just have a lot to think about."

"Okay," Pearl said. "I'll leave you alone tonight and let you get some rest.

"Thanks, Mom." She hugged Pearl and watched as her mother grabbed her bag. "Are you coming up here tomorrow?"

"Oh yes, I will be here. I will call you in the morning to let you know when I am on my way." Pearl smiled at her daughter and left the room.

Heidi slowly sat back down on her bed and thought about the visit from Detective Williams. Something didn't feel right about the brief questioning. She tried to calm her nerves again as she laid down on the bed. A sharp headache forced her to grab the front of her head. She grabbed a small remote control from the side of the bed and summoned the nurse. Within a few moments, Nurse Sonya was poking her head into the room.

"Are you okay?" Nurse Sonya asked.

"No…I have another migraine coming back." Heidi moaned as the pain vibrated from the front to the back of her head.

"Okay…give me one second," Nurse Sonya replied. "I'll get you something for the pain.

Chapter 14

Hillside, New Jersey

**Wednesday November 5, 2008
11:51 a.m.**

Make a left on Elizabeth Avenue, and your destination is 300 feet ahead on the right.

Rhonda was amazed at the precise the computerized voice of the navigation system. She slowly cruised down Elizabeth Avenue in search of the Chopped and Screwed Auto Body Shop. After a few moments, she slammed on her brakes as she realized she was about to pass the location. The outside of the building almost looked abandoned. With the exception of a few auto parts and old hubcaps, the outside of the establishment was relatively empty. The body shop seemed to be a low-key, humble and very *legal* business. But many people were unaware of the shady dealings of the Chopped and Screwed Auto Body Shop. The garage was the final stop for dozens of stolen cars before they were broken down, repainted and re-distributed on the black market at substantial discounts. A good car thief could make a few thousand per week selling cars to Chopped and Screwed. But an excellent one could make thousands of dollars per day. Rhonda was looking for one thief in particular; one that only specialized in strong armed car jacking. She wasn't interested in his larceny abilities; she needed him for an entirely different purpose.

Rhonda parked her car, and then headed to the front entrance of the building. She thought of all the stories Shaheed had told her about the shop. He always confided in her how dangerous the owners were and how much money they were making from stolen cars. He'd advised her never to go to the garage without him. But today she had permission to break that rule.

Rhonda ignored the "Knock First" sign, walking straight into the garage. The loud clanging and screeching of the machinery violated her ears. She was annoyed by the sharp sounds of metal being cut, burned, twisted, reshaped and reassembled. She looked around the garage to find a live body to complain to, but no one was in sight. She walked over to a makeshift counter constructed of wooden legs and old truck parts. Turning her attention to a rusty doorbell that sat atop the counter, she quickly pressed the button, and then leaned on it. To her surprise, the bell was even louder than the machinery. After a few seconds, one of the welding machines suddenly stopped working and a very short man emerged from behind it.

"Okay…okay…okay…" the man yelled. "Take your goddamn finger off the bell…I hear you!"

Rhonda watched as the man took off his gloves, walking over to her. The man's face was covered in so much dust and grease that Rhonda couldn't tell whether he was black or white. He walked behind the counter and glared at her. Rhonda instantly felt uneasy.

"Who the fuck are you?" he snapped. His slight West Indian accent quickly gave him away. Rhonda assumed he was from Jamaica or a nearby island in the Caribbean. She didn't say a word, thrown off by the sharp tone of his question.

"Who the fuck are you?" the mechanic repeated "And what the fuck are you doin' here?"

Rhonda almost clammed up, but she didn't back down. "I'm Rhonda."

"Okay," the man barked. "And what type of business do you have here?"

"I'm looking for Vegas," Rhonda said as she stared at the man.

"Vegas?" the man questioned.

"Yes!"

"You must be blind as a bat. Look around! This is not no goddamn Vegas. Does this look like a casino to you?"

"Vegas…he's a person!" Rhonda yelled. "He's my boyfriend's cousin. I know he works here. Where is he?"

The man gave Rhonda a hesitant look. He unconsciously sized her up and tried to figure out her angle.

"Listen…" she continued. "Stop being a jerk and tell me the last time you saw Vegas. I know you buy cars from him. I need to speak with him as soon as I can. It's about his cousin, Shaheed!"

The man didn't say a word. He slowly reached under the counter and pulled out a twenty-two inch machete and placed it on the counter top. A bright reflection bounced off of the sharp blade and onto the man's dirty t-shirt. He gave Rhonda an intense stare and tried to intimidate her.

"Dawta…I don't know where you getting' your information from," he said. "But you are trespassin' now. And if I was you, I would turn around and walk out the same way I came in."

Despite the large sword on the counter and the mechanic's threatening tone, Rhonda was reluctant to move. She could tell that the man was not telling her all he knew, and she refused to leave before she got the information she came for. Rhonda decided to try another approach. She raised her hands slightly and pleaded to the man.

"I don't want no problems with you," she assured. "My boyfriend made a lot of money for y'all in here for a lot of years. But now he's in trouble…big trouble. And …I didn't come in here to beef with you. I just need to find Vegas. That's it. All I'm asking you is…have you seen him? And if so—"

Rhonda cut herself short when she noticed the West Indian man was suddenly looking at something behind her. His concerned expression automatically made her turn around. To her surprise, she noticed a large man walking over to them. He was wearing a spotless GLB sweat suit and brand new sneakers. His very clean profile was the complete opposite of the grungy man standing behind the counter. She looked at the man's face and immediately recognized him. It was Shaheed's cousin, Vegas.

"Ain't this some shit?" Vegas rhetorically asked as he walked over to Rhonda with a slick grin on his face. "And I thought the first person to find me here was gonna be a cop. Instead it's you."

"What the fuck, Vegas?" Rhonda snapped. "Where the hell you been?"

"Where do you think?" Vegas responded. "Hiding!"

Rhonda shook her head in disgust. "Shaheed is lookin' for you!"

"I know," Vegas calmly said.

"He needs you," Rhonda continued.

"I know."

"So what are you gonna do?"

"Right now, it's nothin' I can do for him."

"What?" Rhonda blurted. "What do you mean? That's your family...you gotta help him out!"

"Rhonda, listen to yourself!" Vegas barked. "That nigga is locked up. He's inside. What the hell can I do for him while he's in there?"

"Are you serious, Vegas?" She was shocked by his attitude about his cousin. "Shaheed is in there holdin' you down, nigga. They are lookin' for you, and Shaheed didn't say shit to them crackers in there."

"No doubt, because Shaheed is a soldier," Vegas proudly said. "He's not a snake."

"So why you out here actin' like a bitch then?" she snapped.

The disrespectful insult hit Vegas like a sledge hammer. He instantly became angry as he stared at his cousin's girlfriend. "Rhonda... just calm the fuck down," he replied with a deadly edge.

His tone scared Rhonda into silence. His huge frame and frightening demeanor had always made her a bit uneasy, but today she found herself downright petrified by his presence.

Vegas moved closer to her. "Listen to me. If I get arrested...it's over. You understand what I'm sayin'? If I get locked up, I'm never gettin' out. And that means that Shah' is never gettin' out...bottom line! So I'm hidin' now. I can't help him out like I want to. I can't go see him and I can't call him. Only you and that muthafuckin' Rasta over there know I'm here. That's it! When you see Shaheed again, tell him that I got him. Just not right now!"

Rhonda gave Vegas a blank expression. She didn't know how to respond to him. He stood over her and waited for her to speak.

"Rhonda?" Vegas blurted. "You understand?"

"Yes!" she answered, clearly shaken by Vegas' tone. "What do you want me to say? You tellin' me you can't do shit for your own blood. What do you want me to say to that?"

Vegas closed his eyes and shook his head in frustration. "I didn't say I couldn't do shit for him. I said…I can't do shit *now*."

"Well…he needs you *now*, Vegas!" Rhonda snapped. "We don't have no money. The trial starts next week and we need some help."

Vegas thought for a moment. He looked over to Rhonda and gave a strange look. "Okay…listen…I'm workin' on somethin'. I think I know where we can get some money from."

Rhonda didn't say a word. Her ears perked up from the news.

"Are you in?"

"Am I in?" Rhonda stuttered. "In what? What do we have to do?"

"I'm plannin' it out," he continued. "But we gotta make that move in a couple of weeks. It's just one day. And we can probably clear some serious money."

"Okay…but you still not tellin' me what I gotta do." Rhonda gave Vegas a suspicious stare.

"Don't worry…it's gonna be easy," Vegas assured. "I just need you to play your part…and we should be good. But like I said…you gotta be ready when I call. We only got one shot at this."

"Don't you worry about me!" Rhonda said as she nodded her head with confidence. "My man is down, and I need to do something drastic. So I *will* be ready."

Chapter 15

Riverview Medical Center
Red Bank, NJ

Tuesday November 11, 2008
9:13 a.m.

I'm going home today, Faith. Can you believe it? After damn near a year...I'm finally leaving this place. I'm nervous, but I'm ready. I hope you are happy for me. I can't wait to get my life back. Don't worry...I will try my best to find those bastards that took you away from me. Please know that I will never forget you. Never! Soon...I will finish what they started. So don't leave me yet. Okay? I miss you...I love you...your road dog...Heidi!

Heidi finished typing the text message and looked outside of her hospital window. The morning rain was slowing and the sun was forcing its way through the dark clouds. The symbolism made her smile for a moment. She, too, was trying to push away a few dark clouds of her own. Turning back her attention to the cell phone, she searched for Faith's name. Just as she did every morning since she'd been in the hospital, she closed her eyes, imagined her best friend's face, then sent the text. Once the message went though, she was relieved. She was now ready to face what would be a very eventful day.

A gentle knock on the door made Heidi turn around. She stood up and gathered herself as she walked toward the middle of the room.

"Come in," she yelled.

Nurse Sonya poked her head around the door and looked at Heidi. "Hey you, are you decent?" Nurse Sonya asked.

"Yes…I was just getting ready to finish packing my things." She turned around and grabbed a few bags and put them on her bed.

"I came to let you know that you have a visitor—the one I told you about before," Nurse Sonya said as she walked all the way into the room.

"Really?" Heidi stammered. She became nervous as she thought about whom else would be visiting her besides her mother or Detective Williams. "A dude, huh?"

"Yes," Nurse Sonya whispered. "And honestly, Heidi…he looks really harmless."

"Harmless, huh?" Heidi suspiciously mumbled. "Shit…I made that mistake before. Who is he?"

"He didn't leave his name—he didn't want to," the nurse responded, shaking her head.

Heidi felt uneasy. She grabbed her phone and thought about calling Detective Williams. "Where is he now?"

"In the waiting area."

"By himself?"

"Yes."

"Is there a security guard up here?"

"Yes. We have two of them on this floor."

"Okay…would you please walk with me to see who this *visitor* is?" Heidi asked.

"Sure," Nurse Sonya quickly answered.

Heidi put her phone in her pocket and walked out the room. Despite her nervousness, she was curious to see who this mystery man was. She felt a knot form in her stomach as the women got closer to the waiting area.

"There he is," Nurse Sonya mumbled as she pointed to a young man sitting quietly by himself in the waiting area. "See…I told you he looks harmless." She nudged Heidi.

"Ummm...hmmm," Heidi grunted. She looked at the man, but didn't recognize him. He looked to be in his late twenties. He was dressed like a street hustler, but something about his demeanor made him appear more conservative. He was well-groomed and all of his clothes were brand new; from the white sneakers on his feet to the fitted baseball cap on his head. She dropped her brows when she noticed he was holding a small gift box in his hands. Heidi took a deep breath as she decided to meet the young man.

She turned to Nurse Sonya. "Wait right here. If he tries some crazy shit, please call security, okay?"

"Not a problem," Nurse Sonya agreed. She stood by the door and watched as Heidi slowly approached the young man.

"Excuse me...but do I know you?" Heidi asked as she walked into the waiting room. Her voice momentarily startled the man.

"Oh damn...Heidi...how are you?" the young man fumbled with his words as he stood to his feet. "I'm sorry...no...you don't know me. Well...not...personally." He cautiously approached Heidi.

She noticed that he was more nervous than she was. "Huh? Have we met?" she asked, skeptically shaking his hand. "You don't look familiar to me. I'm sorry."

"It's okay," he uttered. "My name is Kevin Blackman. I was the first paramedic on the scene the night you got shot."

Heidi didn't respond with words. Instead, she closed her mouth and reared back her face. She was stunned by his introduction.

Kevin picked up on her edgy vibe and tried to make her feel at ease. "Listen Heidi...I'm sorry for just poppin' up on you like this," Kevin continued. "But I had to stop by to thank you."

Heidi nodded to the man and sat down next to the seat adjacent to his.

"Thank me for what?" Heidi was surprised by the man's gratitude. "But, in all seriousness, shouldn't I be thanking you?" From what I hear...you guys made miracles happen that night."

"It wasn't easy," Kevin whispered as he sat back down. "But I think you were strong enough to survive anything that night."

Heidi smiled. "Thanks."

"You know…I really don't want to take up too much of your time. I heard you were leaving the hospital today, and I wanted to make sure you got this." He handed her the gift box.

"You bought a gift for me?" Heidi whispered. "I'm not trying to be funny…but I don't even know you."

"I know this may seem a little crazy on my part," Kevin confessed.

"Uhhh…yea!" Heidi joked as she slowly took the gift.

"I know," Kevin chuckled as he looked at Heidi. "But you really inspired me that night when we found you."

"What?" Heidi uttered as she gave Kevin another skeptical look. "Inspired you to do what?"

"Inspired me to *live*," Kevin said. Heidi gave the young man a serious expression. His words seemed to touch her unexpectedly. "Before I saw you that night I was having major issues in my life. Everything was fucked up. But when I saw you surviving those bullets…that really made something click inside me. It made me want to really get my shit together. The way I see it…if you can come back from being shot like that…then there is no such thing as impossible."

"Whoa…Kevin…I really don't know what to say to that." She was truly at a loss for words.

"It's okay. I really don't mean to intrude like this…I just felt the need to give you something that's brought me luck over the past few years." He nodded as he pointed to the gift.

Heidi looked at the box for a second, and then opened it. Her face twisted with confusion as she grabbed the gift from inside the box and held it in front of her face. "A knife?" Heidi blurted. "You bought me a knife? I don't understand."

A crooked smile came to Kevin's face. "Not just any knife, Heidi. I found this knife when I was only sixteen. Trust me…this knife has been by my side for a minute now. And now I want you to have it."

"Well damn, Kevin…now I really don't know what to say." Heidi stared at the stainless steel handle. She opened up the blade and looked at it for a moment. She marveled at how sharp the knife was. "Kevin…I gotta tell you, this is by far the weirdest gift I've ever got." She continued to look at the knife, then flipped the blade over and noticed two initials on the steel handle. "G.A.?" Heidi asked as she read the letters.

"Those letters were on the knife when I found it," Kevin said. "So I just renamed it…Guardian Angel."

"Guardian Angel!" Heidi repeated with a smirk. "Clever."

"I thought so, too." Kevin smiled. "Well…like I said…I don't want to keep you. I just wanted to give you that gift and wish you the best." He stood up and extended his hand.

Heidi was thrown off by his abruptness, but decided to follow suit. She stood to her feet and shook the young man's hand. They walked toward the hallway and were immediately greeted by Nurse Sonya.

"Is everything okay, Heidi?" Nurse Sonya asked.

"Yes…I'm fine…thanks," Heidi responded, then stood next to her. The women watched as Kevin walked toward the elevator.

"Kevin!" Heidi yelled. The young man turned around and looked at her. "You said this knife brought you good luck…how so?"

Kevin gave her a devilish smirk. "Before I became a paramedic, I used to run the streets. Let's just say that he was a good *friend* to have."

Heidi smiled at Kevin, and then turned around. Nurse Sonya followed Heidi as they walked back to her room.

"What was that about?" Nurse Sonya asked.

"I don't really know," Heidi answered. "I guess a little more *good* luck in my life couldn't hurt."

Nurse Sonya didn't say a word as she tried to figure out what Heidi was referring to. The women walked into Heidi's room and began to gather her bags. Heidi made sure to pack her new gift as she readied herself to be discharged from the hospital.

* * *

9:27 a.m.

A couple of floors down, in the main lobby, Pearl looked at her watch with anticipation as she waited for Heidi to come downstairs. She tried to remain calm, but an ongoing argument with Detective Williams was sucking all of the positive energy out of her already tired body. She glared over to the detective who stood along side her, near the intake area of the hospital.

"Detective, I have no clue whatsoever why you are still here," she snapped as she gave him another unenthusiastic glare. "I told you once before that we don't need no damn officer babysitting us! We'll be fine."

"I understand that *you* believe that you will be fine," Detective Williams stressed. "But you don't see what's going on from my vantage point. This is quickly becoming a very high profile case. A lot of eyes are on your family, and we just want to make sure that no one is in danger."

"Okay, that's fine." She was still upset. "But why are you here today? Can my daughter get one day of rest without seeing the hospital or police or anything like that? Is that possible?"

"I understand that."

"I don't think you do."

"Look, I came up here to make sure everything is good with Heidi," Detective Williams continued. "We're going to need her for the next couple of weeks. This will not be an easy case to prosecute."

There was a silence between the detective and Pearl. She looked at her watch again and pouted in frustration. In Pearl's opinion, Heidi couldn't make it downstairs fast enough so she could escape the detective's presence.

"Ms. Kachina, the last thing I want to do is upset you," Detective Williams assured.

"That's funny…because the *first* thing you're doing *is* upsetting me!" Pearl snapped.

The detective shook his head and walked away from Pearl. He

checked his watch and looked outside the glass doors. He thought for a moment. He was tempted to simply drop the argument and leave, but he decided to press on. He turned around and walked over to Pearl. "What did I do to you, Ms. Kachina?"

"You didn't do nothin' to me!" she rudely responded.

"So what is it? Why don't you like me? What did I do to you? From day one, I can't seem to say the right thing to you. So what is it? You don't like the way I look? The way I act? Is it my cologne? What is it?"

Pearl shook her head and turned away from him. "I know you," she whispered.

"What?" Detective Williams quietly responded. He was confused. "Know me from where?"

"I seen you a hundred times. You try to act like you care. But you don't give a shit. All you care about is gettin' your name in the paper." The detective remained silent. "I did some research of my own on you Detective."

"Did you?" His question was laced with nervousness.

"Yes, I did." She smirked. "And I heard about the Ace Chiles case."

"You know nothing about that case, Pearl." The detective was becoming angry.

"I do now...Harold!" Pearl responded. "I know you set that man up."

Detective Williams emphatically shook his head as if he was on the witness stand. "I didn't set him up," he barked. "Besides, I didn't need to set Ace Chiles up...he was already guilty."

Pearl turned up her nose at the detective's answer. She waved him off and continued to speak. "Well, everybody that I spoke to said that you're a dirty cop. And you're the only person that's saying that you're not...so...I'm sorry...I have to go with everybody else."

"That's ridiculous."

"Well, you wanted to know...so...there it is. I never said I didn't like you Detective. I just don't trust you."

The detective was about to respond to Pearl's words when the elevator doors opened up. Pearl quickly turned her attention to the other side of the lobby where Heidi was struggling with her bags. She quickly walked over to her daughter.

"Hey sweetie, let me help you with those," she offered as Heidi pushed the bags out of the elevator.

"Hey Mom!" Heidi said as she grabbed the last bag. She hugged her mother.

"How are you feelin', baby?" Pearl grabbed the bags and headed toward the exit of the hospital.

"I am feeling good right about now," Heidi answered, following behind Pearl. "I still can't believe that I'm finally leaving."

Detective Williams watched as the women headed for the exit. He waited for them to pass the intake area and approached them.

"Hey, Heidi." He motioned for her. "I'm so glad that everything went well with the discharge."

"Detective," Heidi greeted him. "Thanks...so...are you here to see me off?"

"Uhhh...actually, I'm not." The detective was cautious about revealing his reason for being at the hospital. "I was instructed to give you some extra assistance if you needed it."

"Assistance?" Heidi suspiciously asked. She continued to walk outside and the detective followed alongside her and Pearl. "What type of assistance do I need?"

"Well, I guess we are not really here to assist. We will be providing extra security for you in the form of surveillance."

"Surveillance?" Heidi asked. "So y'all are gonna be followin' us around like Secret Service or something?"

"No, Heidi. It will only be vehicular surveillance," Detective Williams responded. "These street guys are slick. If they get wind that you are out and about...we may have a situation on our hands."

Heidi thought about the detective's words as they walked to the car.

Pearl tried to keep her cool as she opened up the trunk and helped Heidi put the bags in.

"Don't worry, Heidi, we are only here to help."

"Yea…but help who?" Pearl blurted.

Detective Williams didn't take the bait. He smiled at the women. "At this point, I don't want to bother you guys anymore. But just remember, we will be watching you. So if you need us, you can always call my cellular. And if you see anything suspicious going on around you, just let us know."

"Okay Detective," Heidi said. She nodded her head and watched as he walked away and got into an unmarked police car.

Pearl motioned for Heidi to get into the passenger seat. "Come on sweetie, we are late."

"Late for what?" Heidi slammed the trunk shut and got into the car.

"Your auntie took off work today to fix us a big breakfast at the house." Pearl smiled. "She's waiting on us now. And she said she has a big surprise for you."

"Well, I like surprises, especially from Auntie Valerie."

Pearl fired up the engine and pulled out of the parking lot. Heidi rolled down her window to catch the cool breeze. After a few moments, she found herself staring at the entrance to the hospital. Seven months had passed since she'd tasted the fresh air outside. An honest smile came to her face. The feeling of freedom and excitement was beginning to set in as she turned around in her seat, focusing again on the road ahead.

Chapter 16

Garden State Parkway

Tuesday November 11, 2008
10:14 a.m.

*P*earl and her daughter had been driving on the road in silence for almost a half hour. Heidi surprisingly found it difficult to stay awake as the smooth ride on the highway continued to put her to sleep. The excitement of being discharged from the hospital was no match for the comfortable leather seats of her aunt's Audi A8. Pearl realized her daughter needed the sleep, so she let her catch up on some much needed rest. Pearl looked at her watch and estimated that they were only about twenty-five minutes away from her sister's house. She was making good time. She didn't want Heidi to miss her big surprise, so she continued to speed up the highway. After a few moments, Heidi jolted out of her cat nap.

Pearl saw her daughter's body suddenly shake and immediately turned to her. "You okay over there?"

"Damn…I just had another nightmare," Heidi grunted as she tried to gather herself. She sat up in her seat and looked around. "Where are we?"

"We are about twenty minutes from your aunt's house," Pearl responded. "We're almost there."

Heidi rubbed her eyes and tried to shake loose the cobwebs. "Damn, I can't believe I was sleep that long."

"Yes…you were tired. So I just let you rest. So tell me about this nightmare."

Heidi slowly turned to her mother. A few images of the dream flashed into her mind. She was hesitant to tell Pearl about the dream, so she decided to spare her of all the details. "I keep having the same dream. And…it's really not like a scary nightmare," Heidi said. "It's more of a bad feeling nightmare."

"Isn't that the same thing?"

"Hmm…I don't think so. You ever had a nightmare where nothing scary is going on, but you feel scared?"

"No…in most of my nightmares I'm runnin' from something."

Heidi looked at her mother and slowly nodded her head. "Well… in this dream I'm at our old house"

"Which one?" Pearl asked.

"The one down south," Heidi responded. Her mother remained quiet as Heidi continued to speak. "Yup..we are at the old house… and…I'm in my bedroom and I'm scared as hell, but there's nothing going on. No bumping…no crashing, no nothing."

"So who's in the dream with you?" Pearl asked.

Heidi turned away from her mother and thought for a second. She knew her next answer was going to make Pearl emotional. She tried to avoid the question. "You know what, Mom," Heidi continued. "Let's talk about somethin' else."

"What?" Pearl uttered. "Am I in the nightmare with you?"

"No, Mom."

"Well…who's in the dream with you?"

Heidi turned back to her mother. She was reluctant to be truthful with Pearl, but decided to tell her. "Daddy's in the room with me."

"Your dad?" Pearl asked. She turned to her daughter. "What was he doing?"

Heidi shook her head. "Nothing. He was standin' there looking at me, and Faith was behind him. May God rest her soul!"

"Oh wow…so Faith was in the dream too?"

"Yup…I was sittin' on the edge of my bed. Daddy was a few feet away from me, just lookin' at me. Staring. And Faith was right behind him, pointing at him. I don't know why. She was just standing there pointing at him, and he was staring at me."

"And that was the nightmare?" Pearl asked. She was confused.

"That's it. And for some reason, that scares the hell out of me every time I have it."

"Damn...I don't know what to say, baby," Pearl whispered. "I can't explain that one right there."

Heidi turned away from her mother and looked out the window. She thought about her father as the car fell silent.

"You miss him don't you?" Pearl asked.

"Don't you?" Heidi quickly responded. She turned around again and faced her mother.

"Sweetie, your love for your father is different than mine," Pearl continued. "You will always love and miss your father because of the way you remember him. But I knew a different side to that man."

"That's why you left him," Heidi accused with a hint of sarcasm in her voice.

Pearl glanced over to her daughter. She didn't approve of Heidi's tone, but didn't want to upset the moment.

"Baby...let me just say this and we are goin' to drop this subject," Pearl began. "Your father was a good man. And if you're asking me if I loved him...of course, I loved him. But your father had one too many weaknesses. And when it came time for him to protect his family...he didn't. Believe me, sweetie...your father *left us* long before I decided to get away from him."

Heidi nodded at her mother's words. She didn't want to press forward with the conversation, so she dropped it. Discussions about her father had always been delicate. Every time they'd talked about him, Pearl seemed to become defensive and, sometimes, even offended. Heidi knew that there was more to the story, but now was not the time to search for details. She reached over to her mother and rubbed her shoulder as if to say *everything is okay*. Pearl patted her daughter's hand and accepted the truce. Both women remained silent as Pearl continued to speed up the parkway.

* * *

10:19 a.m.

Detective Williams continued to follow closely behind Heidi and Pearl as the Audi weaved in and out of the mid-morning traffic. He tried his best to keep his eyes on the road as he glanced through a stack of papers in his lap. He'd spent the last year gathering case files that centered around Heidi, Pearl, Shaheed and Vegas. He was determined to help end the case with a conviction. With his controversial career as a police detective only a few years from ending, Detective Williams wanted to retire as a respected member of law enforcement. The Kachina case was his golden opportunity to prove that his dirty-cop reputation was just an unproven rumor. But before he could totally redeem himself, he had to make sure the case information was sufficient enough to end in his favor.

"Shit!" the detective yelled as he found himself drifting into another lane. Nervously, he dropped a few papers and tried to grab the wheel with both hands. "Goddammit!" he continued to yell as he got the cruiser back under control. He moved the stack of files off of his lap and grabbed his cell phone. He quickly dialed the police station and waited for someone to pick up on the other line.

"Detective Stewart here, how can I help you?" a male voice answered from the other end of the phone.

"It's me!" Detective Williams informed. "Did any information come back on this Audi?"

"No, Harold. The plates came back clean. It's registered to a Valerie Kachina. And there is no history on her."

"What about Pearl?" Detective Williams asked. "Did you get anything on her?"

"There is no criminal history for Pearl," Detective Stewart continued. "But I did find a complaint in her name filed against a Rick Miller back in 2007 for a domestic dispute."

"Boyfriend, I'm guessing?" Detective Williams asked.

"Looks that way."

"Where is he now?"

"Off the radar," Detective Stewart confirmed. "He's no angel though. He has an extensive arrest record. But nothing as of late."

"Okay…" Detective Williams continued. "What about Heidi? I can't really figure her out. Did you find anything on her?"

"Now this is interesting," Detective Stewart said. "There is no arrest or police record for Heidi. But do you remember a house fire about three years ago, in Newark? A guy named Jayson Carter died in that fire. But his fiancée lived. His fiancée was Heidi Kachina. She'd told the police that he'd beat her real bad right before the fire had started. The firefighters were able to save her, but by the time they got to Jayson…he was already dead."

"I don't remember that incident," Detective Williams confessed. "But are you sure that it's the same girl?"

"One hundred percent positive!" Detective Stewart confirmed. "That's her. There are not too many Heidi Kachina's in the Essex County area. I remember that story very clearly."

"Okay…not sure how that helps, but I will keep that in the back of my mind."

"So what do you want me to do next?" Detective Stewart asked.

"Follow that Rick Miller lead. See if we can bring him in just to question him about Pearl. And also, find out some more information on that house fire in 2007 for me. You can leave the information on my desk. I will be heading back after I find out where Heidi and Pearl are going to be staying."

"Okay…not a problem."

Detective Williams hung up the phone and grabbed his small notepad. He jotted the new information down and tried to piece it all together. He nodded his head and turned his attention back to the Audi as it began to pick up speed. He watched closely as Pearl got off of the highway and made her way to her sister's house.

* * *

Valerie's House
Edison, New Jersey

10:35

Heidi's eyes lit up when Pearl pulled into her sister's driveway. Her Aunt Valerie's house was gorgeous. The colonial-style home was beautifully painted in an intimate white and wheat tone. The architectural accents resembled a home featured on an episode of Home and Garden. From the landscaping to the spotless common areas, Heidi was stunned at how well maintained the house was. As she continued to marvel, she tried to figure out why she hadn't visited her aunt more often before her hospitalization. She felt a tinge of guilt as she gazed at the three-story structure.

"This is amazing," she said as she got out of the car.

"Ain't it?" Pearl agreed. "Your aunt is doing very well these days."

"I see."

The sound of an opening door came from the front of the house. Heidi smiled as she watched her Aunt Valerie walk out onto the porch, closely followed by a nine-year-old ball-of-energy named Janaya. Heidi became even more excited as she watched her young cousin jump off of the porch and run toward her.

"Hey Janabell!" Heidi screamed as her cousin leaped into her arms.

"Oh my goodness, girl. I haven't seen you in ages!"

"Hiyyeee, Auntie Heidi!" Janaya yelled as Heidi picked her up. She was so happy to see her cousin.

"Okay Janabelly…! Heidi teased her cousin. "I see you still callin' me your aunt."

"You will always be my auntie," Janaya said in her playfully sassy voice.

"Oh my God, little girl…look at you." Heidi smiled at her cousin. "You lookin' more like your mother everyday."

"Uhh-Uhhhhh…!" Janaya squeaked as she emphatically shook

124

her head.

"No?" Heidi responded in a childlike voice. "Well, who you look like, then?"

"I look like me!" Janaya said as a sweet smile came to her face.

"Lord, have mercy," Heidi said as she started to laugh at her young cousin. "Well, if you don't look like her…you sure got your mother's mouth."

Heidi continued to laugh at her cousin's joke and put her down, then looked over to her aunt, who was now walking her way. Heidi smiled, reached out her arms, and embraced Valerie.

"Hey, Heidi." Valerie hugged her niece tightly. "I am so glad to see you, baby. Consider this your home for as long as you need it."

"Hey, Auntie!" Heidi responded. "It's so good to see you, too. I'm so happy to finally be out of that hospital."

Pearl got out of the car and nodded to her sister. It was good to see a smile on her daughter's face. She walked around to the rear of the car and opened the trunk. "Janaya…baby… come over here and help an old lady get these bags."

Janaya ran over to Pearl, and then grabbed the smallest bag from the trunk.

"I'm so glad you guys made it back safely," Valerie said. "Me and Janaya made the best breakfast for everyone."

"Ooohh…that's what I wanted to hear. I'm so hungry I can eat a horse," Heidi joked. "I was getting so tired of eating that cardboard-box-tasting hospital food."

"Well, don't you worry, sweetie," Valerie said. "At least our cardboard boxes got some flavor to them."

Heidi, her aunt and cousin laughed while they walked toward the porch. Heidi was still in awe of the house and continued to look around in amazement as she entered the house. Pearl locked up the car and followed everyone inside, then placed the bags near the living room and turned around to close the door. She noticed an unmarked police cruiser passing by the house and saw it was Detective Williams. He took a quick survey of the home and continued on. Pearl slowly shook her head at him and watched as the vehicle disappeared down the street. A nervous feeling came over her as she calmly closed the door.

Chapter 17

Essex County Correctional Facility

Tuesday November 11, 2008
11:07 a.m.

$\mathcal{S}$ haheed calmly leaned back in one of the dayroom's steel chairs to get a better look at the television. The few inmates that were watching the telecast had their eyes fixed on the baby-mama-drama on the Maury Show. Shaheed chuckled as he watched the dead-beat dads and cheating girlfriends try to dance away from their problems. He could only imagine what his life would be like if his problems were as simple as those who he scoffed at on TV. He tried to put himself in the shoes of a deceived husband or misled boyfriend, but his mind couldn't find a correlation. Facing a multiple-murder charge had hardened him a lot more than he'd thought. Everyday his heart raced with anxiety. He'd managed to keep on his game-face in front of the other inmates, but, inside, Shaheed was a trembling child. The cold walls of the facility were closing in on him and it was getting harder for him to breathe at a normal pace. As he watched the stories of deception unfold on the talk show, he decided he didn't want to subject himself to anymore torture from the idiot box. The irony of the lie detector results and DNA testing was too thick to stomach. He stood up and started making his way back to his cell.

"Come on, man...sit the fuck down up there!" a burly voice yelled from two rows behind Shaheed.

"Who the fuck said that?" Shaheed angrily shouted as he turned around to look at the men.

Any type of confrontation in jail could prove to be a dangerous affair, and Shaheed knew it. Having spent a couple of years locked up, he was no stranger to the jungle-like rules of incarceration. He'd refused to be labeled as soft or a coward because of lack of action. Any action, regardless of negative or positive, was better than no action at all, as far as he was concerned. That was a motto he'd lived by during his times in and out of a jail cell. And today, he was close to making an action that could cost him more than he was willing to sacrifice.

"I said it!" A young dude barked as he quickly stood up. He was a short man, but it was apparent that he'd spent a lot of time working out in the weight room. Shaheed knew he'd have his hands full if a fight erupted with the man.

"Nigga...don't get fucked up!" Shaheed yelled, calling out the man. His adrenaline immediately kicked in. He disregarded his better judgment and continued to toss insults at the man. He moved quickly toward the middle of the day room, and the young man moved toward Shaheed. Inmates close to the commotion quickly stood up as everyone realized that a fight was brewing.

An officer ran over to the scene and got between the men. "Porter...get the hell away from here!" The officer yelled and pushed Shaheed back. He then grabbed the other man and aggressively tossed him away from the scene. "Go somewhere, Ali."

Ali resisted for a moment, but then he eventually took the officer's advice and backed off. He turned around and walked to the other side of the day room. Shaheed looked at the man, then walked back to his cell and tried to calm down himself. His frustration was building. He could sense it. He paced back and forth in the tight unit. After a few minutes, the same officer walked near his cell and yelled at Shaheed.

"Porter...lets go...you got visitation!"

Shaheed was shocked. He looked at his calendar and noticed that it was only Tuesday. He wasn't expecting any visitors today. He walked back into the day room and got in line for visitation. As the single-filed line moved through the hallways, Shaheed could only imagine who wanted to see him today.

As usual, Shaheed took the seat in the far corner of the visiting room. He patiently waited while the visitors prepared to enter. After a few moments, the officers opened the exterior doors and allowed everyone inside. Shaheed stood up. He felt uneasy when he saw his girlfriend, Rhonda walking into the room.

"Hey, baby," Rhonda said as she walked over and hugged Shaheed. "I know you are surprised to see me."

"Damn girl…you had me shook for a minute," he confessed. "I thought you was the lawyer comin' with bad news."

Rhonda smiled at her boyfriend. She could sense that he wasn't doing too well today. He seemed agitated and nervous as he sat down next to her.

"I'm sorry to come see you today, baby…but this couldn't wait for tomorrow," Rhonda said.

"What happened?" Nervousness laced his voice.

"Baby…I went by that place you told me to and I found your cousin."

"Vegas!" Shaheed blurted.

"Baby…he was there."

"So what happened…what the fuck did he say?" Shaheed aggressively asked.

Rhonda looked around the visiting room. His voice was too loud. "Shah'…he said he couldn't do nothin' for you right now," she whispered, hoping he'd do the same. "He's broke as hell. But he says he wants me to help him with a job to get some money."

Shaheed thought for a minute, then turned back to his girlfriend. "What the fuck does that mean?" he snapped. His voice echoed again off the concrete walls. A few officers in the room turned their attention on him.

"Baby…calm down. He said he got something lined up. He wants to get some money for the case, but I'm still waitin' on him to call me back."

"Goddammit!" He was beyond frustrated. The pressure of the

situation was clearly getting to him. "And this asshole didn't say nothin' about the case?"

"He didn't. He just kept sayin' he can get some money in a couple of days. Do you want me to go back to see him?"

"What the fuck is wrong with this dude?" Shaheed yelled again, unable to control his anger. His voice drew the attention of a few more guards.

Rhonda began to get nervous as she looked around the visitation room and saw a few more eyes on her table.

"I'm in this fuckin' place because of him," Shaheed continued to vent. "And he didn't say how he was goin' to help me?"

"Not really..." She tried to lower her voice. "Shah' calm down, baby...I don't want you to get into any trouble."

"Don't tell me to calm down, Rhonda! I'm pissed, and all you can say is calm down!"

"Why are you yellin' at me? Relax Shaheed."

"I'm yellin' at you because all you have been tellin' me since you got here is bullshit!" Shaheed barked. "That's all you bring me up here—bad news! You could'a put that bullshit in a letter!"

Rhonda was hurt by Shaheed's words. She realized he was breaking down from the pressure, but his words continued to cut deeper than a dagger.

"What's wrong, baby...relax," Rhonda pleaded. "You are drawin' too much attention to yourself ."

"Fuck that...and fuck them!" Shaheed boomed as he stood up. "Don't bring me no more bad news up here, Rhonda! You hear me? Shit is already fucked up enough!"

Two guards walked over to Shaheed's table. Rhonda looked up to her boyfriend with disappointment in her eyes. She couldn't hold back the tears of rejection and embarrassment. She watched as the guards positioned themselves a few feet from Shaheed, who continued to yell.

"I'm not playin' with you, Rhonda!" Shaheed shouted. "Don't come back up here with no goddamn bad news, I can't take it."

"You know what, nigga...fuck you!" Rhonda spat back as she

stood up. "You don't have to worry about me comin' back up here with *no news*! How 'bout that!?"

"Whatever!" Shaheed shouted.

A guard walked up behind Shaheed and grabbed his shoulder. "Let's go, Porter," he calmly ordered.

"I'm not resistin'," Shaheed yelled to the guard. "I'm ready to go back to my pod anyway."

The guard grabbed Shaheed by his arm and walked him back to the hallway. Rhonda quickly strode to the opposite end of the room, motioning to another guard that she was ready to leave. The tears of frustration were flowing heavy from her eyes now. Shaheed was escorted out of the visitation area by a pack of officers. He never turned around to watch his girlfriend leave.

* * *

Valerie's House
Edison, New Jersey

11:24 a.m.

Back at Valerie's house, the mood was festive. Valerie hadn't lied when she'd said that she'd cooked the best breakfast for them. The Louisiana-style fried catfish, oven-roasted home fries, fried eggs and white-cheddar grits made the house smell like a southern soul food restaurant. The women were just finishing up eating when Heidi turned and looked over to her mother.

"I don't know, Mom. I think you gotta watch your back," Heidi teased. "I think Auntie is gaining on you in the breakfast department. The food tastes great, Auntie Valerie."

"Child…I'm not worried about my sister," Pearl responded. "Who you think she stole the recipes from?"

Valerie winked at her sister and turned to Heidi. "Thank you, baby. I can't cook as good as your mother yet, but I'm doin' just like you young girls say…*gettin' my skills up*!"

Heidi started laughing at her aunt. She turned to her young cousin who was sitting across from her. "Janaya, can you grab some more orange juice for me out of the 'fridge?" Her cousin nodded and got up from the table. Heidi watched as Janaya ran into the kitchen.

Valerie smiled at her granddaughter, and then turned back to Heidi. "So what are your plans for the next few days, Heidi?"

"I need to head to Newark to take care of a few accounts at the bank. And maybe look for a place."

"A place to live?" Valerie quickly asked. "You know you can stay here as long as you want."

"I know, Auntie, I just want to hit the ground runnin'. I got some issues I need to handle so I can move forward."

Valerie felt a strange vibe growing in Heidi as she continued to speak. She appeared to be deep in thought as she expressed herself.

"I want to get my life back in order," Heidi continued. "Or at least try to."

Pearl looked over to her daughter. Janaya walked back into the dining room with the orange juice and placed it on the table.

"I just need to get a couple of things behind me," Heidi said. She grabbed the orange juice and filled her glass. "Once I knock those things out...I can move on."

"Wow!" Pearl blurted. "You sure you don't want to rest up before all of that?"

"I've rested enough, Mom." The dining room fell silent for a moment. "Auntie, I don't want you to think that I don't want to stay here...because I do. But I think the quicker I can stand on my own, the better it will be for me. I have been sitting in that hospital for so long thinkin' about everything I need to get done."

"I understand, Heidi," Valerie said. "You know...we are here for you."

Pearl looked over to her sister. "She's right, Heidi, you know?" Pearl agreed. "I think we all need to get some things behind us."

Valerie nodded at Pearl. "And what are you goin' to get behind you?"

"I need to clean up my house in East Orange and sell it."

"Are you serious, Mom?" Heidi asked.

"Yes…why not?"

"Oh…damn, Sis," Valerie gasped. "You've owned that house for so long."

"I know. And maybe that's the last thing I need to handle so I can move on. I haven't even seen that house since last year, so it's not like I'm using it. And to be honest, I don't think I want to see it for another year. But I know I need to sell it and move on with my life."

"Whoa…!" Heidi said. "I can't imagine you living anywhere else, Mom."

"Yup. It's been a long time in that house," Pearl continued. "I need to get myself a new one, a new man, and a new life."

Heidi started coughing uncontrollably as she tried to get a question out of her mouth too quickly.

Valerie laughed at her niece. "Whoa now…baby, you okay?" she joked.

"Wait a minute, Mom," Heidi blurted when she composed herself. "A new man? Where did that come from?"

Pearl turned to her sister and pointed at Heidi. "I swear for the life of me, I can't figure out why this child thinks she's my mother. Do you see the way she questions me like she carried *me* for nine months?"

"I see it," Valerie concurred.

"Okay…Mom…so tell me…" Heidi said. "A new man? What happened to Rick?"

"Nothin'…I just don't deal with that snake anymore." Her tone silenced the room once again. Heidi was taken aback by the news. Her intuition instructed her not to further pursue Pearl's answer. She decided to let the awkward moment pass without protest. Pearl grabbed her plate and stood up. Heidi watched as she cleaned the table and walked to the kitchen.

Valerie looked over to her niece and put her hand up to her. "Let it go, baby."

Heidi didn't say a word. She nodded to her aunt and decided to take her advice. She stood up and grabbed her plate and headed for the kitchen behind her mother. "So if you had the money…where would you live, Mom?" Heidi asked trying to change the subject. "There are some nice houses around here, right?"

"Yea…I suppose. But it's too expensive around here. I was thinkin' of maybe moving out of New Jersey all together. Maybe I could move somewhere in Pennsylvania. I know the houses are bigger out there and cost less money."

"That's true," Heidi agreed. "Well, whatever you do, let me know so I can help out."

"Help out how?"

"With some money!"

Pearl turned to her daughter. "With some money? Where are you going to get some money from?"

Heidi looked away from her mother. She didn't want to look her in the eyes. "I got some money saved in the bank, Mom. I didn't lose my money."

Pearl didn't know how to respond to Heidi's last statement. A car horn suddenly beeped from just outside Valerie's house, interrupting the women. Pearl's heart jumped as she looked outside. Heidi noticed her mother's mood changing and walked over to the window. Before Heidi could take a look outside, Pearl quickly turned around and stopped her. Heidi noticed a sneaky look on Pearl's face and tried again to look outside.

"Okay, Mom. What's goin' on?"

"I told you we had something for you," Pearl responded. "Well, it's time for your surprise."

A bright smile came to Heidi's face. Valerie walked into the kitchen smiling. Janaya was following close behind.

"Okay Heidi…you gotta play along," Valerie instructed.

"No problem." Heidi tried to hold back her excitement.

Janaya ran over to Heidi and grabbed her hand. "Close your eyes, Auntie Heidi," Janaya said in her sweet little voice.

"Okay, I'm closin' them now," Heidi obeyed.

Valerie turned around and walked to the front door. Pearl followed her. Janaya waited for the signal, then slowly walked Heidi out of the kitchen and toward the front door. Janaya couldn't hold back her laughter and giggled the whole way to the porch.

"Janaya…you can't give me one teensy hint?" Heidi whispered to her young cousin.

"Uhhh-Uhhh…no cheating, Auntie Heidi."

Heidi kept her eyes shut as her cousin guided her outside. She knew she was on the porch when she felt the bright sun warming her face. Janaya guided her a few more steps and told her to stop.

"One more second, baby," Valerie yelled from a short distance away.

Heidi didn't know what to expect. She was tempted to peek but decided to play along. A hundred images ran through her mind. Before Heidi could take another guess, her mother's voice prompted from behind.

"Okay…you can take a look now, Heidi," Pearl whispered.

Heidi slowly opened her eyes. Her jaw dropped at the sight. "Oh, my goodness!" she yelled as she walked off the porch. "Is that my truck?"

Valerie was smiling from ear to ear. She was standing next to an oversized flatbed tow-truck with Heidi's SUV strapped to the back of it.

Heidi walked over to her aunt and stood next to her. "What in the world did you do to my truck?" she asked as she tried to hold back her laughter.

"Well…your mother had me going to the old house checking on things, and I noticed your truck out there one day," Valerie said. "It was looking really old and banged up, so I decided to get some work done to it."

Heidi walked over to the tow truck. She watched as the driver lowered her SUV from the back. "Auntie…it looks like you got a lot of work done to it."

"I had to…I couldn't have my niece coming back to a raggedy truck." Valerie laughed. "I got the whole truck painted black. It looks like they even gave it a wax job. And I know you see those brand new tires on there. It gives the truck more *attitude*."

Heidi walked to the other side of the truck and continued to survey the shiny exterior. Pearl walked over to the women and smiled at Heidi.

"So you like your gift?" Pearl asked. "It was all your aunt's idea."

"I love it."

"And I even got the front of the truck fixed," Valerie continued. "It was all crashed in like somebody hit your car and kept moving."

Heidi tensely looked over to her aunt. "You fixed the front, too?"

"I sure did," Valerie continued. "It's almost like you have a brand new truck."

Heidi started to feel funny about her aunt's gift. The tow truck driver unhooked the SUV, and then gave Valerie the keys. Heidi stared at the grill and thought for a moment. A quick flashback of the crash with Shaheed popped into her mind. As she looked around the new exterior of the car, she thought about that horrific night that had caused all the damage to her truck and to her life. With all the talk of new beginnings and fresh starts, Valerie was doing the right thing in helping her forget the past and focus on the future. Heidi shook the thoughts and looked over to her aunt.

"Thanks," Heidi said. "This really means a lot."

"Don't mention it," Valerie said as she tossed Heidi the keys. "But there is one thing about the truck I didn't change."

Heidi gave her aunt a strange look as she caught the keys. She moved closer to the SUV and looked around. Valerie smile at her niece and pointed toward the bottom of the truck. An empty feeling came over Heidi as she looked down and read the two words she had been reading since the first time she'd bought the truck. But this time, the words were accompanied by so many feelings of emotions, including regret and fear.

Heidi slowly nodded her head and whispered to herself as she read her own license plate. "SO HIGH."

Chapter 18

Valerie's House

Tuesday November 25, 2008
7:02 a.m.
Two Weeks Later

"It felt like somethin' strong was pulling me down. My mind was still working, but I couldn't feel my body. Whatever it was, I couldn't fight it off. . .it was some kind of demon or somethin'. But it couldn't take me under. Now. . .I knew I was shot. . .I could even smell my body burnin'. But there was no emotions there. I wasn't scared or even sad that I was dyin'! Don't look at me like that, I'm tellin' you the truth. I'm serious. I just felt empty. But, like I said, I knew I was still alive. I just concentrated on my heartbeat. That's the only thing that kept me going."

Valerie sat across from Heidi at the kitchen table. Her mouth hung opened as listened to Heidi's intense story of almost being killed at her mother's house. She remained calm as she gave her aunt the intricate details of how a man she'd trusted had betrayed her and tried to take her life over money. Valerie couldn't believe that her young niece went through so much drama without her knowing about it. Heidi was her favorite, and their relationship had always been a close one. Although Heidi had distanced herself from the family over the past few years, Valerie had never held it against her.

She knew the Kachina women were all subject to isolated behaviors and lives, but she had found hope in knowing they'd all eventually be reunited. She'd just never imagined they're getting together would be under such drastic circumstances.

"So you are tellin' me that a demon was tuggin' on you?" Valerie questioned. "Like the devil?"

"I think it was the devil," Heidi responded. She looked down at her coffee. "I don't believe in the devil on earth. But when you close your eyes for too long, I think that mutha is somewhere in there."

"Hmph," Valerie grunted. "Somewhere in *where*? Your mind?"

"Oh yes…That's what I think. How else are people so capable of doing so many evil things?"

"Sweetie, some folks are just bad people." She stood up from the kitchen table and poured another cup of coffee. They'd been talking for almost an hour now. And like most of the morning, they were again switching subjects.

Valerie checked the time on the microwave, noticing she had another thirty minutes to spare before she had to get ready for work. She sat down and continued the conversation. "I don't believe in the devil. But I do believe in good people and bad people."

"Well…I believe in the devil." Heidi nodded her head. "I don't think I'm goin' to see him walking down the street any time soon, but I do believe that he makes a lot of people do some crazy shit."

Valerie thought for a minute and looked at her niece. "I have a question for you. Have you ever done anything evil before?"

Heidi gave her aunt a skeptical look. She paused for a moment and tried to avoid the question.

"You don't have to tell me what it was," Valerie assured. "We have all done somethin' crazy in our lifetime. God knows that your mother and me were no angels growing up. I know I've done some evil things in my life and so has she."

Heidi began to feel more comfortable with the question. She slowly nodded her head and stared at her aunt to see where she was going with the conversation.

"Okay…think about that evil thing for a minute." She took a

moment to let Heidi think about her evil action. "Now, I have another question for you. That evil thing that you done before…did you benefit from it?"

Heidi was stumped by the question. She turned away from her aunt and reflected again. She thought long and hard and turned back to Valerie.

"Now when I ask you…if you benefited from it…I want you to think about everything. You may have gotten some money out of the situation, a raise, a bonus, a free meal…or even just a good feeling. I want you to think about this… did that evil act bring you some physical, emotional or sexual satisfaction?"

"Damn Auntie!" Heidi said. "You got me thinkin' too heavy early this morning."

"Well, I will keep it simple for you," Valerie continued. "Were you happy or even satisfied after you did that evil shit?"

"Yes. I was."

"So how can you say that the devil made you do somethin' when it was you that got the pleasure from it?" Valerie pointed out. "Anything that we do in life will either hurt us or help us. There is no in between. And usually when you do some evil shit, you are trying to help yourself. Or help somebody around you, which is the same thing."

"I never thought about it like that," Heidi whispered as she reflected on her aunt's words.

"Me neither until your grandmother beat it into me one day." Valerie smiled. "So from that day on, I always believed that there are some people in this world that are just evil and there are just some people in this world that do evil things. But the devil has nothing to do with it. We all have a choice."

"And some people just choose to do evil things in this world and to each other."

"That's right. Just look at the guy you were just telling me about. What is his name?"

"Aaron!"

"Yes, look at how Aaron turned out to be. That was a choice."

"You are right," Heidi said quietly.

"Or better yet, what about how Rick did your mother?" Valerie blurted. "Even the people you think are supposed to have your back can turn out to be snakes."

Heidi looked at her aunt and closed her mouth. The words echoed in her head for a moment. Something in her aunt's tone made Heidi curious. "Auntie…what do you mean how Rick did my mother? Did he do something to her when I was in the hospital?"

"I don't think so. I doubt if she's seen him after she found out he was helping them guys out."

Heidi felt a lump come to her throat. "Wait a second," she stuttered. "What guys? What are you talkin' about, Auntie?"

"The guys you was just tellin' me about," Valerie responded. She was confused by Heidi's cloudy memory. "Didn't your mother tell you about Rick?"

"Oh my God…hell no!" Heidi's voice raised a few decibels. "Rick was involved with that shit at my mother's house last year?" She couldn't contain her anger. She almost dropped the hot coffee on the table as she struggled to keep her hands from shaking.

"Damn, sweetie…I thought you and your mother talked about this," Valerie whispered. She felt sad knowing her niece was in the dark about Rick.

"That muthafuckin' bastard!" Heidi unapologetically shouted. "How did she find out that Rick was involved? Did he kill Lamar?" she quickly added.

Valerie's eyes lit up as she watched as her niece transform into another person. "Sweetie…calm down!" Her heart began to race. She tried to soothe her niece, but nothing she said seemed to work. "I don't think he killed Lamar. Actually…we don't know. Your mother told me that she saw Rick carrying one of the guys into the hospital when she was there. She said she knew it was him. She was one hundred percent sure."

"This is ridiculous!" Heidi stood up.

"That's probably why your mother didn't say anything to you," Valerie continued. "He went missing after that. Nobody has seen him or heard from him since."

"Oh, somebody has heard from him," Heidi quickly snapped. She turned around and stormed out of the kitchen. Valerie didn't like Heidi's body language and decided to follow her. "Mom!" Heidi yelled as she made her way through the living room and to the stairs. Her frantic voice seemed to shake the entire house.

"Heidi...what are you doing?" Valerie whispered. She tried to catch up to her niece, but Heidi was already running up the stairs to the second floor. "Your mother is sleeping."

Heidi ignored her aunt. She quickly reached the second floor and headed straight for the guestroom where her mother was sleeping.

"Mom...I hope you're up!" she yelled. Her anger made her voice crack. "We gotta talk, Mom. Get up!"

Heidi reached the guestroom and banged on the door. The loud thumping caused Valerie to move faster up the steps. Before she could reach her niece, the door to the guestroom opened up. Pearl was obviously shaken by the commotion as she tried to cover herself with her nightgown. She rubbed her eyes and tried to focus on her daughter.

"What happened?" Pearl asked nervously. "What's going on? Why are you yelling?" She looked behind Heidi and saw her sister rushing toward her room. "What's the problem?"

Heidi gave her mother a hard stare. "Mom? Why didn't you tell me that bullshit about Rick being at the hospital?"

Pearl's heart dropped to her stomach. She gave her daughter a disappointed look, and then turned to her sister.

"Pearl, I'm sorry," Valerie apologized. She rushed to get in between Pearl and her daughter. "I never realized you didn't tell her about Rick. It was a slip-up, Sis'...I swear."

"Forget all of that," Heidi rudely interrupted. "Mom, why didn't you tell me?"

Pearl turned around and walked back into the guestroom. She sat on the edge of the bed and looked away from her daughter. Heidi followed her inside and stared. The room seemed to get hotter as the tension began to thicken.

"I didn't tell you because I didn't think it was the right time," she said in barely a whisper. She was still trying to gather herself after being awakened suddenly from her sleep. "You haven't even been home a month yet."

"I understand that, Mom. But all those times you came to visit me at the hospital...why didn't you tell me then?"

"Because I didn't want you to think about all the bullshit going on out here." She was getting more agitated with the discussion. "I wanted you to get better."

"Mom, they killed Lamar," Heidi snapped. "Or did you forget that?"

"Don't talk to me like a goddamn child, Heidi!" she snapped with a fierce tone, returning a hard stare at her daughter.

"So if he had somethin' to do with it, why didn't you tell the police that?" Heidi asked. "We need to find this goddamn snake."

"Stop cursin' at me!" Pearl yelled "I'm not your fuckin' child!"

The room fell silent as Pearl's words bounced off the walls. She was clearly angry with her daughter's interrogating her.

Heidi hesitated to speak again.

"She's right, Heidi," Valerie said from the other side of the room. "Show some respect. That's your mother you are speaking to."

Before Heidi could speak again, Pearl cut her off. "I was thinkin' about *you* when I didn't tell *you*! Just so you know. I wanted you to get better. That's it. I was just protecting you."

Heidi thought about her mother's explanation and decided to press forward. "So why didn't you tell Detective Williams?" She lowered her voice and tried her best to be less combative. "He's out there lookin' for Vegas...when he could have been lookin' for Rick. I know he has to know somethin' about this whole situation. Even if he didn't pull the trigger...he knows something!"

Pearl didn't say a word. She turned away from her daughter and put her head down. Heidi noticed a change in her mood and knelt down beside her mom. She knew somethin' else was weighing heavy on Pearl's mind.

"Mom, I have to ask you somethin'...and please be honest with me," Heidi whispered. "Did Rick try to contact you anytime after that night?"

Pearl looked at her daughter and pursed her lips together. She was reluctant to give the answer. She looked down again and slowly nodded her head. "He called me like a month after Lamar got killed," she whispered.

"Goddammit!" Heidi yelled. She stood up and paced back and forth.

Valerie couldn't believe her ears. She walked over to her sister and sat next to her on the bed. "You spoke to Rick, Sis'?" Valerie nervously mumbled.

Pearl was embarrassed, and refused to look at her sister. She simply nodded her head again, thinking about the conversation.

"Mom?" Heidi said. "What did he say?"

"It's wasn't nothin' like y'all thinkin' it was," Pearl defended.

"Then what was it like?" Heidi snapped. She was clearly pressed to hear the details.

"I saw a restricted number on my cell phone one day," Pearl revealed. "I answered it and it was Rick. He sounded like he was crying or drinking or both. I was so shocked and nervous, I didn't even get to say much. He did all the talking. He kept sayin' how he was sorry and he can't come back to me because he would get killed if he ever showed his face again. That's all he kept sayin'. That he was sorry and that he was scared."

"And that's it?" Heidi asked. "Did he say where he was?"

"No," Pearl shook her head and answered. "He didn't say where he was. Didn't say where he was goin'. He didn't even say goodbye." She was getting emotional as she thought about her ex-boyfriend, Rick. Her mixed emotions about him were beginning to show.

Valerie sensed her sister's state. She put her arm around Pearl and spoke to her. "Maybe it was for the best. This whole situation is too much for anybody to stomach... so I feel your pain, Sis'."

"You know what, Mom!" Heidi said as she walked toward the front door of the guestroom. "That nigga got another reason to be scared."

Pearl looked up to her daughter. "What do you mean?"

"Mom, I don't know if you *want* to believe it or not…But Rick had somethin' to do with Lamar dying! I've been trying to piece this whole situation together since I woke up in that hospital! I was thinkin' that Rick had somethin' to do with all of this, but I never brought it to you. There was no proof then to say he did or didn't, until this. I really wish you would have told me about him being at the hospital earlier. And after hearin' all of this, now I know he's the snake."

Pearl listened to her daughter vent. The conviction in her voice was thick enough to slice. She was beyond angry. The fire in Heidi's eyes was familiar. Pearl also felt a lust for vengeance for the death of her son. She tried her best to suppress the thirst, but this morning her daughter was stirring up old feelings deep within her.

"So what do you want to do now?" Pearl asked. Her eyes were filling with tears.

"I'm goin' to find him," Heidi stated flatly. "I will ask around myself until we figure out something. But he can't get away with this shit. Him…nor those others bastards. Somebody has to pay!"

Valerie looked at her niece with fear. She never saw Heidi filled with so much anger. She stood up and walked over to her. "You are not seriously considering lookin' for Rick are you? By the way it sounds…he is pretty dangerous."

"Fuck him!" Heidi snarled. "I lost my best friend, brother, and almost got killed because of him. I think he should be worried about whether or not I'm dangerous." Heidi abruptly ended the conversation with her aunt and left the room.

Valerie watched as Heidi walked into another guestroom and began to pack a small bag. She turned back to Pearl, who was now holding her head in her hands. "Did I just miss something?" She was confused. "Are you goin' to let her leave and go look for that man?"

"I don't know what else to do," Pearl whispered. "She's right… somebody has to pay."

Valerie felt nervous for her family. She watched her sister wipe a few tears from her eyes.

"The detective is outside," Pearl said quietly. She looked up to Valerie, who was still standing near the door. "He'll watch her. Let her go. When she gets angry like that...it's best to just leave her be."

Valerie didn't want to meddle, so she nodded toward her sister. "Are you okay?"

"I will be. Just let me get myself together."

Valerie turned around and left the room. She passed by the other guestroom and noticed that Heidi was getting ready to leave. She thought about trying to stop her niece, but decided against it. She saw how emotional Heidi was, and felt it was best to take Pearl's advice.

Heidi grabbed her bag and left the room. She passed by her aunt and didn't say a word. She stormed out the house and headed for her car. She was on a mission to find Rick.

Chapter 19

Edison, New Jersey

Tuesday November 25, 2008
7:38 a.m.

etective Williams let out a boisterous yawn as he pulled up
to the neighborhood Dunkin' Donuts. His exhausted eyes
could barely focus on the bright images of the drive-thru window.

"Good morning, how can I help you?" a tiny voice asked over
the loud speaker.

"Yes, good morning. Can I get a toasted blueberry bagel and a
large coffee…black!?"

"No problem…please drive around."

Detective Williams pulled up to the second window of the donut
shop. Like every other morning for the past two weeks, he'd ordered
a caffeine-and-sugar-filled breakfast to keep him awake during his
shift. The stress from the Kachina case was weighing heavy on him,
but he refused to give up. He had been working day and night on this
case, and the long hours continued to punish his aging body. As the
young employee walked over to the window, Detective Williams
gave her a familiar look.

"That coffee is black, right?" Detective Williams asked.

"Pitch black!" the young woman playfully responded. She
handed the detective his order. "Be careful with that…it's very
hot."

The detective gave the young woman a smile and grabbed his

breakfast. "See you tomorrow."

"Have a good day, Officer," the young employee responded. She returned the smile.

Detective Williams put the coffee in his elevated cup holder and pulled out of the parking lot. He checked his cell phone for any new messages as he made his way to Valerie Kachina's residence. Nothing much had been going on at the house since he'd begun to watch Heidi and her mother. But with the case heating up, he didn't want to take any chances and let this case slip by.

As he pulled up, he saw the front door was opened wide. He cautiously pulled his police cruiser to the side of the road and parked across the street. As he looked around the front of the house, Detective Williams began to sense that something was wrong. He put the cruiser in park and got out of the car. He looked around the house one last time and took a deep breath. He'd only made it a few steps in the middle of the street when he saw Heidi storming out of the house with a small bag in her hand. She slammed the front door shut and angrily walked to her truck.

Detective Williams couldn't believe that she hadn't noticed him standing in the street. She quickly jumped into the freshly painted 4Runner, and then fired up the engine. He stood motionless as she revved the SUVs engine. The heavy tires screeched out of the driveway as Heidi slammed the truck into gear. Detective Williams rushed back to his car. He had no idea where she was speeding off to, but he quickly realized that he had to follow her.

Heidi backed away from the house, then tore down the opposite side of the street. Detective Williams quickly shoved his police car into gear and began to make a u-turn. The clunky cruiser almost spun out of control as he tried to quickly whip the car around. He was in the middle of the u-turn when he heard the worst sound he could've possibly heard this morning: the cardboard coffee cup toppling in the cup holder. Before he could reach out and catch it, the entire cup of hot coffee flew into the air and landed directly in his lap.

"Owwww…shitttt!" he yelled. The searing coffee burned through his pants in a split second. Slamming on his brakes, he threw the car into gear and jumped out. "Whattttt the fuccccckkkk…!" he continued to yell. He tried to pull his pants away from his skin, but the hot coffee continued to burn his thighs. His loud screaming made a few of the neighbors look outside of their windows, including Pearl. She noticed the detective screaming near the car and rushed downstairs.

When Pearl opened the front door she saw him leaning on the front of the car, looking at himself. The hot coffee was now cooling down, but Detective Williams was still a mess. Pearl walked out to the middle of the street and approached him.

She covered her mouth when she saw the enormous wet spot on the detective's pants. "What the hell are you yellin' about early this morning?" she questioned. She continued to look down to his crotch area. "Please don't tell me that you pissed yourself."

Detective Williams was not amused by her joke. He tried to hide his embarrassment and brushed himself off. "It's coffee," he grunted. "I just burned the shit out of my legs."

"Wow…I'm sorry. I didn't know." She watched him as he tried to shake some of the leftover coffee off of him. He grimaced in pain as the coffee ran down his leg. Pearl saw the look on his face and felt sorry for him. "I got some towels inside if you want to dry off."

"That's okay, I'll be fine."

"You're not fine. Look at you…it looks like somebody dumped a bucket of soda on you. Come inside and dry yourself off. It's okay."

Detective Williams looked at Pearl. She had a different look in her eyes that made him comfortable. He looked down the street, noticing Heidi's truck was long gone. There was no use trying to follow her now. Pearl watched him as he carefully got back into his car, and then parked it in front of the house. He was clearly upset as he looked at the spilled coffee all around his front seat.

"Let's go, mister," Pearl said with a smirk on her face. "Before you make a bigger mess than you already have."

The detective never responded to Pearl. He got out of the car and followed her toward the front door. He tried to hide his embarrassment, but his body language defied him. He followed her into the house and instantly became amazed at how immaculate Valerie's house was.

"Damn…this place looks even better than it does from the outside," he marveled. "What does your sister do for a living?"

Pearl turned around and glared at the detective. "Are you asking me as a cop?" she sternly asked. "Or as somebody that genuinely cares?"

The detective looked at Pearl and gave her a slick grin. "I guess a little bit of both." He chuckled.

Pearl returned the smile. She respected his honesty. "Valerie is an accountant for Bristol Myer-Squibb. All she does is work. And as you can see…the girl works hard."

"I see!" He continued to follow Pearl as she walked into the kitchen.

"Have a seat, Detective. I will get you a couple of towels."

"Please call me Harold. You make me sound so official when you call me Detective."

Pearl looked at Detective Williams for moment as he took a seat at the kitchen table. "Are you sure?"

"Yes, I'm sure. Call me Harold. That's what my *friends* call me."

Pearl picked up on his clever comment and shook her head. "Okay…Harold. Sit tight…I will be right back."

He gave Pearl a small grin and watched as she walked away. He looked around the clean kitchen. He was clearly impressed by the house. Most of his cases lead him to the rundown houses and low income dwellings of Essex County. After nearly thirteen years on the job, he'd almost forgot about the nice homes that were sprinkled throughout the state. As Harold looked around the kitchen, he began to have thoughts about his upcoming retirement and where he would spend his next years enjoying the fruits of his labor.

A few moments later, Pearl re-entered the kitchen with a handful of towels. She walked over and placed them on the table. "I also have a hair dryer upstairs if you want it."

"It's really okay…these are fine," Harold said as he grabbed the towels. "Whatever I don't get now will dry up later."

Pearl shrugged her shoulders and headed for the counter. "I'm about to make me some coffee. Do you want me to make you one?"

"Oh God…no…!" Harold emphatically gasped as he tried to scrub the wet stains from his paints.

Pearl chuckled at his stiff answer. She'd known he would refuse, so she poured him a cup of apple juice instead. She set the juice on the table, and then leaned against the counter. She watched Harold dry off his pants as she waited for her coffee. After a few moments of silence in the kitchen, Pearl decided to make small talk with the detective.

"So how long do you think you will be watching us?" she asked.

Harold continued to scrub his pants. He tried his best to ignore the question, but he could feel Pearl watching him from across the kitchen.

"Until the Porter case is finished," he answered, still drying his pants. But…you do know…we are watching you for your own protection."

"And I'm not complaining," Pearl quickly responded. "But my question to you is…why are you guys watching us…and not going after whoever else was involved in this nonsense?"

Harold took a deep break. He tossed one of the damp towels onto the kitchen table and looked over to Pearl. "Is that why you invited me in here? To give me a tongue lashing?"

Pearl smiled. "Child, you call this a tongue lashing? You lucky I'm not really mad at you. I don't think you will be able to handle it." She turned around and poured herself a cup of coffee.

"We have men waiting and watching for a few people that have something to do with this case. We're hoping for a conviction so we can get him to turn over on everybody else. Trust me, we are doing everything possible."

"Are you?" she asked.

"Yes we are!" Harold snapped. He was growing more agitated with Pearl's tone.

She turned around, then leaned on the counter. She noticed his frustration and decided to change the subject. "So what's your story, Detective? You never struck me as a type of man that would devote his life to being a cop."

"Okay…?" Harold grunted. "What does that mean?"

"Well, I'm sorry if you took offense to that. All I'm saying is… you have a different look to you. I mean…don't take this the wrong way…but you walk and you talk like you're from the streets."

"Because I am," Harold quickly responded. He stopped scrubbing his pants and looked over to Pearl.

"Oh…!" she stuttered.

"Yup…that was a long time ago…Used to do a lot of dirt back in the day."

"Is that right?"

"Yes…before I became I cop I used to do a lot of dumb shit," he confessed. "Right after high school, I used to run with a group of guys, and all we did was steal from people and, of course, run the streets."

"So how in the world did they let you become a cop?"

"I never got caught. All those years…all that dirt…and I never got arrested. But one day my best friend got killed out there. He robbed the wrong person, and they did him dirty. So that was my wake up call. I was about to go to the army, but the police academy called me back first. So here I am chasing the people I use to be like. Life is funny like that, I guess."

"Hmph…interesting…!" Pearl mumbled. "That explains the crooked look in your eyes."

"I will take that as a compliment," Harold said with a slight chuckle. "That's why I'm good at what I do. I understand these guys out here. Not all of them…but my past helps me get into the mind of a criminal in order to cut them off."

"And you never feel the urge to go back?"

"To the streets?"

"Yes, to the streets?"

"Not a chance," Harold answered. "I help put a lot of people behind them walls. And I don't want to see any of them from the other side. Trust me, there's a reason we need the prison system out here. There are some real animals in the world that need to be caged."

Pearl took a sip of her coffee and thought for a moment. The detective's tone made her look at him in a different light. He sounded sincere about his work, which seemed to put her more at ease. "So who's at home waiting on you?" she asked never changing her facial expression.

"You mean like a family?"

"Yes…who do you work so hard to please?" Pearl added.

"Well, I don't have any kids. And my wife is gone."

"Gone?"

"Yes…she died a few years back. But that story is too sad to tell."

"I am so sorry," Pearl whispered. "I apologize for asking that question."

"It's okay. You didn't know. Maybe one day I will tell you the story. But right now, it's just me and my badge."

The kitchen fell silent as Pearl continued to feel uncomfortable about Harold's revelation about his wife. She took a sip of her coffee and looked around the kitchen.

Harold noticed the thick silence and decided to change the subject. "So what about you?"

"What?"

"Your story?" Harold asked. "What's your story?"

"Well, I'm not a cop or a criminal, if that is what you're asking."

Harold smiled and shook his head. "No…I mean…why are you such a hard-ass?"

"I'm just a hard-ass to people who rub me the wrong way." Pearl took another sip of her coffee. The detective picked up on her double meaning as she continued to speak. "I don't know where I got it from…but at some point in my life, I picked up this nasty habit of trusting the wrong people. I think I trusted the wrong people my whole life. And now…everyone is guilty unless they can prove otherwise. It's just safer for me to be like that."

"I understand," Harold quietly said. He looked down to his pants and noticed they were drying up. "Well…I'm not going to hold you up any longer. I have to get back to my post." Harold reached out and grabbed the rest of the towels from the kitchen table. "Can I take these with me outside? If you want, I will wash them and bring them back."

"No…it's okay. You can have those. Consider those a gift from a friend."

Harold smiled at Pearl, who returned the gesture. He stood up and began to walk to the door. Pearl followed close behind.

"So if you need anything else…if we can help…just knock on the door," Pearl offered.

Harold nodded his head and continued to the door. "I do have one more question. Do you have any idea where Heidi was going? I would like to get a unit to find her, you know…to make sure she is not in danger."

"Detective…I mean…Harold, I have no clue. She was pretty upset, so who knows where she's headed."

"Okay…well, if you find out anything…please let me know. We want to make sure you guys are safe."

"No problem."

Harold walked out the door and headed to his cruiser. As he got inside the car, he noticed his had a missed call from the police department. He promptly returned the call, praying he was about to receive some good news about the case.

Chapter 20

Datakorp Office Tower
Newark, NJ

Tuesday November 25, 2008
9:21 a.m.

"*Like I said Sir, you are calling the wrong department. This is the office of the Vice President of Communications. If you have a problem with your brokerage account, you have to call the customer support department.*"

Twenty-six-year-old Judith Smith was tempted to hang up on the unruly customer. As the haggling man continued to yell directly into her ear, she couldn't help but think of why she was still employed at the online brokerage firm. Being the executive assistant to the Communications department had its perks, but today Judith was becoming very tired of her position. Despite being with the company for almost six years, she was unable to save much money and, with the exploding economic crisis, there wasn't a month that went by that she couldn't help but notice her 401k fund was dwindling right before her eyes.

The voice of the angry customer brought her back to reality as she thought about escaping the office. She had only been at her desk for a few minutes, and she was already considering taking a quick smoke break. Judith looked at her watch and shook her head.

"Okay Sir, this is what I'm going to do," she said, interrupting the customer. "It sounds like I may be able to help you with this problem. I am going to place you on hold for one second and grab my supervisor."

When the customer became silent on the other line, Judith disconnected the call and logged out of her phone. She waved her hand at her computer, then grabbed her jacket. Before anyone else in the office could interrupt her, she quickly made her escape to the elevator.

It didn't take long for her to make it to the lobby of the Datakorp Corporate Tower. People whizzed by each other trying to make it in and out of the building. *Just a typical morning in this place.* Judith pushed her way past a few people, then made her way out to the street. She felt relieved as she finally made it outside of the building.

She looked at her watch and began to pick up the pace. She knew she only had a few minutes to spare and wanted to milk every second she had away from the office. Judith walked toward the side of the building. Too focused on leaving, she never noticed a young woman, wearing a too big baseball cap, trailing close behind. As she neared Judith, the woman gently tapped her on the shoulder. Judith nervously turned around and stared.

"I know you're from Datakorp. I just need to speak with you for a second," the mystery woman whispered.

Judith gave the woman a strange stare. She knew the woman looked familiar, but couldn't quite place her face. The woman's cheap disguise also added to the memory lapse. Judith's mouth fell opened when the woman removed her shades. Although she hadn't seen her in nearly three years she instantly recognized Heidi Kachina.

"Oh my God," Judith stuttered. "Heidi, is that you?"

Heidi nodded her head and put back on her shades. "Yup, it's me."

"My goodness…what are…what are you doing here?" Judith said nervously. She couldn't believe Heidi was actually standing in front of her. "I heard about what happened to you and your family. It was all over the news."

"I know," Heidi somberly said, cutting Judith short. "I didn't come here to talk about them."

"Of course. I'm sorry. What's going on? Are you okay?"

"No, not really," Heidi responded as she looked around the busy street. "But not here. Let's walk."

Judith nodded her head and turned around.

Heidi followed closely behind and began to speak. "Judith, I need to ask you something, and I need you to be very honest with me. I'm not going to be mad at whatever you say. Please believe me. I just need you to be really honest with me so I can clear up some things on my end. Okay?"

Judith nervously looked over to Heidi. "Yes, I'll be honest," she assured. "What do you want to know? I hope I can help you with this."

"Was Jayson cheating on me? Please tell me the truth...I need to know."

Judith stopped dead in her tracks, then turned to Heidi. "No, sweetie." She grabbed Heidi's arms and attempted to console her. "Jayson loved you, Heidi. He spoke so highly about you all the time. He never cheated on you—not to my knowledge. But, then again, we only had a working relationship. I don't know what he did on his down time."

Heidi shook her head in disgust. "Don't fuckin' patronize me, Judith. Don't give me that he *loved me* shit."

Judith was stunned by her words. She let go of Heidi's arms and became nervous. She could feel the heat emitting from behind Heidi's sunglasses.

"I said don't lie to me, Judith," Heidi continued her rant. "This shit has gotten way beyond Jayson now. He's dead and gone! Don't try to stick up for him anymore. Now he worked with you the whole time he was up there...so you probably knew his habits better than I did. So please tell me...did you ever see anything around that place that would tell you that he was seeing somebody else down there?"

Judith slowly shook her head. Her expression became very serious. "I swear, Heidi. As far as I know, Jayson never cheated on you. Now I answered the phones for him for almost four years, and nothing happened up there that I can pinpoint that would make me think he was cheating on you."

"What about you?" Heidi quickly snapped.

"What about me?" Judith countered.

"Did you cheat with him?"

Judith's closed her mouth as she became frustrated with the question. She looked around the busy block in disbelief, and then turned back to Heidi. "Take off your glasses."

"Excuse me?"

"Take off your glasses," Judith repeated. "I want you to see this."

Heidi took off her shades and gave Judith a hard stare.

Judith raised her left arm and showed Heidi the back of her left hand.

"I'm married, Heidi," she said, revealing her wedding ring. "I've known my husband for almost eight years, and never once did I step out on him. I never even thought about touching Jayson. You told me to be honest, and I'm being totally straight up with you. I swear on my eyes, as far as I can remember, Jayson was not seeing anybody outside of you. Now if he was doin' something outside of the office...that's a whole other story that I know nothing about. But from where I was sitting...it was all about you!"

Heidi continued to stare into Judith's eyes. She saw everything except dishonesty in her demeanor. Judith was clearly nervous, but she never turned away from Heidi. She watched as Heidi put her shades back on and began to walk up the street. She remained quiet as she thought about the situation. Closely, she watched Heidi turn away and walk up the block. Now Judith was the one that was closely following behind. There was a cold silence between the two women. After a few seconds, Judith tried to break the ice.

"So you think Jayson was cheating on you?" she quietly asked, trying her best not to offend Heidi again.

"I don't know. I really don't know. Either he was cheating or he was involved in something dirty up there."

"Something dirty? Up where?" Judith quickly asked. "At Datakorp?"

"Hell yes." She hesitated. "Can I trust you Judith?"

"I don't think that's the question, Heidi. The question is whether or not you're *going* to trust me."

Heidi stopped in her tracks. She looked over to Judith. After a quiet moment, she looked around the busy street once again. "This is very serious, Judith. I really need to know if I can trust you. I have somethin' important to tell you, and I need your help."

Judith's eyes became wide as two stop signs. Heidi's tone made her nervous. She nodded her head. "You can trust me. What do you want from me?"

"I have a proposition for you." Heidi looked around again. "If you don't want to help me with this...I understand. But you can't tell a single soul about this."

"Of course!" Judith uttered. She was eager to hear what was on Heidi's mind.

"How long does it take to transfer money from a Datakorp account to a regular bank account?"

"Hmmmm...most of the time it takes about three business days." Judith gave Heidi another wary glance. "Sometimes it can be as long as seven business days. But the longest I have seen was like a month."

"Oh, okay!" Heidi grunted, nodding her head. "Well, here is what I need you to do—if you're interested. I opened up a new account with Datakorp about a year ago, but it was never approved. I need a senior broker up there to simply process my account so I can transfer the funds out."

"Did you open the account online or with a representative at the office?" Judith asked.

"I opened it up online," Heidi lied. She thought about the night she illegally opened the account at the Datakorp office, but decided not to reveal the true source of the account. "For some reason it was never cleared," she continued. "And with the drama with my family last year, I just never got around to coming down here."

"Ok...I can do that," Judith said. "I have a few friends in that department and I can get that approved today for you. Do you have the account number?"

"Yes." Heidi pulled out a small piece of paper from her bag.

Judith took the paper and read it. "There are two sets of numbers on this." She was confused.

"The top one is my account."

"And the bottom number?"

"That's the second part of the proposition," Heidi whispered. Her tone grew more guarded as she talked about the purpose of the second number. She looked around momentarily, then turned back to Judith. "I need you to find out who owns this account. I'm not gonna lie to you...I got that number from Jayson, and I think he's dead because of it. So if you're going to do this for me...I need you to be careful."

"I don't...understand," Judith stammered.

"I'll explain all of that later," she said, interrupting Judith. "I just need you to get my account approved and the name of the person who owns that second account number. That's it. If you do that for me...I'll give you five thousand dollars once my money is transferred."

"Holy shit, Heidi!" Judith yelled. "Are you serious?"

"As a heart attack! Just do that for me and I will give you that in cash. No bullshit!"

Judith did the math in her head. She could use the money and the work seemed simple enough. She found herself becoming just as paranoid as Heidi as she looked around the busy street. "So that's all you want me to do?"

"That's it. Think you can handle that?"

"For five thousand in cash? Hell yes!"

"Okay...my number is on the other side of that piece of paper. Text me your cell number later today," Heidi instructed. "When the account is cleared, call me and I will transfer the money to my personal account today. As soon as the money is cleared in my account, I will pay you."

"Okay...I'll do that," Judith said.

"Don't forget what I said. I don't know who that other account is attached to, so please be careful."

"No problem."

"Okay…I will talk to you later." Heidi abruptly turned around and walked away from Judith. She never looked back as she tried to blend in with the busy foot traffic of downtown Newark.

Judith thought about Heidi's offer for a moment. The cautionary words replayed in her mind as she made her way back to Datakorp.

Chapter 21

Elizabeth, NJ

Tuesday November 25, 2008
11:38 a.m.

A few miles away in Elizabeth, a 2006 marine-blue Range Rover sped around the corner of Prince Street and stopped on a dime in front of a white townhouse. The driver impatiently honked the horn four times and rolled down the driver side window of the luxury SUV.

"Let's go…!" The driver yelled.

Rhonda looked outside of her apartment window and noticed that the Range Rover was waiting on her. She grabbed her purse and checked herself in the mirror one last time. Her silver-pink Juicy Couture tracksuit firmly hugged her curvaceous body. She was definitely dressed to impress. She took a deep breath as she put on her Gucci shades. *Perfect.* Her stunning outfit was ideal for today's events. Now satisfied with her appearance, she rushed out of her apartment and headed downstairs, where her ride was waiting on her.

Rhonda only got a few feet out of her front door when she heard the honking sound of the car horn again. "I'm here…gosh! You can't see me?"

The driver poked his head out of the window and looked over to Rhonda. It was her boyfriend's cousin, Vegas. You gotta hurry up, girl," he barked. "Dude is goin' over there for lunch right now!"

Rhonda hustled her way over to the Range Rover. Vegas directed her to the back seat, and Rhonda hopped in.

"What's good, Rhonda?" he greeted her. "I'm glad you wit' doin' this shit today. We only got one chance to bag this dude."

Rhonda didn't say a word. She looked away from Vegas and noticed a young woman sitting silently in the passenger seat. The brown skinned vixen was cutely dressed in an all white sheer t-shirt that clearly complimented her model-like appearance. Even though the woman was sitting down, Rhonda could see her shapely body protruding through her True Religion jeans. From her five-inch-stilettos, to the flawless makeup on her face, to the expensive jewelry that draped her fingers and neck, Rhonda could tell that this young woman was definitely a get-money-chick.

"Who's this?" Rhonda asked as she tapped Vegas on the shoulder."

"*This*!?" the woman harshly snapped. She turned around and gave Rhonda a very sharp stare. "I am not a *this*! I have a name... chica!"

Vegas quickly put his hand up in the air. "Ladies...please...don't even start. Rhonda...my bad...I didn't introduce you. This is my friend...her name is Skittles. And Skittles...this is my cousin-in-law, Rhonda. Y'all are workin' together today... so just chill out!"

"Workin' together!? What are you talkin' about Vegas?" Rhonda yelled. "I thought you wanted me to do this for you...by myself!"

Vegas put the Range Rover in gear and pulled off. He sped down the road and looked at his watch. "I know I told you I wanted you to help me out today...but I needed Ms. Skittles here because of her... special talents."

Rhonda looked over to the young woman in the passenger seat and frowned her face. As much as she tried to hate on Skittles, Rhonda was impressed with how she put herself together.

"So how are we gonna do this?" Rhonda asked.

Vegas never took his eyes off the road. He continued to speed down the streets of Elizabeth until he reached the Weequahic section of Newark.

"There's a slight change of plans," he shouted so Rhonda could hear him. "This cat is leaving town tomorrow, so he won't be where I thought he was gonna be. So I had to improvise."

"Alright…so what do you want me to do?" Rhonda asked.

"Skittles is goin' to take the point on this one. She knows what to do," he said.

"Okay…that's cool with me…whatever…as long as I get the same money you promised," she snapped with a slight attitude. "Shaheed needs this money, and I gotta get it for him."

"Don't worry Rhonda…we gonna get it," he assured. "Skittles is a pro'…she knows what she's doin'. Just make sure you follow her lead and do what she says. The money is there waitin on us."

Rhonda didn't respond as she continued to study her new partner, Skittles. She began to have an edgy feeling about the little plan that Vegas had put together. She thought about her boyfriend, Shaheed sitting in the county jail, and tried her best to shake the negative thoughts. She was down for her man, and she was going to do whatever it took to help him out. Whatever his cousin had planned for today, Rhonda decided to go along for the whole ride no matter where it was going.

Chapter 22

Maplewood, NJ

Tuesday November 25, 2008
11:47 a.m.

Good morning, Faith. I am so pissed off today! I always had my suspicions about Rick, but today my mother confirmed that he is a true snake. I don't know how deep he is involved, but I pray that he didn't touch you or my brother. I know he is scared to show his face... and he should be!!! But don't sweat it, Faith...I will find him and I will punish him for what he did. Please don't leave me yet. I miss you...I love you...your road dog...Heidi!

The loud horn of a city bus jolted Heidi as she waited at a stop light. As she sat in her truck, she never noticed the traffic light turning green. She scrolled down to Faith's name on her cell phone and sent her best friend the daily text message. Slowly, she nodded when the text message was successfully delivered. She calmly flipped the bus driver her middle finger, then proceeded through the intersection.

Heidi sped down the street until she entered the town of Maplewood. She was making her way to a familiar location to visit an old friend. She pulled out a small black notepad from her purse and double checked the address. The building she was searching for was only a few blocks away.

The neighborhood had changed much in a year. Heidi almost

164

didn't recognize the new department stores and businesses that had sprouted throughout the small town. As she pulled up to the familiar building, a smile came to her face. She nodded her head and read the sign: The Call and Response Regional Headquarters.

Heidi parked her truck in the front and grabbed her bag. Just as she exited her SUV, a loud ringing blared from her cell phone. Heidi fumbled through the bag and answered the call. "This is Heidi," she answered.

"Heidi…this is Judith from Datakorp. I hope I'm not calling at a bad time."

"No, this is a good time…what's up?"

"I just want you to know that I was able to clear that account for you."

"That's a good thing." Heidi was excited. "So I can transfer the money today?"

"Yes…but…" Judith stopped herself.

"But what?"

"You lied to me, Heidi. I can see everything on my computer screen. You opened this account here…at Datakorp."

She picked up on the change in Judith's voice and immediately became defensive. "Okay…so what if I did? Is that a problem?"

"Don't do me like that!" Judith was exasperated. "I'm on your side. How you got that money in the account is none of my business. But this definitely changes the price."

Heidi almost slammed the phone down to the concrete as she became enraged by Judith's words. "What's with you, Judith?" she yelled. "Why can't you just do what you're told?"

"I did, but look at it from my perspective. You didn't tell me the whole story. I can get fired for this. So now…it's twenty-five thousand—or you can try to get somebody else up here to make it happen for you."

Heidi chuckled to herself in an effort to hold back her anger. She hated the fact that Judith was boxing her into a corner, but she admired her gall to get more money. She looked at the phone and calmed herself. "Done deal!" Twenty-five it is…like I said before, as soon as the money is transferred into my account I will contact you…bye!"

Before Judith could say another word, Heidi hung up. She shoved the cell phone back into her purse and headed to the front of the building. She shook her head, quickly erasing Judith's face from her mind. She turned back her focus to the issue in front of her.

She hadn't seen the Call and Response building in a few years. And although she only visited the headquarters once to register for the program, Heidi had grown close to an older woman named Abbie Sutton who'd helped her with the process. As she walked into the building and headed for the front desk, Heidi was hoping that she would once again help her with a major problem.

"Hello…I need to speak with Abbie Sutton," Heidi requested as she walked into the front office.

The young clerk at the front desk gave Heidi a strange look. "Ma'am…I'm so sorry to tell you this…but Ms. Sutton passed away about a half-year ago."

"Oh no…are you serious?"

"Yes…I'm sorry you didn't know," the clerk said. "Did you want to see her specifically about something or are you signing up for our services?"

Heidi took a moment to think. She thought about turning away and leaving, but something made her stay. She looked at the young clerk again.

"I…umm…had a question for her," she whispered. She found herself getting slightly emotional over the news. "I met her a few years ago…I mean, I signed up for the program back then…and she was always very nice to me."

"Oh yes…Ms. Sutton was the best," the clerk responded. "I started here right before she died, and she was always there for me."

"That is tragic."

"I know…I'm so sorry to be the one to tell you the news."

"It's okay…I just been goin' through a lot myself," Heidi said. "I wasn't really ready for that type of news just now. Is someone handling her clients here?"

"Yes. Mr. Wakefield has taken on all of her clients. He is the acting Department Chief. If you wait one moment, I will dial him up and have him come out here."

Heidi dropped her eyebrows and thought for a moment. "Mr. Wakefield? That name sounds so familiar to me."

As the clerk dialed the number and summoned the acting Department Chief, Heidi took a seat in the waiting area. A few moments later, a well-dressed gentleman emerged from one of the offices. Heidi took notice of the man and rose to her feet. Her mouth almost dropped to the floor at the sight of his commanding appearance. He was sharply dressed in an executive-style two-button wool suit that fell smoothly on top of his Eaton-Moc-Toe shoes. Heidi was overly impressed when she noticed how the oxford-grey suit meshed beautifully with the man's dark chocolate skin. *Jesus Christ.* The man gracefully moved through the hallway. Her heart started racing when he reached out his hand to shake hers. She was instantly attracted to him.

"How are you this afternoon? My name is Tycen Wakefield," he said.

Heidi gave him a strange look and shook his hand. "I know you."

"You do look familiar, too," Tycen agreed. "I know I met you somewhere…are you part of the Call and Response program?"

"I am," she responded as she continued to stare into Tycen's eyes. "But I don't know you from here. I met you some years ago."

"Where did you go to school?"

"Oh my God!" Heidi screamed. "That's it! We both went to Kean College!"

Tycen erupted into a joyous chuckle and nodded his head. "I can't believe this," he blurted. "Heidi…right?"

"Yes…Heidi Kachina. That is so funny."

"I know…I can't believe it," Tycen said. He turned around and pointed down the hallway. "Follow me, let's talk in my office."

"Alright." A wide smile grew on Heidi's face as she followed Tycen. She nearly let out a playful giggle as she found herself trying to identify the intoxicating cologne that lingered in his wake. Heidi shook her head at the irony of the moment. To her, Tycen's profile fit that of a GQ model more than an Essex County social worker.

"Have a seat," Tycen offered as they walked into his office.

"Thank you," Heidi said. Heidi looked around his office and marveled at his plaques and certificates. Tycen clearly loved his job and was obviously good at it. Before she said a word, she noticed what seemed to be a family portrait of Tycen with two young children. She instantly became disappointed at the fact that he was obviously already hitched to some lucky woman.

"So what have you been up to?" he asked, interrupting her train of thought. "I haven't seen you since school."

"Oh my goodness…where do I start? I have been through so much since school. But to be honest…it's so much drama…that I can't even explain it all. Let's just say that these past few years have been somethin' straight out of a Lifetime Original Movie."

Tycen let out a hardy laugh, exposing all of his pearly whites.

"What about you?" she asked. "It looks like you're doin' very well for yourself. I'm impressed."

"Thank you. I do okay here. It's really about the clients, in my book. I knew I was going to work in this field even back at Kean. Right after undergrad I got my Masters in Social Work, and now they have me working on my doctorate. So I have been a busy body."

"Oh wow…it really sounds like it."

"Yup…and now that we are expanding the program throughout the entire State of New Jersey, I will be even busier than ever because I'll be heading up my own division soon."

"Damn…look at you," Heidi said. "I am so glad to hear that your hard work is paying off. That's wonderful. It's must be hard to juggle this career and the family, right?" Heidi gave Tycen a faint smile as she decided to do some indirect probing into his personal life.

"Yes…the work is overwhelming sometimes…but the good news is…I have yet to start a family of my own," he said with a smile. "I only have two nephews, who I treat as my own." Tycen turned to the photo of his nephews and smiled. "But it's just me…so that gives me a lot of free time to maximize my opportunities here."

Heidi internally let out a sigh of relief. She knew she would have to probe a lot more to figure out why such a talented and attractive man was still single. "I have to admit, that's good to hear," Heidi said as she nodded her head. "It's good to know that expensive education at Kean was not all in vain."

Tycen smiled at Heidi and leaned back in his chair. She returned the smile and unconsciously licked her lips. He immediately picked up on her flirtatious vibe. She had matured a lot since he'd last seen her back in college. And although she wasn't looking her best today, Tycen could see her beauty escaping through her ragged clothes. He tried his best to stay professional, but he was clearly growing more attracted to her as the conversation progressed.

"So how can I help you today, Heidi?" his question was kind.

Heidi changed positions in her chair and looked around the office again. "I came down to speak to Ms. Sutton about something."

"Oh...okay. Is there anything that you think I will be able to help you with?"

"I hope so. I was looking for some information about a guy that was my partner in the Call and Response program last year."

"Alrighty...what's his name?" Tycen asked as he logged on to his computer.

"Aaron Smith. I was paired up with him in the summer of 2007. We lost contact last year. He was a really good partner. I just needed to know if you have a current phone number or address for him?"

Tycen punched a few keys and pulled up his list of clients on the computer screen. After a few seconds, he came to Aaron's name and read the details about his contact info.

"It looks like he hasn't shown to a meeting since 2007," Tycen said. "And the latest phone number has a *NG* by it."

"NG?"

"No good."

"Oh...okay...damn!"

"Have you tried to go by his house?" Tycen asked.

"I sent a few letters over there, but all of them were returned,"

Heidi responded. "Does it show if his physical address was updated at all?"

"No. Looks like we have the same info that he gave us once he started the program."

Heidi was upset. She knew that she'd hit a major roadblock in finding Aaron. She looked away from Tycen and thought for a moment.

"How bad do you need to find Mr. Smith?" he asked quietly.

Heidi turned back to him and gave him a very sincere glare. "Like somebody's life depended on it."

Something in her tone made Tycen realize that this missing person meant more to Heidi than she was letting on. He couldn't place her vibe so he decided to go the extra mile for her. "Heidi… I'll let you in on a little secret. Whenever we lose a client or we really need to locate what we call a high-risk individual, we call on our sister agency to track them down. They have local and federal resources to find them for us. If you like, I will make a few phone calls and try to see if we can locate him for you. But you have to keep two things in mind."

"Okay…what's that?" Heidi said as she sat up in her chair.

"Number one…this will take a while to do. Sometimes a few months. So you have to be patient."

"That's not a problem." Heidi nodded her head. "And what's the second thing."

"If I do this for you…I have to ask you for a favor back," Tycen said with a flirtatious smirk on his face.

"Hmm…depends on what the favor is," Heidi smiled.

"Let me buy you dinner."

Heidi's heart fluttered for a moment. An instant feeling of flattery rushed through her. She tried to hide her excitement, but it was written all over her face as her cheeks filled with color. "Damn…I didn't expect that to be number two."

"So is that a yes?"

"Yes…Mr. Wakefield. I would love for you to take me out for dinner. But only on one condition."

"What's the condition?"

"I have to choose the place."

Tycen smiled at Heidi and reached out his hand over the desk. She met him halfway and shook his hand as if they were finalizing a major business transaction. "Deal!"

Heidi smiled and grabbed a pen off his desk. She wrote down her phone number and handed it to Tycen. "That's my cell. Call me anytime, and let me know when you want to buy me this dinner. I know a very nice place we can go to. I can call over there and make reservations for us. Trust me…you are goin' to love it."

"Sounds good to me," Tycen said as he grabbed a business card from his desk and gave it to Heidi. "That's my number right there. Please don't be a stranger and, more importantly, don't forget about our date."

Heidi stood up and prepared herself to leave. As she walked out of his office, Tycen followed her out to the hallway.

"Thanks again for helping me out with this problem I have," she said.

"No problem. It was so good seeing you again. It's been almost ten years, right?"

"At least! Well, you have my number so don't be a stranger."

Tycen shook Heidi's hand again and watched her walk toward the exit. He couldn't believe she was still so attractive after all these years. A genuine smile came to his face as he thought about the next time he would see her again.

As Heidi made her way out the door, she grabbed her cell phone from her bag. She was about to make one more stop, but first she wanted to call her mother and make sure that everything was good at her aunt's house. Before she could dial the number, a call quickly came in. It was Judith. Heidi reluctantly answered the phone with an attitude.

"What now?" Heidi snapped. "You callin' to ask me to raise the price again?"

"No…not at all!" Judith responded from the other line. "You gave me two account numbers and I wanted to let you know that I found the other account information."

"Oh okay, one second," Heidi said as she rushed to her truck. She quickly got in and grabbed a pen. "Okay…go ahead. Who does the account belong to?"

"I see right here that it belongs to a Rick Miller of East Orange, New Jersey."

Heidi almost choked on her own shock. Her body tensed with anger and confusion. "Rick? Are you sure? Is someone else listed on the account or is it just him?"

"Shows here…that he is the only one on that account."

"Is there any money in it?"

"Nope. The account has been closed."

"I can't believe this…Rick?" Heidi whispered. "Is there an address on that account?"

"Because the account is closed…I won't be able to pull up any personal information on the account holder."

"Okay…see if you can find some information on him for me," Heidi said. "I will throw in an extra five thousand if you can find me some information I can use."

"Okay, I will keep you posted."

This time Judith hung up on Heidi before she could say another word. Heidi slammed the phone down in frustration of the news. She couldn't believe that Rick was involved in all this chaos from the beginning. Her mind immediately focused on revenge. Now she had another individual to add to her personal hit list. She grabbed her black book and wrote down some notes. She fired up her engine, deciding that the rest of her day would be dedicated to finding her mother's soon-to-be-dead ex-boyfriend.

Chapter 23

*M*eanwhile, back in Newark, Vegas drove past Kings Restaurant on Lyons Avenue. He took a quick survey of the parking lot, then smiled when he saw the alpine-white BMW 750i parked near the entrance. He never forgot a vehicle. And because most street hustlers in Newark could be identified by their cars, he was one hundred percent sure that his mark was in the restaurant. Vegas drove a few feet ahead and quickly pulled over.

"Okay Skittles...he's definitely in there." He pulled out his cell phone and showed her a picture of his mark. "This is the dude. Try to remember his face." Rhonda sat up and looked at the photo. She didn't recognize the man but now she was never going to forget him. "Remember to sit directly across from him. He always watches the door."

"Vegas...stop stressin'!" Skittles said. She looked in the mirror and reapplied some cherry gloss to her lips. After a few moments, she put the lip gloss inside her Fendi handbag and pulled out a jet black P229 handgun. She double checked the clip to make sure her .40 caliber bullets were filled to the tip. Rhonda immediately realized that her new partner meant business. She watched Skittles closely as she put the automatic weapon back into her purse and looked at Vegas. "You didn't bring me out here because you thought I was gonna fuck this up. So let me do me!"

Vegas nodded his head and watched the women exit the vehicle.

"Take care of my cousin-in-law!" he yelled as Skittles slammed the door. He watched the women in his rearview mirror as they walked up the street. He smoothly drove off and searched for a spot to keep eye on the restaurant.

"So what's the plan?" Rhonda nervously asked as she walked with Skittles.

"Right now…there is no plan," Skittles confessed. "The goal now is just to get next to this dude, and we'll make up the rest as we go. Just follow my lead…okay?"

"Whatever you say!" Rhonda was beyond confused. She had no idea what was going on or what was about to happen. The women quickly entered the soul food restaurant. Skittles looked around the dining room. It didn't take long for her to identify the man on Vegas' cell phone sitting alone near the window. Without warning, Skittles aggressively grabbed Rhonda by the arm and pulled her toward the register.

"C'mon bitch!" Skittles yelled. "You said you wanted some lunch…so here we are!" Rhonda was instantly shocked at Skittles' behavior. Her voice was loud enough for everyone in the restaurant to hear them.

"Wait a goddamn minute, who you callin' a bitch?" Rhonda snapped as she pulled away from Skittles.

"Oh…it's like that now?" Skittles yelled. "You not my *bitch* now… after all these years…what…you don't want to be with me no more? I told you I was sorry."

Rhonda gave Skittles a funny stare. She paused for a moment and suddenly picked up on the game. "Whatever, girl…whatever you want to do." Rhonda looked around the restaurant in embarrassment.

"So…are we gonna eat or not?" Skittles yelled again. "You gonna forgive me and let me buy you lunch? Huh?"

Rhonda shook her head at Skittles and gave her a peculiar stare. She now understood why Skittles never told her of the plan today. Rhonda was leery about pretending to be Skittles' girlfriend, but her mind changed once she thought about Shaheed. Besides, it was only acting to get money, she reasoned.

"I'm here, ain't I?" Rhonda yelled.

Skittles smiled at Rhonda, knowing that she was down with the plan. She turned around and spoke to the waitress who'd greeted them near the entrance to the dining area.

"How are you today? Table for two?" the waitress sweetly asked.

"Oh yes, chica…and can you put us near the window. My baby loves the view of the streets." Skittles turned to Rhonda and smiled. They followed the waitress as she led them to the end of the dining room. Skittles smiled and looked at the man sitting at a round table by himself near the window. The half Black-half Spanish man was clearly a hustler type. He wore a red and white skull-n-bones t-shirt with a very expensive diamond chain *blinging* on top of it. The ice in the chain matched the ones wrapped around his wrist and fingers. He had very expensive taste to be so young. He was clearly bringing in a hefty salary with his craft. His clean style was a perfect compliment to his boyish face. From a distance, the man fit the profile of a typical drug dealer from Newark. His name was Raeford "Ray" Hunter.

As the women sat down at their table, Ray gave them a smile and returned his focus back to his lunch.

"Give me one minute guys. I will be back to take your order," the waitress said.

Rhonda smiled at the young woman and watched her leave.

"Can I sit next to you, baby?" Skittles asked Rhonda in a playful voice. Rhonda rolled her eyes at Skittles, remaining silent as she looked at the menu. Skittles slowly got up and walked around the table and sat next to Rhonda. Both women, sitting catty corner to Ray, had a clear view of the young man. More importantly, he had a clear view of them. "So you know I'm sorry, right?" she apologized to Rhonda just loud enough so Ray could hear her.

Rhonda turned to Skittles and laughed at how serious she was about her role. "It's okay…really…let's just eat," she said not knowing exactly what to do to play along.

"Noooo…!" Skittles wined. "I really want to make it up to you. I really didn't mean to make you mad."

"It's okay…I'm fine."

Skittles moved her chair closer to Rhonda's, then put her arm around her. Rhonda froze for a second and looked over to Skittles. "I hope you're not mad at me anymore." Rhonda almost jumped up from the chair as she felt Skittles' other hand slide up her thighs.

"What are you doin'?" Rhonda whispered.

"It's okay, sweetie…let me make it up to you," she moaned as she moved closer and began to kiss her softly on her neck. Rhonda's heart started pounding as she felt Skittles' tongue sliding up and down her skin.

"Wait…Skittles…please," Rhonda whispered. She started to feel uncomfortable but, surprisingly, she wasn't turned off by Skittles' actions.

Skittles' warm breath teased Rhonda's skin as she moved to her ear. "Is he lookin'?" she whispered.

Rhonda slowly turned toward Ray and smiled as she noticed him putting his head back down. He was clearly enjoying the show from across the room, but must've felt embarrassed that he'd gotten caught being nosey. "Hmmm… yes," she moaned, starting to play along.

"Good. Go to the bathroom for two minutes and let me do my thing."

Skittles slowly backed away from Rhonda and grinned at her. Rhonda was clearly thrown for a loop, but she was down for the cause. She returned Skittles' smile, then rose to her feet.

"Don't be long, baby…I'll order your drink for you," Skittles sang.

Rhonda got up from the table and slowly walked to the bathroom. Skittles turned around and seductively watched Rhonda as her tight body slowly moved through the restaurant. She smiled and turned back around. Just as she thought he would, Ray was also looking. She saw this as her best opportunity and decided to seize the moment.

"She's somethin', aint she?" she asked Ray with a devious smile.

"I'm sorry for lookin'…but she is fine…!" Ray mumbled and put his head down. He was embarrassed that he'd gotten caught looking again.

"It's okay, daddy…that's why imma marry her sexy ass…very soon," Skittles bragged.

Ray looked up to Skittles and smiled at her. "So that's your girl?"

"Yea…she's my girl. But she has a boyfriend, and I'm trying to put an end to that."

"Is that right?" he mumbled, happy to learn that they were still into men. He took a sip of his drink and noticed Skittles standing up and walking over to him. She stood directly over him and reached out her hand."

"What's your name, baby?"

"Raeford…but my people call me Ray," he answered as the two shook hands.

"Good to meet you…Ray…my name is Skittles."

Ray smiled at her and chuckled. "Skittles?" he asked and placed his hand on his chin.

Skittles raised her white shirt just above her navel and exposed a sexy tattoo of a multi-colored rainbow that barely arched above her waistline. Ray's heart jumped for a moment as he stared at her sexy stomach.

"Yes…I'm Skittles…!" she responded. "Taste the rainbow, baby."

Ray smiled and chuckled at Skittles' joke. He was digging her style already. She was a very attractive girl, and Ray was loved that she was far from shy.

"I only got a minute before she comes back," Skittles whispered as she turned around and looked toward the bathroom. "I got a confession, Ray. My girlfriend is mad at me, and I want to do somethin' nice for her."

"Okay," Ray said.

"I don't want you to think we're crazy or no shit like that," she continued. "But...she always wanted somebody to watch us."

"What?" Ray questioned. "Watch you do what?"

Skittles gave Ray a crazy look. She smiled and raised her left eyebrow. After a brief moment of confusion, Ray had finally gotten the message.

"Oh shit...!" he laughed again. He started to rub the dark hairs on his chin. "Damn...so you want me to watch y'all get busy?"

"Could you?" Skittles asked in her best seductive voice.

"No disrespect, homegirl...but I don't even know y'all."

"That's why it's perfect." Her response was quick. "C'mon Ray...be a big boy...don't tell me you afraid of us."

Ray shook his head and smiled again. "I haven't been scared of nothin' since I was a kid."

"So what's the problem? Don't you like what you see?" She gave him another seductive gesture.

"Baby...you sexy as hell...no doubt about that...!" Ray said. "But I'm not a trick...I don't pay for pussy...so you gotta take that shit somewhere else."

"What!" Skittles yelled. She played like she was offended. "What you mean you ain't no trick? Baby...you must don't know 'bout me or something...daddy...I got my own money!" Skittles pulled out a bankroll the size of a small hamburger. She flashed it in Ray's line of sight.

Rhonda returned from the bathroom and walked over to Skittles. "Everything good?" she asked when she noticed Skittles was upset. "What happened?"

"This dude think we some ho's or somethin'," Skittles blurted. "He don't know that we probably cakin' more than him out this bitch!"

Rhonda didn't know what was going on and decided to stay quiet. She watched as Skittles peeled off two one-hundred-dollar bills from her bankroll and tossed it on the table. "There you go, Ray, baby...your lunch is on me today." Skittles smiled. She turned to Rhonda and motioned for the exit. "Let's go, baby…I don't like the view in here no more!"

Ray's face became serious. He looked down at the crisp money and took it as an insult. He watched as Skittles grabbed Rhonda by the waist and exited the restaurant.

"What the fuck are you doin', girl?" Rhonda snapped as the women walked outside. "You just blew our chance."

"Baby girl…relax…please," Skittles whispered as she looked inside of the restaurant window. "Be patient."

"What do you mean be patient?" Rhonda continued to yell. "How the hell are we supposed to get next to his ass now?"

"Cat and mouse baby!" Skittles whispered as she continued to look into the window. Rhonda was upset. She began to walk away from the restaurant, and Skittles quickly ran off the steps to catch her. "Be patient Rhonda…trust me…come here."

Rhonda turned around and looked at Skittles. Before she could say a word, Skittles grabbed her by the face and gave her a deep and passionate tongue kiss. Rhonda tried to pull away, but Skittles had a tight grip on her. The kiss lasted just long enough for Ray to come rushing out the door. He saw them and smiled at the sight. He was instantly turned on.

"Hey!" Ray yelled to the women as he walked over to them. Skittles winked at Rhonda and turned around to face Ray as he continued to walk over to her. "Don't ever do that shit again," he barked.

"What shit?" Skittles asked. She played dumb.

"I don't like to be embarrassed," Ray said.

"And I don't like to be rejected."

"So what now?" he asked as he gave Skittles a long and hard stare. He'd hoped to read her like a book, but she was too complicated. And after looking her up and down once again, it quickly dawned on him that she was also too sexy to pass on.

"You tell me what's next, Ray. Like I said…all you have to do is watch."

"Watch what?" Rhonda quickly interjected.

Skittles turned to her. She seductively looked her up and down and licked her lips. Rhonda's heart started racing, but she tried her best to stay in character.

"You can come to our place if you like," Skittles said as she turned back to Ray. She slowly ran her index finger over her bottom lip and smiled at him.

"You know what? That's okay. Not to say that I don't trust you like that…but…I say we go back to my place," Ray suggested. "I think we all will feel safer back there."

Skittles turned back to Rhonda and smiled. "What you think, baby? I told you I would get you what you wanted if you'd be patient with me."

Rhonda quickly picked up on her double talk and turned to Ray. "Fuck it…why not?" she said as she thought about what was about to go down.

"Y'all can leave your car here. I'll drive. I just gotta make a few stops and we can be on our way."

Skittles nodded her head and grabbed Rhonda by the arm. As the women followed Ray to his car, Skittles simply smiled as her mark fell helplessly into her well designed man-trap.

Chapter 24

Dirty Betty's Bar
Patterson, NJ

Tuesday November 25, 2008
2:10 p.m.

*L*ater that afternoon, Heidi pulled into the parking lot of Dirty Betty's Go-Go Bar. Judging by the amount of cars parked outside it seemed that the lunchtime crowd was already arriving. She felt strange coming to the bar, but didn't have any additional options left to get some answers to her burning questions. After calling around and trying to find some leads that would give her some insight on where to find Rick, she found herself coming to Dirty Betty's bar as a last resort. Heidi figured this would be her last stop before she headed back to her aunt's house for the evening.

She grabbed her cell phone and got out of the truck. The fall air was warmer than usual this afternoon, which put her at ease as she walked to the front of the club. A huge man stood near the front entrance. He was over six-feet tall and a few sandwiches short of three hundred pounds. He was obviously doing security for the club. After one of his partners called out to him, Heidi discovered his name was Rueben. Slowly, she walked over to the big bouncer and smiled at him.

"Hey," Heidi opened humbly. "I need to see Betty for a minute."

Rueben looked Heidi up and down. She was clearly out of place. She was dressed rather raggedly and looked more like she was going to the gym instead of a strip club. He decided to pry before he let her in. "Is this a professional visit? Or are you looking for a job or something?"

Heidi calmly shook her head. "No, not exactly. I'm here to talk to her about my best friend, Faith. She—"

"Faith...the bartender?" Rueben quickly asked, cutting off Heidi.

"Yes, she was my best friend."

Rueben's mood changed. "I heard about what happened to her." There was a hint of frustration in his voice. "She was my favorite bartender here. Always cool and down to help a nigga out...for real. With money, advice...whatever!"

Heidi nodded. She felt herself becoming emotional as she thought about the praises coming from the bouncer.

"Yeah," Heidi continued. "That was my girl right there. Ride or die chick."

"It's fucked up what happened to her," Rueben stated angrily. "So a nigga shot her in the head? What type of fool would do that shit to such a pretty girl?"

"That's what I'm trying to figure out," Heidi whispered, almost getting choked up.

"Well, if you find out let me know," Rueben said. His eyes were more serious than the tone in his voice. "I can't stand a coward nigga that would do some foul shit like that. And she was a good girl. So anything you need, let me know. I don't mind puttin' a nigga on his back for Faith. Shit...I do it here all day just for the hell of it."

Heidi smiled at Rueben. "I sure will."

"Come on," Rueben said as he turned around. "I will walk you downstairs."

Heidi followed Rueben into the club. Although she had never been inside Dirty Betty's, she was impressed by the bar's layout. The oversized stage with neon lights gave the club a New York City feel. Women of all races swayed seductively on stage to smooth R &B music.

Rueben made his way through a thick crowd of men and women who were steadily making cat-calls at the women on stage. He grabbed Heidi's hand as they passed the bar. Heidi felt like she was walking into another world as they got into an elevator and went downstairs. With gold handrails, crystal clear mirrors, and deep burgundy carpet, the elevator had a plush feel to it.

"No disrespect, but this place looks a lot better on the inside," she broke the silence in the elevator.

"Yeah, we just did some renovations to the club. Business is good."

"I see."

"Besides, Betty spends the whole day in this place, so she wanted it to feel like home."

The elevator doors opened, and Heidi followed Rueben down the corridor. She remained silent as they both walked to the end of the hallway to a jet black door that seemed to be bolted shut. Rueben rang the doorbell and waited for a response. After a few seconds, Heidi heard a raspy voice yelling from the other side.

"Who is that with you, Rueben?" the voice demanded an answer.

"She's cool, DB. It's okay. She's Faith's friend."

The words were almost like a pass code. Heidi heard about six locks being removed from the other side.

"Come on in," the voice yelled.

Rueben opened the door and they walked inside. Heidi's jaw dropped. Just when she didn't think she could be more impressed with the establishment, she couldn't believe how magnificent Betty's office was. There were paintings and small statues throughout the room. The thick carpet and hard oak tables looked like a set that would be on the final showcase of The Price is Right. The entire room was a direct contrast to Betty's style. Betty was dressed in what seemed to be a vintage two-tone Puma sweat suit. Her hair was a mess, but Betty seemed like the type of person who didn't care. She was almost fifty eight years old, but she was still going strong. Her lust for money clearly outlived her fashion sense.

Heidi watched as Betty sat down behind her desk and put a glass of red wine to her lips.

"Have a seat friend," Betty greeted Heidi, motioning to a chair that was directly on the opposite side of the desk. Heidi slowly sat down across from Betty, who took another smooth sip of her drink. Rueben sat down on the other side of the office behind Betty.

"Do you want a drink?" Betty asked.

"No…I'm okay…thank you."

"So you are the infamous Heidi?" Betty asked rhetorically, staring directly at her visitor.

"Yes." She gave Betty a strange look, knowing the two had never before met.

"I remember your face from the newspapers," Betty uttered, noticing that Heidi was becoming confused. "Honey, you don't get this old ignoring the news. You gotta keep up on what's going on around you to avoid the riff raff."

Heidi remained silent. She didn't know how to respond to Betty.

"I'm sorry to hear about your family," Betty continued, sipping on her wine again. "That story was on the local news for about two straight months. Sad story too…just sad how a robbery can turn into such a blood bath."

Heidi thought about interrupting Betty, but decided against it. She remained quiet as Betty continued to speak.

"When I first heard about it, I really wasn't surprised. When you play with guns somebody is bound to get shot," Betty continued. "That's what my daddy would always say. When people play with guns, you wanna make sure you're on the right side of that trigger. Right Rueben?"

"Damn right!" Rueben mumbled from behind Betty.

"So when I heard Faith got killed that night, I don't think I was all that shocked."

Heidi became uncomfortable with Betty's tone.

"Don't get me wrong, Faith was a sweet girl. God Bless the dead." Betty mumbled. She took another sip of the wine and looked at Heidi. "But when you roll around in the dirt with killers, all is fair. You start to roll in that dirt until it gets muddy. And when the dirt gets muddy, it's hard to see who's the good guys and who's the bad guys anymore. Because…after a while, of all that rollin'…everyone becomes dirty. You get where I'm coming from?"

Heidi nodded her head. She finally began to understand what Betty's rambling was all about.

"So is that why you came to see me?" Betty asked. Her face was hard as stone as she continued to stare at Heidi. "You ready to get dirty again?"

Heidi readjusted her jaw as she contemplated the question. It was almost eerie the way Betty read her like an open magazine. But being so deep in the game for as long as she was, Betty was filled with wisdom. Heidi thought for another second and decided to answer the question.

"I don't know what I want to do," she mumbled. She was clearly nervous, but she was still seeking answers. "I don't have a lot of friends. The only two people I trusted besides my mother are dead now." Betty nodded her head and put her drink down on her desk. "Before she died, Faith trusted you," Heidi continued. "For whatever reason, she felt like you was the go-to person when shit got thick. So that's really why I'm here. I'm hoping you can point me in the right direction. I need to find those bastards that put my brother down. And you already know that Faith was my best friend, so there is no way I can even think about moving on with my life until these motherfuckers are severely punished for takin' her away from me."

"That happened like what…a year ago, Rueben?" Betty asked without looking at him. She kept her eyes fixed on Heidi.

"Yes, DB…somethin' like that," Rueben mumbled. "But a year is nothing. The dead are gone forever."

Betty slowly turned around and looked at Rueben. "That's right, Rue…that was your friend too."

Rueben didn't say a word; he just nodded his head in agreement.

Betty turned around and faced Heidi again. "You young people take everything so personal." She took another sip of wine. "I guess that's why the game is so screwed up. Nobody really does business these days. Everyone is so caught up on revenge and making people pay."

Heidi slowly became frustrated. She couldn't hold back her silence any longer. "Betty, look, if you don't want to help me, then say so," Heidi blurted. "I really don't have time for your lectures." Heidi stood up without warning.

"Sit the fuck down!" Betty yelled coldly. Her wrinkled face turned almost demonic with a slight shift of her eyebrows. The mood in the room thickened, and Heidi nervously sat down without a thought. Betty's commanding voice sent a shot of fear through Heidi. "You interrupted my day, Heidi," Betty lowered her tone. "You come into my office and ask me for help, and you can't give me the respect to listen to what I have to say?"

Heidi didn't speak. She gave Betty a blank stare.

"Maybe if you take the time to listen to what people have to say, then you might find the answers you're looking for," Betty barked. She was clearly becoming angry. "Despite what you think little lady, the world doesn't revolve around you and what you want. Understand?"

"I do, Betty. I'm sorry," Heidi conceded. "I'm just hurting, and I really need some help."

"What do you want from me?"

"I just need some information. I'm lookin' for a dude named Rick Miller. He used to date my mother, and I'm positive that he's the reason why my brother and best friend are dead. He may even have somethin' to do with my ex-fiancé dying a few years back. I think he's from Newark, but I'm not sure. He's dirty as hell, and I was just wondering if you heard his name before."

"I never heard his name before. Does he have a lot of money?"

"I don't think so. When he was dating my mom he was a broke ass nigga."

"Well…if he was broke…I definitely don't know him," Betty responded.

"What if I paid you?" Heidi asked. "If I paid you…do you think you can find him for me?"

"Do I look like a bounty hunter?" Betty snapped.

"No…but everybody knows you," Heidi quickly said. She began to sound desperate. "And I don't know a soul that don't respect you. I really need to find this dude. I will pay you ten thousand dollars to find him."

Betty started laughing and looked back to Rueben. "This girl is dead serious!"

"I am, Betty…this is not a joke. I will pay you. All you have to do is find him for me."

"And then what?" Betty snapped.

"What do you mean?"

"Then what are you gonna do?" Betty snapped again. Clearly growing more agitated with the exchange. "What are you gonna do…kill him?"

"I might," Heidi blurted. Her face stiffened around the words.

Betty chuckled and shook her head. She grabbed her wine again. After taking another sip she sat back in her chair. "You ever saw somebody die, Heidi?"

"I have seen a dead body before."

"Did you see them die?"

"No."

"Well, let me tell you what happens when you do," Betty whispered.

"If you look into a man's eyes when he dies, you will notice that he transforms. His body gets cold and lifeless…almost like a mannequin. And that's because his soul has left this earth for good. Everything that made him what he is…is gone from his body and away from this place. And if you're watching very closely, your soul almost becomes jealous and wants to leave this world of pain behind. But it can't because it's not your time. But you know what does happen? A piece of your soul does tag along. And you lose a piece of yourself. You become colder. The world becomes darker, and that piece of you that use to *give a fuck* doesn't anymore," Betty's tone became harsher with every word. Heidi could tell she was speaking from a very familiar place deep inside her. "And if you watch enough people die in your lifetime, after a while you find there is nothing left of your soul for yourself. And then you just walk this earth…with no conscious…and no remorse…and…no heart."

The room fell silent. Even Rueben sat quietly behind Betty and contemplated on her words.

"So I ask you again, Heidi," Betty continued. "Are you sure that you want to get dirty again?"

Heidi thought for a second. She didn't expect Betty's wisdom to be so morbid. After a few moments, she began to understand why Betty forewarned her of the road that was ahead. After taking another second to think, Heidi looked up to Betty and responded to her question.

"At this point, Betty," she whispered. "I have nothing else to lose."

"We'll see. I'll find this Rick dude for you. But I don't get out of the bed for nothing less than twenty-thousand dollars. So if I find him dead or alive, I want my money."

"You got it, Betty. Thank you so much."

"Give your number to Rueben, and we'll be in touch."

Heidi got up and nodded to Betty. She turned around and Rueben followed her to the door. As he forced opened the heavy door, Heidi thought about Betty's bleak lesson on life and death.

Chapter 25

Garden State Parkway

Tuesday November 25, 2008
2:31 p.m.

"*O*kay this bullshit is gettin' real tired," Rhonda yelled over the loud music as she sat in the back seat of Ray's BMW. "You said that we were goin' back to your house, Ray. What the hell is goin' on? You takin' us all the way around New Jersey!"

Ray tried to ignore Rhonda, but she managed to raise her angry voice over the loud stereo. He turned down the volume and looked at her through his rearview mirror.

"I told y'all that I needed to make a few stops. But like I said… I'm finished for today. Straight up…really! We only about ten minutes from my crib!"

Skittles looked over to Ray for a moment. "Are you sure?" she asked from the front seat. She was noticeably just as tired as Rhonda was of the long ride to his house.

Ray had taken the women on his errand-run for the last three hours. He'd stopped by and visited a few of his clients and had managed to collect a sizeable amount of money. After each stop, he'd secretly tossed the money in the trunk of his car. He had never told the women why he was making the stops, but now that his business was finished, Ray was ready to head back to his house for a very exciting break.

"Word to everything. I'm done." Ray pumped up the music and

turned his focus back to the road. Skittles shook her head, then turned around and looked at Rhonda in the back seat. She gave Rhonda a confident look and smiled at her.

"Just hang in there, baby," Skittles said. "I'll make it up to you."

Rhonda didn't respond. She looked outside of the car and tried to locate the marine-blue Range Rover. Ray had managed to lose Vegas about three stops ago, and Rhonda was getting nervous that Vegas would never find them. She had text messaged him a few times to give him an update on where they were, but he never responded. It appeared that Rhonda and Skittles would have to go at this alone.

Skittles turned around and looked at Ray again. "So where you live at...on Mars?" she joked.

Ray ignored her.

After a few moments, Skittles turned down the music and repeated the question. "Where do you live, Ray?"

"You must never heard Chris Tucker. You know...you can get your ass whooped for that!"

"For what?" Skittles quickly asked.

"For touchin' a Black man's radio!" Ray smiled.

"Boy, please!" Skittles snapped. "You gonna tell me or not?"

"I live in Teaneck."

"Damn...baby, why you live so far from the hood?" Skittles asked. "I guess we are never comin' to visit you."

Rhonda quickly sent a text to Vegas, telling him what city they were headed to. When there was no response, she knew something was wrong. Skittles continued to make small talk with Ray as he got off the highway and continued to drive into Teaneck's city limits. Rhonda kept a close eye out for the street signs and continued texting Vegas the directions.

"Wow...these are some bomb-ass cribs up here," Skittles gasped as she looked at the expensive homes.

"Well...I don't live in none of these big cribs...I live alone...so I didn't get a big house," Ray continued. "Just some small shit for me. But it's hot."

Ray turned off the main road and began to drive into a secluded neighborhood. Rhonda continued to type the street names into her phone. After a few moments, Ray pulled into the driveway of a two-story townhouse.

"Here it is," Ray announced. He pulled into the long driveway and parked the car. Rhonda took a look at the house from the back seat. The all white exterior seemed oddly clean for Ray's style.

"And you live here alone?" Rhonda inquired. "You don't have any roommates?" She wanted to make sure that Ray didn't have any surprise guests waiting inside for them.

Ray quickly turned off the engine to the BMV and exited the car. He opened his trunk and grabbed a green duffle bag. He tossed the bag over his shoulder and continued to walk around to the other side of the car. He watched as Skittles grabbed her purse and got out. Rhonda followed suit and got out of the car.

"Nope, I don't have no roommates...all of this is mine," he said as he pointed at the house. "Now before we go in...I gotta ask y'all to do one thing."

Rhonda looked over to Skittles, who was giving Ray a strange stare. "What's that?" Skittles asked.

"Y'all gotta leave those bags in the car."

"What?" Rhonda snapped.

Skittles didn't say a word, but she gave Ray a defiant gesture.

"I just met y'all...and on the real...I don't trust y'all," he said. "A nigga like me can never be too careful."

"This is some bullshit...let's just go back home," Rhonda said.

Skittles shook her head at Rhonda and turned to Ray. "And what about you?"

"What about me?"

"How do we know we can trust you?"

"Remember...you pushed up on me. So if you wanna get what you want...you gonna have to trust me."

Skittles thought for a moment, then tossed her purse in the front seat of the car. She looked over to Rhonda and nodded her head toward the backseat.

"All I need to get this party started is already on me," Skittles said. She playfully tapped herself on the butt and winked at Rhonda. "C'mon, baby…let's go have some fun."

Rhonda became more nervous that Skittles was leaving behind the only protection they had. She reluctantly put her purse in the backseat and slammed the door.

"Okay ladies, let's go."

The women followed him inside the house and looked around. Rhonda stayed close behind Skittles and quickly surveyed the house. Ray lived in a typical bachelor pad, and Rhonda wasn't the least bit surprised when she saw a huge leather sectional wrapping around an oversized flat screen television in the middle of his living room. Posters of Scarface, Tupac, Biggie and Bob Marley were scattered about the walls. She simply nodded her head at the tacky decor.

"I know this nigga don't have a girlfriend," she whispered. Skittles took notice to Rhonda's observation and laughed at her joke.

"Have a seat," Ray said, pointing to the leather couch. "Y'all want something to drink?"

"Hell yes!" Skittles yelled. "Do you have any Nuvo?"

"Goddamn right I do! You too, shortie?"

"Yes," Rhonda answered. Ray left the living room and went into the kitchen. He kept the duffle bag draped around his shoulder as he left the women. Skittles watched the bag, making a mental note. Both women took a seat on the sofa and continued to look around. Rhonda was clearly nervous.

"Just flow with me," Skittles whispered, trying to put her at ease. Rhonda nodded her head as Ray came out of the kitchen with two glasses of the sparkling liquor.

"That's what I'm talkin' 'bout right there," Skittles said. She stood up and grabbed the wine glasses. She gave one to Rhonda. "Where's the music at, Ray? What kind of host are you?"

Ray grabbed the remote to the plasma television and tossed it to Skittles. "It's all yours…get comfortable ladies. I will be right back. Gonna change my clothes."

Ray went back into the kitchen and retrieved the duffle bag, then headed to his bedroom, passing by the women as he did so.

Skittles waved at Ray and turned her attention back to Rhonda, who remained on the sofa.

"Get comfortable, baby," Skittles whispered. Rhonda sat back on the sofa and took a sip of the Nuvo. Skittles looked at her watch and turned on the television. She found the music channel and turned up the volume. As the smooth R&B music blared through the speakers, she turned back to Rhonda and gave her a seductive look.

"I don't know why you lookin' at me like that," Rhonda said. She gave Skittles an uncomfortable smile. "Ain't nothin' happenin' over here."

Skittles chuckled and walked over to Rhonda. Before Rhonda could stand up, Skittles slowly got on top of her and straddled her lap.

"C'mon, Skittles," Rhonda whispered harshly. She tried to move, but Skittles was too heavy. "I don't get down like that. I'm sorry… you gotta come up with a new plan."

Skittles took a sip of the drink and looked Rhonda in her eyes. "There is no other plan," she whispered. "What we gonna rob him with? Unless you got somethin' on you I don't know about."

Rhonda didn't answer.

"Look…I will do all the work. Just follow my lead. But when the shit goes down…I need you right there with me, cool?"

Rhonda took a moment to think. She couldn't believe that she had a woman in her lap and was contemplating sex with her. She'd never had a sexual encounter with a woman or considered herself bisexual or bi-curious. She took a long swig of the drink. The liquor shot straight to her head and made her more relaxed. She thought about her boyfriend, and looked at Skittles. "Okay," she whispered. "I'm in. But I swear that nigga Shaheed owe me big time."

Skittles heard Ray walking down the stairs and took another sip of her drink. "Showtime," she murmured.

Ray headed straight for the kitchen and fixed himself a glass of Hennessey and Coke. He returned to the living room wearing nothing but a pair of sweatpants and a bright-white tank top. He smiled when he saw Skittles on top of Rhonda. He watched her as she slowly started kissing on Rhonda's neck.

"Damn," Ray whispered. "Y'all don't play around."

He was instantly turned on watching Skittles rub her hands against Rhonda's neck, then over her breast. He walked over to the women and slowly grabbed the wine glass out of Skittles' hand, then placed it on the table next to them. "Let me help you with that, shortie."

His masculine voice seemed to put Rhonda more at ease as she slowly handed him the drink. Skittles was totally into character now. She forcefully pulled Rhonda's shirt over her head and dove into her chest with fervor. Rhonda was thrown off by the move and suddenly moaned out loud. Skittle's wet tongue attacked Rhonda's nipples like she was angry with them.

"Oh my, God," Rhonda moaned as she felt Skittles' tongue aggressively teasing her breast. She unconsciously grabbed the back of Skittles' head as the sensation shot from her nipples to the back of her neck.

"That's what you like, right?" Skittles whispered. Rhonda could feel her warm breath grazing over her stomach as Skittles slowly moved down her body.

"Yes," Rhonda moaned. She found herself getting lost in the moment.

Ray took a seat on the leather sectional. Although he was on the opposite side of the sofa, he had an orchestra-pit-view of the action. He instantly became aroused, watching Skittles move down Rhonda's body and unzip her jeans. Although Rhonda's moans were taking him to another level, he didn't realize the show was just beginning.

Skittles quickly undressed Rhonda down to her naked ass and stood in front of her. She smiled at the sight of Rhonda's mocha brown body and licked her lips. Rhonda's heart fluttered as she felt a rush of excitement go through her. She started breathing heavy with anticipation. The combination of fear and passion was driving her crazy. Amazingly, Rhonda's embarrassment slowly began to fade as Skittles looked at her trembling body with appreciation. Something in Skittles' glance made Rhonda want to expose more of her naked body. A sinful grin came to Rhonda's face. She lifted her right leg and placed her foot squarely on the edge of the sofa. She rocked her leg back and forth as Skittles continued to watch her. Rhonda's smile seemed to invite Skittles in for a taste.

The room began to heat up like an oven. Ray watched the women's intense stares and became more aroused. He had never seen two women so attracted to each other, and the sight was taking his mind on a sexual ride. He reached down into his sweatpants, then put a firm grip on his throbbing dick. He moaned under his breath and realized he was just as excited as the women.

Ray watched as Skittles took off her shirt and wiggled out of her tight jeans. She left on her five-inch-stilettos and kneeled down in front of Rhonda. She didn't waste a moment as she quickly placed her face squarely between Rhonda's legs.

"Ohhh…Goddd," Rhonda moaned. Her head fell back and sunk into the sofa as the feeling was too much to handle.

"Ummm…hmmm," Skittles moaned as she licked, teased and sucked Rhonda into her first orgasm. She felt Rhonda aggressively grab the back of her head as her body began to shake and quiver with pleasure. Rhonda couldn't believe how good Skittles was making her body feel. Skittles knew every button to push and every weak spot to tease. She concentrated on every little detail about Rhonda's body to keep her trembling. Rhonda couldn't help but think that Skittles was pleasing her better than any man had ever done before. She'd never climaxed so much from oral sex. But today, she was becoming hornier and hornier by the second. As she reached another orgasm, Skittles screamed out in pain as Rhonda's dug her fingernails into Skittles' shoulder.

"Wait…Skittles," she moaned. "Please stop…please…this is not right," Rhonda moaned louder.

Skittles ignored Rhonda's pleading and continued to lick between her thighs. The more Rhonda tried to fight it, the harder Skittles worked to make her climax again. She continued to taste Rhonda and looked over to Ray. He was now stroking himself and his hard dick was totally exposed. Skittles smiled at him as they made eye contact. Skittles was already turned on by eating another woman's pussy, but there was nothing in the world better to her than an erect penis. She winked at Ray and motioned for him to come join them. He didn't hesitate to accept the invitation.

Ray stood up from the other end of the sofa and walked up behind Skittles as she continued to please Rhonda. Skittles knew that Ray was standing over her and decided to give him a sneak peek at what he was missing. She took both of her hands and lowered her satin thong for him. She exposed her ass and began to play with her pussy. Ray salivated over the sight until he couldn't take it anymore. He grabbed a Trojan condom out of his pocket and stripped naked. He quickly got on his knees, grabbing Skittles' ass.

"Hurry up, baby," Skittles moaned. "I want you."

Ray put on the condom in a rush and inched up behind her. She moaned like a porno star when Ray's solid dick entered her from behind. She squeezed Rhonda's thighs as she tried to take the pain. Ray's size had caught her off guard.

"Damn, nigga!" Skittles moaned. She dropped her head back into Rhonda's lap as Ray forced himself inside of her. He grunted like an animal as he mercilessly tore into Skittles' tight pussy. The louder Skittles panted, the harder he stroked her. She loved it. She moaned to the top of her lungs when she felt Ray forcing himself deeper. Rhonda raised her head and watched the incredible sex scene. The sight of the threesome sent chills up Rhonda's spine. Another orgasm rushed through her body as Skittles' tongue became more vibrant.

"Whew…girl…this pussy is crazy!" Ray blurted out of no-where.

Skittles felt Ray getting more excited and turned around to look at him. She didn't want him to climax too soon so, without warning, she backed him off her and stood up. Rhonda and Ray were both shocked by her move.

"You want her?" Skittles asked Ray. She pointed to Rhonda, who sat motionless on the leather sofa.

"What?" Ray gasped.

"My girlfriend...you want her?" Skittles repeated. "She needs to feel some of that good dick!"

Rhonda's mouth fell opened as she looked at Ray. A provocative smile came to Skittles' face. She winked at Rhonda and nodded her head.

"Come on, baby...do this for mama," Skittles whispered and nodded her head again.

Rhonda picked up on the cue and gave Ray a crooked smile. She was clearly uncomfortable with letting another man touch her, but she knew that she had to go through with this to help her boyfriend, Shaheed.

Rhonda opened her legs wider on the sofa and watched as Ray's eyes widened. He stayed on his knees and moved closer to her. His eyes were fixated on Rhonda's thick body. Rhonda tried her best to play it cool, but she was beyond nervous. Her body shook as she felt Ray's rough hands rub up against her legs. He started to kiss on her stomach, then moved his way up to her chest. For a moment, he was in complete euphoria.

Rhonda turned her head. She didn't want to watch anymore. She looked over to Skittles and noticed her calmly walking up behind Ray. She seductively rubbed his back as he ran his tongue across Rhonda's breast. His attention was now solely on Rhonda. He squeezed her body and prepared himself for another round.

Skittles looked down at Ray. Her expression slightly changed and her mood became very sinister. Rhonda lowered her brows as she tried to figure out what Skittles was up to. Skittles raised her right leg and grabbed the bottom of her five-inch-stiletto heel. She held onto Ray's back to maintain her balance. Rhonda's heart started beating faster. She watched Skittles unscrew the plastic heel and reveal what appeared to be a sharp surgical knife.

"Oh shit...!" Rhonda gasped. She didn't realize how loud she was. Ray reacted to her gesture. He looked at Rhonda's eyes and quickly turned around. Before he could react, Skittles swung the sharp blade directly at his head. He tried to avoid the blow, but it was too late. Skittles sliced the young hustler on the side of the face with the small knife. A thick stream of blood shot from the side of his cheek and spilled onto the couch. Ray yelled at the top of his lungs. Rhonda jumped up from the sofa and grabbed her clothes. Ray was in total shock as he fell to the floor and held his face. His naked body shook like a leaf as the blood gushed onto the carpet. Skittles rushed over to Ray and stood over him.

"Where's the money, nigga?" she yelled as she waved the knife in front of his face. "Hurry up…tell me!"

"What money?" Ray yelled as he tried to cover his face.

Skittles took another swing at Ray. This time she cut a huge gash into his left shoulder. Ray screamed again.

"Stop!" Ray yelled. "What the fuck are you doin, you crazy bitch!?"

"What am I doin'?" Skittles yelled. "I'm killin yo ass if you don't tell me where the money is."

Rhonda ran to the other side of the room and quickly got dressed.

"Grab his keys!" Skittles yelled to Rhonda, who barely heard her over the loud music. Skittles held the blade directly at Ray. "I'm not gonna ask you again. Where is the money?"

Ray didn't answer. Rhonda ran over to the table near the door and grabbed the car keys. She was fully dressed now. She turned and saw Skittles take another swing at Ray, cutting his other arm.

"What the fuck!" Ray yelled. He was almost in tears from the pain. "Wait…please…wait…I'm bleedin' to death over here."

"I don't give a fuck, Ray…where's the money?" Skittles repeated. She was about to take another swing when she heard a loud banging on his front door. Rhonda froze with fear as she turned to the door. Everyone in the room looked in shock. Skittles quickly turned back around and moved closer to Ray. He continued to bleed from his face. "See who it is." Skittles motioned to Rhonda. Ray became more nervous as he couldn't imagine who could be knocking. He prayed that it was the police.

Rhonda crept to the front door and took a look. A feeling of relief came to her. "It's Vegas!" she yelled.

"Good shit!" Skittles said. "Now it's really time to get it poppin'!

Let him in!"

Rhonda quickly unlocked the door and watched as Vegas coldly walked inside. He was carrying a black pistol in his hand and wearing a serious expression on his face. He quickly moved into the house and walked over toward Skittles. Ray nearly passed out at the sight of Vegas' enormous frame walking toward him.

"I got it from here, Skittles," Vegas ordered. He watched as Skittles dropped the knife and quickly got dressed.

She looked over to Rhonda, who was still standing near the door. "Go grab our stuff from this nigga's car."

Rhonda nodded her head and rushed out the front door.

Vegas turned back to Ray, who continued to lay naked on the floor bleeding from his face and arms. "Where's the money?" Vegas asked as he stood over Ray with his gun pointed at him.

Ray put up his hands as if he was surrendering. "Okay…wait…!" he pleaded. "Wait…don't shoot, man. I got money all around this place."

"Where's the green bag?" Vegas asked. "I know the money's in there. I been watchin' yo dumbass the whole time!"

"It's upstairs. In my room…under the bed." Ray was beyond scared now that he had a gun pointed directly at him.

Skittles didn't waste another moment. She darted upstairs to the second floor to retrieve the bag.

"Don't kill me, fam," Ray mumbled. He was bleeding badly now.

Vegas gave him a cold grin. He enjoyed watching Ray in pain. After a few moments, Skittles ran back downstairs with the green duffle bag in her hands. Vegas nodded at her and pointed to the door. "Grab Rhonda, and y'all wait in the car," he ordered. "I'll meet you outside in a minute."

"No way, Vegas…let's go!" Skittles yelled. "We got what we came for…let's get outta here before the cops come."

"Wait in the fuckin' car!" he yelled and gave Skittles an ice-cold stare. Skittles scoffed at him and darted out the door. Vegas turned his attention back to Ray with malice in his eyes.

"Dog…you don't have to do this," Ray pleaded. His voice was thick with fear.

"I don't?" Vegas toyed with Ray.

"I know somebody set me up, man!" Ray cried out. "Whatever they payin' you to do this…I will double it!"

"You will?" Vegas mumbled with a sinister tone.

"I swear!" Ray shouted. His voice sounded desperate as he continued to bleed. "Whatever they payin' you, I will double—"

Vegas quickly raised his gun and pointed it directly at Ray's chest. Before Ray could finish his statement, Vegas pulled the trigger and murderously put three bullets in Ray's body. The bullets tore into Ray's chest like acid. He never made another sound.

"You will double my money, huh?" Vegas whispered coldly as he watched Ray take his last breath. He thought about the duffle bag and a small grin came to his face. "You already did."

Vegas looked around the living room and thought for a minute. He pulled out a book of matches and began to set fire to Ray's house. He placed the gun next to Ray and left the townhome. He prayed that the blaze would destroy any trace of the gruesome murder that had occurred.

Chapter 26

First National Bank
Newark, New Jersey

Tuesday January 20, 2009
10:03 a.m.
Two Months Later

*H*eidi tensely wrung her hands as she sat in the parking lot of the First National Bank. She suspiciously looked around the bank property for a moment and surveyed the area. She tried to calm herself as she exited her truck and proceeded toward the entrance to the bank. Earlier that morning, she'd received a call from the bank manager asking her to visit the main branch regarding her checking account. The manager had never revealed the nature of the problem, but insisted Heidi resolve her account issues immediately. As she walked toward the entrance of the bank, she began to feel light-headed. She knew her account was only days away from receiving an immense deposit from the Datakorp account, and she was hoping that her plans were not going to be delayed or even worse; derailed.

Slowly, Heidi opened the glass doors to the bank and walked inside. She made her way to the back of the branch and sought out the bank manager. As Heidi got closer to the rear offices, she was greeted by a very short and professional looking Jewish man. Joseph Clayden. He had been the bank manager for over six years at First National Bank. He was well known throughout his region for being a renaissance man of the bank industry. His knack for retaining high-end customers and attracting new money was uncanny. His branch was one of the best performing locations throughout the network, and it was obvious that Mr. Clayden was an efficient employee. But what Heidi didn't know from looking at his clean-cut appearance was that Joseph Clayden was a bloodhound when it came to fraud. In order to maintain a high level of service and quality at the branch, Mr. Clayden made it his business to seek out fraudulent activities of the customers and snuff them out. She never suspected that his suspicions about her were one of his ulterior motives for asking her to visit the bank today. As he greeted Heidi, he gave a warm smile and invited her inside his office.

"How are you, Sir?" Heidi nervously greeted him. "I'm Heidi Kachina…I spoke to you earlier today on the phone."

"Yes…of course," Mr. Clayden responded. "Please come in and take a seat. I was just reviewing your account files."

Heidi felt a knot form in her stomach as she looked at his desk. She noticed Mr. Clayden was viewing an opened folder with her information scattered about.

"Is everything okay with my account?" Heidi asked. Her voice tensed with anxiety.

"Ummm…I have to honest with you, Ms. Kachina," Mr. Clayden continued. "I have worked in the banking industry for a long time, and I have never had a customer try to transfer this type of money into one account."

Heidi's eyes widen at Mr. Clayden's words. She realized that her worse fear was close to becoming a reality. With her Datakorp transfer beginning to raise too many red flags, she realized the money was now in jeopardy of being investigated. She had to calm herself. Heidi looked down and noticed that her hands began to slightly shiver.

"I'm not sure what to say to that, Mr. Clayden," she stammered. "I was simply tired of having my money in my brokerage account. And I'm ready to make some life changing moves with it."

"So why not get a few accounts and spread it out?" he asked. "That's what most of our premium customers do."

Heidi thought to herself and groaned. She sneered at her own inexperience with dealing with large sums of money. She tried to make light of the situation and calm down the mood in the room.

"I have a bad habit of losing things…so this way, I have one account and I won't lose my money ever again," she joked.

Mr. Clayden gave Heidi an insincere smile. He slowly stood up, walked behind her, and closed his office door. Heidi looked up to Mr. Clayden and gave him a nervous glance. She could feel his mood change.

"Listen Heidi…I am going to be frank with you. There are two things I know in life like the back of my hands. One thing I know is money…and the second thing I know is people." Heidi didn't budge as she stared directly at the bank manager. "Now I have been studying this money since we got the request for the transfer two days ago. And now that I am looking at you…I know for a fact… that this money…does not belong to you."

Heidi felt a cold chill rush through her body. She began to envision a dark prison cell as she listened to the manager's words. She thought about running out of the office and bank, but something made her sit motionless in her chair as Mr. Clayden continued to speak.

"Now, I don't know where this money came from…and I don't know where you came from…but I know this money and you don't mix. Like I said, I have been working in this business for a long time, and I can tell when something doesn't add up."

"Mr. Clayden, let me explain," Heidi pleaded. Her voice became defensive as she leaned up from her chair and gave the bank manager a sympathetic expression. "I can't tell you everything. But I can explain where the money came from—"

"I don't care where the money is from," he interrupted Heidi. "The less I know the better."

Heidi raised her eyebrows. She gave Mr. Clayden a strange look as her mouth fell open. "What do you mean…the less you know?" She was surprised.

"I didn't get this far in life being a moron, Heidi," Mr. Clayden responded. "I know a good opportunity when I see one."

"Opportunity?"

"Yes…opportunity. You need something that I can offer. And judging by your demeanor, you could use every bit of my help now."

Heidi was clueless. She felt the bank manager's vibe softening and wanted to know more about what he was offering. "So what's this opportunity you are talkin' about?"

"I know this money didn't come from a bonus check from Wall Street," he joked. "And I know you didn't get a large inheritance from a dead relative. So when the IRS gets a hold of this transaction, you are screwed. And I don't mean to be a jerk to you, Ms. Kachina… but the fact that you tried to transfer all of this money into a basic free-checking account tells me that you need to brush up on your financial knowledge."

"Okay…so I don't own a Fortune 500 company," Heidi snapped. "The money is still mine."

"Indeed it is," Mr. Clayden countered. "But if you want to keep it that way…you are going to need my help." He turned his computer around and logged into the system. After typing a few pass codes and punching a few keys, he turned his attention back to Heidi. "Now, the way I see it...you can let me open a few more accounts for you, and help you filter this money for you...or…"

"Or what?" Heidi sternly asked.

"Or...? Or...I can call the FBI down here and you can explain to them the legitimacy of the money."

Heidi sat back in her chair and nervously smiled at Mr. Clayden. "You're blackmailing me?"

"Don't say that, Ms. Kachina. You make it sound so...illegal! Just think of me as your new financial advisor." Mr. Clayden smiled at Heidi, but she could tell that he was very serious about his proposition.

"So what do you want?" She realized that Mr. Clayden was just as dirty as she was.

"First off...I am not going to allow you to transfer all this money at once. I will allow about half of the account to clear."

"So how much is that?" Heidi quickly asked.

Mr. Clayden punched a few buttons on the keyboard and waited for a moment. "That's a little over one million dollars. The rest of the money will have to stay in your Datakorp account until later."

Heidi tried to hold back her enthusiasm. Dollar signs danced in her mind as she thought about the money clearing. The words from the manager's mouth seemed surreal to her. She couldn't believe that she was about to have full access to so much money. "So what do I owe you for this?" Heidi whispered. She was still shocked from the good news.

Mr. Clayden calmly printed out some paperwork for Heidi to sign.

"I am going to give you one of our high-yield banking accounts. You are going to earn about five percent on your money and I want two percent of that....every month."

"Okay...whatever." She scowled at Mr. Clayden's predatory nature, but he clearly had her backed into a corner.

"So I take it that you agree to the terms?" he asked with a devilish smile.

Heidi reluctantly nodded her head. "That's it?"

"What about today? Will you be making a withdrawal today?"

Heidi's phone rung before she could answer the manager's question. She grabbed her cell and turned off the ringer. She noticed it was her new friend, Tycen calling. She sent his call to voicemail, then turned her attention back to the bank manager. "I want to take out fifty thousand right now."

Mr. Clayden nodded his head. "That's it?"

"That's it," Heidi confirmed. She watched him closely as he printed out more papers and handed them to her. He got up from his desk and headed out the door.

"Sit tight, I will return shortly."

Heidi smiled at the manager as he left the office. She quickly grabbed the papers from the desk and signed each one of the forms. She thought about Tycen and pulled out her cell phone from her bag. She decided to text him while she waited for the bank manager to return. *I can't talk, I am in a meeting*, Heidi typed and waited for his response.

Okay, I do apologize. I wanted to say hi and find out when we can do dinner. I am eager to see you again, Tycen's reply read.

Heidi smiled at her phone and responded. *Don't make me blush. I will call you once I leave the bank. okay?*

Okay beautiful. Talk to you soon, Tycen responded.

Heidi put her phone away and thought about her new friend for a moment. She heard a noise behind her and realized Mr. Clayden was returning into the office. He was carrying a mid-sized, vinyl bank bag with the First National Bank logo on it. He put the bag on the table in front of Heidi, and then took a seat across from her. He handed her a stack of papers, including her account information and two debit cards. Heidi curiously put the bag in her lap and unzipped it. Her face lit up when she noticed six stacks of tightly wrapped one-hundred-dollar-bills inside.

"Hmmmm. This is fifty thousand dollars?"

"Actually, that is sixty thousand dollars," Mr. Clayden said as he gave Heidi a cunning grin.

Heidi looked at the bank manager and dropped her eyebrows. She watched as the manager opened the top drawer to his desk and nodded toward the bag. Heidi finally picked up on the hint. She reached in the bag and grabbed a stack of bills and placed it on the table. Mr. Clayden grabbed for the stack of money, but before he could get a good grip on the bills, Heidi slammed her hand on the table, covering one end of the money stack. She gave the bank manager a hard stare as he froze.

"Let me just say one thing before we complete this business," she said in a very low tone. Her face was hard as stone as she stared directly into his eyes. "You may know money and people, but I know people too. And I know that you're a greedy son-of-a-bitch!" The bank manager flinched at Heidi's words. "I'm goin' to give you this money and your bullshit two percent per month. But if you try any funny shit with me or my money...I will come back down here and I will personally fuck you up!" In an unexpected move, Heidi smiled at the bank manager. Her words echoed in his mind as he watched her slowly release the money and sit back in her chair. He thought about her threat for a second and slowly put the money in his drawer. He calmly nodded to Heidi.

"So when do you advise that I transfer the rest of the money?"

"Umm…I would say to transfer the rest of the money in another month or so," he said, clearing his voice. He was still shaken by Heidi's threat.

"Okay…thanks." She looked at her watch and stood up to leave. "I will come back down here tomorrow to get my new account info. Is that okay?"

"Yes…of course. I will be here."

Heidi put a tighter grip on her bag and left the office. Her adrenaline took over as she thought about all the amount of money she was carrying out of the bank. She focused on her truck and picked up her pace. She totally ignored the people around her as she made her way out of the bank and into the parking lot.

"I can't believe this," she whispered to herself. She was excited and nervous about the money under her arm. She rushed to her truck and tossed the bag into the back seat. She fired up her engine and peeled out the parking lot. Her mind raced as she unconsciously sped down the street and made her way to the highway. She screamed with excitement as it finally dawned on her that she was a rich girl. She fumbled for her bag and grabbed her cell phone. She dialed the one person that she wanted to be with.

"Hello?" a sweet voice answered from the other line.

"Auntie Valerie, is my mother there?"

"Hey Heidi…your mother left out a while ago," Valerie responded. "I'm not sure where she went."

"Damn…I wanted to pick her up and take her out to celebrate."

"Celebrate?" Valerie quickly asked. "Celebrate what?"

"I'll explain it later," Heidi said. "Is Janaya there?"

"You know she is…sitting right here eating up everything."

"Okay…meet me at Menlo Park Mall in about an hour."

"What…Menlo Park Mall? For what?"

"Don't bring a thing but yourself and Janaya," Heidi blurted. "We are goin' shoppin'!"

❖

Chapter 27

St. Mary's Cemetery
Newark, NJ

Tuesday January 20, 2009
11:13 a.m.

*P*earl sat quietly with her thoughts, staring at a gravestone near the edge of the cemetery. She continued to read the chiseled words on the marble stone and became emotional. She couldn't believe her son, Lamar was dead and gone forever. His violent death not only left a gaping whole in her immediate family, but she felt a heavy sense of emptiness as she thought about her family's structure and history. Lamar was the last adult male of the Kachina family. His death symbolized much more than just a loss of a son. His death marked the beginning of the end of her grandfather's name and legacy. Pearl found herself fretfully staring at the Kachina name on the gravestone.

"Please forgive me," Pearl whispered as a few tears came to her eyes.

For the past few months, she had been faithfully visiting Lamar's burial site. Since his death, she felt responsible for not protecting him when he had needed her the most. Visiting his gravesite gave her an opportunity to be with her son again, even if it was only for a spiritual reunion.

A light drizzle began to fall over the cemetery. Pearl looked to the sky for a moment as the cold rain drenched her face. She was totally caught off guard by the weather as the clouds moved over the city in a hurry. She stood and folded her wooden chair. She took one last look at her son's headstone, then nodded her head.

"See you again soon," she whispered.

She turned around and rushed to her car to escape the escalating rain. As she neared the car, she noticed an unmarked police vehicle parked about a hundred yards away. She was surprised to see the cruiser. She put her chair in the trunk of the car and grabbed her umbrella. *Who is this?* She opened the umbrella and walked over to the cruiser. A feeling of frustration came over her as she approached the vehicle. Detective Harold Williams sitting in the driver seat.

"You guys are unbelievable!" Pearl snapped as the detective rolled down his window. "Can I get any privacy?"

"I'm sorry, Pearl. I had to see you," Detective Harold Williams said.

His tone was very different from what Pearl was used to. She gave him a strained expression. "And this couldn't wait until later?"

"It really couldn't," Harold responded. "I just came from court."

"And..." Pearl asked as the rain began to pour.

"We should talk. Can you get in for a second?"

Pearl rolled her eyes in annoyance. She ran around the car, then got inside of the police cruiser.

"I apologize for coming here," Harold said. His voice cracked with a hint of anger.

"What happened at court?"

"Shaheed's lawyer requested a motion for dismissal from the judge again today."

"What does that mean?" Pearl quickly asked. "Can they do that?"

"I'm not gonna lie to you, Pearl...the case doesn't look good." He turned away for a moment. "This lawyer they're using has a knack for turning the evidence around on us."

"Us?" Pearl grunted.

"The police department," Harold answered. "Right now, the strongest case we have is an accessory conviction. But I doubt that this DA can get this murder case to stick."

"What about our testimony?" Pearl interrupted. "Doesn't that count for something?"

"It does!" Harold responded. "And I think we will get a conviction...but I'm hard pressed to say that it's gonna be more than aiding and abetting."

"Goddamn...this is really not fair," Pearl whispered. She dropped her head in disappointment.

Harold looked over to her. "I'm sorry, Pearl...really I am. Closing arguments are tomorrow. I just came over here to tell you that I think you and your family need to be in court tomorrow. It will really help get some sympathy from the jury."

Pearl raised her head and looked over to Harold. "What is this? A game to you?" she asked with an irritated tone.

"What do you mean?" He was totally thrown off by the question. Pearl shook her head in disgust, and then quickly opened the door to the police cruiser. The sound of the hard rain startled Harold momentarily. "Pearl?" Harold yelled as he watched her storm out of the car. "Where are you going?"

Pearl's emotions took over as she began to walk up the short hill. She was too upset to even bother raising the umbrella.

Harold jumped out of the car and ran to catch up to her. "Pearl, wait....what did I say?" he asked as he caught up to her. He grabbed her by the arm and swung her around. "What the hell is the matter with you?"

"You! *You* are what's the matter with me! You think this is a game. Like cops and robbers. All this bullshit talk about jury sympathy and DAs and fancy lawyers. You taking this situation like it's a game. This is my family we are talking about!"

"No Pearl!" Harold pleaded. He vigorously shook his head. "I am takin' this serious—"

"The jury wants *sympathy*?" Pearl yelled, interrupting the detective. "Tell them to come down here to this cemetery and see how real this grief is. Show them the pictures of my house...all the blood they had to clean up back there," she continued in a fit of anger. Her eyes were turning red with pain. "Tell them if they want some goddamn sympathy to dig up my son and look at the hole he got in his head from those animals who put him there!" She was breaking down. The rain began to flow harder as the drops added to the tears on her face.

Harold up balled his lips. He hated to see Pearl become emotionally unraveled. "Pearl, come on...please! I'm sorry," he attempted to calm her down. "I didn't mean to explain it like that. This is *not* a game. You are right. And I was stupid to say that shit to you. But I'm on your side. I am tryin' everything in my power to make sure this coward never sees the streets again. Believe me, Pearl...I understand what you are goin' through. We are in this fight together."

"No, we're not!" Pearl snapped. "We are not in this together. You weren't there...you didn't see the look on his face. He was helpless. He couldn't hurt them...and they just killed him. Why? Huh? You tell me that! What gave them the right to take him away from me... away from us!?" Pearl's face was full of tears. The pain from her loss had finally boiled over. She turned around to walk away and Harold grabbed her by her arm again. "Get off me Detective! I don't have nothing else to say to you! You don't know what it's like. You don't know how it feels...and you don't know what I'm goin' through...so please leave me alone." Pearl gave Harold an intense stare through the rain. She angrily pulled her arm away from him, then stormed off.

Harold felt frozen. He watched Pearl walk a few feet away from him and he yelled at her. "They killed her!" he yelled.

Pearl heard the hurt in his voice, then stopped in her tracks. She slowly turned around and looked at Harold.

"My wife...remember I was going to tell you how she died? They killed her! Some cowards just like Shaheed and Vegas killed her."

Pearl covered her mouth. A cold chill rushed through her entire body as she watched his eyes fill with water.

"I know what you are goin' through," Harold said. "I know what it feels like to sit in front of a grave for hours wishing a voice could be heard again or a smile could be seen. I know the feeling."

Pearl still didn't say a word. She couldn't. She simply stared at the anguished detective and felt his pain.

"No, I wasn't there. I wasn't with her like you were with Lamar... but I know what it feels like." Harold wiped his face and tried to hide his tears from Pearl. "All I'm asking you to do is bring your family tomorrow. That's it. I don't know what's going to happen. I don't know if the State made a good enough case against Shaheed. All I know is...the more cases I lose and the more these hoodlums run the streets, the more I feel like I failed my wife. And people like Lamar." Harold turned around and headed back to his car. The combination of the rain and his emotions made him move with a purpose.

Before Harold could get too far, Pearl yelled to him. "Detective!"

Harold quickly turned around and glanced at her.

"We will be there tomorrow. I promise...I want to see that animal go down too."

Harold nodded his head at Pearl. His expression never changed. She gave him a reassuring smile and watched as he jogged off to make it out of the rain. She turned around and headed toward her car. A feeling of guilt came over her as she realized that she was not the only person dealing with a lost loved one.

Chapter 28

Tuesday January 20, 2009
12:18 p.m.

*S*haheed slammed down the payphone in frustration. He had been trying to reach Rhonda all morning, but she was not accepting his collect-calls from the facility. He hadn't spoken to his girlfriend since he had yelled at her during her last visit to the county jail. Shaheed and Rhonda had had many arguments in the past, but this time she seemed beyond fed-up with his temper. Aggressively, he picked up the phone again and dialed zero. The operator tried to connect his call once more, but there was no answer at Rhonda's house.

"Dammit!" Shaheed yelled as he slammed the receiver down again. He stood up from the phone, walked out of the day room and back to his cell. He was stressed. Between Rhonda's absence and his ongoing trial, he felt like the facility walls were closing in on him fast. Shaheed paced back and forth in his cell and thought about his case. He found himself thinking about how complicated his life had become since he ran into the problem with his ex street-hustling employer, Abdul. With just a few bad decisions, his life had spun out of control, his brother Robert was dead, and he was facing a multiple-murder case.

He was not a murderer, but the State of New Jersey was trying him as a hardened killer. From Shaheed's point of view, the case against him was a solid one. And because the police were unsuccessful in tracking down Vegas, it looked like Shaheed was going to take the fall for him. His feeling of abandonment ran deeper now that his girlfriend was staying away from him. As he thought about his bleak reality, he stopped pacing. He sat on the edge of his bunk and dropped his head in his hands.

"Porter!" a harsh voice yelled from the entrance of his cell.

Shaheed looked up and saw an oversized officer approaching him. He quickly stood up expecting trouble. "What's goin' on CO?" he nervously asked as the officer walked into the cell. "What happened?"

"Take this!" the officer whispered as he handed Shaheed a small leather pouch.

Shaheed gave the officer a confused look as he took the object.

"You got some generous friends out there, Porter," the officer said. "You got ten minutes with this, and I have to take it back." The officer turned around and walked outside of Shaheed's cell. He stood next to the entrance as Shaheed continued to look at him.

What the hell is going on? Before Shaheed could open it, the pouch began to vibrate in his hand. He almost dropped it as the buzzing startled him. He anxiously opened the pouch and saw a mobile phone. "Oh shit!" Shaheed whispered as he turned to the officer, who continued to guard the entrance to his cell. He looked at the vibrating phone and sat down again. After a brief moment he decided to answer the call.

"Hello," Shaheed quietly answered not wanting to bring any attention to himself.

"How you holdin' up, Cousin?" a familiar voice asked from the other line.

"Vegas!?" Shaheed gasped.

"No doubt, Shah'....don't flip out!" Vegas quickly said.

"What the fuck, nigga....where you been?" Shaheed angrily asked. "I'm lookin' at three bodies in this bitch 'cause of you!"

"Calm down, fam...I already talked to your lawyer about that,"

Vegas said. "They got no case on you. Trust me!"

"Trust you?" Shaheed barked in a harsh whisper. "You left me for dead, nigga! Why the hell should I trust you?" There was silence on the phone. "Hello?"

"I'm here, fam...but you gots 'ta calm down, Cousin," Vegas continued. "I had to get out of there, Shah'. Think about it...if we both got locked up that night...there is no way we would'a seen the light of day after that."

"You mean...you wouldn't have seen the light of day. I didn't kill nobody!" Shaheed words were ice.

"I hear you, Cousin...for real...and I know you pissed off. But you gotta calm down...man, you are goin' to give yourself an ulcer."

"Fuck you, nigga...see what I'm sayin'...everything is a joke to you!" Shaheed was not smiling. "This is my life, Vegas...they are tryin' to bury me over here."

"Yo Cousin...check this!" Vegas coldly said. His voice sounded serious now. "I spoke to the lawyer right before I called you and she said you are good. Just calm down and listen to me," Vegas' tone caused Shaheed to remain silent. He listened as his older cousin tried to reason with him. "Now for the amount of money we are payin' her....trust me...she knows what she's doin'. She said the State has no case. And I believe her. They have no weapon and you got shot on the scene. The most they could do is a few years and she can appeal that...so just sit tight, Cousin."

"Sit tight?" Shaheed whispered. "What else can I do?"

"No doubt, Shah'...man...that was my bad for leavin' you," Vegas continued. "But there was nothin' I could do. I had to bounce like that. But I been out here gettin' this money up and tryin' to stay on the low. But I didn't forget about you, fam."

"Who is we?" Shaheed asked as he cut Vegas off. "You said *we* paid the lawyer...who is we?"

"Me and Rhonda," Vegas answered. "We put the money up for the lawyer."

"You saw Rhonda?"

"No doubt...she helped me get the money for your case," Vegas responded. "She said y'all was beefin' the last time I saw her."

Shaheed squeezed his forehead as he began to stress again. "Where is she now? I can't find her. And she hasn't been up here to visit me."

"I don't know, Shah'. After we paid the lawyer she disappeared."

"What the fuck?" Shaheed gasped. "If you speak to her, tell her I need her to come up here. The case is almost over, and I don't know what's gonna happen tomorrow."

"I got you, Cousin," Vegas assured.

The officer turned around and summoned Shaheed's attention. He pointed at his watch.

"I think my time is up on this phone."

"Cool!" Vegas responded. "I just wanted you to know that I'm workin' on gettin' another crack at that money. Good luck tomorrow, fam! Don't worry...I will be somewhere close."

"No doubt...peace." Shaheed hung up the phone and replaced it in the leather case. He handed the phone back to the officer and watched as the officer left his cell. He stood slowly and leaned face forward against the wall. He was haunted by his mixed feelings for his cousin, Vegas. Although he was still angry and disappointed that Vegas had left him to get arrested by himself last year, he was feeling grateful that his cousin was still working hard to help him beat the charges.

Chapter 29

Melo Park Mall
Edison, NJ

Tuesday January 20, 2009
12:41 p.m.

"I love you more."
    "What did I say. . .I love you more!"
    "No. . .I love you more."
    "Well today. . . I love you more!"

Heidi and her nine-year-old cousin, Janaya continued to have their playful argument as they walked through the mall. Valerie smiled at the two as Heidi toyed with her younger cousin. Heidi was visibly in a great mood this afternoon. Things were looking up for her. She was overly excited about her new money and was itching to flaunt her new wealth.

"So what if I told you that I can *show* you that I love you more?" Heidi asked as she playfully pinched her cousin.

"I bet you can't," Janaya yelled as she tried to run away from Heidi.

"Watch this." She grabbed Janaya by the hand and led her into the Disney Store. Valerie followed closed behind and continued to chuckle at her family. Janaya's face lit up with excitement when she saw all the toys and games scattered about the store.

"Pick out anything you want?" Heidi said.

"Anythingggg!" Janaya yelled. Her animated voice echoed throughout the toy store. Heidi laughed at her cousin's jubilance. Janaya ran around the store and looked at the toys. "What should I get?" She looked back to her grandmother, Valerie.

"Janaya…if I tell you that…then it wouldn't be a gift for you, right?" Valerie responded.

Janaya's smile widen as she ran up and down the aisles. There were so many toys and games to choose from. After a few minutes, she stopped in front of a huge toy and pointed at it. "That's what I want!" Janaya commanded.

Heidi smiled as she looked at the biggest toy in the store. It was over four-feet tall and weighed almost twenty-five pounds. "Winnie The Pooh? That's what you want?"

Janaya emphatically nodded her head and looked at Heidi. "Can I?"

"Yes…but as long as you know that I love you more," Heidi bragged.

Janaya smiled at her cousin and hugged her.

Heidi took Janaya's hand and walked over to the cashier. She grabbed a pen and a slip of paper and began to write a note. "I'll take one of those humongous *Winnie The Pooh* stuffed dolls. Please box it up and mail it to this address." Heidi gave the slip to the clerk and opened her handbag.

Valerie almost gagged as she watched Heidi peel off a few bills from an enormous stack of money in her bag. Heidi noticed her aunt's face and smiled at her.

"Wow Beyoncé," Valerie joked. "I didn't know you had another platinum album out."

Heidi turned back to the money in her bag, laughing at her aunt's joke. "Yea…I kind of came into some money today," she said as the women turned to exit the store.

"Came into some money?" Valerie skeptically asked.

"Yup...that's why I'm excited today. I sort of invested in something at Jayson's job last year, and it finally came through. So I just wanted to come out and celebrate today."

218

Valerie gave her niece a hesitant look. The women made their way through the mall as they continued to talk. "What kind of investment, sweetie? Something legal, right?"

"Of course," Heidi lied to her aunt.

"Hmmm…" Valerie groaned. Heidi's quick answer didn't sit right with her. "You know Heidi, if you ever needed to tell me something…you know you can come to me, right? No matter what it is…anything."

"I know that, Auntie."

"Okay…I'm serious…anything!" Valerie repeated. "I won't be mad at you and I won't judge you."

"Don't worry, Auntie. I know you're worried about me. But I'm fine. Especially now…I just want to put the past behind me and look to the future."

"I understand," Valerie said.

Heidi smiled at her aunt and pointed to a bright store sign. "Let's go to Zales. I want to get some jewelry for my mom."

Valerie smiled at Heidi. "Okay…let's go. I will help you pick out something nice for her."

* * *

Maplewood, NJ

1:01 p.m.

Tycen Wakefield stretched out his long athletic arms and released a primal scream as he sat at his desk. His eyes burned like fire from his four hour marathon in front of the computer screen. He knew his days of long meetings and tedious reports were soon behind him. A much overdue promotion, along with a handsome salary increase, was just on the horizon for Mr. Wakefield. He smiled as he thought about how his hard work was only days away from paying dividends. He thought about his bright future and imagined how it was going to feel to be running his own division of the Call and

Response program. Another wide smile grew on his face. Tycen picked up the phone, deciding to make one more call before he headed to lunch. After a few rings, a young female voice answered from the other line.

"Hello?"

"Hey Heidi, how are you today? It's Tycen from Call and Response."

"Oh…hey," Heidi replied as she smiled through her words. "This is a surprise."

"Yes, I wanted to call you before I left out for lunch. I haven't spoken to you besides texting. I wanted to see if everything was good with you."

"That's sweet of you. I'm good…been spending time with my family. I am at the mall now with my auntie and my little cousin," Heidi continued. "How are you doing?"

"I'm great. I wanted to call you to let you know that I am still waiting on some information to come back about your ex-partner, Aaron Smith. My friends at the other agency haven't found any direct information on him, but their department is waiting on some bank records to come back we may be able to use to track him down."

"Is that right?" Heidi quickly asked. "So what are the chances that you guys can find him?"

"The chances are very good that we *will* find him," Tycen assertively said. "You know there are so many traceable things we do everyday from bank transactions to sending out mail to simply buying a plane ticket. So my people really just need to do some more research and put the pieces together. But if we don't find the person, we will find at least a current address or a phone number for him."

"Okay…so that gives me some hope."

"Yes. Don't give up on us yet. We are working it out for you."

"Well, I have to say that I'm happy that you called me. You really made my day just a little bit better."

"I hope so. That's another reason why I'm calling," Tycen flirted.

"I do remember us discussing something about a date or dinner or something like that."

Heidi chuckled for a moment. "So you remembered that?"

"How could I forget?" Tycen responded. "I can't get you out of my mind."

"Wow!" Heidi grunted. "I haven't heard that line used in a long time. Wasn't that a SWV song back in the day?"

"Damn, now why you gotta diss me like that," Tycen said as he laughed at the joke. "Can't a brother be honest these days without being compared to a washed-up singing group?"

Heidi continued to laugh from the other end of the phone. "Okay. You got that. I'll take that joke back." Heidi chuckled. "It's good to know that I was on your mind. I do appreciate being missed sometimes."

"Well…I didn't want to bother and hound you like some kind of stalker. So I figured I would wait for you to reach out…and you did with the text message."

"That's understandable," Heidi continued. "I was goin' to call you a few times…but can I be totally honest with you?"

"Yes…please do."

"Before I talked to you that day in your office, I was goin' through a lot," Heidi admitted. "And today…I'm still goin' through a lot of that bullshit that I was goin' through when you met me."

"Okay…"

"And right now…I just don't want to subject you to that side of me," she confessed. "I don't think that would be fair to you."

Tycen could sense the sincerity in her voice. "I understand. Now you know…I help people for a living. So pardon me if I try to help you. Do you think that there's anything that I can help you out with? I know you just met me…and you don't know me from a whole in the wall other than remembering my face from college. But if there's anything I can do within my power to help you…I surely will."

"You are sweet, Tycen. Really…you are…and I'm letting you know…that in my book…I think you are a good man. But there are just some wounds that have to heal on their own."

There was a brief silence on the phone. Tycen thought about Heidi's words and decided not to push the issue. "I understand. And just know that I'm just a phone call away."

"And so am I," she responded sweetly. "I don't want to tell you to wait by the phone…but when it is our time, I hope you will be available."

Tycen smiled. "Just give me the word, and I'll be there."

"Well damn, Mr. Wakefield…you are just full of songs today," Heidi joked.

Tycen laughed at Heidi's tease. "Damn…I didn't even notice that one."

"It's okay." Heidi chuckled. "Just make sure I'm the only person you use those one-liners on."

Heidi and Tycen laughed in unison.

"You are too much. I'm not going to hold you any longer. I really just wanted to say hello and check in with you."

"Thanks, sweetie," Heidi responded. "Don't forget. When I call…please be ready."

"I will be. Have a good day today, and I look forward to speaking with you again soon."

"Okay, Mr. Wakefield. Goodbye."

"Goodbye."

Tycen hung up the phone and smiled. He caught a chill as he thought about how things seemed to be coming together nicely for him. Although he had just really met Heidi, he felt a strong connection with her. He began to get excited about the mutual attraction between the two. He grabbed his phone and made another call.

"Call and Response," a male voice answered.

"This is Wakefield from the Maplewood Office," Tycen announced. "Did you guys find any more information about Aaron Smith?"

"We are still looking in to that, Wakefield," the man informed.

"Okay…but please use every resource we have over there to get what we can on him," Tycen sternly said.

"We surely will," the man continued. "This sounds like it's

important to you. Is this a personal matter?"

Tycen remained silent for a moment. He thought about Heidi's face when she'd made the request for him to find Aaron. "Yes... actually this is a personal matter!" Tycen replied. "This is a very personal matter. So treat it like somebody's life depends on it."

* * *

Melo Park Mall

1:12 p.m.

Back in the mall, Heidi was blushing like an embarrassed schoolgirl. As much as she tried to hide it, she was a little more than just curious about Tycen. There was something genuine about him that aroused her interest. As she thought about his voice, she never noticed Janaya poking fun at her.

"Little girl what are you grinning for?" Heidi asked as she looked down at her.

"You got a boyfriend," Janaya giggled as she covered her mouth.

Heidi smiled. "No, I don't got a boyfriend...Miss Nosey!"

"He's not your boyfriend?" Janaya said.

"Nope!"

"Do you like him?"

"Yup."

"And he likes you?"

"Yup."

"And he's not your boyfriend?"

"Nope!"

"Why not?"

"Because it's a little more complicated than that, Heidi answered as they continued to walk through the mall.

"I don't know why grown-ups always say that," Janaya sassed. "If he likes you and you like him...I don't care if you like it or not... he is your boyfriend."

Heidi smiled at Janaya's logic, then turned to Valerie.

Valerie looked over to Heidi and laughed. "Don't look at me! Now you see what I go through everyday with her. This girl is nine going on twenty-nine."

"Tell me about it." Heidi gave Janaya a playful angry-face.

"So who is he?" Valerie asked as watched her niece.

"His name is Tycen."

"And what does he do?"

"He's the acting director of the Call and Response program."

"Okay…that's good." Valerie nodded as she gave her approval. "So he's a corporate man?"

"Yup…but if you seen him…" Heidi continued. "Auntie, let me tell you…you would swear this dude should be on television or in a magazine."

"Is that right? Brother's fine like that?"

"Like that!" Heidi smiled. "And he got somethin' on his brain. Not just a bunch of nonsense."

"So what do you think?" Valerie asked. "You think he's The One?"

"I don't even care. I'm not lookin' for The One. I'm not lookin' for someone to save me or try to make me happy....nothin' like that. I just don't want nobody to hurt me."

Valerie looked over to Heidi. She felt bad to hear such pessimistic words come from such a beautiful young girl, but she understood why Heidi felt that way. She realized her niece had been through a lot in the past few years, and she empathized with her.

"So I'm guessing the plan is to take it slow with Mr. Tycen?" Valerie asked.

"Well, he wants to go out to a dinner with me. But I was thinkin' of just inviting him to Lamar's birthday party."

"Lamar's birthday party?" Valerie gasped. "When is that?"

"Dammit…I'm sorry, Auntie. I forgot to tell you that I'm planning a big party in Lamar's name in a few weeks. I was goin' to tell you guys, but I wanted it to be a surprise once I got some money together."

"Ooooooo…a party? Can I come?" Janaya asked.

"Of course you can come. It's for your Uncle Lamar."

"That is a great idea, Heidi," Valerie said. "Do you need any help with it?"

"No, Auntie…I want to do this by myself. I owe this to my brother. I already booked the hall in Newark, and I got two catering places doing the food. It's going to be very nice."

"Wow…that is great. How many people are you going to invite?"

"I am goin' to invite everybody. It's going to be free to the public. I just want to celebrate Lamar, and maybe it can turn into something I can do every year for him. Free food…free drinks and free music for the community…in his name."

"Wow, Heidi…that is very impressive." Valerie reached over and rubbed Heidi on the shoulder. "I am so proud of you. I can't wait for the party."

"Me neither. And I know Lamar is going to love it."

Chapter 30

Valerie's House
Edison, New Jersey

6:15 p.m.

*P*earl pulled up to Valerie's house and turned off the engine. Nightfall was just settling in as the rain continued to pour. She noticed the house was dark as she grabbed her things and hurried into the house. She was surprised to see that no one was home this late in the day.

"Hellooo!" she yelled as she walked through the house. "Valerie! Janaya!"

The silence confirmed she was home alone. She set her bags on the dining room table, then pulled out her cell phone. After looking at the display screen, she noticed she'd missed a number of calls. She'd forgotten to turn back on the ringer, and had missed almost eight calls from her sister and Heidi. Quickly, she dialed her daughter and waited for an answer.

"Heyyyy, Mommy Dearest!" Heidi answered in a bubbly mood. "You missed all the fun."

"What fun? Where are you?"

"We are on our way home now," Heidi responded.

"We?"

"Me…Auntie Valerie and Janaya spent the day together," Heidi continued. "We went to the mall…to the nail salon…and I even went to look at a new car."

"New car…what in the world?" Pearl uttered. "Hmmm okay… did you hit the lotto?"

Heidi chuckled from the other line. "Not exactly, Mother!" Heidi said in her best suburban voice. "I will explain it to you later. We should be there in about ten minutes."

"Good…because we need to talk."

"Is everything okay?"

"I spoke to Detective Williams today. He told me that tomorrow's a big day in court and we need to be there," Pearl informed. "But…I will give you all the details when you get here."

"Okay, Mom…I will see you in a minute."

"See you guys soon."

Pearl hung up the phone and began to put away her things. She couldn't help but think about her long day and discussion with Detective Williams. She prayed that Harold was wrong about his prediction of the case's outcome. She wanted justice for her son, and she had no idea what her family would do if the case didn't turn out in their favor. Pearl forced the thought from her mind and continued to put away her bags.

The rhythmic clanging of Valerie's doorbell startled her for a moment. She looked at the clock on the microwave. *I thought she said ten minutes.* She figured it was Heidi and her sister. She calmly walked to the front door and opened it.

"Oh my goodness…Melissa!?" Pearl yelled in shock. She covered her mouth as she laid eyes on a face she hadn't seen since her son had died. It had been a little over a year since she'd last laid eyes on Melissa. She knew Melissa was beyond broken-up over Lamar's death, so she'd assumed it was too much for her to be around the family. The last thing she'd expected out of Melissa was for her to show up at Valerie's house.

Melissa looked nervous as she stood on the porch. She didn't say a word.

"My God, Melissa…what are you doing here?"

"I didn't know where else to go…" Melissa said quietly, a strange tone wrapped around her words.

Pearl immediately realized that something was not right with her deceased son's last girlfriend. She motioned for Melissa to come inside, then reached out and hugged her. "Damn, child...I haven't seen you in so long. Are you okay?"

"Honestly? I was good..." Melissa uttered. "But tonight I really started to break down. I can't do it in that apartment anymore. I had to get out of there."

Pearl walked Melissa to the living room and invited her to take a seat on the sofa. "You want something to drink? Water...juice?"

"No...I'm fine," Melissa respectfully responded and sat down on the sofa.

"So where have you been, Melissa? I was thinking about you a couple of days ago. I was wondering how you was holding up."

"I have been good...but it's been hard to adjust," Melissa whispered. "Since Lamar died, it's been hard for me to be normal again."

"Tell me about it...I totally understand where you are coming from," Pearl quietly said. "I think all of us are going through the same thing. Lamar was just that type of person. We all miss him. Lord knows we do."

Melissa never responded. She seemed to drift into deep thought as she reflected on how much she missed her boyfriend.

Pearl noticed Melissa's mood changing. "You still live near Philadelphia?" She tried to ease the mood in the room.

"Yes...I'm still there," Melissa somberly answered. "I couldn't bring myself to move out yet. I got too many memories of your son in there."

"So you drove all the way up here—" Pearl stopped herself before she could finish her own question. "Wait a minute...how did you find us, Melissa? How did you know we lived here?"

Melissa hesitated to answer. Pearl gave her a strange look. Melissa turned to her and stayed quiet.

"Well..." Pearl uttered waiting for an answer from Melissa.

"I got the address from the hospital Heidi was staying at," she confessed.

"What?" Pearl whispered. She thought for a moment and looked at Melissa. "So that was *you* showing up to the hospital to see my daughter? Why?"

"I really don't know. I wanted to visit Heidi…but every time I got there…I chickened out and left."

Pearl was extremely suspicious of Melissa. She looked at her son's girlfriend and tried to understand her odd behavior.

Melissa continued to mumble under her breath. "I just needed to know!" Melissa whispered.

"Huh? You wanted to know what? You are acting funny, Melissa. What did you want to know?"

"I needed to know the truth," Melissa continued as she looked directly at Pearl. "I needed to know if Heidi—" Before Melissa could finish her last statement, a rumble sounded out from the front door. She turned around in time to see Heidi and the rest of the family struggling in with bags.

Pearl gasped, realizing the moment was passing. She forced a fake smile to her face as her grand-niece. Janaya ran into the house in a joyous mood. She was carrying two bags filled with toys.

"Auntieee Pearlyyy…look!" Janaya yelled as she rushed over to Pearl and dumped the toys onto the carpet. "Auntie Heidi said today was Christmas again for me."

"Wow!" Pearl uttered as Janaya showed her each of the toys one by one.

"Hey Mom," Heidi smiled as she and Valerie struggled with what looked like a merchandise bag from every store in the mall.

Pearl turned her attention from Janaya, and then looked at Heidi near the door. She didn't know how to react as she looked at the massive bags filled with designer purses, shoes, clothes and jewelry. She stood up and looked at Valerie. "Val'…how in the world did y'all get all of that stuff?"

"Ask your daughter," Valerie responded. "I thought I was a shopaholic…child…this girl was like Ivana Trump today. I need a drink," she joked as she headed straight for the kitchen.

Heidi chuckled and put down her bags. She walked over to greet her mother, then noticed Melissa. Heidi stopped in the middle of her stride and gave Melissa a hard stare. "What are you doin' here?" she asked sharply.

Melissa timidly stood up and looked at Heidi. She instantly picked up on Heidi's cold tone. The two women hadn't seen each other in years. Lamar had refused to bring Melissa around Heidi because of their bitter relationship. Heidi had never liked Melissa, and her ill feelings for her were crystal clear tonight. The room temperature seemed to drop ten degrees as the tension mounted between the two.

"What am I doin' here?" Melissa nervously mumbled. "I wanted to visit my family."

"So why did you come here?" Heidi responded rudely. "I thought your family was in Pennsylvania?"

Melissa closed her mouth and scowled at Heidi. "This is my family!"

"Is it? I didn't know you and Lamar had got married!" Heidi blurted.

"Heidi, stop it!" Pearl interrupted as she grilled her daughter. "Stop acting like that."

"Why should I?" Heidi snapped back. "This bitch is not our family!"

"Okaayyyy…" Pearl yelled. She immediately turned her attention to her grand-niece. "Janaya, go to your room!"

"Whyyyy… didn't do nothing," Janaya whined.

"Now!" Pearl shouted and pointed toward the stairs. Janaya pouted and ran up to her bedroom. Valerie heard the commotion from the kitchen and ran into the living room.

"What's your problem with me?" Melissa yelled as she stared at Heidi. "You know…I'm really fed up with you treating me like shit."

Heidi walked over toward Melissa. "So make me stop treatin' you like shit! Just because my brother accepted you…don't mean that I have to kiss your ass for the rest of your life!"

"What!?" Melissa yelled.

"Heidi, what the hell has gotten into you?" Pearl shouted as she grabbed her daughter by the shoulders. She separated the women. "Calm down, Heidi."

"I am calm!" Heidi barked. "I just want to know why she's here?"

Valerie rushed over to her niece and pulled her away from Melissa. "Okay enough, Heidi…you gotta calm down," Valerie said as she tried her best to restrain Heidi. "You know I don't like all this drama in my house."

Heidi looked at her aunt and calmed herself. She walked to the opposite side of the living room with Valerie following close behind.

Pearl turned around and looked at Melissa. "Baby, I know you mean well…but I don't think it's a good idea for you to be here," Pearl advised.

Melissa coolly nodded her head. "It's okay. I didn't want to stay anyway," she continued to speak as she gathered herself. "I guess Heidi already answered my question."

"What question?" Heidi shouted as she moved toward Melissa again.

"Look around, Heidi," Melissa said as she pointed to her shopping bags. "I guess you got some money out of the deal, too."

"What deal…" Heidi uttered. "I don't know what you are talking about."

"Melissa, what are you saying?" Pearl whispered as she moved closer to her. "What deal are you talking about?"

"Well, I don't know all the details…but after Lamar died there was a rumor that he'd gotten killed over some money at a company called Datakorp."

"No shit, Sherlock!" Heidi snapped. "It was in the newspapers."

"Wait a minute Heidi, let her finished!" Pearl yelled.

"When I found out that Lamar died because of Datakorp, I got suspicious because of Heidi," Melissa said.

"What the hell are you sayin'?" Heidi yelled. "Suspicious of me…for what!?"

"This is all I'm saying…Jayson worked at Datakorp, right? And he's dead," Melissa raised her voice. "And now Lamar is dead because some guys wanted some money from Datakorp. So you tell me, Heidi…what the hell is going on?"

"I don't know what's going on!" Heidi responded. "What are you trying to say?"

"What am I trying to say?" Melissa shouted her question. "People are dying around you because of Datakorp, and you are still goin' up there. Why?"

"You need to mind your business!" Heidi shouted from across the room.

"See!" Melissa blurted as she turned to Pearl. "I knew she was goin' to play dumb. That's why I followed her when she got out of the hospital."

"What?" Valerie whispered as she looked over to Melissa. Heidi was shocked. She remained silent as Melissa continued to speak.

"You goddamn right," Melissa snapped as she turned back to Heidi. "I knew you couldn't be trusted, Heidi…that's why I needed to find out for myself."

"Find out what?" Heidi snapped. She was becoming more upset with Melissa. "I don't have shit to hide."

"Did you ask her where she got the money from?" Melissa quickly asked as she turned to Heidi's mother. The room fell silent.

Pearl was speechless. She looked at her daughter with confusion and turned to Melissa. Pearl slowly shook her head.

"Mom…don't listen to her!" Heidi walked toward her mother. Her aunt tried to grab her, but Heidi was moving too fast. "Mom, come here. Trust me…she has no idea what she's talking about."

"I don't know what I'm talkin' about? So ask her where she got the money from!" Melissa yelled as she tried to move closer to Pearl. Heidi raised her hand and reached out for her mother.

"What money? What is she talking about, Heidi?" Pearl continued to ask her daughter a string of questions as Heidi continued walking toward her.

"You got that money from Datakorp, didn't you?" Melissa

accused as she pointed her finger directly into Heidi's face. "You can't hide behind your lies no more! Who knows what other type of shit you into! For all we know, you're the *real* reason why Lamar got killed!"

Melissa's words set off a violent rage in Heidi. Before Melissa could react, Heidi pushed Pearl to the side and rushed toward Melissa. Heidi swung an opened hand at Melissa, smacking her square on the left cheek. Her skinny palm stung the side of Melissa's face like a table tennis paddle.

"You need to shut your fuckin' mouth!" Heidi screamed.

Melissa hollered in pain and stumbled to the floor. Heidi rushed over to Melissa and jumped on top of her. She grabbed her by the head and continued to punch her. Pearl grabbed Heidi's shoulders before her daughter could do any further damage. Valerie rushed over and helped Pearl grab Heidi. They pulled her away Melissa.

"You need to mind your business, bitch!" Heidi taunted Melissa. "Next time...Imma really make it hurt."

"My God, Heidi!" Valerie yelled at her niece. She held back Heidi as she continued to throw insults at Melissa.

Pearl turned around and looked at Heidi, who was still enraged. "Goddamn Heidi...what is with you?" She turned around and noticed Melissa trying to pick herself up from the floor. Melissa seemed to be more embarrassed than injured by Heidi's attack. Pearl walked over to her and tried to help her up. "Are you okay?" she whispered as she gently grabbed Melissa by the shoulder.

"I'm fine!" Melissa snapped as she pulled her arm away from Pearl. "Get away from me."

Pearl quickly stood back from Melissa, who continued to give her an angry expression. Melissa spit out a mouthful of blood onto Valerie's carpet and stood to her feet. The living room fell silent. All three women closely watched Melissa and tried to anticipate her reaction. But Melissa did nothing. She wiped a few tears that came to her face, and then headed for the front door.

"This ain't over, Heidi," Melissa whispered. "Enjoy that money while it lasts." Melissa slammed the front door and left without incident.

Valerie looked over to Heidi and shook her head. "What the hell was that all about?" Valerie gasped. She walked over to her living room window and watched as Melissa got into her car and sped off down the street. Heidi never answered her aunt's question. She looked over to her mother as Pearl gave her a disappointed look.

"What is she talking about, Heidi?" Pearl sternly asked her daughter.

"What do you mean?" Heidi nervously asked.

"Don't start that shit, child!" Pearl shouted. "Tell me, what the hell is Melissa talking about? What money?"

Valerie turned around and walked toward Pearl. Both women looked at Heidi.

"Mom...it is nothin' like you're thinkin'."

"So tell me what it's like. I'm listening."

"I wanted to tell you, Mom...I did...but I knew you would be mad at me," Heidi said.

"Mad at what?" Pearl was becoming emotional. "What did you do?"

"Last year when they told me to go to Datakorp to transfer the money, I started another account," Heidi confessed. Valerie's mouth fell opened as she listen to her niece explain the details about the switch. "I don't know why I did it at the time, but I figured if something else went wrong we could use the money to help us."

"So, you stole the money...from the company?" Pearl stuttered. Her voice struggled to rise above her emotions. "What is wrong with you?"

"Yes, Mom...I took the money. I had to!" Heidi said, raising her voice.

"I don't understand you," Pearl continued to scold her daughter. "You stole that money. You didn't have to do shit! Do you understand that? It's not yours."

"See, Mom...this is why I didn't tell you sooner because I knew you would overreact."

"So all of this..." Pearl yelled as she pointed at the bags from the mall. "All of this is from that stolen money?"

Heidi didn't say a word. Pearl nodded her head in disappointment and slowly sat down on the sofa.

"You are a criminal now, Heidi," Pearl said as she looked at her daughter with fear in her eyes. "Your brother died over that money. Why would you do that?"

Heidi didn't know what to say. She looked away from her mother and turned to Valerie. He aunt was speechless. Heidi could tell that Valerie shared in Pearl's ill feeling toward her.

"I took the money for us, Mom."

"I never asked for it," Pearl whispered. "You have to give it back, baby."

Heidi frowned her face at her mother and instantly became belligerent. "Are you serious? I'm not givin' it back. That's my money!"

"It's not yours…" Pearl fired back. "It's stolen!"

"I'm not givin' it back, Mom! I don't care what you say!"

Pearl stood up and walked over to her daughter. She grabbed Heidi by the shoulders and tried to reason with her. "Heidi, that is *not* your money. Don't you know that if you keep that money…then you're no different than those thugs that killed your brother? Maybe even worse…because you know better."

"Mom, I can't give that money back," Heidi whispered. "We finally got a chance to live a better life. We even got a chance to get away from here."

"And go where?" Pearl whispered. "I won't be able to live with myself knowing that this is blood money. And no matter where you go…you can't run from yourself."

Heidi dropped her head. Her mother's words were beginning to make sense, but her greed overpowered her emotions. "I'm sorry, Mom. I can't do it. I won't do it. I'm keeping the money."

"Okay Heidi, if that is your choice, then I'm sorry."

"Sorry for what?" Heidi asked.

"I have to turn my back on you," Pearl mumbled. "You gotta leave here. I can't have you around me."

Heidi was shocked by her mother's words. "What are you

saying, Mom?"

"You got blood money around you," Pearl whispered. "And nothing but more blood will follow that money, Heidi. Believe me. You said it yourself…you think somebody killed Jayson over that money, and now Lamar is dead over the same money. And right now…you are tellin' me that you have been spending that same money. No baby…I'm sorry…you gotta leave here or give that money back."

A chill rushed through Heidi's body. Her mother's words slowly eased into her mind and settled in her conscious. She looked over to Valerie, who remained silent. Heidi slowly turned back to her mother. "I'm guess I'm sorry too, Mom," Heidi uttered. "The money is staying with me."

A tear fell from the corner of Pearl's eyes. She nodded her head and walked away from her daughter. Heidi grabbed the bags from the living room floor and placed them next to the door.

"Wait a minute, Pearl," Valerie said, breaking the silence in the house. "You are goin' to let your daughter leave?"

"It's okay, Auntie," Heidi said. "She's right. This is really my decision." She grabbed Janaya's toys from the floor and placed them back in the shopping bag.

Pearl sat quietly on the sofa as Heidi began taking the bags outside to her truck. None of the women said a word as Heidi returned, retrieving a few things from upstairs in her bedroom. After Heidi had put the last bag inside of her truck, she returned holding a small gift box.

"Mom, before I go…I have to give you this," she said as she walked back into the house.

Pearl turned to her daughter as she walked over to her near the sofa. She looked at the small gold box with caution. "What is this?"

"I got it from a jewelry store. Don't worry, Mom. I bought this with my own money. I had it made for you before and I picked it up today," Heidi said. Pearl accepted the small gift box and placed it in her lap. "You don't have to open it now," she continued. "But please don't throw it away. I got it made especially for you."

236

Pearl looked up to her daughter and nodded her head. Heidi hugged Pearl and said goodbye to her. Pearl was becoming emotional, but she fought back her tears. Heidi smiled at her Aunt Valerie and headed for the front door.

"Where are you going to go?" Valerie asked, concerned about her niece.

"Don't worry about me, Auntie." Heidi smiled. "I will find a place and settle in real quick. Just make sure you take care of my mother."

"I will." Valerie smiled at her niece. She watched as Heidi calmly turned around and headed out into the dark night.

Chapter 31

Essex County Superior Court
Newark, New Jersey

**Wednesday January 21, 2009
10:25a.m.**

"May it please the court, ladies and gentlemen of the jury. My name is Kenneth Townsend, as I'm sure you already know this by now. This is my first opportunity to address you directly, and I want to begin by thanking you for the long hours and exhaustive attention you have given this case. I would like to first apologize to each and every person in this jury box and those who have been subject to the graphic details surrounding this case. Especially the disturbing photos and explicit testimony that will haunt us all for many years to come. But today...I assure you...we will put those demons to rest in this courtroom."

The authoritative voice of the prosecuting attorney echoed boldly throughout the trial courtroom. Kenneth Townsend had always been known for his strong finishes in the Essex County Courtroom. He was eyeing his tenth murder conviction in his short, yet illustrious career, and he could smell an easy victory for the Prosecutor's Office. He glanced at Shaheed Porter as Shaheed nervously wrung his hands together from the defense-side of the courtroom. Knowing that he had successfully painted Shaheed as a hardened criminal, Kenneth turned his attention back to his audience and began to pace back and forth in front of the jury box.

"On November 4, 2007…carnage occurred right in our own backyard!" he continued to speak as he gazed at each juror. "It was a Sunday morning…the Lord's morning…when two men entered the home of Pearl Kachina and turned her peaceful residence into a house of horror. These men committed a multiple murder that would shake up this community for a really long time. It is a stretch for me to even call them men. The unspeakable slaughter of three individuals in that house could have only been carried out by men with no souls… *animals*…if you may. Now folks…I have dedicated my entire career to making sure that I do everything in my power to prove that those who are not fit to walk among the decent and civilized people of this community be put away just long enough to exceed *forever*. When I was handed this case almost two years ago, I want you folks to know that I knew Shaheed Porter was guilty of these crimes. There is overwhelming physical evidence that places him at the scene. And the motive for the murders is clear and beyond a shadow of a doubt, present…in this case. Now the defense has mounted a theory that Mr. Porter was not alone that night when the murders occurred. I don't doubt this fact for one minute. In fact…I do believe there was another man who helped Mr. Porter murder the helpless victims. I think Mr. Porter is the real killer and his so-called assistant is too scared to come forward for fear of Mr. Porter taking his life, too. And my question to you…the jury…and the question I want you to ask yourself when you commence with your deliberation today…is… if Shaheed Porter didn't kill those people that night…and he didn't have any intentions on committing the murders…why didn't he do anything to prevent the massacre?"

The courtroom became dead silent. A fierce chill rushed from Shaheed's hands and throughout his body. He felt numb as he thought about the Prosecutor's question. The energy from the jury box told him a grim story. One by one, each of the jurors began to glance at him with judgmental eyes. His heart skipped a beat as he heard the voice of the Superior Court Judge ask his Defense Attorney for her closing arguments. As his lawyer looked over her notes, Shaheed quickly turned around and scanned the courtroom. Where was Rhonda? He felt alone as he soon realized that there was nothing but angry faces staring back at him. Rhonda was nowhere to be found.

Continuing to scan the courtroom, he noticed Pearl and some woman sitting near the back. Pearl fixed her attention on him. She never flinched as the two looked at each other. Fear and anguish filled her eyes. She was clearly seeking justice for her son, Lamar. She knew Shaheed was not the only person who deserved to be punished for her pain; but justice served in portions would feel a lot better than none at all. Shaheed stared at her coldly for a moment, then turned around. He glanced at his lawyer as she prepared to plead her client's case one final time.

Michelle Miles confidently stood to her feet and coolly brushed a few wrinkles from her Burberry Prorsum pantsuit. She nodded to the judge and gracefully approached the jury box as the lead prosecutor returned to his seat. Michelle had been a dynamic defense attorney in the Essex County area for many years. With almost twenty years of experience, she was every prosecutor's nightmare. She possessed an uncanny knack for hypnotizing even the most callus jurors, making them acquit her clients. Known for her sarcastic tongue and sharp attention to detail, she had a tendency to use the courtroom as a place to discredit and, sometimes, even embarrass her opponents. Shaheed took a deep breath and slowly exhaled as Michelle walked in front of the jury box. She looked at each one of the jurors for a brief moment and nodded her head. In an unexpected move, she turned around and pointed directly at her client.

"Guilty!" Michelle yelled as the courtroom let out a collective gasp. Shaheed's mouth fell opened as he looked at his lawyer. He had no idea what she was up to. Before he could react, Michelle turned back to the jurors and began to speak again very loudly. "Guilty as hell! Right? Yes…I agree with you! I do believe my client is guilty. And he deserves whatever the punishment that a guilty person should get!"

The courtroom was still in awe of Michelle's admission. The

entire courtroom fell silent as everyone began to hang on her every word. She lowered her voice and continued to speak, "But…before you condemn my client…I want you to ask yourself…what exactly is my client guilty of?" She turned around and walked toward the defense section. "Someone please answer me that…what *crime* is my client…guilty of? The crime of loyalty? The crime of being in the wrong place at the wrong time? The crime of being misinformed by a deranged family member? Maybe so…but guilty of murder? Absolutely not…"

Michelle turned around and began to walk toward the prosecutor's table. "…Now folks, before I continue with my closing arguments I must give a round of applause to the wonderful work the State of New Jersey did in making my case for me." She sarcastically began to clap her hands toward the direction of the lead attorney. A few groans came from the rear of the courtroom. "Throughout this trial, you've heard the prosecutors continuously admit that my client's fingerprints were not present on the murder weapons and his fingers showed no signs of powder burns or residue. The very gun that was found on the scene has absolutely no connection to my client. So how could my client be guilty of pulling the trigger that killed the victims? Also, all of the witnesses called to the stand by the prosecution…including the very people that were in the house that evening…admitted that my client's cousin appeared to be a very intimidating figure when it came to Mr. Porter. In fact…if my client is guilty of anything…Mr. Porter is guilty of being the *victim*—coerced by another party...guilty of being a *victim* of a gunshot wound…and also, being the *victim* of police brutality." Michelle readjusted her posture and began to move back toward the jury box. "And now, for the grand finale. I would also like to thank the State of New Jersey for using the testimony of a detective that has been under investigation for God knows how many allegations of misconduct from his department. I do appreciate the hard work and dedication of Detective Harold Williams. But if his testimony is the glue that is holding their case together, you must treat it like the apple picked from a putrid tree. Although it looks nice and shiny on the outside…once you dissect it…you will find that it is rotten to the core..."

Michelle turned toward the prosecution table and gave the lawyers a subtle taunting gesture. After a brief moment of silence she turned her attention back to the jurors. "...So ladies and gentlemen of the jury...please remember that my client is guilty, but not of murder. Mr. Porter is no killer. He has no prior history of violence, and once you examine the evidence again, you will realize that wrongfully convicting this man will take the focus off of finding the real killer who remains a fugitive from the law. Thank you for your time." She returned to the defense table and smiled at Shaheed.

Shaheed's heart skipped a beat as he heard the voice of the Superior Court Judge call for recess so the jury could deliberate his fate. His face stiffened as three oversized court officers approached him. Shaheed's defense lawyer gave him a confident smile.

"Don't worry, Mr. Porter," Michelle mumbled. "I think we nailed this one down."

Shaheed didn't say a word as the court officers placed the steel shackles around his wrists and ankles. He just lowered his head in shame as they escorted him out of the courtroom to await the jury's verdict.

***

Datakorp Towers
Newark, NJ

11:32 a.m.

"I still don't understand why you need the pass code to my account!" Heidi angrily stated as she looked at a frustrated Judith. Both women had been arguing for nearly twenty minutes inside the women's bathroom located in the main lobby of the Datakorp building.

Judith shook her head with disgust and looked at her watch. "Heidi, please stop it. You are wasting time now. How many times do I have to tell you things have changed at Datakorp? The company

242

doesn't operate the same as it did a couple years ago. If you don't open a new account they will investigate the one you have. And I know you don't want that. Just give me the pass code and I will handle everything for you."

"So why can't I just open up another account on my own and transfer the funds myself?" Heidi asked suspiciously. She tried to lower her voice as she realized her words were bouncing off the bathroom walls.

"Because...you still need a supervisor on the floor to approve the new account," Judith explained. "And I will tell you...Heidi... you don't want somebody else in that office diggin' into this account history. People are searching for a way to get promoted up there. They will find out the details about that account and turn you in without a second thought."

Heidi waved her hand at the thought of getting caught with the money. She turned toward the huge mirror located on the bathroom wall and looked at her own reflection. "So let me get this straight," she uttered. "I give you the pass code and you close my current account and open up a new one? What type of account will it be?"

"You have to get a business account," Judith pointed out. She walked closer to Heidi and leaned on the sink next to her. "For the amount of money you have in the account, it would be easier to hide from the big bosses up here."

"And how long will this take? When will I have access to the money again? I really don't want this money held up too long. I got plans."

Judith gave Heidi a shifty look. "What kind of plans? You're holding out on me?"

"Don't worry about me. Just don't fuck this transaction up."

Judith didn't like Heidi's tone, but she ignored her pride. "So are you going to give me the pass code?"

"Not yet," Heidi quickly answered. "Let me think about it. Nothing personal...but I don't fully trust you, yet."

Judith walked away from Heidi to the other side of the bathroom. "Whatever Heidi...do whatever you want! I'm just trying to help.

You asked for my help…and now…you don't want it. Whatever… can I get my money now?"

Heidi turned to Judith and looked at her. She grabbed a large yellow envelope from her bag and tossed it. "Don't worry...it's all there."

Judith ignored Heidi's last statement and counted the money anyway. "Don't take it personal that I'm counting it," she mumbled. "I don't fully trust you either."

A smirk came to Heidi's face as she watched Judith count the money and place it back in the envelope.

"Okay, I have to get back to work." Judith closed the envelope and stuffed it in a larger shopping bag. "You just let me know when you want to give me the pass code. I'm not goin' keep breakin' my neck to help you, Heidi! Just remember that you only got a few weeks left before they transfer the servers and overhaul all of the accounts. So please keep that in mind."

"No problem!" Heidi said. "I will do that."

Judith gave Heidi a disgusted look and shook her head. She turned to walk out of the bathroom when she heard Heidi's voice.

"Judith!" Heidi whispered. "Thanks for helping me out with this."

Judith looked at her strangely. She noticed that Heidi was being sincere and nodded toward her. "No problem."

"Hey listen, I'm throwing a party for my brother, Lamar in a few weeks…in his name. You're more than welcome to come out. It's goin' to be insane. All of my family and most of his friends will be there. Maybe you can come and hang out with us, if you're not busy."

Judith nodded her head for a moment and thought about the offer. "You know I haven't been to a party in a while, so maybe that will be good for me."

"Maybe…" Heidi agreed. "Just think about it. If you want to come, let me know and I will give you the details."

"Okay Heidi, thanks for the invite." Judith smiled at Heidi and left the bathroom.

Heidi looked at her watch and grabbed her phone from her bag. She exited the bathroom and headed out of the main lobby of the

Datakorp building. Before Heidi could reach her car, her cell phone rang. She quickly answered it.

"Hello?"

"Heidi, where are you?" a female voice frantically asked from the other line. She immediately picked up on the voice and realized it was her mother.

"Hey, Mom. I just got finished running a few errands. Is everything alright?"

"I hope you are close...we need you to get down here to the courtroom now!" Pearl shouted.

Heidi heard a lot of noise in the background and immediately became worried. "Mom, are you okay?"

"They are saying that the jury is finishing up the deliberation." Pearl was hysterical.

"That quick?"

"Hell yes, that quick!" Pearl responded. "It don't take that long to figure out that he's guilty of this shit! I told you to be down here earlier. I told you that the closing arguments were today."

Heidi felt excited and nervous at the news and started to rush down the street. "Mom, I had to take care of a couple of things that couldn't wait. I'm sorry. I'm hauling ass to get down there right now. I am right downtown. I'll be up there in a minute."

"Hurry up!" Pearl continued. "We are about to go back into the courtroom in a few minutes."

"Okay...I am on my way!" Heidi hung up the phone and bolted to her truck. She didn't waste a second as she started up her engine and sped down the busy street en route to the courthouse.

* * *

Essex County Superior Court
Newark, NJ

12:16 p.m.

Detective Harold Williams nearly stumbled up the courthouse steps as he rushed into the front entrance of the Superior Court. Harold was on duty when he'd gotten the call that the jury was nearing the end of their deliberation. He had dropped everything he was doing at the precinct, then bolted over to the courthouse. It seemed that the entire courtroom was buzzing with the news of the quick deliberation of the Porter case. The entrance to the courtroom was packed with reporters, police, and a number of people who were generally interested in the case. He noticed Pearl and Valerie standing off to the side and walked over to them.

"Hello, Pearl. I rushed over here as soon as I got the call," Harold stated as he reached out and shook her hand. Her face was blank, and Harold could tell that she was very nervous.

Valerie reached out and shook the detective's hand and greeted him. "I'm glad you could make it. We're still waiting to go back inside. Everyone is saying that the jury has made a decision and we should be called back into the courtroom soon."

"I know, I heard," Harold said. "These quick deliberations usually mean a conviction."

"Please God!" Pearl uttered as her voice cracked with emotion.

"It will…don't you worry, Sis. He is going down today," Valerie whispered as she hugged her sister.

A loud commotion came from the adjacent side of the courtroom lobby. Detective Williams quickly swung around and noticed the noise.

Heidi pushed her way through a crowd of reporters and made her way to her mother. "Mom, I'm so sorry I'm late," she shouted as she walked by the detective and hugged her mother. "What happened? Did the jury decide yet?"

"Hey baby!" Pearl uttered. Despite their dispute last night, Pearl was relieved to see her daughter. She returned the hug and rubbed Heidi's back. "No…they still haven't called us back in there yet."

"It should be any minute now," Valerie added as she took her turn hugging her niece.

"Are you okay?" Heidi asked as she looked at her mother.

"I'm trying," Pearl responded. "This is nerve wracking."

"Don't worry, ladies," Harold said as he tried to comfort the women. "This was a strong case against him. Let's just see how this plays out."

"I agree," Valerie said.

A loud thump came from the entrance to the courtroom as a very tall officer emerged from behind the doors. Everyone in the lobby immediately turned their attention to him as he looked around.

"Everyone please return to the courtroom in an orderly fashion," the officer instructed. "The jury has concluded its deliberation process."

Pearl's heart dropped to her stomach. She covered her mouth as everyone rushed to re-enter the courtroom. Heidi grabbed her by the hand as the women walked back to take their seats. Harold followed closely behind.

"This is it," Pearl whispered as the family sat in the row directly behind the prosecutor's table. Heidi was visibly nervous as she sat next to her mother and wrapped her arms around her. She couldn't stop her hands from shaking as she looked at the empty jury box.

Another loud bang came from the front of the courtroom as a few court officers and Sheriffs escorted Shaheed back inside. He was flanked closely by his defense lawyer Michelle Miles. He tried his best to appear unfazed by his shackles as he slowly shuffled toward the defense table, looking around at the courtroom spectators. A small grin came to his otherwise hardened face when turned his attention to the rear. His girlfriend, Rhonda was slowly entering the courtroom. She gazed at her boyfriend for a moment and tried her best to smile for him. Relief moved through him, seeing that Rhonda had come to support him. She gave him a gentle nod and blew a kiss his way. In return, he gave her a crooked smile, then nodded at her as he watched her take a seat in the last row.

Heidi watched Shaheed the whole time as he was escorted into the courtroom. She followed his eyes and turned around. She wanted to know who he was smiling at. Curiously, she looked at Rhonda. She had never seen her before, and took a mental picture of her. Turning back around, she fixed her glare on Shaheed. A dark feeling came over Heidi as she stared at him. Although he was fully restrained, she couldn't help but feel nervous as she sat in his presence. Her emotions mounted as she thought about her brother, Lamar and her best friend, Faith. She thought about how Shaheed and Vegas took them away from her. Her energy seemed to touch Shaheed as he turned around and looked directly at her. His eyes froze her for a moment. Heidi tensed up and instantly felt angry. The officers forced him to sit down at the table. They walked away from him, never noticing that he was still staring at a member of one of the victim's family. He discreetly placed his thumb near the side of his neck and made a throat-slashing gesture to Heidi. She instantly became infuriated.

"You murderin' muthafucker!" Heidi yelled as she stood up and pointed at Shaheed. A court officer immediately rushed over to her and tried to grab her.

Detective Williams stood up and forced her to sit back down. "Heidi…no…don't lose it in here!" he shouted as he tried to calm her.

Pearl turned to her daughter and gave her a strange look. "Oh my God…Heidi…please…what are you doing?" she whispered.

"Y'all didn't see that?" Heidi yelled as she pointed to Shaheed.

"See what?" Harold quickly asked.

"He's taunting us!"

"Ma'am, we can't have that type of outburst in here," an officer stated as he looked at Heidi.

"It's okay, Officer," Harold assured. "I will take care of this. She's fine."

The officer nodded to the detective and walked away.

Harold turned his attention back to Heidi. "You have to keep your emotions in check now, Heidi. If the judge was in here they could hold you in contempt and lock you up for that."

Heidi bit her tongue and didn't say a word. She turned back to Shaheed, who'd quickly turned around as if nothing had happened. Heidi shook her head and took a deep breath. "I'm okay, Harold."

Pearl looked at her daughter and grabbed her hand. Before Pearl could say a word, the bailiff entered the courtroom.

"All rise, court is now back in session," the bailiff yelled. "The Honorable Judge Hector DeSoto now presiding."

Everyone in the courtroom came to their feet as a very short and pudgy man walked out of the chambers and approached the bench.

"Please be seated," Judge DeSoto instructed as he sat down. "I would like to thank everyone for their patience. In the interest of time, I will keep my final remarks to a minimum. I simply want to thank the counsels of both the State and the Defendant for your professionalism in my courtroom throughout these proceedings. Now…if I can ask the clerk to bring in the jury."

The courtroom was cemetery-silent as the twelve members of the jury entered into the courtroom. Heidi looked over to her mother, who was near tears due to the gravity of the moment. Heidi grabbed her hand and squeezed it. The judge looked over to the jury box and continued to speak.

"Good afternoon, members of the jury," Judge DeSoto said. "I was informed by the courtroom clerk that you have reached a verdict in the case of the State of New Jersey vs. Shaheed Porter. Is this true Mr. Foreman?"

An Irish man near the end of the jury box stood up and nodded toward the judge. "I am the Foreman, Your Honor. And yes…we have reached a verdict."

Judge DeSoto nodded his head to the Foreman. "Would you please hand the verdicts to the clerk? I direct the clerk to read the verdicts."

The clerk slowly walked over to the Foreman and retrieved a small index card from him. He walked away from the jury box to the adjacent side of the courtroom. Heidi grabbed Valerie's hands as the women sat at attention, anxiously awaiting the verdicts. The clerk read over the notes, then cleared his throat. Shaheed placed his palms together and bowed his head. He seemed to be praying for a miracle.

"In the case of the State of New Jersey versus Shaheed Porter…" the clerk began. "We, the jury, find the defendant, Shaheed Porter… guilty of Count I of the indictment of reckless endangerment…"

A subtle cheer came from the prosecutor's side of the courtroom. Pearl let out a sigh of relief as the guilty verdict was read. She smiled and turned to Harold, who didn't budge. He knew there were still two more counts to be read. The clerk continued to read the index card.

"In regards to Count II of the indictment of kidnapping…we, the jury, find the defendant…not guilty as charged."

"Oh my God!" A voice yelled from the rear of the courtroom. Heidi's mouth fell opened as she turned to her mother.

"Not guilty?" Pearl yelled. "How could that be?"

A few groans began to rise from the courtroom.

Judge DeSoto slammed down his gavel and demanded order. "Please respect my courtroom!" he yelled. "Mr. Clerk, would you please read the final verdict."

The courtroom once again fell silent. Pearl continued to shake her head as a few tears fell uncontrollably from her face. Valerie looked over to her sister and became emotional. Heidi felt herself becoming numb as the clerk read the last verdict.

"In regard to Count III and Count IV of the indictments of murder in the second degree of Lamar Kachina and Faith Jowler…we, the jury, find the defendant…not guilty as charged!"

"Jesus…No!" Pearl yelled as she immediately dropped to her knees from her seat.

Heidi jumped to her feet and began to yell at the courtroom clerk. "Are you fuckin' kidding me? That can't be right…not guilty!?" Heidi yelled. "He killed my brother."

"Lady, sit down!" Judge DeSoto yelled from the bench. "I will have order in my courtroom."

A commotion broke out as Heidi quickly left her seat and jumped over the wood divider behind the prosecutor's table. Before any of the court officers could grab her, Heidi grabbed whatever she could from the prosecutor's table and tossed it at Shaheed and his defense attorney. Papers and notebooks flew everywhere as Heidi continued her onslaught. She screamed to the top of her lungs and tried to make her way over to Shaheed.

"You fuckin' killed my brother, you bastard!" she yelled as she charged the defense table.

Shaheed stood up and backed away. He saw fire in Heidi's eyes as she rushed toward the defense table. Michelle Miles bolted from the table to escape Heidi's wrath. Before Heidi could reach Shaheed, two court officers tackled her to the courtroom floor.

"He's guilty!" Heidi yelled. "He did it!"

Pearl screamed with emotion as the courtroom exploded into chaos.

Valerie couldn't bear to watch as the court officers tussled with Heidi, then handcuffed her.

"Get her out of my courtroom now!" Judge DeSoto yelled.

Heidi continued to yell insults toward Shaheed. She tried her best to pull away from the officers, but they were too strong. They aggressively pulled Heidi to her feet and shoved her toward the exit. Pearl cried as she watched her daughter being forced out of the courtroom. Detective Williams noticed Pearl on the courtroom floor and reached down to help her to her feet.

"Pearl…come on let's go," he whispered.

Jude DeSoto slammed down his gavel again. "Would the court officers please remove the defendant from the courtroom! I hereby order this court adjourned until the sentencing exactly two weeks from this day."

"Oh my Lord…why!" Pearl continued to yell. "They killed my son…they killed him!"

Harold helped Pearl to her feet and hugged her. "I know, Pearl. It's not fair. But we have to get you out of here and make sure your daughter is okay." Harold motioned for Valerie to assist him.

Valerie's face was full of tears. She grabbed her sister by the arm as Harold helped her out of the chaotic courtroom.

❖

Chapter 32

Valerie's House
Edison, New Jersey

Thursday February 12, 2009
10:18 a.m.
Three Weeks Later

A cool breeze blew by Valerie's house and momentarily jolted
Pearl out of her daydream. She had been sitting on the porch
of her sister's house for nearly two hours, staring off into space.
Images of the chaotic court scene flashed in and out of her mind.
It had been almost three weeks since she'd left the house. It was
hard for her to get over the pain of watching the court system deny
her family the right to justice for the death of her son. As each day
passed, it became harder for Pearl grasp that closure for Lamar's
death was possibly never within her reach.

A white unmarked police cruiser pulled up to the front of
Valerie's house. Pearl took one look at the cop car and realized it
was Detective Williams. She watched him as he exited the car and
cautiously greeted her from the yard.

"Good morning, Pearl," Harold said as he continued to make his
way to the porch.

"Good morning, Detective," Pearl calmly replied.

"How are you holding up?"

"I'm trying."

"I understand," Harold continued. "I wanted to stop by to give you some good news. They have decided to drop the contempt charges against Heidi."

Pearl slowly nodded. "That is good news. I will have to tell her that when I see her."

"Heidi's not here?"

"I haven't seen my daughter in over a week. She doesn't live here anymore." Pearl turned away from Harold and continued to speak, "She drops in every once in a while. I don't know what's gotten into her, but she's definitely changed since she's been out of the hospital."

"Oh, okay…is she alright?"

"I hope so. But I think the whole family has changed since she's been out of the hospital…even me."

Harold took a seat on the porch next to Pearl. "I have to be honest with you. I also came over to see you."

"See me?" Pearl turned to Harold and looked at him. "Why?"

"I wanted to apologize for how things turned out. You know… with the verdict and all," Harold continued. "I got the news the other day that Shaheed will be back on the street any day now."

"I know…I got the same news." Pearl was disappointed. "I guess his lawyer worked some sort of deal for time served?"

"Yes."

"It's okay," Pearl whispered. "It's not your fault. You did everything you could. It just wasn't in the cards, I guess."

"Is that how you truly feel?" Harold asked. He was surprised to hear Pearl sound so defeated.

"When I was younger, I used to believe that the world would just do what I wanted it to do for me," Pearl said. "I remember when things came easy to me. But then I had to remember that I was a child and the real world doesn't work that way. So as I got older, I realized that life is really a game of chances. You win some, you lose some…just that simple."

"Damn…that sounds so cold." Harold looked away from Pearl. "But I agree with you. That's the way of the world…cold and bitter."

"Damn right," Pearl said sharply. "So what are you going to do with yourself, now that the case is over?"

"Well…we still have to find Vegas," Harold responded. "And the State will appeal the Porter decision, so there is still a lot of work to be done. So the case isn't over."

Pearl looked at Harold for a moment. "You think they will find him?" she asked with concern in her voice.

"I hope so, Pearl," Harold honestly responded. "I hope so."

* * *

Patterson, NJ

11:02 a.m.

Heidi pulled up into the parking lot of Dirty Betty's Go-Go Bar and turned off the engine. She looked at her watch and pulled her cell phone from her purse. For the past few weeks, she'd been desperately trying to find her mother's ex boyfriend, Rick. Since the acquittal of Shaheed, she'd begun to feel a lot less confident with the legal system. She knew one day she would have to confront Vegas and Shaheed herself. But at the moment, the cousins were a distant target in her mind. She had set her sights on Rick.

Heidi looked at her cell phone for a moment. She scrolled through the contacts and found Rueben's name. She called the bouncer and waited for him to pick up.

"What's goin' on, Heidi?" Rueben answered.

"I'm outside."

"Cool…meet me at the front door."

Heidi hung up the phone and put it back in her purse. She turned off her engine and exited the truck. As she walked to the front door of the club, she noticed Rueben opening the door for her. She smiled at him.

"Okay, Ms. Heidi." Rueben nodded as he gave her a wide smile. "Long time no see."

"Hey, Rueben. I'm so glad you came over to meet with me."

"No problem." Rueben watched Heidi enter the bar. He closed the door behind her and locked it. "Do you want something to drink?"

"No…I'm good. I'm gonna grab something to eat when I leave here. I just wanted to stop by and give you this." Heidi handed Rueben a FedEx box.

"What's this?" Rueben asked.

"It's five thousand dollars. Cash," Heidi responded. "I didn't know what else to put the money in."

Rueben was shocked at Heidi's move. "We didn't find the guy for you, Heidi. Why are you giving me this?"

"Honestly…I really need your help," Heidi confessed. "You can have the money or you can split it with Betty. I don't care. But I need to find this guy like yesterday. I'm very serious about this, Rueben. I just found out that Shaheed…one of the guys that killed my brother…will be getting out soon. And I don't want to rely on the cops to handle this shit no more. I don't care if you have to pay people to get some information on him. But I really need to find Rick."

"No bullshit?" Rueben uttered as he opened the box and looked at the money. "Damn…I see you are dead serious. I will step it up over here."

"Please do," Heidi said. "I really don't have no one else to turn to. So you are my last resort."

"Heidi…don't stress it another second. If we can't find him…we will find someone who knows where he is."

"That's what I wanted to hear," Heidi said with a sadistic grin. "Just call me when you got some information on him." She passed Rueben and headed for the door. "By the way, I am having a party for my brother in a couple of days out in Newark. If you are not working…maybe you can come by."

"Cool…hit me with the info, and I might slide through."

"I will. Don't forget to call me. Thanks again." Heidi gave Rueben one final smile and left the bar. She was making her way back to her car when she heard her phone ringing. Heidi smiled as she answered the phone.

"Hey, Tycen."

"Hey, Sweetie," Tycen answered from the other end of the phone. "Where have you been? I have been trying to reach you."

"I know…don't kill me, baby," Heidi said. "Been busy with some family things over here."

"Are you okay?"

"I'm fine…we can talk about it later. It's just too much to discuss. How are you doing, honey?"

"I'm good, Heidi," Tycen quickly answered. "I just was thinking about you, and wanted to know when we were going to get together?"

Heidi thought for a moment as she reached her truck. It had been a couple of weeks since she had spoken to Tycen. He had been trying to reach out to her, but she hadn't been ready to take his calls. She felt bad for ignoring him.

"I have been so busy lately, Tycen," Heidi explained. "I haven't really been in the mood, and I didn't want to take it out on you."

"Okay…I understand. The last thing I want to do is add to your stress. But you know I can't wait to see you."

"Is that right?"

"That is one-hundred and ten percent right," he joked. "All of this chasing you has gotten me all worked up."

"Hmmm…worked up you say?" Heidi whispered. She immediately picked up on his flirting. "And how worked up are you, exactly?"

"Well…if you must know…I feel like I'm about to bust if I don't see you soon."

"Damn…Tycen…mmm hmmm…you are bad."

"You have no idea."

Heidi could feel him smiling through the phone. "Baby, I'm goin' to tell you like my mother always told me. Be very careful what you wish for…and I think you know the rest."

"Yup! I think the rest goes something like…once you get what you ask for…you have to cherish every moment you have it…and treat it like it's the most beautiful thing on earth."

"Oh boy…you been cooped up in that office too long," Heidi joked as she laughed at Tycen. "I think you need a break. You are starting to sound a little delirious."

Tycen laughed. "I guess I am. So when are you going to save me from this place?"

"Just give me a little bit more time. I got you, boo. Just hang in there."

"I will, Heidi. Just don't take too long. I'll sit tight and wait for you to hit me up."

"Sounds good to me, sweetie. Have a good day…okay?"

"I will."

Heidi hung up the phone and drove out of the parking lot. A warm feeling came over her as she realized that Tycen was slowly becoming just one of the few people in her life who actually made her smile.

Chapter 33

Newark Penn Station
Newark, New Jersey

Friday February 20, 2009
12:04 p.m.

*R*honda looked at her watch and let out a frustrated gasp of air. She couldn't believe it was already noon as she sat impatiently in her car, in the tow-away zone in front of the busy Newark Rail Terminal. An uneasy feeling came over her as she looked around at the unfamiliar faces rushing in and out of the train station. She thought for a moment and prayed that she'd correctly heard her instructions just a few hours earlier. She was just about to reach for her phone when she noticed a familiar face walking up behind her car. Her face lit up with excitement. She didn't waste another moment. She hopped out of the car and rushed over to the man as he quickly approached. It was her boyfriend, Shaheed.

"Oh God, baby…you don't know how happy I am to see you," Rhonda shouted as she rushed over and gave him a long overdue hug. Shaheed almost toppled over as he caught her in his arms. She immediately grabbed the sides of his face and gave him a passionate kiss. "Baby, ummm…damn…hmmm…I missed you so goddamned much. You don't even know, boy!" She continued to kiss Shaheed. "Please don't leave me like that again, baby…please…promise me." Shaheed tried to speak but Rhonda continued to put her tongue in his mouth. She had missed Shaheed and it wasn't hard for him to realize it.

"Rhonda, I promise I won't," he grunted. He pulled his face away from her for a moment, smiling. Rhonda knew Shaheed would be leaving the county jail today and had prepared for him. She looked good from head to toe.

"Damn…you look like a stallion today." He smiled and licked his bottom lip.

Rhonda loved when he did that. She blushed at his compliment and playfully fixed her hair. "Shiittt…you been down for almost two years, baby. You know I had to show you what you was missing."

"Damn, girl…don't remind me…I already feel like I'm out of touch on these streets."

"It's okay, baby. Forget these streets," Rhonda sang as she moved closer to him. "I got something else you can touch." Rhonda seductively began to rub on Shaheed's chest. She moaned as she started to kiss his neck. She stood on the tips of her toes to reach his left ear. "I got something that needs a lot of touching right about now."

"Hell yea…!" he said, nodding his head. "We are gonna handle that. I got a couple things that need touching too!"

"Let's go then!" Rhonda blurted as she turned around and headed back to the car. Shaheed walked to the passenger side. He put his bag in the back seat and got in the car. He smiled at Rhonda as she put the car into gear and pulled into traffic. "So where do you want to go?" she asked. "Back to my place? Or do you want to get a hotel?"

"Actually, we have to make one stop first, before I do anything else." Shaheed responded. "Did you bring the money I asked for?"

"Yes…it's in the glove box."

"Bet." Shaheed looked inside the glove box. He noticed the white envelope and nodded his head. "Good lookin', Rhonda."

"What do you mean we have to make a stop first?" she inquired, turning to Shaheed with a disappointed look. "I thought we were goin' to spend some time together first."

"I'm sorry, baby. I have to make this run first."

"Baby…you just got out. Who do you have to see?"

"I have to see an old friend," Shaheed said. "It wont' take long. Seriously…but I have to see him today."

Rhonda slammed on the brakes of the car and stopped in the middle of the street.

Shaheed's heart started to race as he turned to his girlfriend. "What the hell are you doin'?" he yelled as she looked out the window. Car horns and angry screams blared from the other drivers as Rhonda's car created a mini traffic jam.

She looked over to Shaheed. "I will not move this car another inch if you don't tell me where we are going."

"Baby…please drive the car," Shaheed said. He tried his best not to raise his voice. "You are drawing too much attention to us!"

"So…let them go around!" Rhonda barked. "Now tell me… what the hell is so important? You just got out. You haven't been home a goddamn hour yet, and you want to go around your *old friends* already?"

"It's not like that!" Shaheed said. His voice became angry.

"So tell me who it is?" Rhonda yelled.

"What the fuck, Rhonda…calm down!" Shaheed shouted. "You know I got this problem with Adbul. Now…I'm back on the street…I need to know how safe I am. Remember…he never got paid."

Rhonda didn't say a word. She shook her head and turned away from her boyfriend.

"Come on, Rhonda. Just drive the car. I have to go to New York to make sure everything is good. It won't take that long at all. If these niggas still got beef with me…I gotta know if it's coming head on. That's why I have to go. Come on, Rhonda…just drive the car."

"I can't do it," Rhonda whispered as she looked out the window.

"What do you mean you *can't* do it?" Shaheed barked. "Okay… get in the passenger side…I will drive."

"No Shaheed!" Rhonda yelled. She turned back to him. "I mean…I can't do this no more!"

"What?"

"I can't," Rhonda whispered. "I just spent almost sixteen months wondering if I was gonna ever see you again. You don't even realize how lucky you are for getting out of there."

"Where is all this comin' from, Rhonda?" Shaheed asked. "I just need to make one stop, then I'm all yours."

"You just don't get it, Shah'!" Rhonda shouted. "You was gone! Double murder! Don't you get it? They was gonna send you away forever and then some." A few more car horns blared from behind them as Rhonda refused to move her car. She looked out the window and continued to speak. "So after all that...you still want to be around your old friends?"

Shaheed thought for a moment and turned to Rhonda. "I have to, baby. I need to find out if I'm in the clear or not."

"Okay," Rhonda said as she looked over to Shaheed. She gave her boyfriend a strange expression. "I understand. I'm not gonna stress you no more. You can drive." Rhonda gave Shaheed an uneasy smile and got out of the car.

Shaheed opened the passenger door and walked around to the driver's side. Instead of walking around the car, Rhonda kept walking down Broad Street.

Shaheed noticed his girlfriend was leaving him on foot and screamed out to her. "Rhonda...where are you going?" he yelled. "Rhonda...I know you hear me!"

Rhonda turned around and kept walking backwards. She threw both of her hands in the air as if she was surrendering. "Nigga... when you are tired of playing these street games...you know where I live at!" she yelled. She turned back around and made haste up the street.

A few car horns brought Shaheed back to reality. He waved the cars off and turned back to look at Rhonda. She was halfway down the block. He looked at his watch and thought for a minute. He shook his head and got back in the car. He decided to go along with his plan and headed up to New York City.

* * *

125th Street
Harlem, New York

3: 20 p.m.

"If you got feet, I got socks! Come on, New York! I'm not playing out here today! Get two pair of socks for just six bucks. No gimmicks, no games! Let's go!"

The powerful voice of a street vendor could be heard on the busy sidewalk of 125th street in Harlem. Despite the loud backdrop of car horns, blasting music and screaming shoppers, the voice of the yelling sock seller could be heard clearly over all the noise. The stocky man held two pair of socks in his hands as he paced back and forth a few feet in front of his table. The flea market-like atmosphere was chaotic, but the man seemed to thrive in the environment. His intense hustle, along with his piercing stare, seemed to draw shoppers by the dozen. New Yorkers and tourists alike felt compelled to buy from him; even if they didn't need socks. Twelve years of battling the harsh life of street vending had made his a household name in Harlem. His name was Rashad Parris.

"That's right people, step right up," Rashad said as a few buyers approached his table. "No doubt, y'all. I got a play like back in the day for y'all. How many pairs you need?"

Rashad walked behind the table as more people walked over to buy from him. He made a few sells and kept yelling for more shoppers to stop by. A tall man in a hooded sweatshirt slowly approached the table. The man suspiciously kept his head low. The black hood was nearly covering his entire face. Rashad took a quick glance, but was too busy taking money to get a better look at him.

"What's good, famo'? What you need today?" Rashad asked as the man got closer to the table. Rashad watched him as he slowly reached out and grabbed a pair of socks. "Those are two for six," Rashad said to the man. "Need a bag for those?" Without warning

262

the man stuffed the socks under his sweater and ran off. "What the fuck!?" Rashad yelled as he watched the man disappear quicker than a bolt of lightning.

No one had ever gotten away with stealing socks from Rashad in the twelve years that he had been selling in Harlem. And he was in no mood to break that streak today. Rashad sprung into action. He jumped over the table like an Olympic hurdler.

"Gimme back those socks motherfucker!" he yelled as he chased the man down the crowded sidewalk. Both men were shoving shoppers to the side as the pursuit intensified. People began to yell as the chase electrified 125th Street. Rashad kept a sharp eye on the thief. He watched him turn the corner, and balled up his lip. He picked up his speed fearing he might lose the sock snatcher. A few people dove out of his way as his two-hundred-plus pound body barreled down the street. Again, he yelled for the man to stop as he turned the corner. The man never looked back as he approached another corner and made a quick right down 124th street.

"Fuck!" Rashad yelled. His chest began to hurt but he was focused on getting his product back. He kept running until he got to 124th street and made a right.

"Aye Rashad, hold up," the man yelled as he turned the corner. Rashad's heart dropped as the man quickly wrapped him up in a bear hug and smiled at him. "Hold up, Rashad. It's me, man. Calm down. It's me!" the man said.

Rashad tussled with the would-be thief for a brief moment until he broke free from his grip. "Get the fuck off of me, nigga!" Rashad yelled. "Gimme back my shit."

"Rashad, calm down, man. It's me," the man repeated. "Look man…it's me."

Rashad took a moment to calm himself. He looked into the man's eyes and a wide smile grew on his face. He instantly recognized him. It was his old friend, Shaheed Porter.

"Word to my mother, homeboy, you was about to get rocked," Rashad yelled as he put out his arms and hugged Shaheed.

"Damn boy, it's good seein' you out here," Shaheed said returning the love.

Rashad started laughing uncontrollably as he thought about the sight of the two of them running down the street. His entire mood lightened as he stepped back from Shaheed and looked at him. "What the hell is wrong with you, boy?" Rashad said, trying to catch his breath. He was still laughing. "Why the hell you make me chase you all the way over here? You had to take the joke that far, man?"

Shaheed started laughing too as he leaned up against the building.

"Man, on the way up here I tried to think of how I was gonna get you away from that table. And I know how much you take pride in gettin' ya shit back."

"Damn straight," Rashad said. "Twelve years. Ain't a nigga got me yet!"

"I bet not," Shaheed continued. "Not as fast as you was runnin'." Both men started laughing loud again. Shaheed started shaking his head at Rashad, who was almost in tears. "Damn, man," Shaheed continued. "I haven't laughed this hard in years."

"Yea, man. That is too funny. So what's goin' on with you, Shah'? What are you doin' up this way?"

"Man, I got some serious business to take care of." Shaheed looked around. "I'm not even supposed to be on these streets up here. That's why I had to get you to come over here so we can build."

Rashad nodded his head and gave Shaheed a peculiar look.

"Okay. You still workin' for Abdul?"

The mention of Abdul's name brought Shaheed back to reality. He was tempted to turn away as his laughter quickly subsided.

Rashad picked up on the vibe and continued to probe. "I haven't seen Abdul in a while, now that I think about it. But I heard he's getting' crazy paper right now."

"Actually, my dude. That's why I came out here to see you. I need your help."

"My help?" Rashad stuttered.

"Yea, homie. Your help," Shaheed said. "Damn, man. Don't tell me I'm not good for a favor."

264

"C'mon, fam. You know I got you," Rashad assured. "Just that you never asked me for a favor before."

Shaheed nodded his head and looked around for a moment.

"So true, homie. So you know I'm in the shit pretty bad if I'm comin' to you." Shaheed looked around again, then handed Rashad a white envelope. "In a nut shell, I need you to give that to Abdul for me. This nigga had a bounty out on my head for like two years now, and I'm ready to get this shit off my back. I know you don't like to get in the middle of this shit, but I really don't have nobody else to turn to."

A look of disappointed emerged on Rashad's face. "C'mon, Shah. This feels like money is in this thing." He was reluctant to take the envelope.

"It is money, family. I know you feel some kind of way 'bout this, Rashad. But please do me this favor. I can't go see him. I can't really trust him."

"What?" Rashad said. His disappointed look turned to anger. "You think he's gonna hurt you...so you want to send me in there?"

"Man, that nigga would never touch you," Shaheed said as he twisted his face up. "You know them dudes got mad respect for you."

"They only got respect for me 'cause I never get involved in this shit," Rashad said. "Now you involving me."

Shaheed didn't say a word. Rashad could tell that Shaheed was scared about the entire ordeal. He didn't want to know any more details, but decided to ask more questions as he went against his better judgment.

"So what happened?"

"Long story, Rah," Shaheed began. "But to cut it short, I got into some shit out in Chicago and Adbul gave me a pass. But I had to pay him for it. I tried to do a few things with my cousin."

"Who Vegas?" Rashad quickly asked. He shook his head. "Man, that boy right there is certified crazy."

Shaheed smiled. "Hell yea. But he's family. We tried to do some shit out in Jersey but it didn't work. I caught a bullet and everything fuckin' with that shit."

"Say word!" Rashad watched as Shaheed pulled up his sweater and revealed the bullet scars on his stomach. "Whoa!" Rashad shook his head. "So how much you owe Abdul?"

"It was twenty five thousand. But that was two years ago," Shaheed said. "It's probably fifty by now."

"Damn, Shah. You lucky you like family to me." Rashad took the envelope and shoved it down his pants.

"Thanks, man," Shaheed said as he hugged Rashad. He felt relieved. "Listen, man. Just tell him that I will have the rest in a few weeks. But I need to know that he's gonna leave me alone after I give him the money."

Rashad nodded his head and looked at Shaheed. "So that's what you needed from me? You want me to drop some money off for you?"

"Hell yea. That's it. Trust me, this is a big deal. This nigga Abdul got me shook to death."

Rashad shook his head and chuckled at the statement. "How many times, Shah?" Rashad rhetorically asked. "How many times I asked you to come down to the Masjid and get out of that nonsense?"

"I know Rashad," Shaheed said. "Man, I wish I could be a better Muslim like you. But you know I'm not big on religion. It's been tough out here, man."

"No doubt, fam," Rashad continued. "But Allah makes it hard for us—"

"Because he loves us!" Shaheed blurted, cutting off Rashad. He rolled his eyes and looked away.

"Wallahi Akhi," Rashad said. "But you're right, I'm not gonna preach to you. You are definitely your own man and you are gonna make your own decisions. But if I'm gonna do this for you, you gotta promise me one thing, Shah'."

Shaheed turned and looked at Rashad. "What's that?"

"I don't know where you goin' in the next chapter of your life. But when the time comes to make another major life decision, I don't want you to think about the next five minutes, five days for five months. I want you to think about the rest of your life and then make that decision."

Shaheed nodded his head. Something in Rashad's tone made him pay close attention. "I feel you. That's it?"

"That's it. And don't worry about this money. I will handle that today for you."

"Damn man, that's wassup." He looked around again and shook Rashad's hand. "I gotta skate outta here before somebody sees me. You still got the same house number, right?"

"For the last fifteen years," Rashad said proudly. "It's never gonna change."

"Cool. I'll call you in a few days and give you some updates on what's goin' on with me."

"Say no more," Rashad said. He watched as Shaheed turned around and began to walk off. A feeling of regret came over him as he thought about the conversation. He knew Shaheed was in way over his head with Abdul, but he was going to try his best to make it right for him. Before Shaheed could get too far, he yelled for him. "Yo Shah! Come back for a second."

Shaheed turned around and gave him a strange look. He quickly walked back over to Rashad and stood in front of him. "Yea, what's up?"

Rashad didn't answer. He held out his hand and looked at Shaheed.

Shaheed gave him another strange look. "What?"

"Gimme back my goddamn socks!" Rashad said as a huge smile came to his face.

Shaheed tossed the socks to Rashad. Both men were laughing now. Shaheed shook his head and gave his friend a pound. He didn't say a word as he turned around and started to jog back down the block. Rashad watched him as he ran up the street and disappeared into the crowd.

❖

Chapter 34

Bristol-Myers Squibb
New Brunswick, NJ

Thursday February 26, 2009
11:30 a.m.

It rained all week, Faith. You wouldn't believe how much water we got in Jersey over the past few days. It was coming down in buckets. I know I haven't written you in a couple of weeks. My mind has been so preoccupied with all that's going on. I finally got that tattoo I told you about before. I got a black rose tattooed on my chest. It is so cute. And I have your name on one of the leaves. You would love it. I tried to tell my mom about it but she is mad at me. Me and her still having problems, but, hopefully, she will come around soon. I know you heard the news...that coward Shaheed got off. Those jurors didn't have the guts to find him guilty. But it's okay, it's always more than one way to skin a cat. We'll cross paths again. But first I have to keep my mind on Rick. I know he had a lot to do with this shit. So just stay patient with me. I miss...I love you...your road dog...Heidi!

Heidi looked outside of her car window as she sat alone in the parking lot of her Aunt Valerie's job. She read the text message one last time before she sent it to her best friend, Faith. As the message disappeared from her mobile phone, she tried her best to fight her emotions. The past few weeks had been dreadfully lonely for her. With no one to talk to now that she and Pearl were not speaking, Heidi found herself feeling hopelessly alone. Not having Faith near was becoming more difficult for her with each passing day. She decided she needed someone to talk to this morning. After being unsuccessful in reaching her mother, she decided to take a chance and visit her Aunt Valerie at her job. After a few moments, she felt relieved to see Valerie exiting her job and walking toward her car.

"Hey, Auntie!" Heidi said as she got out of her car to greet her aunt. "I know it's such a short notice, but thanks for coming to lunch with me today."

"Good morning, sweetie!" Valerie said as she gave her niece a hug. "Honestly, I won't be able to do lunch today. I am extremely busy up there and I really can't get away."

"Awww damn!" Heidi uttered. She was clearly disappointed. "Not even for a half hour?"

Valerie slowly shook her head. "I'm very sorry, sweetie. I really can't."

"Damn…alright."

"You okay, Heidi?" Valerie asked.

"Not really…but I'm trying my best to be okay."

"So what's wrong…how is the new apartment?"

"I like it," Heidi whispered. "I guess I'm just lonely. And I'm still having these damn headaches."

"Are they getting worse?" Valerie asked. "The headaches?"

"Yes…I called my doctor and they don't know what it is."

"Sounds to me like you really need a release or something close to it," Valerie suggested.

Heidi turned to her aunt. "What do you mean?"

"Heidi, since you've been out of the hospital you have been ripping and running around like you're on a mission. The only time I really seen you having any fun was when we went to the mall together. Other than that…it has been nothing but stress. I told your mom the same thing."

"You think that is where these headaches are coming from?"

"I really don't know…but you need to get out. Go have some fun. Take a minute to yourself and have some fun, sweetie. Stop carrying all that stress around with you. Let go!"

Heidi thought for a moment and turned away from her aunt. "So, is it that bad? You can tell that I'm stressing too much?"

"Absolutely!" Valerie uttered. "Just take my advice and try to have some fun okay?"

Heidi looked at her aunt and rubbed her head. "I may have to do that, Auntie. I know I have to do something. These headaches are really beginning to bother me."

"Well, you have to do a better job of taking care of yourself," Valerie said as she looked at her watch. "I really have to get back to work, honey. Are you going to be alright?"

Heidi nodded her head. "I'll be okay, Auntie. Too bad we can't hang out today. Are you still coming to Lamar's party tomorrow night?"

"I'll be there."

"Is my mother coming with you?"

"I hope so…but don't worry…I will get her to come."

"Thank you." Heidi gave her aunt a hug. "Call me later, and I'll let you know how my non-stressful day went."

Valerie smiled at her niece. "Okay…I will do that." Valerie waved to Heidi and walked back to the office building. Heidi returned to her car and drove out of the parking lot.

As she made her way through town, she realized the day was still young. With everything set for her brother's party tomorrow, she found herself struggling with finding something to do to keep her busy. She looked at her watch again as she pulled up to a traffic light. A bright neon blare caught her attention from the sidewalk. Quickly, Heidi read the sign and thought for a moment. *Empire Luxury Car Rentals*? She read the sign again and a thought moved her. A devilish smile came to her face as Heidi quickly pulled her truck over to the side of the road. She decided to take her aunt's advice, and came up with an idea to help relieve her stress.

* * *

Elizabeth, NJ

12:57 p.m.

"Rhonndaaaaa…!" Shaheed yelled as he stood on the porch of his girlfriend's house. He had been yelling for her for over ten minutes, and hadn't received a response. "Rhonda…I know you're up there…stop playin' and open the goddamn door!" he continued to yell as people began to take notice of the commotion he was causing. Shaheed disregarded the nosey neighbors and continued to bark toward the second floor of the building. "Come on, Rhonda… please…I know you're up there! Let me in!" Shaheed banged on the front door.

An older woman walked by the porch and gave him a disappointed expression. "I don't know who Rhonda is…but I can see why she's ignoring you," the woman said. "You are annoying."

"Mind ya business…!" Shaheed barked as he waved off the woman. He turned his attention back to Rhonda's front door and continued the intense banging. "What the hell is wrong with you, Rhonda…open the door! I said I'm sorry! Come on, baby… I'm sorry!"

The apology seemed to work like a secret password as the front door swung opened. Rhonda stood near the entrance to the house and looked at her boyfriend, who remained outside on the porch.

"You lucky I love you, nigga…I swear," Rhonda whispered. She gave him a small grin. "I should make you stand out there and beg some more."

Shaheed gave his girlfriend a blank expression. He was clearly mad at her for making him wait outside, but he didn't want to piss her off again. He returned a smile. "Baby…if I have to do anymore begging…can I at least do it inside the house?" he asked humbly.

Rhonda nodded her head and turned around. She headed back upstairs and left the front door opened for her boyfriend.

Shaheed looked around the neighborhood one last time and entered the house. He followed Rhonda to the second floor apartment and walked inside the living room. There were suitcases and brown boxes scattered about. He looked around in confusion and saw all the photos and posters were removed from the wall and the living room furniture was gone.

"What's goin' on, Rhonda?" Shaheed asked. "Where is all of your stuff?"

"I sold it," Rhonda responded as she sat on the edge of a milk crate in the middle of the living room.

"What? Why?" Shaheed gasped.

"Because I'm leaving, baby. I have to get out of Jersey."

"What the hell are you sayin'?" Shaheed asked. He was thrown off by Rhonda's decision and walked over to her. "When did you make this decision?"

"When you got shot…and then got arrested!"

"So are you leaving me?"

"No, baby!" Rhonda said as she stood up. "I want you to come with me. We talked about his before, Shah'. I'm not like you. Seeing you shackled down in that courtroom really scared me. I am not built like you, baby. I can't be that *down-ass chick* runnin' back and forth upstate to see her man behind bars. That's not me. I want a regular life. And I want to spend that regular life with you."

"Damn, Rhonda…why didn't you tell me this before?" Shaheed asked. He walked to the other side of the room and rubbed his head in frustration. "You know I got a lot of court shit I gotta deal with, right? And what about Abdul? I just can't up and leave like that."

Rhonda walked over and hugged him. "Baby, listen to me," Rhonda continued. "Fuck all of that…seriously! We can leave all of that bullshit behind. Shah', look around, baby…I sold most of my shit. And I got almost eighty-five hundred dollars. I know it's not a lot of money, but I know it's enough to start over with. Nobody don't even have to know where we're goin'. Not even my mom. We can just leave."

"And go where, Rhonda?" Shaheed raised his voice.

"Down south!" Rhonda answered.

I don't know nobody down there."

"But I do," Rhonda quickly fired back. "Trust me, Shaheed. I know you don't want to trust me...or my judgment. But I got you. We don't have to wait here until somethin' else bad happens...we can leave today...tomorrow. I don't care. It's up to you. But I have to leave, Shaheed...and I would love for you to come with me."

He thought for a moment and looked at his girlfriend. "You are dead serious about this move, huh?"

"Baby, you know I don't talk just to hear my own voice. I am very serious," Rhonda said. She looked into Shaheed's eyes and nodded her head. "I am getting rid of everything else today. I already got people who are either going to buy or take this stuff. So it's up to you, Shah'...but I'm leaving. Are you coming with me?"

Shaheed slowly waked by Rhonda and looked out the window. The abruptness of his girlfriend's plan made him uncomfortable, but something about the move was attractive to him. He was now presented with a good opportunity to leave Jersey and all of his street problems behind him without going to prison. He knew his future would not turn out positive if he continued down the same destructive path. No matter how rough things would become with Rhonda, nothing would be worse than spending the rest of his life in jail. He turned back to Rhonda as she stood in the middle of the taped up boxes and packed up suitcases.

"You know, Rhonda...a crazy thing happens when you're behind bars." Shaheed leaned against the wall near the window. "When you're locked up...it's like your mind all of a sudden becomes focused. Before I was locked up...I remember how my mind would ramble on shit and stray away from the real shit...and how hard it was for me to focus on one thing. But when I got caged...that's the first thing my mind did for me—got focused!"

Rhonda gave her boyfriend a strange look. She didn't know where he was going with his words, so she decided to remain quiet.

"Some niggas in there focused on the wrong shit. They focused on getting' high...or stabbin' a nigga. Some of them even focused on who they girl was fuckin' with on the outside... ya know, shit like that. But the only thing I could focus on was getting' out of that box.

I didn't want to be there. And everyday I was trying to figure out how to make it out." Shaheed turned away from Rhonda and looked out the window. He continued to speak, "And one day this cat spoke to me about my bid. And I was tellin' him how I needed to get out of there. He told me not to focus on getting out because that would only drive me crazier and make my time move slower. He told me to focus on *why* I wanted to get out. No matter what it was. He told me to focus on the reasons why I wanted to see the streets again." Shaheed turned back to Rhonda and walked over to her. "And it took a couple of days for me to figure it out…but besides havin' my freedom…you were the only reason why I wanted to leave."

Rhonda dropped her head. A wide smile came to her face. She looked up to Shaheed and smiled. "Damn, Shah'…why can't you be this sweet all the time?" she whispered. "You know I love you, right?"

"You betta," he responded. He kissed her on the lips. "I'm with you, baby. Let's leave tomorrow. We can say goodbye to all this bullshit up here. I'm goin' to trust you. I hope you know what you're doin'."

Rhonda gave Shaheed a tight hug. Her heart started racing as she realized that her and her man were about to act on a major move. "We'll be okay, Shah'…trust me…as long as we're together."

Chapter 35

Call And Response Headquarters
Maplewood, New Jersey

Thursday February 26, 2009
2:51 p.m.

*B*ack in Maplewood, Tycen paced back and forth in his office as he yelled into his Bluetooth headset. He had been on the phone for nearly twenty minutes confirming instructions to the mid-managers of the Call and Response program. It was difficult to adjust to his new role as the official Department Chief of the program. Managing five offices and almost two hundred employees proved to be a major task for the young executive. Tycen stopped in the middle of the office and read from a sheet of paper he held.

"All we have to do is schedule less clients on Fridays and move the meetings to Tuesdays. That way people will come out with no problems. People want to relax on Fridays; they don't want to feel pressured to meet with each other on party nights," Tycen yelled.

He continued to pace around the office, listening to the few voices battle with him from the other line. He looked at his watch and realized he hadn't left the office all day. Tycen shook his head in frustration as his stress level grew. A knock on the door made him turn around. He became more agitated when he saw his young assistant entering his office. She waited patiently near the door as Tycen continued his conversation.

"Guys...wait a minute. Let me speak," Tycen snapped into his headset. The men on the other line became silent. "Let's make this very simple, okay? I will be sending out an email later today to all the offices requesting that we change the days of the meetings to Tuesday. We will try it out for ninety days. If the response is positive, we will implement a full schedule change." Tycen walked over to his desk and took a seat. "Now guys, I have a lot of work to do so I'm going to hang up. The meetings are now officially on Tuesdays, so plan accordingly! Goodbye."

He disconnected his call, and removed the Bluetooth from his ear. He tried to calm himself, but he was aggravated from the phone conference. He looked at his assistant and shrugged his shoulders. "I don't know why they are giving me such a hard time," Tycen said, referring to his call. "I guess some people don't like change."

"Don't let them stress you," the young assistant said, smiling him. "They are going to test you because you're new to the position. I have seen it happen a few times in this place. Just hang in there."

Tycen shuffled through a stack of papers on his desk and nodded his head. "Thanks for the advice."

"No problem, Mr. Wakefield," the assistant replied. "I was coming in here to let you know you have a strange visitor waiting for you in the lobby."

Tycen looked up to his assistant. "Strange? What do you mean by *strange*?"

"I can't really explain it, Sir. You really have to see for yourself."

Tycen looked oddly, and then stood to his feet. "Okay...is this a bad *strange* or a good *strange*?" he asked, giving the assistant a pressing glance.

"Mr. Wakefield, I have been around a long time," the assistant continued. "And I have never seen anything like this." She smiled at Tycen as he walked around his desk, then led him out of the office and down the hall to meet his visitor.

Tycen became unsure as he walked into the lobby area and noticed a man standing near the front entrance to the building. The assistant walked over to the man, then called for Tycen's attention.

"Mr. Wakefield, this is Mr. Jean Cantor," the assistant introduced.

"Hello." Tycen reached out and shook the man's hand.

Mr. Cantor was dressed in a jet-black chauffeur uniform. The double-breasted suit and chauffeur hat fit snugly on the small man. He looked up to Tycen and gave him a professional smile.

"Mr. Wakefield, how are you today," Mr. Cantor inquired. "I was instructed to come here and save you from this place."

"Save me?" Tycen mumbled. He looked over to his assistant, who was trying to hold back her giggles.

"That's what he told me too," the assistant said as she let out a chuckle. "I told you it was a strange visit."

Tycen smiled and shook his head. "Who are you?" he asked the man.

"I'm your chauffeur for the day, Mr. Wakefield," Mr. Cantor replied. "Take a look for yourself." Mr. Cantor pointed to the front door of the building.

Tycen walked outside with his assistant following closely behind. He'd only made it a few feet outdoors before stopping dead in his tracks. He was instantly taken aback by the sight of an English-white Rolls-Royce Phantom parked in the front of the building.

"Oh my…!" the assistant gasped behind her boss.

"Damn…is that what you're driving?" Tycen asked.

"Yes," Mr. Cantor replied. "I have clear instructions to take you away from this place, even if I have to do it with you kicking and screaming."

"Is that right?" Tycen asked. He turned around to the chauffeur and sized him up. "And where exactly did these instructions come from?"

Mr. Cantor reached inside his jacket pocket and pulled out a small card. He handed it to Tycen and waited for him to read it. Tycen flipped the card around and quietly read the note.

I hope you like the car. I think a man like you deserves to ride in style. I want to spend some time with you tonight. A few weeks ago you asked me to SAVE you from your job. And today, I have my SUPERWOMAN-CAPE on! So grab your stuff and get in! Don't worry about a thing. This is all on me. Tonight will be a night you will never forget. – Your Friend, Heidi Kachina.

Tycen smiled from ear to ear. He put the note in his pocket, then looked at the car. The sexy design of the luxury sedan hypnotized him for a moment. He turned around and gave his assistant a crooked smile. "You think I should go?"

"Hell yes!" The assistant yelled to her boss. "Don't worry about this place. It will be here when you get back."

He considered going or not, rubbing his chin. He thought about how he needed a break from the Call and Response Headquarters, and today was the perfect day to make it happen. He turned to his assistant. "Please cancel my appointments for the day and hold my calls," he instructed.

His assistant nodded her head and gave him a thumps-up. She watched as he turned back to the car. "Okay, Mr. Wakefield. Just call and let me know if you will be making it in tomorrow...or the next day."

"Will do," Tycen said, ignoring his assistant's last request. He walked down the stairs and towards the car.

Mr. Cantor scurried to get in front of Tycen, then quickly opened the back door.

Tycen looked inside the backseat. "Where is she? Where's Heidi?"

"She left some money in the back, and instructed me to take you shopping first," Mr. Cantor replied.

"Wow," Tyson whispered. He was overwhelmed by Heidi's gift to him.

"She wants to meet for dinner around eight this evening, so we have some time," Mr. Cantor informed. "Shall we?" He directed Tycen to the plush interior of the Phantom.

Tycen nodded his head and got in, at a loss for words.

"Okay." Mr. Cantor hopped in the driver seat and fired up the

V-12 engine. Tycen felt like a king as he got comfortable in the back of the vehicle. He melted into the seashell leather, and tried to imagine what else Heidi had in store for him this evening.

* * *

New York City

3:18 p.m.

"Excuse me!" Heidi yelled as she pushed her way past a cluster of rude pedestrians in midtown Manhattan's busy shopping district. She couldn't believe the amount of people walking up and down Fifth Avenue. She continued to push and shove people out of her way as she tried her best to avoid being trampled by the herd. "Pardon me…damn!" she snapped, lugging three large shopping bags down the congested block. Heidi had been shopping all afternoon, trying to find the right outfit. She walked down a few more blocks as she thought about one final item to add to her ensemble.

Reaching her destination, she looked up to the enormous store sign. She smiled like a child at an amusement park as she read the fancy letters. *Saks Fifth Avenue.* Her smile widened as she walked through the glass doors, entering into an expensive world of fashion and prestige. The store reminded her of a place right out of the movies. The French-Style décor and wide selection of high-end items added to the storybook atmosphere. Heidi felt like she was in a shopper's dream as she made her way through the enormous store. She headed straight for the Women's department. She grabbed her phone and decided to check in on her friend before she got lost in her shopping spree.

"Hey sweetie, how are you making out?" she asked when Tycen answered the phone.

"Well, hello Ms. Superwoman," Tycen joked with a short chuckle. "I'm doing a lot better now. I'm starting to feel a little special right now."

"Well…that's because you are special," Heidi replied with a smile.

"Did you go shopping yet? I hope you don't mind my leaving the money…I wanted to treat you to something nice."

"Yes…I got the money, and we're stopping by a few more stores," Tycen continued. "I don't mind at all. To be honest, I'm a bit excited about later."

"I hope so. We're going to have a wonderful time."

"So have you picked out a nice spot for dinner yet?" Tycen asked.

"I have," Heidi whispered as she searched the racks for another item. "I found a nice place in New York. Don't worry…Mr. Cantor knows how to get there."

"Sounds good to me. I guess I will buy something nice to throw on, then call you when I'm on my way."

"Okay sweetie," Heidi said. "I told the driver to have you there by eight tonight."

"Cool…I will be there."

"Before I let you go," Heidi continued. "I want to wear something nice for you, and I never got a chance to ask you what your favorite color was."

"Hmm…that's easy, baby," Tycen said. "I love red."

"Wow, I was hoping you said that." Heidi smiled and nodded her head. "Now I know this will be a night to remember."

Chapter 36

Trump International Hotel
New York City

Thursday February 26, 2009
8:34 p.m.

"*S*o this was a very creative place to have dinner, Ms. Superwoman," Tycen joked as he sat across from a beautifully dressed Heidi.

"Yes…I always wanted to have dinner in a nice hotel suite away from people." Heidi smoothly put a glass of red wine to her lips and took a few sips. "I got the idea from a magazine I was reading while in the hospital late last year."

Tycen listened to Heidi speak as he finished up his drink. For the past half hour the two had been having a beautiful dinner in the Presidential Suite of the Trump International Hotel. Heidi decided to rent the loft for the evening so they could be alone. The oversized suite overlooked New York City's beautiful night life. Although Heidi and Tycen were on the 44th floor, the luxurious view made them feel like they were on top of the world.

"Would you like another glass?" Heidi asked, giving Tycen a warm smile.

"Yes…please," Tycen uttered.

"You so polite," Heidi teased as she got up from the glass table and walked backwards to a small countertop near the window. "I know you are not a corporate guy all the time, Tycen. I know there's a bad boy somewhere inside of there." Heidi smirked as she pointed at Tycen.

"I don't know, Heidi," Tycen responded with a sly smile. Heidi turned around and poured two glasses of white wine this time. Tycen looked at Heidi's shapely body and licked his lips. "It's been a long time since the bad boy's been out of the cage."

Heidi shook her head as she slowly grabbed the glasses and headed back to the table. Tycen marveled at her style. The geranium-red silk dress she wore hugged her body like a movie star. From the flawless hairstyle up top, to the strapless dress in the middle, to the Loeffler Randall pumps on the bottom, she was red-carpet-ready from head to toe. Tycen couldn't believe how much she had changed since meeting her in the office. She was beautiful.

"So how long has it been since the bad boy has surfaced?" she asked as she handed Tycen his drink.

"I would say—" Tycen uttered.

"Actually…I don't want to know. I didn't mean to cut you off. But I'm really looking to start fresh, and I don't even care what happened before me," Heidi said.

Tycen gave her a strong stare and took a sip of his drink. "So is there anything that you want to know about me?"

Heidi looked over to Tycen and smiled. It had been a while since she was in an intimate setting with a man, and she was clearly feeling it. Heidi found herself getting slightly nervous as she looked over to Tycen. He sat confidently on the other side of the table with his hand on his chin. His solid physique filled out every crease of his Marc Jacobs outfit. Every time he smiled at her, Heidi felt herself becoming more curious about him. She stood to her feet and put her drink down on the table. She grabbed Tycen by the hand, then walked him over to the far window overlooking Central Park.

"New York City is so beautiful at night," she whispered. She turned around and looked out the window as Tycen stood behind her. She grabbed his hands and slowly placed them around her waist. "Don't you agree?" she asked as Tycen moved closer to her. She felt his solid frame pressing against her back, then closed her eyes.

"It's romantic," Tycen responded. His deep voice caused the hairs on the back of Heidi's neck to rise. Her heart fluttered as she felt herself becoming more nervous. The combination of the drinks and Tycen's presence was making her warm.

"I want to tell you something, and I don't want you to get upset or take it the wrong way," she whispered.

"Okay I won't," Tycen responded.

Heidi hesitated to speak as she continued to look out of the window. The room was silent. "Hmmmm," Heidi moaned as she found herself enjoying the quiet moment in the room. The view was turning Heidi on, but she wanted to say something before it was too late. She turned around and looked Tycen in his eyes. She found herself sinking into the moment. She opened her mouth to speak and let out an awkward chuckle. "I know you will think this is silly but," she continued as she gave Tycen a smile. "I just wanted you to know that I don't want anything from you. I mean…I want somethin' from you," Heidi said as she blushed. "But I don't want you to think I'm tryin' to lock you down or something. I've had a pretty rough past two years and right now…I just ask one thing from you, Tycen."

"Okay," Tycen said as he looked at Heidi. "What is it that you want?"

"Just don't lie to me, baby," Heidi whispered. "Just keep it real with me, and I can live with that. It's been a long time since I even wanted to get this close to somebody. But I don't want to put no pressure on you. I just want to be able to trust you."

Tycen nodded his head, giving Heidi a serious look. Her vulnerability made Tycen comfort her. "You can trust me, Heidi."

The sincerity in his voice made Heidi feel more at ease. She looked into his eyes and tried to read him. There was no lying in Tycen's eyes. Heidi grabbed Tycen by the shoulders and smiled at him. She reached up and kissed him on the lips. The electricity from the kiss made her moan with pleasure. He was instantly turned on by her reaction. He pulled her closer as the kiss became more intense. Heidi decided not to waste another second. She was feeling Tycen more than she realized, and she shivered with anticipation. His strong hands moved down the arch in her back, making her quiver. Heidi had to smile as she began to realize that it wasn't taking much to get her started tonight. It had been a long time and her body begged for some attention. She gently placed her palms on his chest, then slowly pushed herself away from him.

She kept her eyes fixed on him as she backed up against the large window. He couldn't help but smile as Heidi's silhouette blended seductively with the bright lights of New York. He watched her closely as she unzipped her red dress and let it fall to the carpet. His eyes grew wide as he stared at her nakedness. She slowly pressed her back up against the window, then easily caressed her body. Her rhythmic tease silently invited Tycen to join her. He quickly removed his button-down shirt, exposing his sculpted chest to her. Heidi became even more excited at the sight.

Tycen kicked off his shoes and moved toward her. He pressed his body up against hers and started kissing her again. His warm tongue danced around her lips before starting to make its way down to her neck.

"Damn baby…it's been so long," Heidi admitted, moaning as she felt his tongue massaging her neck. She grabbed the back of his head as he made his way down her body and started to suck on her nipples. It didn't take long for them to react to Tycen's attention as they stood fully erected for him. Heidi let out another seductive groan. "Move down, baby." She wanted to feel his tongue between her thighs.

Tycen picked up on the vibe and started to kiss on her stomach. Before she could react, Tycen got on his knees and quickly threw her left leg over his shoulder. Her wet pussy was hungry for him.

"Oh my God…" Heidi moaned as she felt Tycen's strong tongue dive into her walls with passion. She grabbed onto his shoulders as he ate her pussy like a sex slave. Her head fell back in bliss as her body trembled from the sensation. His tongue danced over her love button until Heidi started to scream through her first orgasm. She held onto him tightly as her body oozed with ecstasy.

"Oh yes, baby…please don't stop," Heidi stammered as her body gyrated against the window. Tycen almost chuckled at how fast the multiple-orgasms came. The oral sex was clearly long overdue for Heidi. He kissed her thighs, then stood to his feet. Heidi was ready for the next level. She reached for his waist, then quickly removed his belt. Tycen backed away from Heidi and pulled down his pants. One look at Tycen's dick, and Heidi smiled like a teenaged school girl. He had more than enough to please her, and she realized it more and more as he moved closer to her. She grabbed his dick and slowly massaged it. She leaned against the large window again as a seductive smile came to her face.

"I knew you had a bad boy somewhere in there," Heidi groaned with a smirk. Tycen returned the smile and moved closer. "So how do you want to do it?"

Tycen never said a word. Without warning, he picked her up, making sure she was raised a few feet above the floor. She spread her arms out against the window to maintain her balance. Tycen quickly moved under her. As Heidi slowly slid down the window, she felt Tycen's hard dick slowly enter her yearning pussy.

"Oh yes, Tycen…hell yes!" she moaned as she felt the thickness of Tycen open her wider. He grabbed Heidi by the ass and started to work on her against the window. It didn't take long for another chill to rush up Heidi's spine as another orgasm made her body tremble. Tycen seemed to fit perfectly inside of her. Heidi held onto Tycen's neck as he held her higher in the air. He started to go deeper and deeper as he became more excited. Heidi couldn't hold on any longer as she felt his strong dick bounce off of every one of her inner secret spots.

"Wait…Tycen…wait…I'm comin' again!" She couldn't believe how incredible the sex was. As another orgasm gripped her, Tycen gently let her down. She stood in front of him, shaking her head. "Goddamn boy…you are somethin'." He quickly spun her around, then gently pushed her up against the window. "That's right, baby," Heidi moaned. "I love it from the back." Heidi bent over and placed her hands squarely on the large glass. "Oh…shit…" Heidi gasped as she felt Tycen enter her from behind.

"That's how you like it?" Tycen groaned. Heidi's silky body turned him on even more as he watched her bounce back and forth off of his hips.

"Yes, baby…I like that…please don't stop…goddamn." Heidi became more aggressive as the sex intensified, and moaned as he ravished her sexy body. The windows began to fog as the fervor from their bodies heated up the room. Heidi looked out into the night sky. She was beyond paradise. Tycen was giving her the best sex she had had in years.

"Damn Heidi…I am lovin' this right now!" Tycen moaned.

Heidi felt his stroke intensify as she reacted. Tycen went deeper inside of her as another orgasm began to build. "Damn baby…don't stop…I'm about to come again."

"Me too, baby!" Tycen yelled.

Heidi screamed as she felt Tycen pushed himself deeper. His body shook as his powerful orgasm rocked her insides. Heidi collapsed against the large window and tried to catch her breath. She closed her eyes and moaned in pleasure. Tycen pressed his body up against hers. They both were leaning against the window now.

"That was amazing, Heidi."

"I can really get use to that, baby," Heidi whispered. Her body was still shaking from the sensation. "That was great."

Tycen kissed Heidi on the back of her neck. "Damn, I guess you brought the bad boy out of me, baby."

"I'm glad I could help," Heidi joked. She let out a playful laugh, and then looked back at Tycen. "You think that was somethin'… wait until round two." Tycen smiled and kissed Heidi on the side of the cheek. She closed her eyes and melted into his arms as he squeezed her tightly from behind.

Chapter 37

Trump International Hotel
New York City

**Friday February 27, 2009
10:12 a.m.**

*T*he late morning sunshine crept through the hotel room's velvet curtains and slowly moved over Heidi's peaceful face. The amber sunlight caused her to slowly open her eyes as she awoke from a well deserved slumber. She thought about her incredible night with Tycen and smiled. Images of her fairytale-style evening flashed into her mind. From the romantic dinner to the unbelievable sex sessions, she felt like she was floating on a cloud. If only every night could be like last night. Turning over, she decided to wake him. Immediately, she sat up. She was alone in the bed. Heidi looked around the suite, but there was no sign of Tycen anywhere.

"Baby?" Heidi called out for him. There was no answer. She got out of the bed and walked around the suite. All the lights were off and all of Tycen's clothes were gone. He had left her alone. She walked into the bathroom and saw a note on the mirror.

"Sorry Superwoman...I had an emergency at the office. Call me when you wake up," he'd written.

She shook her head and smiled. She loved that he was so dedicated to his work. She slowly walked back to the bedroom and grabbed her phone. It didn't take long for him to answer after she'd dialed his number.

"Good morning, sunshine," Tycen greeted.

"Hey baby," she moaned her words. "What a night."

"Yes…that was a total surprise. You have great taste."

"So do you," Heidi replied. "You are definitely a smooth one…I have to give you that."

"Well, thank you, baby." Tycen smiled from the other line. "I'm sorry I had to leave. My phone was ringing all morning, and I didn't want to wake you."

"It's okay, really," Heidi assured. "I have some last minute things to do before my brother's party tonight."

"Okay…great," he uttered. "So am I still invited?"

"Hell yes!" Heidi blurted, wearing her feelings on her exterior. "I'm looking forward to seeing you again, so I hope you can make it tonight."

"Don't worry, Heidi," Tycen continued. "I will be there."

"Thank you, sweetie. I'll let you get back to work. I will see you tonight."

"Okay, baby. Have a good one. Talk to you later."

"Goodbye." Heidi hung up the phone and sat on the edge of the bed. After such a wonderful night, she couldn't help but feel like her brother's party was going to be the icing on the cake. Heidi scrolled down her phone and decided to make another call. She found the name she was looking for and quickly dialed the number. She waited a few moments for someone to answer on the other line.

"Good morning," a soft female voice answered.

"Judith…it's me!"

"Oh…hey…I didn't even look at the phone I just answered it," Judith responded.

"Are you at work right now?"

"You know it," Judith replied. "What's goin' on?"

"I just wanted to know if you were coming to the party tonight?"

"I'm thinking about it," Judith continued. "I just need to find something to wear."

"Just wear something nice. It's going to be fun."

"That's cool. I need to hang out tonight. This job is still getting on my nerves."

"Speaking of which, that's another reason why I was calling," Heidi said. "Do I still have to transfer that money to a new account?"

"Yes, especially if you want to keep it on the low."

"Okay…you are catching me on a really good morning," Heidi said. "I'm going to give you the pass code right now. You got a pen?"

"Seriously?" Judith gasped. "Damn, you must be in a good mood. I got a pen."

"Okay…the pass code is 1-0-2-2."

"Oh damn, why that number sound so familiar?" Judith blurted as she wrote down the number.

"What do you mean?" Heidi asked, immediately becoming suspicious. "You know that number?"

"I don't think so…it's not ringing a bell," Judith said. "It just feels like I saw it somewhere before."

Heidi didn't know what to say as she thought about Judith's comment. Heidi knew the four digit number very well. It was the month and date of her late fiancé Jayson's birthday.

"Are you sure you don't know that number?" Heidi asked again with a hint of distrust.

"I'm sorry, Heidi. I forgot where I seen it before but when it comes back to me I will let you know."

Heidi decided to drop the subject. She was in a great mood this morning, and she was not going to allow her suspicions to ruin her day. She stood up from the bed, and decided to wrap up the call with Judith. "So how long is this going to take?"

"Only a few days," Judith responded. "Don't worry…I got you."

"Okay Judith, I trust you."

"Well it's about time you trust somebody." Judith laughed.

"Whatever…bye, girl!" Heidi mumbled.

"Okay…I will see you later."

Heidi hung up the phone and walked over to the large window near the bed. She pulled the curtains back and immediately stood in awe of the beautiful sight of Central Park in the morning. The massive landscape put her in a reflective mood, making her think about her brother, Lamar and his party. She looked at her phone and decided to call her mother to find out if she would be attending the event. Although the two hadn't spoken in over a week, Heidi decided to press her luck. She quickly dialed her mother and waited for her to answer the phone. After a few attempts, Heidi was unsuccessful. Pearl hadn't call her daughter in some time, and refused to answer her calls. Heidi felt bad. She decided to call her aunt Valerie to see how her mother was doing. After a few rings, her aunt answered the other line.

"Hey Heidi," Valerie whispered from the other line.

"Hey Auntie!"

"Good morning, sweetie. How are you doing?"

"Oh my God …Auntie…I'm feeling a lot better!" Heidi gasped. "I took your advice and I did something nice for myself."

"That's wonderful, honey. What did you do?"

"I finally spent some time with that guy I told you about from Kean."

"Good for you. So you finally opened up to him?"

Heidi almost choked as she laughed at the irony of her aunt's question. "Well…I can't tell you everything, Auntie. But let's just say that we had a wonderful evening together."

"I am so happy for you, honey." Valerie smiled through her words. "So are you feeling any better?"

"Well…I still have the headache," Heidi confessed. "But it's not as bad as it was yesterday. I am going to take some Motrin and see if that helps."

"I'm sorry about the headaches. I hope the medicine helps."

"Me too," Heidi continued. "But I was calling about tonight. I wanted to make sure you were coming out to the party."

"Of course I'm coming. I wouldn't miss this for the world."

"What about my mother?" Heidi asked. "Did she say if she was going to come out?"

"We only spoke for a second last night when I got home. But I will ask her again tonight. I think she will come."

"I hope so."

"What time are you going to be there?"

"I need to be there by seven," Heidi replied. "So anytime after that is good."

"Okay…well let me get back to work so I can get out of here early," Valerie said. "I will see you tonight."

"Okay, Auntie. See you tonight."

Heidi hung up the phone, turning her back on the beautiful view. She gathered her things and readied herself for a busy day back in Newark. She only had a few hours before she had to get ready for Lamar's party, and she wanted to make sure everything went well without a hitch.

* * *

Elizabeth, New Jersey

2:08 p.m.

Later that afternoon, Rhonda and Shaheed were calmly walking around Rhonda's empty apartment. For most of the day, they had been throwing out the rest of her belongings or giving them to people in her neighborhood. Rhonda was excited about taking this big step. The very thought of moving down south and starting a brand new life with her boyfriend, Shaheed was surreal. As she grabbed one of the last boxes in the living room, she thought about all the memories she'd had in her apartment and neighborhood. She was going to miss her friends and family, but she was also excited about leaving a lot of her problems behind.

"Do you want me to put this in the car, too?" Shaheed asked as he grabbed a huge box from the corner. "Or is this garbage?"

"Everything except this box I got in my hands is trash," Rhonda said. "So you can throw that one away." She watched as Shaheed picked up the box and followed her downstairs.

Shaheed was less excited about the move than she was. He was nervous about leaving his legal issues behind, but he trusted his girlfriend would stick by him. She didn't have much money left, and he was nervous that they wouldn't have enough funds to live comfortable in their new surroundings. As the two walked to her car, Shaheed couldn't help but wonder if her plan would actually work.

"So…you sure that's everything?" he asked as he turned to his girlfriend.

She packed the last box in the trunk of her car and turned him. "That's it, Shah,'" Rhonda confirmed. "I just need you to grab that last box in the middle of the kitchen floor, and we can go."

Shaheed nodded his head, then headed back upstairs. Rhonda walked around her car and made sure all of their bags were packed securely for the trip. The couple was heading nearly eighteen hours away, and she wanted to make sure that their trip would be as smooth as possible. She opened the back door to her car and ducked her head inside. She was rearranging the luggage when she heard the sound of screeching tires just over her right shoulder. She turned around just in time to see a blue Range Rover speeding down the street. She felt a knot come to her stomach as she immediately recognized the speeding vehicle. The SUV quickly pulled up behind Rhonda's car. She put her hands on her hips as she watched the driver exit the truck. It was Shaheed's cousin, Vegas.

"What the hell are you doin' here?" Rhonda yelled as Vegas quickly approached her car.

"Where's my cousin?" Vegas barked as he ignored her question.

"He's not here!" Rhonda lied. "Why are you here?"

"What the hell are you talkin' about, Rhonda!" Vegas scowled at his cousin's girlfriend. "I know he's here!"

Rhonda shook her head and turned away from Vegas. She crossed her arms with an attitude. She couldn't believe his timing. Before she could say another word, Shaheed walked out of the front door and looked at his cousin, Vegas.

"I'll be damned…it's a miracle. He is here!" Vegas yelled sarcastically as he looked at Rhonda.

"What are you doin' here, Vegas?" Shaheed asked as he walked over to his cousin.

"That's not important, Cuzzo," Vegas responded sharply. "The real question is: where you been? I tried to call you mad times, and you don't pick up my calls."

Shaheed didn't say a word. He didn't know what to say to his cousin. Vegas looked behind Shaheed and noticed that Rhonda's car was packed with luggage.

"Goin' somewhere, playboy?" Vegas asked as he walked over to the car.

Shaheed nervously followed Vegas. "We takin' a small trip."

"A small trip?" Vegas suspiciously mumbled as he looked inside the car. "To where…Canada? That's a lot of shit for a small trip, Shah'."

"Come on, Shaheed," Rhonda snapped with a clear attitude. "We are goin' to be late!"

"I gotta go, Vegas. I'll call you when we get settled, and let you know what's up!" Shaheed mumbled as he tried to move toward the car.

Vegas blocked his path and got in front of Shaheed. "Wait a minute, fam'," Vegas whispered. "We gotta talk right now."

"Well…it's gonna have to wait!" Rhonda yelled as she waved her hand toward Vegas. "We have to go…*right now.*"

Shaheed looked over to his girlfriend, who wore a look of anger and worry. He turned back to Vegas and shook his head. "I can't talk right now," Shaheed said. "I can call you from the road and we can talk then."

"Shah' listen…we need to talk right now!" Vegas barked. The tone in his voice made Shaheed nervous. He looked over to Rhonda and flipped up his finger to her.

"Give me one minute," Shaheed mumbled. Rhonda threw her hands in the air. She was beyond angry.

Vegas put his arm around Shaheed and walked him towards the

Range Rover. "So where are you goin'?" Vegas asked as the cousins walked near the passenger side of the truck. "Looks like she got her whole apartment in that car."

Shaheed looked at his cousin. He felt uneasy about his tone. "I'm outta here, Vee," Shaheed admitted. "We are movin' down south."

"Today?"

"Right now. I can't take it up here no more. Shit is really gettin' fucked up."

"So what you gonna do?" Vegas mumbled. "Ride off into the sunset?"

"That's the plan"

"You got money?" Vegas asked.

"We got a little bit."

"What the fuck you gonna do when that *little bit* run out?"

"Shit...I don't know," Shaheed admitted. "We'll figure out somethin'."

"Look nigga...you can't leave yet," Vegas said sternly. He gave his cousin a hard stare. "We got one more job to do."

Shaheed felt his heart jump for a moment. He looked away from his older cousin. "C'mon Vegas, what the fuck!" Shaheed said incredulously. "Don't do this shit to me. We are out the door, man. This shit is over."

"Not yet, Shah'," Vegas snapped. "This shit ain't over until we get that fuckin' money. For real!"

The very mention of money made Shaheed turn back to his cousin. "What money?" Shaheed asked.

Vegas reached in his pocket, pulled out a red cellphone and a party flyer. He showed Shaheed what he held as a cunning grin came to his face.

Shaheed looked at the phone in Vegas' hand and grabbed the flyer. Shaheed's face became twisted as he read the flyer. "So Heidi is throwin' a party tonight?"

"In Newark!" Vegas added "And that bitch got the money."

"How do you know she got that money?" Shaheed asked with a skeptical expression.

"Trust me," Vegas assured. "She got that fuckin' money—and we can get it tonight. It won't take long. One last job…and you can ride off with your girl and never come back here."

Shaheed thought for a second and looked back to Rhonda. She was leaning on the car with her arms folded. Rhonda was clearly angry with her boyfriend. Shaheed picked up the vibe and turned back to Vegas.

"Cuzzo…I can't do it," Shaheed mumbled. "I can't do that dumb shit no more. I know what you are askin' me to do, and I just can't do it."

Vegas' face became hard as ice. "Shaheed…I don't think you understand what I'm sayin'," Vegas whispered. "Right now…I'm *not* askin'!" His voice froze Shaheed to the street. His hard glare spoke louder than his voice. "When that nigga Abdul wanted that money from you…I held you down, fam'," Vegas pointed out. "And when it was time to get that money for that lawyer…nigga… you don't even wanna know what I did to get that paper for you. So right now, you *owe* me this last job. Let's get this money tonight and we even. Don't *bitch* up on me right now!"

Shaheed didn't say a word. Vegas' tone toward him made Shaheed angry, but he held back his emotions. He turned back to Rhonda and shook his head. "How long is this gonna take?"

"Not long…Heidi is doin' that party tonight downtown. The flyer says seven o'clock. I say we lay on her…and pick the right time. Get the money from her, then be out. And like I said…then it's over. I won't ask you for shit else."

Shaheed took another few moments to think. He turned to Rhonda one last time and thought about the plan. "Okay Vegas, I'm in. I gotta tell Rhonda that I'll be right back. Just wait in the truck for me."

Vegas nodded his head and turned around. He headed back to the Range Rover.

Shaheed took a deep breath, preparing himself for attitude. He walked over to Rhonda and gave her a nervous smile.

"What the hell was that all about?" Rhonda asked quickly.

"I'm sorry, baby," Shaheed mumbled. He was reluctant to speak again.

"Sorry for what?"

"I got to make one more run before we leave," he whispered.

"Baby…no…not with that dude." Rhonda shook her head. "What does Vegas want you to do now?"

"It's nothin', Rhonda," Shaheed said. "Trust me…I just need to pick up somethin', and then I'll be right back. I just need a few hours. Can you wait at your mom's house for me?"

"Baby, why are you doin' this to yourself?" Rhonda asked as she gave her boyfriend a sympathetic expression.

"It's no big deal. I just need a few hours."

"I can't believe this, Shah'. You are doin' the same—"

"Rhonda!" Shaheed barked as he cut his girlfriend short. "Not right now. Please! Just give me a few hours…wait at your mother's house, and as soon as I'm done I will call you." Rhonda saw something different in Shaheed's eyes. She could see that he was torn between what he wanted to do and what he had to. He slightly lowered his head and continued to speak to her. "I'm just gonna take this ride with him and pick something up. Okay? Will you wait for me?"

Rhonda slowly nodded her head. She noticed that Shaheed was battling with something deeper than just making her happy. He walked over to his girlfriend and hugged her. Rhonda squeezed him tight and gave him quick kiss. "Just come back to me in one piece, okay?"

"I will," Shaheed whispered. He turned around and walked to the Range Rover.

Vegas fired up the engine as Shaheed hopped into the passenger side of the truck. Rhonda kept her eyes on Shaheed as the SUV sped passed her, then disappeared down the block.

❖

Chapter 38

Terrace Ballroom
Newark, New Jersey

Friday February 27, 2009
8:02 p.m.

"*I'm feelin' a lot better today, Faith, but I still got these terrible headaches. I don't know what it is, but they keep coming back. After this party tonight, I will catch up on some rest. The party looks like its goin' to be really nice. I see a lot of cars out here, so I hope it's packed. I really wish you were here. I miss you. . .I love you. . .your road dog. . .Heidi!*"

Heidi sat quietly in her truck and glanced at the busy entrance to the ballroom. Although she was an hour late to Lamar's party, she refused to enter the party before sending her thoughts to her best friend first. She scrolled down to Faith's name and calmly sent out the text message. Instantly, she felt relieved. She locked her phone and put it away in her handbag. She looked around the busy street and noticed that the crowd for the party was growing larger by the minute. She was shocked to see so many people arriving to celebrate her brother's birthday. As Heidi watched the crowd become larger, she couldn't help but feel nervous about the amount of people who continued to file into the ballroom. She continued to scan the crowd for a moment. A sense of fear came over her. Heidi couldn't recognize a lot of the faces in the crowd, and she didn't want to take any chances with someone getting out of line. She reached into her glove compartment and pushed a few papers to the side. She pulled out a small box and opened it. A nervous grin came to her face as she pulled out the flip-action knife she'd received as a gift a few months ago. Heidi thought about the young paramedic who'd given her the knife in the hospital. *Let's hope I don't have to use this tonight.* She put the knife in her front pocket and tossed the box in the backseat. She was now ready to party.

Heidi turned off her truck's engine and hopped out the vehicle. She made her way to the front entrance of the ballroom, cautiously looking around at all the unfamiliar faces. She was still in awe at the amount of people who showed to the event.

A loud roar erupted from inside the party. Heidi waved to security at the door, hurried down the tunnel and into the ballroom. A smile came to her face when she saw a large crowd of partygoers moving on the dance floor. The music was loud enough to wake the dead, but the large crowd every second of it. DJ Symphony was spinning the latest hits from some of the biggest Hip-Hop and R&B stars. Heidi nodded her head to the music and waved at the DJ.

DJ Symphony smiled when he saw Heidi making her way through the crowd. "Okay Brick City…the party is about to go to another level…the Diva of the hour just stepped into the building!"

Heidi blushed when she heard DJ Symphony announcing her arrival. She decided to walk to the VIP section and settle down until her aunt arrived. Heidi was nearing the back of the club when she felt a large hand grab her by the shoulder.

"What the fuck?" Heidi yelled as she turned around in attack mode.

"Whoa…it's me!" a male voice yelled as the young man took a few steps back from Heidi.

She sized the man up and immediately covered her mouth. "I'm so sorry, Tycen." Heidi smiled at her friend. "I didn't know it was you." She rushed over and hugged him, then kissed him on the lips and looked at him. "Why are you here so early?"

"I thought I was late," Tycen said as he looked at his watch. "I thought you said you were going to be here by seven, so I tried to meet you here."

Heidi smiled. "Well…you know, sometimes I am fashionably late. How long have you been here?"

"I got here about a half hour ago, and I saw this woman that looks like you," Tycen smiled and continued to speak. "I introduced myself ,and she said she was your aunt."

"Are you serious?" Another wide smile came to her face. "My aunt is already here? Where is she?" Heidi asked as she looked around the crowded dance floor.

"She's in the VIP section in the back. I'll take you to her." Tycen grabbed Heidi by the arm and led her through the crowd. They made their way through the dance floor to a bright room near the rear of the ballroom. Heidi's face lit up as she walked into the room. Valerie was standing near the juice bar.

"Auntieee…you made it!" Heidi shouted as she rushed over to Valerie and hugged her.

"I told you I was going to make it tonight." She gave Heidi a hug and looked at her. "Damn, sister girl…I see you threw it on tonight," Valerie teased as she looked at her niece's party outfit.

"You know it, Auntie," Heidi responded. "I had to look good for the paparazzi."

"You're too much, girl." Valerie laughed at the joke. "I got a surprise for you." Valerie smiled as she turned her niece around.

Heidi's heart raced with excitement as she saw her mother and Janaya walking towards her from the other side of the room.

"Auntieeee Heidddiii!" Janaya yelled as she ran over to her older cousin.

"Oh my goodness…what are you doing here little girl." Heidi smiled as she hugged Janaya.

"Auntie Pearl said I can be with the grown-ups today," Janaya said in her sassy voice.

"But not for too long," Pearl added as she walked up behind Janaya. "Only for a couple of more minutes." Pearl looked at her daughter and gave her a small grin. "Hello, Heidi."

"Hey Mom," Heidi whispered as she looked at her mother. She could tell that Pearl was still upset with her, and approached her slowly. "I'm glad you made it out." She gave Pearl a tight hug. Despite the problems the two were having recently, it was clear that they missed each other. Valerie smiled at the sight.

"I thought about it, and I wanted to come out and support what you were doing," Pearl said as she proudly looked at her daughter. "I think Lamar would have been very happy with the turn out."

"Well…when you invite folks to a free party with free drinks… black people are going to show up," Heidi said.

"And show up early!" Valerie shouted from across the room. The women laughed at the joke.

Heidi looked at her mother's neck and saw that she wore the locket she'd gifted her with a few days ago. "I see you are wearing my gift." Heidi nodded towards the platinum chain.

"Oh yes." Pearl smiled as she slowly grazed over the charm. "I didn't open the locket yet. I was afraid to."

Heidi smiled at Pearl. "It's okay, Mom. Open it when you're ready. I'm pretty sure you are going to love it." Heidi turned around and looked at Tycen. He was still standing by the door. She invited him in. "Mom…I want to introduce you to my friend, Tycen." Heidi said as he approached.

"We already met him," Valerie replied as she walked over to Heidi and Pearl.

Tycen walked over and shook Pearl's hand again. "Yes…we met a few minutes ago," he said as he humbly stood next to the women.

"And you were right child," Valerie whispered with a smile. "Brother is fine like that." Pearl playfully nudged her sister and smiled at Tycen. Heidi shook her head and looked at her aunt.

"And you say that I'm too much?" Heidi joked, winking at Valerie. "So how long are you guys staying for?"

"We can't stay long," Pearl responded. "We have to get Janaya home. I'm nervous about having her around all this chaos."

"I understand, Mom. So I will do it now."

"Do what?" Pearl asked.

"I wrote a small dedication to Lamar," Heidi responded and reached in her bag. She grabbed a small piece of paper and quickly looked it over. "Tycen can you take my family to the dance floor and look after them? I'm goin' to the DJ booth to grab the microphone."

"Okay," Tycen agreed, nodding his head.

Valerie and Pearl looked at each other as Heidi left the VIP room. They followed closely behind Tycen as he led them through the thick crowd. Heidi walked over to the elevated stage where DJ Symphony continued to spin records.

The DJ noticed Heidi walking towards him. Reaching out his hand, he helped Heidi up onto the stage. "This party is crazy, Heidi," DJ Symphony yelled as he took off his headphones.

"I know...I didn't think this many people needed a drink tonight," Heidi joked. DJ Symphony smiled at Heidi. "I need the mic, baby. I want to get this out the way before these people get too crazy in here."

"Okay...just give me the cue, and I will turn you up." The DJ gave Heidi the microphone. Heidi felt her cellphone buzzing in her bag, but decided to ignore the call. She gave DJ Symphony the thumbs-up and nodded her head. The music slowly faded out as everyone in the ballroom turned their attention to the DJ booth.

"One...two...testin' one-two..." Heidi spoke into the microphone and adjusted her voice to the volume. "I want to give a shout out to everyone that came out to celebrate the birthday of Lamar Kachina." The crowd erupted into a boisterous cheer. The festive crowd clapped and yelled Lamar's name as Heidi continued to speak. "Now I know some of you knew my brother from when he was runnin' the streets back in the day. And some of you knew him from doin' time with him. But I know some of you don't even know him at all...y'all just wanted to come out and get drunk for free!" Laughter came from the audience. Valerie and Pearl laughed at the joke as Heidi continued to speak. "But in all seriousness...if you ever met my brother and sat with him...then you know what type of person we are celebrating today. Not only was my brother very intelligent…but he had a big heart." Heidi paused for a moment as she continued to read the small paper. She began to get emotional about Lamar. "He was always there for me and my family, and although he is gone forever…his spirit will live on through his family." Another loud cheer erupted from the crowd. Pearl found herself becoming emotional as well and clapped her hands along with the rest of the crowd. Heidi continued to speak about Lamar. "So tonight I don't want this to be a sad occasion. I want you guys to party hard for the memory of my brother. So everything is on me tonight. I don't want you guys to reach in your pocket for a dime. I know my brother is watching us wherever he is, and I just want to tell him that I love him and I miss him. Thank you."

DJ Symphony played another song and the crowd clapped for Heidi. The mood in the ballroom remained joyful. People began to dance and celebrate as the DJ turned up the music. Heidi smiled at DJ Symphony and carefully got off the stage. Pearl and her family walked towards the VIP room and Heidi followed them.

"That was beautiful Heidi," Pearl said as they walked into the bright room. "Seriously."

"Yes, it was," Valerie agreed. "I'm so proud of you."

Heidi hugged her mother and her aunt. "I know Lamar would love to see all these people here for him tonight." Heidi's phone started buzzing again. "Damn…this phone was buzzing the whole time I was up on stage." Heidi shook her head. "Let me get this." She walked to the other side of the room and reached for her phone.

Valerie and Pearl took a seat.

"Would you guys like something to drink?" Tycen asked as he looked at Pearl.

"Why yes, young man." Valerie smiled at Tycen. "Can you get me a cranberry juice?"

"I sure can."

"I'll take the same thing," Pearl added. "Janaya…do you want something to drink?"

Janaya shook her head.

"Okay…just two cranberry juices," Tycen confirmed. "I will be right back."

Heidi watched Tycen leave the room and looked at her phone. Her heart skipped a beat when she saw that she'd missed six calls from Rueben. She became nervous as she frantically called Rueben's phone and waited for him to answer.

"Heidi where are you?" Rueben yelled from the other line. He sounded out of breath.

"I'm at my brother's birthday party. What's goin' on?"

"No…I mean are you close by?" Rueben quickly asked.

"To where?"

"Betty's place?"

"I'm in Newark right now."

"I need you over here like right now!" Rueben barked. His voice sounded angry. Heidi heard a few strange noises in the background and became nervous.

"What's going on, Rueben?" Heidi asked. "You are scaring me."

"We found this motherfuckin' nigga, Rick!" Rueben shouted.

"Holy shit!" Heidi gasped. "Seriously?" Her voice echoed in the VIP room. Pearl turned to her daughter and looked at her.

"He's here right now! We got this nigga," Rueben continued. "But he told us somethin' that I think you should hear for yourself."

"What did he say?" Heidi asked. Her adrenaline caused her to speak louder into the phone.

"Just come here now, Heidi," Rueben urged. "Trust me…I think you really wanna hear this shit."

Heidi turned and looked at her mother. She thought for moment and continued to speak into the phone. "Okay…I am on my way right now. Keep him there." Heidi hung up the phone and walked over to her mother.

"What was that all about Heidi?" Pearl asked as she gave her daughter a worried expression.

"I have to go, Mom," Heidi said.

"Right now?" Pearl asked as she stood up.

"Yes."

"You just got here! Who was that on the phone?"

"Not right now, Mom…really…I have to go. I will be right back," she snapped.

Pearl sensed apprehension in her daughter's voice. Heidi turned around to leave and Pearl grabbed her arm. "Heidi …wait…" Pearl whispered. "What's going on?"

"Mom, I can say right now. I have to take care of something… but I have to go now."

Pearl gave her daughter another worried look. "Is it that serious? You have that *look* in your eyes, baby. Are you sure you have to go now?"

"Yes, Mom…I gotta do this!" Heidi uttered. "This may be my only chance to handle this."

Pearl's looked at her daughter for a moment. She could tell that Heidi was up to something, but she decided not to press the issue. "Just be careful. Please."

Heidi nodded her head and left the VIP room. She fought her way through the thick crowd, rushing outside. It didn't take long for her to hop in her truck and fire up the engine. Heidi punched the gas and peeled out of the parking space. The loud sound of the screeching tires startled the crowd in front of the ballroom. Heidi made a quick u-turn and barely missed a marine-blue Range Rover that was parked on the other side of the street. She pushed her truck to the limit and sped up the street en route to Dirty Betty's Go-Go Bar.

Chapter 39

Patterson, NJ

Friday February 27, 2009
9:14 p.m.

*T*he back streets of Patterson where extremely dark as Heidi made her way to Betty's bar. The V-6 engine in her SUV screamed as she pushed the gas pedal to the floor. Although she was only a few blocks away from the club, Heidi felt like she couldn't make it there fast enough. Her body trembled with excitement and anxiety as she thought about the news from Rueben. She couldn't wait to find out just how much Rick knew about the death of her brother, Lamar and her best friend, Faith.

The front of the strip club was just like any typical Friday night. Men and women alike lined the side of the club, impatiently waiting to get in. The bouncers near the entrance were frisking the patrons before they walked into the bar. Heidi immediately noticed that Rueben was not on the door. She quickly pulled into the parking lot and grabbed her phone. She noticed that she missed a few more calls from Rueben and quickly dialed his number.

Rueben wasted no time in answering the call. "Please tell me that you're here!" he barked. He sounded strange.

Heidi immediately picked up on his aggressive tone. "Yes…I'm outside!" she fired back. "I just pulled up."

"Okay, I'll meet you outside." Before Heidi could say another word Rueben disconnected the call.

Heidi shook her head and put the cellphone in her glove box. She got out of the truck and rushed towards the front entrance of the club. She was contemplating cutting the long line when she heard a burly voice yelling her name from the other side of the building. It was Rueben. He pushed the door wide opened and motioned for Heidi to come toward him.

"This way!" Rueben yelled, waving his hand. Heidi made a bee-line and rushed over. "We are goin' in this way!" Rueben continued. "We got this nigga in the basement, in the second kitchen."

Heidi's eyes widened as she followed Rueben into the side door and down a flight of stairs. She felt her heart pounding as she walked through the dark rooms below the club. She could hear the muffled sound of music coming from the main lounge above them.

"You wouldn't believe how we found this dude," Rueben said as he continued to maneuver through the dimly lit space.

"Where was he?" Heidi asked as she found herself stumbling over a pile of trash in the junkie basement.

"He was gettin' drunk with some cats I know down in Jersey City. He was so fuckin' wasted that he started talkin' 'bout some money scheme he wished he could do again."

"Are you serious?" Heidi asked.

"Hell yea! I don't know where y'all found this dude...but he's not too bright," Rueben joked. "And on top of that...he starts talkin' about how he been tryin' to get some money from some girl for the past couple of years now."

Heidi stopped in her tracks. "Who's the girl? Me?"

Rueben turned around and looked at Heidi. "I don't know. That's why I wanted you to come here. We had him here for a couple of hours. He's been tellin' us all types of shit tonight."

"Us?" Heidi asked.

Rueben ignored the question and continued down the dimly lit hall.

Heidi picked up the pace and followed close behind as Rueben approached a large brown door. He banged on the door and waited for a moment. Heidi started to feel nervous again as she heard footsteps just beyond the other side of the door. Rueben stepped back as the large door slowly opened.

"Is she with you?" A raspy female voice asked.

Heidi couldn't see the face, but she immediately recognized the voice. Dirty Betty. Rueben nodded his head and walked into the room. He grabbed Heidi by the arm and pulled her inside. Heidi immediately covered her mouth and nose. The smell in the room was beyond rancid. She was becoming more nauseous with every breath. Betty and Rueben continued to walk towards the back. Heidi followed them and twisted her face as she looked around. She noticed the large room was actually an old kitchen like Rueben had said. Heidi assumed the smell was coming from the spoiled food in the sinks and possibly a few dead rodents, but as she rounded a corner Heidi made a grisly discovery.

Ruben approached two men as they stood near the back of the kitchen. They were hovering over another man tied to a chair. The man was stripped down to his boxers and bleeding from his head and chest. His right arm and leg were badly burned. Heidi almost gagged at the sight of the torture. She looked closely at the man and instantly recognized him. Rick. He was breathing heavy as he sat helplessly in the chair. Heidi could clearly see the fear that was beaten into his eyes. Betty walked over to Rick and stood over him.

"We brought somebody to see you, Ricky," Betty sinisterly mocked as she stood over him. "Come over here," Betty motioned for Heidi.

Heidi slowly walked over to Betty and looked at Rick. He slowly lifted his head and looked up to her.

"Heidi, please help me," Rick managed to moan through the pain, beginning to weep.

"Shut the fuck up!" Rueben yelled. He punched Rick square in the face, then shouted another insult to him.

Heidi turned away from Rick as blood flew from his mouth.

"Goddamn girl…don't tell me that you scared of a little blood," Betty said as she laughed at Heidi. Betty was clearly detached from the horrific scene as a devilish smile came to her face. "Boys…it looks like we got a rookie on our hands."

Heidi looked over to Betty, but decided not to respond to her. She continued to cringe as Betty's goons smacked and punched Rick. "Okay enough!" Heidi yelled as she moved closer to Rick. "Don't kill him yet. Jesus!" Betty took a step back from Rick and made room for Heidi. "Rick can you hear me?" Heidi asked as she moved closer to him. "You brought this shit on yourself, Rick! I can't help you right now."

Rick slowly shook his head. Blood dripped from the side of his mouth as he struggled to hold his head up. "It wasn't me," he whispered.

"What do you mean...*it wasn't you?*" Heidi mumbled as a confused look came to her face. "I didn't ask you nothin' yet!"

"He's been sayin' that shit all night," Betty said.

"It wasn't me," Rick whispered again. "I didn't kill her."

"Kill who?" Heidi asked.

"Faith." His voice was weak.

"Then who did it?" Rueben barked as he reached back to hit Rick again.

Heidi quickly grabbed his arm to stop him. "Wait...not yet!' Heidi ordered. "Tell me Rick...what happened that night? Who killed Faith and my brother?"

Rick looked up to Heidi and slowly exhaled. "Vegas did that shit...it wasn't me. I swear," he confessed. "He went crazy that night and started poppin' everybody."

"So why the fuck were you helpin' them?" Heidi yelled, becoming angrier.

Rick didn't say a word.

"Answer me!" Heidi yelled. Her voice echoed in the kitchen and shook Rick.

"I needed the money," Rick uttered.

"So because you needed the money, my brother had to die that night?" Heidi shouted. She couldn't restrain her emotions any longer. Heidi smacked Rick on the side of the head, then quickly backhanded him on the bridge of his nose. "You a fuckin' snake,

Rick!" Heidi hollered as she continued to hit Rick. Betty laughed with excitement as she watched the beating. "You crossed my family over some goddamn money?"

"Please Heidi…stop!" Rick yelled. "I know I fucked up…but it was my money. I had to get it!"

Heidi paused for a moment and stared at Rick. "What do you mean *it was your money?*"

"It was my money," Rick continued. "Jayson promised me that money."

"What?" Heidi whispered. She almost lost her breath when she heard Jayson's name. "My fiancé, Jayson?"

Rick's head fell back as he realized his mistake. He looked up to Heidi, who was anticipating his next words. "Heidi, you gotta let me go." "Fuck that…tell me!" Heidi shouted. "What do you mean Jayson promised you money? What the hell is goin' on here?"

"I can't Heidi," Rick mumbled. "You are goin' to kill me if I tell you."

"I'm gonna kill you if you don't!"

"Tell her," Rueben snapped.

Rick dropped his head and closed his eyes. He emphatically shook his head, and didn't say another word.

Rueben grabbed a coffee mug from a counter next to him. "This will make him talk."

Before Rick could react, Rueben dumped the liquid out of the cup onto Ricks left leg. Rick yelled to the top of his lungs. Heidi watched the liquid burn through Rick's skin in a matter of seconds. She frowned at the disgusting smell of burning flesh. Heidi looked over to Rueben in shock.

"Battery acid," Rueben revealed. "He's gonna tell you anything you wanna know now."

Heidi turned back to Rick trembling with pain. He continued to yell as the acid burned his skin like a hot iron. "Don't make this any worse than what it has to be, Rick." Heidi said. "Now what does all this have to do with Jayson?"

Rick dropped his head again. He was in tears. Rick started to mumble to himself. He was praying.

"Rick!" Rueben yelled. "Focus nigga!"

"Talk to me, Rick...was Jayson involved in this shit?" Heidi asked.

"Yes Heidi," Rick whispered. His voice was trembling as he forced himself to speak through the pain. "Jayson came to me a few years ago..." Rick paused, reflecting for a moment. "Jayson came to me and said he was approached by some girl with an idea to take some money from Datakorp."

"What?" Heidi said as she covered her mouth.

"Yes, he told me that all I had to do was open up a new account and give him the account number, then he would do the rest," Rick continued. "So that's what I did. I opened the account and sent him some flowers with the account number attached to them."

Heidi covered her face and walked away from Rick. "So you sent him the flowers?" she asked as she turned around. Rick nodded his head. "I can't believe this shit. So you were involved the whole time?"

"Not like that." Rick became more nervous. "I was out of the mix until that girl called me last year. She told me that they were goin' to try it again, and asked me to help them. So I did. But I swear I didn't know anybody was goin' to get killed."

"Whatever Rick!" Heidi calmly said. She was clearly holding back her anger. "Somebody did get killed. My family."

"Heidi, you gotta believe me," Rick pleaded. "I swear I didn't know it was goin' to go down that way."

"So where's Aaron?" Heidi quickly asked.

"I don't know who that is."

"You're lying!" Heidi snapped.

Rueben reached for the cup again and looked at Rick.

"Please...don't...please," Rick pleaded. "I don't know who that is. I swear."

"So who was the girl?" Heidi asked as she stared at Rick. "Who was the girl that Jayson was working with?"

"Her name is Judith Smith," Rick responded. "I think she still works at Datakorp."

All the blood rushed from Heidi's head and flooded her stomach. She almost collapsed at the revelation as she stumbled against Rueben.

"Are you okay?" Rueben asked.

"That bitch played me the whole time," Heidi blurted. She thought about the money in her Datakorp account and grabbed her head with both hands. "*Fuck*! I gotta go!" Heidi turned around and headed for the exit.

"Whoa, Heidi!" Betty yelled. "Where are you goin'?"

"I gotta find this bitch Judith. She has access to my account."

"What about him?" Betty asked as she pointed at Rick.

Heidi turned to Rick and gave him a cold stare. "Fuck him!" she whispered, coldly condemning Rick. She turned around and rushed through the dark hallway. She needed to get back to her phone in the car. Heidi made her way through the dark rooms and quickly approached the side door to the outside. She heard a single gunshot echo from the old kitchen and knew Rick was dead. A major score was finally settled, but Heidi's problems were only mounting.

Chapter 40

Newark, New Jersey

Friday February 27, 2009
10:22 p.m.

We're sorry, but the number you have reached is not in service at this time. Please hang up and try your call again.

"Shit!" Heidi yelled in frustration. She slammed the phone in her lap, and turned her attention back to the road. Heidi found herself speeding down the highway as she made her way back to Newark. Her tires hugged the road as she made a quick exit onto Broad Street, making her way back to Lamar's party.

She called Judith's phone once again and got the same message. Judith's phone was disconnected. A million thoughts raced through Heidi's mind. The news from Rick's mouth hit her like a ton of bricks. She couldn't believe Judith was involved with the Datakorp scheme from the beginning. Heidi thought for a moment and tried to call Judith once again. Before she could dial the number, another call popped up on her screen. It was Tycen.

"Hey beautiful!" Tycen uttered as Heidi answered the call.

"I'm sorry, baby…I have to call you right back," Heidi blurted. Her voice sounded desperate. She rushed through another green light and continued to speak to Tycen. "I'm only a few blocks away from the ballroom."

"Is everything okay?" Tycen asked. "I just wanted to let you know that I left the party already."

"You did?" Heidi gasped. "Is my mom still there?"

"I don't know," Tycen responded. "Your aunt said they were leaving, but they were still there when I left the party."

"How long ago was that?"

"About an hour ago."

"Damn." Heidi approached the ballroom. There were police cars and fire engines scattered about the block. A large crowd of people were standing in front of the building. Heidi's heart pounded with fear. "What happened here?" Heidi unconsciously whispered.

"Where?" Tycen asked from the other line.

"What the fuck?" Heidi mumbled. She almost forgot she was on the phone as she approached the front of the ballroom. It appeared as if everyone from the party was outside in the front. The sight reminded Heidi of a large protest as police and fireman tried to maintain order in front of the building. "I gotta go." She hung up the phone on Tycen, quickly parking the SUV. Her mouth was wide opened as she got out of her vehicle and looked around. There were no signs of her mother or Valerie. Heidi pushed her way through the large crowd and made her way to the front door. There were a few policemen forcing the remaining club-goers out of the building. "What happened here?" Heidi yelled as she approached the policemen.

"You have to back up, Ma'am," one officer ordered.

"My name is Heidi Kachina. I put this party together," Heidi continued to yell as she moved closer to the door. "What happened?"

Another officer walked over to the front door. "This is your party?" the officer asked.

"Yes. What's goin' on?"

"Around 9:30 tonight somebody called in a bomb threat for this building."

"What?" Heidi covered her mouth.

"The bomb threat came from an anonymous caller, but we have to take it serious," the officer continued. "We are making sure everyone gets out of the building safely."

Heidi became nervous. She grabbed her phone and called her

mother. She walked away from the officers and waited for the call to connect. After a few rings the call was redirected to the voicemail. "Mom…where are you?" Heidi whispered into the phone. "Call me back, I'm at the club." Heidi ended the call and looked around the crowded street. She became emotional as she scanned a sea of strange faces in the crowd. Heidi did a double take when she saw a woman that looked like Judith a few feet from her. Heidi became angry. She momentarily shook the ugly feeling when she realized her mind was playing tricks on her. The woman was a complete stranger. Heidi shook her head when she walked by the woman and looked at her phone. She decided to call Valerie. After a few rings, her aunt's phone also went to voicemail. Heidi decided not to leave a message. She disconnected the call with disgust. She continued to call her mother's phone as she walked through the crowd, searching for her family.

"Heidi!" a familiar voice yelled from a distance. Heidi turned around and noticed a young man quickly walking up behind her. It was DJ Symphony. He pushed his way through the crowd.

"Hey…I'm tryin' to find my mother," Heidi yelled over the loud crowd as she approached the DJ. "Have you seen my mother and my family?"

"What's good, Heidi?" DJ Symphony asked. "I saw them earlier before the cops came in and told everybody to leave. But that was about forty-five minutes ago. I think they left already. The cops said it was a bomb threat or something."

"They told me the same thing…this is some bullshit!" Heidi shouted. "So you think my mother left already?"

"A lot of people left after they made that announcement," DJ Symphony continued. "Is everything good, Heidi?"

"I really don't know. If you see them, please call me!" Heidi past DJ Symphony, walking back to her truck. She looked at her phone again and dialed her mother. There was still no answer. Heidi became extremely worried. She couldn't imagine why Pearl was not picking up the phone. Heidi felt powerless as she scrolled down her list of contacts. She didn't have many options to reach out to.

314

She decided to get the police involved. She selected a familiar name and called the number. After a few rings, a male voice answered from the other line.

"Detective Williams, this is Heidi. I'm so sorry to bother you so late."

"Hello, Heidi. It's not a problem," Harold said. "Where are you? There's a lot of noise behind you."

"I'm at my brother's party down here in Newark," Heidi continued. "There was a bomb scare here, and I can't find my mother."

"Holy shit!" Harold mumbled. "I heard that call go over the radio, but I didn't know it was your party. Are you okay?" Harold asked.

"I'm just worried out of my mind right now. I been calling my mother for the past twenty minutes, and I'm getting' no answer. Are you working now?"

"I just got off not too long ago. If you want, I can go by your aunt's house and make sure everything is okay."

"Oh God…thank you so much!" Heidi shouted. "I'm trying to get back to my truck now. It's so many goddamn people out here. I will meet you down at my aunt's house, Detective."

"Okay…I am on my way right now," Harold said. "I should be there in about fifteen minutes."

"Great…I will meet you there." Heidi disconnected the call and tucked the phone in her fist.

She continued to push her way through the rowdy crowd and walk toward her truck. The Newark Police continued to force people away from the scene, fearing that a bomb would level the building at any moment. Heidi ignored the cops and fought her way back to the SUV. She unlocked her doors and hurried into the driver's seat. Heidi started the truck, and honked her horn as a few people stood in front of the vehicle. As the small group rushed to get out of her way, a strange noise chimed from Heidi's cell phone. She was receiving a text message. Heidi quickly looked at the message, hoping it was from her mother. Heidi had to adjust her focus as she looked at her phone with a horrified expression. She couldn't believe what she was reading.

"*Faith*!?" Heidi whispered as she read the incoming message. Heidi stopped breathing. She couldn't believe she was getting a message from her best friend's phone. Heidi exhaled a lung full of air as her heart started to pound through her chest. She put her palm on the front of her head, and nervously read the messages to herself: "*It looks like ya best friend was good for something after all, Heidi. We have ya family bitch, so don't get cute. You know who this is and you know what this is about. Meet us at the house if you ever wanna see ya family alive again. We got some unfinished business that needs to get handled tonight!*"

Heidi's face erupted into tears. Her entire body trembled with fear as she read the message again. Before she could finish rereading the first sentence, another message came in from Faith's cellphone. This time it was a Picture-Mail. Heidi began to feel light-headed. She was reluctant to look at the photo. But before she could stop herself, her thumbs were clicking on her phone and opening the file. Heidi covered her mouth as the image loaded. She sunk further into her seat as she stared at a shocking image of Vegas pointing a gun directly at Pearl and Valerie as they sat on a familiar looking sofa. Heidi's tears continued to flow as she looked closer at the photo. She screamed when she saw her baby cousin, Janaya sitting next to her aunt. Heidi felt a thick stream of anger rush through her body. She looked at the photo again, concentrating on the background. She knew exactly where Vegas was holding her family. Heidi forced the truck into drive and sped down Broad Street. She wiped away the tears from her angry face and reached under the car seat. Revenge gripped her mind as she grabbed a black pistol and placed it on her lap. Heidi never looked back as she sped up the dark road ahead.

Chapter 41

Valerie's House
Edison, New Jersey

Friday February 27, 2009
10:46 p.m.

A feeling of déjà vu came over Detective Harold Williams as he carefully turned onto Valerie's block. The neighborhood was calm this evening, and Harold almost felt like he was the only live body moving about the quiet street. He suspiciously surveyed the area as he slowed his vehicle down to a crawl. All of the houses were illuminated by street lamps and porch lights until he pulled up to Valerie's home. He parked his car in the front of the residence and looked around. The house was completely dark. Harold immediately noticed that there were no cars in the driveway. He became slightly confused as he turned off the police cruiser and got out. The neighborhood was extremely still. Harold slowly walked through the gate and approached the front door. He tried to listen for any strange noises, but the house was completely quiet. He rang the doorbell and waited for a response. After a few more attempts, he realized there was no movement in the house. Harold looked through the front window.

"Helloooo…!" the detective called out as he looked into the house. The front room was completely silent. It was clear that neither Pearl nor Valerie was home, but Harold wanted to make certain. He cautiously walked around to the rear of the house. He looked closely at the backyard area for any signs of foul play. After a careful eye test, Harold determined that everything was in order. He decided to try knocking on the backdoor.

"Helloooo…!" Harold yelled again as he pounded on the back window. There was still no answer. He looked around the dark yard again, and headed back to the front of the house.

A nervous feeling came over him as he walked back toward his police car. He grabbed his cell phone and dialed Pearl's number. After a few rings, he was redirected to her voicemail. Harold stood next to his car and shook his head. *Where are you?* He decided to call Heidi to see how far she was from Valerie's house. After a few rings, Heidi picked up the phone.

"I'm at your aunt's house now, Heidi."

"My mother's not there," Heidi coldly said from the other line. Her tone seemed to be angry.

"I know that, Heidi…I'm here now." Harold immediately picked up on her dark tone. "Are you okay? Where are you?"

"On my way to take care of some unfinished business," Heidi blurted.

"What…" Harold whispered. "What are you talking about? Where are you going?"

"Just stay there detective," Heidi snapped. "I'm goin' to go get my family. This bullshit ends tonight!"

"Wait Hei—"

Heidi disconnected the call.

He tried to call Heidi back, but she refused to answer the phone. Harold called Pearl again and got no answer. *What the hell is going on?*. He slowly took a seat in the police cruiser and tried to figure out where Heidi was headed.

* * *

Pearl's House
East Orange, New Jersey

Friday February 27, 2009
11:21 p.m.

"Everybody sit down right there and don't say shit!" Vegas ordered as he raised his gun to Pearl and Valerie. The women didn't say a word as they obeyed the order, quietly sitting on the sofa in the living room. Vegas took a seat in a wooden chair directly across from the women. He continued to point his gun at them. Valerie held onto her granddaughter, Janaya, who continued to shake like a leaf. She was beyond petrified. Janaya tried her best not to cry, but the fear caused her little heart to work overtime.

Pearl looked over to her grand-niece and shook her head. She was angry with Shaheed and Vegas, but she tried her best to disguise it. She knew they were in a bad situation that could turn severe at any moment. She looked around the living room, and tried to come up with a plan to get out of the house. Vegas had pushed the sofa in front of the door so no one could come in or out it. The only way out of the house was through the back door. With no weapons or phones, Pearl and Valerie would have to pull off the impossible to make it to safety.

Pearl's mood started to darken as she looked around the familiar surroundings. She hadn't stepped foot inside her old house since the night her son died. Although the house had since been cleaned and repainted, the stark aura of fear and death was still present. She tried to shake the images, but they continued to flash in and out of her memory. Pearl unconsciously turned to Vegas as recollections of her son, Lamar haunted her mind.

Vegas noticed Pearl looking at him and gave her a hard stare. "I bet you never thought you would see me again, huh?" his whisper was cold.

Pearl didn't say a word. Her heart raced with adrenaline, but she never changed her facial expression.

"But don't worry…" Vegas continued. "After tonight…you will never see me again." Vegas had a menacing smirk. Something in his tone scared Pearl.

She turned to her sister, who was clearly gripped by fear. Pearl tried to give her a reassuring gesture, but Valerie could see that Pearl was just as scared as she was.

A noise came from the kitchen causing everyone to turn their attention toward the back of the house. It was Shaheed walking into the living room. He held a red cell phone in one hand and a pistol in the other. He looked over to Vegas and gave him a tense look.

"Heidi is still not pickin' up her phone," Shaheed said. "And I think she turned her shit off."

Vegas didn't say a word. He turned around and continued to stare at Pearl and Valerie.

"Did you hear what I just said?" Shaheed snapped as he stood over his cousin.

Vegas slowly looked up to a nervous Shaheed. "Nigga…I heard you. I'm not deaf," he responded. "It's cool."

"What you mean *it's cool*…I can't find her," Shaheed said.

Vegas picked up on the fear in his cousin's voice and stood up. He pulled Shaheed to the back of the living room, away from the women, but he still kept his gun on them. "What the fuck is your problem, Shah'?" He tried to whisper but his deep voice nearly echoed throughout the entire house.

"Homie, this is all wrong," Shaheed said as he looked at his cousin. "I thought we was gonna snatch Heidi. That's it. You didn't say shit about bringin' her family here."

"So what!" Vegas shouted. "Heidi is comin' here, and we gonna get the money from her…that's it. It ain't shit else to talk about, Shah'."

"So what if she bring somebody with her?" Shaheed asked.

Pearl turned to Vegas and paid close attention to the argument.

"Like who?" Vegas asked.

"Like the cops, nigga…" Shaheed responded.

"Man…would you calm the fuck down?" Vegas waved his

cousin off.

"I'm calm, man...but I'm not goin' back!" Shaheed snapped at Vegas.

"What?"

"To jail...I'm not goin' back," Shaheed responded. "Or did you forget that shit. I'm the one that went to jail...*not you*. And I'm not goin' back. Not for this shit...you can forget that."

Vegas shook his head and pointed to the kitchen with his left thumb. "Man...go 'head with that shit. This is not the time for *bitchin' up*. Take a walk, and make sure Heidi doesn't come through that back door. That's what you need to do. And you need to stop bein' a bitch about all this. What the fuck, Shah'...you worse than your brother, Robert."

Shaheed gave his older cousin a cold stare. He was clearly growing more disgusted with Vegas with each passing moment. His disrespectful words cut into Shaheed's pride like a rusty blade. Shaheed was beyond upset with Vegas' derogatory reference to his dead brother. He shook his head and looked away from his cousin. He thought about confronting Vegas, but decided against it. Shaheed slowly turned around and headed toward the kitchen without incident.

Vegas waved his cousin off, then turned his attention back to the women on the living room sofa. He slowly walked toward the wooden chair, keeping his gun raised and pointed at Pearl. Vegas was agitated. His grey eyes glanced over Pearl with contempt. "So where is she hiding the money?" Vegas stared at Pearl.

She gave him a confused look and closed her mouth.

"Heidi has some money that doesn't belong to her," Vegas continued. "Where is it?"

Pearl's eyes grew wider. She looked over to Valerie and shook her head. "I don't know what you are talking about," Pearl whispered as she turned back to Vegas.

"You're lying to me," Vegas said as he raised his voice. "Don't lie to me again...I'm goin' to ask you one more time. Where is the fuckin' money Heidi took from us?"

Pearl didn't know how to answer the question. She looked over to Valerie and Janaya a second time, then turned back to Vegas. "I don't know about no money...I'm sorry," Pearl lied.

Vegas lowered his eyebrows and gave Pearl a threatening gesture. He looked over to her sister, Valerie for a moment. "What about you?" Vegas asked. "Where's the money? Do you know?"

Valerie shook her head. "I don't know," she mumbled. Valerie's voice trembled with fear. "Heidi never mentioned any money to us."

Vegas slowly nodded his head.

Pearl felt uneasy about the look on his face. She could tell that his patience was wearing thin.

Vegas turned his attention to Janaya. "What about you, little girl...do *you* know?" he whispered to Janaya, who frightfully turned away from him. "No...you don't know either, huh?" he mocked Janaya as he angrily shook his head. He looked back to Pearl. "I'm gonna ask y'all one more time. Where is the fuckin' money?"

The entire living room fell silent. Pearl nervously stared at Vegas, speechless. Valerie tightly grabbed Janaya.

Vegas balled up his lip in anger. "Sha'...!" he yelled. His angry voice shook the living room. He turned around as Shaheed walked out of the kitchen. "Grab me a knife out of there."

"What?" Shaheed asked as he moved closer to Vegas.

"Just do it," Vegas ordered. "Grab me the sharpest knife you can find."

Shaheed walked back to the kitchen. Pearl's heart started to pound as she thought about Vegas' request. Her mind raced again as she sensed that the women were running out of time. Shaheed returned with the knife and gave it to his cousin. Vegas looked at Pearl and gave her a dreadful look.

"I'm goin' to get y'all to talk one way or another," Vegas said. He quickly tucked his gun away between his beltline and his stomach. He gripped the kitchen knife in his right palm, walking over toward Valerie. Before she could react, Vegas reached out and snatched Janaya by the arm. His brute strength surprised Valerie as he pulled the little girl up and out of her clutches like a ragdoll.

"Oh God!" Valerie shouted as she reached out for Janaya. Vegas reacted by swinging at Valerie, smashing her on the side of the head with the back of his fist. The momentum from the blow caused the knife to cut Valerie on the side of her face. Pearl screamed in horror.

Shaheed was stunned by the move, and quickly raised his gun and pointed it at Pearl. "Don't move!" he shouted.

"Sit down, bitch!" Vegas yelled at Valerie.

Blood began to slowly trickle from Valerie's face, closely followed by tears. Valerie grabbed the side of her face, groaning in pain. She was dazed, but still conscious.

Vegas pulled Janaya to the other side of the room, and turned her around so she faced Pearl. Vegas put a tight grip on Janaya's shoulder, then put the sharp blade to the little girl's neck.

"Wait…Vegas, don't do that," Pearl uttered as she stood to her feet.

"Sit the fuck down!" Shaheed nervously shouted as he put a tighter grip on his gun.

"Tell me where the money is," Vegas yelled.

"Leave her out of this," Pearl pleaded. "She's just a child." Pearl looked at Janaya's frightened face, which was full of tears. She watched helplessly as Vegas continued to put the kitchen knife closer and closer to Janaya's neck. "Vegas…I am tellin' you the truth. We don't know shit about no money Heidi got."

"You're fuckin' lying again!" Vegas yelled.

"No…I'm not lying," Pearl whispered as she continued to stand on the other side of the room. She kept her eyes on Janaya, and tried to keep her calm. "Janaya, baby…don't move. It's gonna be okay."

"I don't know about that," Vegas responded to Pearl's comments.

"Owwwww…" Janaya whined as Vegas slightly poked the knife into the side of her neck. Janaya's voice caused a few tears to come to Pearl's eyes.

"Vegas…you don't want to do that," Pearl whispered as her heart raced out of control.

"How do you know I don't wanna do this?" Vegas said. "Where is the fuckin' money?"

Shaheed looked over to his cousin, then down to Janaya. He noticed a slight drop of blood coming from the young girl's neck, and became emotional. He tried to keep his game face on, but the scene was becoming unbearable. "Vegas…what are you doin' man?" Shaheed mumbled. "This was not part of the plan."

"Fuck the plan," Vegas blurted. "I'm tired of this shit. Bitch… where is the money?" Vegas yelled at Pearl.

Shaheed kept his gun on Pearl and moved closer to Vegas. Valerie started to come back around as she stared at her granddaughter.

"Man…this is not the way to go, Cousin," Shaheed pleaded as he walked over to Vegas. "She's a little girl." Shaheed looked down to Janaya. Her face was overflowing with tears.

Vegas continued to hold the knife to her throat. Shaheed's conscious slowly began to get the best of him as he looked at the frightened eyes of Janaya.

"I'm gonna ask you one more time," Vegas said as he gave Pearl a colder stare. "And I think you know what's gonna happen next."

The entire living room fell silent. Pearl felt helpless as she looked at Janaya.

"Let her go," Shaheed whispered to his cousin. His words shocked Vegas.

"What the fuck you say?" Vegas snapped.

"I can't let you do that, Cousin," Shaheed whispered. "This is crazy. Let her go, man. This is insane."

Vegas looked over to Shaheed with distain. "What the hell is wrong with you, nigga. Don't tell me that you bitchin' up on me again."

"It ain't about that," Shaheed shouted. He became angrier. Shaheed decided it was time to put an end to his cousin's madness. "Let her go Vegas…she's a little girl." Shaheed looked down to Janaya and noticed that his cousin was drawing more blood from her fragile neck. He rushed over toward Vegas and grabbed his arm. Pearl gasped as she watched a power struggle ensue. Shaheed grabbed Vegas by the wrist and tried to pull the knife away from

Janaya's neck.

"What the fuck are you doin', Shah'?" Vegas yelled. "Are you stupid?" He continued to force the knife towards Janya's neck, clearly too strong for his cousin.

Shaheed realized he was losing the battle as Vegas pushed the knife to her throat. Shaheed gave his cousin an evil gesture and made a desperate move. Before Vegas could react, he quickly swung at Vegas' head, hitting and him square in the face with the side of his gun. Vegas yelled in pain, stumbling backward toward the wall. All hell broke loose in the small living room. As Vegas tumbled, Shaheed pulled Janaya from his grasp. Valerie sprung into action and grabbed her granddaughter.

"Run!" Pearl shouted as she grabbed her sister by the arm. The women and Janaya bolted toward the back door.

Shaheed noticed the commotion and turned around. He grabbed Pearl by the arm. Valerie never looked back as she managed to make it through the kitchen, rushing outside with Janaya in tow. Pearl tried to break free from Shaheed's grip but he held her tightly. She didn't know what to expect as Shaheed gave her a strange look.

Blood rushed from Vegas' face as he tried to regain his balance. Instinctively, he reached for his nose. The sight of his own blood caused him to snap out. He threw the knife down and reached for his gun. His face was flushed with rage as he pointed the pistol at his cousin. Shaheed never knew what hit him as Vegas fired three shots.

"Jesus. No!" Pearl yelled as the bullets maliciously tore into Shaheed's back and spun him around. Pearl continued to scream in shock as Vegas kept firing at his cousin as if he was a total stranger. Two more bullets hit Shaheed in the shoulders, crumbling him to the floor. Pearl tried to run into the kitchen, but Vegas' wild firing caught her in the right thigh. She screamed in pain as the hot bullet tore into her flesh. She fell to the floor and cried out as she crawled into the kitchen. She couldn't believe she'd been shot.

Vegas seemed to be a man possessed as he kept firing inside the house. The bullets flew over Pearl's head until his gun emptied.

Pearl was petrified as she lay on her stomach. The clicking of Vegas' gun made her cringe in fear. She heard the deep pounding of his footsteps and turned around. She watched as Vegas tossed his empty gun and walked toward her like a stalker. Before she could scream, Vegas quickly reached down, grabbing her by the collar. His large hands pulled Pearl a few feet off the ground. Her feet dangled mid-air as he held her up by her sweater, like a bag of laundry. He forced her face close to his. His soulless eyes cut deep into her.

"Bitch, you got one more chance to tell me," Vegas grunted. "Where is Heidi keepin' the money?"

"Please…don't…" Pearl cried out.

Vegas never gave her a second chance to respond. He raised her up a few more feet, then threw Pearl's frail body clear across the kitchen. Pearl was instantly knocked unconscious when the back of her head slammed into the wooden cabinets. The loud crash shook the house.

Vegas looked at Pearl's battered body as an evil smile came to his face. His anger began to subside as he looked around, realizing he was the last man standing in the house. He turned his attention to his cousin on the floor. He had no remorse for Shaheed. He walked over to his cousin's bullet- riddled body and, for the first time tonight, reality began to set in. His plan to get the money from Heidi had seriously gone wrong. Valerie had escaped the house and now his cousin lay dying on the living room floor. He knew it was just a matter of time before the police would investigate the gunshots and storm the house.

He decided to abandon his plan. He walked out of the living room and looked at Pearl. She was out cold. He panicked. He rushed toward the back of the kitchen and reached for the doorknob. As Vegas swung opened the door, his heart jumped out of his chest. Heidi was standing near the entrance of the back door holding a shovel in her hand like a baseball bat. Before Vegas could react, Heidi mustered all the strength she could and swung the metal shovel. Vegas yelled like a wounded animal as the steel connected with the side of his head. She rushed him as he fell to the floor. He tried to shield himself, but Heidi continued to beat him.

"You should'a left my family alone!" she yelled.

Vegas became angrier with every blow. He waited for Heidi to lift her weapon again, then decided to make his move. She raised the shovel above her head once more, about to deliver a serious hit when Vegas cocked his left leg back, kicking her directly in her knee cap. The impact momentarily felt like Vegas broke her leg.

"Oww…fuck!" Heidi yelled as she found herself reeling backward.

Vegas quickly jumped to his feet and rushed Heidi. She tried to raise the shovel again, but she was too late. Before she knew it, Vegas was on her. He balled up his fist and punched her in the face like she was a man. The swift punch dazed her, but she continued to fight. She swung back, hitting him in the face and chest. Her light punches barely phased him as Vegas swung back, doing major damage to her face with each hit. Heidi's face began to bleed, but she kept fighting. She grabbed Vegas' neck with both of her hands, and began to choke him, digging her fingernails into his neck like an orange peel. She squeezed harder as she saw blood come through his skin. Vegas seemed to be oblivious to the pain. He continued to ruthlessly punish Heidi. She squeezed harder, trying to ignore her own demise. All of a sudden, Vegas made a bold move, picking Heidi up and off of her feet. He turned around with Heidi in his hands, slamming her to the floor. Heidi let out a primal cry as her back met the hard surface. All of the air rushed from her lungs, freezing her for a moment.

Vegas stared down at his victim, then wiped the blood from his neck. His adrenaline caused his hands to shake as he walked over to Heidi, who moaned in pain. Without a second thought, he decided to finish the job. He knelt down next to Heidi, then straddled her. He placed both of his large hands around her neck and slammed her head to the floor.

"Don't you fuckin' die on me yet, bitch!" Vegas yelled as he squeezed her neck. "Where it the fuckin' money?"

Heidi slowly opened her eyes and glared at Vegas. Her vision was blurred from the tears that started to form. She couldn't breathe with his hands around her neck so tightly. She slowly moved her lips and tried to answer him.

"What's that?" Vegas mumbled. "Where is it?"

Heidi continued to move her lips.

Vegas eased up on his grip, trying to hear what Heidi was trying to say. "Where's the money?" he asked again, moving closer to her face.

"Please don't kill me if I tell you where the money is," she whispered. She tried to catch her breath with Vegas sitting on top of her.

Vegas gave her a strange look. "I won't do it…I'll spare you," Vegas continued. "Just tell me where the money is."

"Okay," Heidi whispered. She purposely spoke very low so that Vegas could come closer to her. "I will tell you where the money is," she said, barely audible as she closed her eyes.

"Where is it?" Vegas asked.

Heidi started to move her mouth, but she didn't say a word.

Vegas moved closer to her face and tried to listen. "Where is it?"

"It's with—" Heidi cut herself short and grunted in pain.

Vegas moved closer to her face. "What?" Vegas frowned as he tried to figure out what Heidi was trying to say.

"It's with my brother, Lamar. You son of a bitch!" Heidi blurted.

Vegas eyes grew wide.

He never noticed Heidi reaching for the flip-action knife in her front pocket. She quickly flipped the sharp blade opened and ripped into the side of Vegas' neck. The blood spilled from his throat like a thick stream of water.

Vegas grabbed his neck and backed off of Heidi. He quickly stood up in shock, but there was nothing he could do. Heidi had delivered a fatal cut to his neck. He tried to speak, but he began to drown from his own blood. Heidi coldly watched as Vegas stumbled backward and fell against the kitchen wall. He tried to cover his wound, but the blood continued to flow. He was dying.

Heidi composed herself and stood to her feet just in time to watch Vegas fall to the floor. She wiped his blood from her face and stared.

She felt no pity as his hands dropped limply to his sides. Vegas looked at Heidi and never made another sound. With once last gasp of air, his grey eyes began to stare into eternity. He was dead.

Heidi dropped her head and stumbled her way over to her mother. She knelt down next to Pearl, and held her in her arms. She became emotional after realizing her mother was still alive. *Thank God.* She grabbed the cell phone out of her back pocket and called the police. She gave them her address and placed the phone by her side. Heidi closed her eyes and said a quick prayer for Pearl. She held her in her arms, waiting for help to arrive.

Epilogue

Valerie's House
Edison, New Jersey

Monday July 23, 2009
1:29 p.m.

Five Months Later

*T*he loud clanging of the front doorbell shook Valerie from her daydream. She had been quietly sitting on her living room sofa for over twenty minutes waiting on her ride to the airport. She yelled for Pearl and Janaya to come downstairs, assuming the car service had arrived to pick them up. Valerie slowly stood to her feet, then walked toward the front door. She counted the suitcases and bags on the living room floor one more time. She wanted to make sure she had all of her belongings for the long trip.

After the vicious episode a few months ago at Pearl's house, Valerie and her sister decided to move away from New Jersey and leave the dark memories behind. Valerie elected to transfer to another position within her company with better pay and better benefits. She'd asked her sister, Pearl to come along in exchange for helping her with raising Janaya. Pearl had agreed. The sisters decided to sell their respective houses and relocate to Chicago. The move would allow them to start their lives over again. Still, Valerie had mixed feelings about the move. She loved her house and never thought she would be leaving it behind so soon. But for the safety of Janaya and her family, Valerie had no other choice but to move away and avoid the risk of more bloodshed.

"Just one minute," Valerie called out as she walked toward the front door. She unlocked the top and bottom locks, then opened the door. Her mouth fell as she stared at her niece Heidi. "Oh my goodness, baby…what are you doing here, sweetie?" Valerie smiled and hugged her. "Come in."

Heidi gave her aunt an uneven smile and walked inside the house. "Hey Auntie," Heidi whispered. She walked by the bags on the floor and stood in the middle of the living room. "I just stopped by to say goodbye. I know I came by last night…but…I wanted to see you guys one more time."

"Oh okay, sweetie," Valerie said as she walked over to Heidi. "We're just getting ready to leave. I'm waiting for the car service now."

Heidi slowly nodded her head and looked at her aunt. The look on her face was distant. Valerie picked up on her niece's unusual mood and immediately became concerned.

"Are you okay, Heidi?"

"I don't know," Heidi replied, staring at her aunt.

Valerie moved closer and grabbed her niece by the arms. "Are you sure you don't want to come with us? You know I have more than enough room for you."

"It's not that," Heidi said. "I just feel…different."

Valerie gave her niece a sympathetic gesture and nodded her head. "Heidi…I want to say something to you." Valerie looked her niece squarely in the eyes and continued to speak. "I *can't* honestly say that I know what you're going through. But it took a lot of heart to do what you did that night,sweetie. You saved us all." Heidi dropped her head as she listened to her aunt's words. "I know it's tough for you," Valerie continued. "You did what you had to do. So don't feel guilty about what happened."

"That's just the thing, Auntie," Heidi whispered as she lifted her head. "I don't feel guilty. I don't feel sad. I don't feel happy. To be honest, I don't *feel* at all. I woke up last week and my headaches just stopped."

"Well, that's a good thing, right?" Valerie asked as she cut her niece short.

"I don't know. I haven't taken a pill in almost a month, and I don't feel anything. No pain…no stress…no excitement…nothing." Heidi paused for a moment and thought about her own words. "I absolutely…don't feel…nothing. It's like…I lost a major part of me that night."

Before Valerie could respond to her niece a loud sound came from the second floor. Pearl and Janaya were making their way down to the ground level with two handfuls of luggage. Heidi walked over to her mother and helped her with her bags. Pearl was still walking with a minor limp, but she was making a full recovery from her injuries.

Pear gave her daughter a gentle smile as she approached her. "Hey Heidi," she whispered as they walked near the front door, setting down her bags. "So you changed your mind about Chicago?"

"No…I just wanted to come by and say goodbye again," Heidi said. "Are you okay, Mom?"

"I am doing good," Pearl said. "Just taking things one day at a time."

"I can relate to that. Are you ready for a fresh start?"

"As ready as I'm goin' to be," Pearl responded. "I don't know why you won't come with us."

"I will…but just not now," Heidi assured. "I got a few loose ends to tie up here, and then I will make a move."

"Not to mention…she don't want to leave that beautiful man behind," Valerie added.

"That too. Thanks Auntie!" Heidi jokingly said and smiled at Valerie. "But when the time is right, I will make it out there."

"Okay, I'm not going to rush you. Just be careful out here."

Heidi closed her eyes and nodded toward her mother. "So did you get a chance to look at your locket, Mom?"

"I didn't look at it yet," Pearl responded as she reached for the chain around her neck. "I'm still not ready."

"Okay…I understand. When you open it and look at it…let me know what you think," Heidi said. She gave her mother a hug and smiled at her. "You guys have a safe trip, okay?"

"We will," Valerie said as she hugged her niece.

Janaya rushed over to Heidi and hugged her.

"I'm goin' to miss you, Janabell," Heidi said as her young cousin smiled at her.

Heidi headed for the door and waved to her family. She didn't look back as she walked outside and headed for her car. Pearl walked to the front door and watched as her daughter fired up the engine to her truck, then sped off down the quiet street.

Heidi got halfway down the block when her cell phone started ringing. She kept her concentration on the road and reached for her phone. She read the caller's name and smiled. It was Tycen.

"Hey baby," Heidi greeted as she answered the call.

"Well, hello gorgeous," Tycen said from the other line. "How are you feeling today?"

"I'm doing good," Heidi responded. "I'm on my way back to my apartment. Just had to say goodbye to my family."

"Okay," Tycen replied. "Are we still on for dinner later?"

"Absolutely."

"Good. Because I have some good news for you."

"Good news?"

"Yup!" Tycen continued. "Remember you asked me to find that guy Aaron for you?"

"Of course." Heidi's heart starting beating faster from the very mention of Aaron's name.

"One of the managers from the Pennsylvania office gave me a solid address on him."

"No shit?" Heidi asked as her mind started to work.

"Yes…the address he gave me is for a small town right outside of Philadelphia."

"Is that right?" Heidi whispered. Her entire mood slowly turned ominous as she thought about Aaron. "And this manager is positive that he lives there."

"Yes…he is one hundred and fifty percent positive on this one," Tycen said. "That's why it took so long to get it."

Heidi thought for moment and pulled her truck over to the side of the road. She felt her heart pounding through her chest and her hands beginning to tremble. Her adrenaline rushed through her veins like a power surge as she tensed by the second. Old feelings of betrayal came over her as her mind immediately dragged her back a few years ago to that fateful night at her mother's house. Images of Aaron pointing his gun at her flashed in and out of her mind. Heidi quickly exhaled as an imaginary gunshot woke her from her momentary daydream.

"Heidi!" Tycen shouted from the other end of the phone. "Are you still there?"

"I'm sorry…yes…I'm here," Heidi gasped as she tried to catch her breath. "I zoned out for a minute."

"Damn…I thought I lost you," Tycen nervously said. "Are you okay?"

"Yes, I'm fine. Ummm…can you text me that address right now?"

"Yes, of course I can."

"Please do that," Heidi said. "And I will call you back later."

"Okay, but is there anything you need my help with?" Tycen asked. He was growing more concerned for Heidi.

"No baby," Heidi said. "This is something I have to take care of myself."

Heidi abruptly disconnected the call. She looked at her hands as they continued to tremble. She tried to calm herself down, but there was no use. A strange noise came from her cell phone. Heidi was receiving a text message. She opened the message and noticed that Tycen was sending her Aaron's address. *Finally!*

Heidi put her truck into gear and prepared herself to get back on the road. She looked in the rearview mirror and paused for a moment. She found herself feeling strange as she stared back at a lifeless pair of eyes. Heidi couldn't recognize the woman who was staring back at her in the mirror. She was clearly a changed woman. The person Betty had warned her about was slowly taking over her body. A demonic smile came to Heidi's face as she punched the gas.

The thought of being betrayed by Aaron and now Judith caused her heart to pound with fury. One word danced around in her mind as she sped down the road en route to an unfamiliar destination.

Revenge.

To Be Continued . . .

NEXT LEVEL PUBLISHING

Name: _____

Address: _____

City/State: _____

Zip: _____

QTY	TITLE	PRICE
	From Poverty To Power Moves $15	
	Kissed By The Devil I $15	
	Kissed By The Devil II $15	
	FREE SHIPPING	

TOTAL $ _____

We Ship To All Institutions Within the USA

Send cashiers check or money order to:

Next Level Publishing
P.O. Box 83
Newark, NJ 07101

Order online at:
www.nextlevelpublishing.com